I0629353

GRITS AND GLORY

(PLANTATION SHADOWS SERIES, BOOK 1)

HALEY WHITEHALL

EXPANDING HORIZONS PRESS

 **Expanding Horizons Press**

Published by Expanding Horizons Press
1250 N. Wenatchee Ave., Suite H #322
Wenatchee, WA 98801

Grits and Glory

Manufactured in the United States of America

ISBN: 978-0-9851828-2-3
E-ISBN: 978-0-9851828-4-7
LCCN: 2012942277

ACKNOWLEDGEMENTS

This book has been a labor of love long in the making. The character Peter Warren has been in my mind since high school. I am grateful to my parents for not only putting up with my imaginary friend—er muse for so many years but fostering this story and my passion for the Civil War. Thank you to my friend Angie Pike who has also known Peter since high school, believed in the story, and encouraged me to continue polishing it even when I wanted to give up. She patiently helped me hone my craft and read many drafts over the years. Thank you to the Coffee Cabin Writers Group for their continued support and guidance. Thank you to my amazing critique partners for their critical eye and encouragement: Janet Brooks, Carmen Fox, Greg Henry, and Carrie Murgittroyd. This book would not be possible without all of you.

CHAPTER 1

September 7, 1862
Pittsfield, New Hampshire

MOLLY ADMIRED THEIR unfinished house with a critical inspection. Their kitchen would be warm when they brought in the stove, but right now it was chilly. "I talked to mother again yesterday about moving up the wedding. She said no."

Peter tipped his head back and took a deep breath. Of course she did. For the millionth time. How was he going to tell her he had enlisted?

"I know you are not looking forward to the big ceremony. We could go to the next town and get married in secret. Dan can come with us to be a witness."

Peter pressed his lips together. Molly had accepted that Dan was going to be his best man, but her mother had not yet made peace with having a negro in the wedding party. It was a good thing that Molly took after her father and Peter didn't take after his.

Dan was going to be a witness all right. A witness to Peter boarding a train with his fellow soldiers.

"I know it is late, but we could wake up the judge." The daring in Molly's voice made Peter's pulse quicken. She had always been headstrong and defying tradition was nothing new, but this proposition was surprising.

He was sure Molly would find him donning a blue uniform surprising, too.

"No," Peter said although it was painful. He didn't want strained relations with her mother; they were going to have children after all. "We need your parents' blessings. I don't want us to do something you will regret later."

"Mother is the one enamored with high society. I just want to be with you. I don't care if our wedding is the social event of the year."

Peter forced out a weak laugh. He didn't know if he could survive without her. He loved Molly with every breath in his body. She always put him first. But he couldn't do what she wanted.

"One day you will look back at that wrinkled newspaper clipping of our wedding. It is something you will want to show our children." Would she instead be looking a newspaper clipping of his name among the dead?

Molly nodded. "I suppose you are right. I know Mother would make me regret my hasty decision." She giggled.

Speaking of things he might regret later, there was the big news Peter couldn't hold back any longer. He loosened the collar of his shirt. His heart palpitated. She had no idea why he suddenly wanted to marry sooner than planned. And he was running out of time to tell her. Their unfinished house, the home they had built and dreamed of, would have to be the place.

He wrapped his arms around her slender frame, pressing her back tightly against his chest, her height mere inches shorter than his. The heat of her body warmed him. Could he make it through every day without her tender caress? Maybe he shouldn't go. Their future together didn't involve him dodging cannonballs. Or maybe that was an excuse. Would people think him a coward? What kind of man would he be if he didn't fight? Would he still have honor? Would he be shunned from Molly's social circle?

Then again, what kind of man would he be if he *did* leave Molly behind? Would she still want to marry him? He didn't know how long he was going to be gone. Would she refuse to wait for him and meet someone else? No. He knew Molly's heart belonged to him. And he'd made up his mind.

He ran a couple fingers along her collarbone and she shivered. Did she know something was wrong? She knew him so well, after all, as if they were destined for each other. One look at him, and she'd burrowed inside his soul. Maybe that ability would help her understand why he needed to do this. If he didn't tell her now, he never would. "Molly," he stammered, "I need to tell you something important."

Molly tilted her head back. "What?"

Peter opened his mouth, but the words refused to come. He didn't want to hurt her. He had vowed to always be there for her, to protect her. But he had to leave.

He kissed her on the top of the head, inhaling her perfume and a faint scent of wildflowers. They had picked wildflowers earlier and she had woven them into a circlet for her head which she had worn proudly until they had faded. Wildflowers had special meaning for them. A bouquet of wildflowers had helped bring them together and Molly planned to hold a similar bouquet at their wedding.

Molly gently elbowed him. "Don't just stand there with your mouth open. What is it?"

Peter whispered, "I have enlisted in the army. The train leaves tomorrow."

Molly broke free from his embrace and spun around. Her eyes pierced the shadowy dusk; her words pierced his soul. An uncharacteristic roughness invaded her well-bred speech. "How can you make me a widow before I'm a bride? How dare you run off and play soldier."

How could she think he was volunteering for glory? He had much purer motives. He had to right his father's wrongs.

"This isn't a game, Molly," Peter said. "You know about my past. You know about my father's cruelty and my feelings towards the South. I had hoped you'd understand." His father loved the whip, loved the power, loved the fear in a slave's eyes or his son's eyes. He fed off of it as if was his daily bread.

Tightening the ivory shawl around her shoulders, Molly worried the fabric between her fingers. "I know this is serious. But do you? Why did you wait till the last minute to tell me?"

Peter stroked the nape of his neck. Standing in the kitchen, he gazed at the stars above their unroofed house. A cold wind blew. Should he give her his coat? He wanted to avoid her question. He didn't have a good answer. "It is late. I should take you back to your parents' house."

In the glow of lamplight, Molly's face flushed. Folding her arms across her chest, she confronted him. "You are not going to tell me something of this nature and then take me home as if nothing is wrong! We are going to talk about this." Her voice tripled in volume.

"I didn't know how to tell you. I love you, Molly. I didn't want to hurt you."

"The same way you told me just now." She jutted out her chin. "Didn't you think this was something we should discuss first? Or do my concerns mean nothing?"

Peter closed his eyes. "You are right. I should have summoned the courage to bring this up sooner."

"But you didn't. You were only thinking about yourself. I expect my future husband to be open with me."

"I understand." He reached for her hand, but she pulled away.

"Why can't you enlist after we're married? Can't it wait two weeks?" The sorrow Peter had feared entered her voice and tears filled her eyes.

The two weeks would easily stretch on to two months. No. He had to go now. "If I want to be in the same company as everyone else in Pittsfield I need to enlist now. And considering my past, considering what my father has done, it is my duty—"

"You know this war isn't really about slavery."

"When the South seceded from the Union, they made it about slavery."

Molly took short, rapid breaths. "I know this is important to you. My family gives money to the cause. There is no reason you have to get yourself shot."

Peter's gut twisted, his blood simmered. He wasn't angry with her, but with himself. His words carried the weight of the past, the weight of the responsibility he'd thrust upon his shoulders. "I have to be a man. I have to do what I think is right. I have to fight or I won't be able to—"

"A real man takes care of his wife. At least he makes her feel involved in important decisions."

Her words carried a bite, teeth sinking into his heart. If she wanted him to feel guilty, she'd just won a blue ribbon.

Peter straightened his wiry frame and met her wounded gaze. "I knew you would try to sway me from risking my life. And, as you know, I can be easily swayed." His voice was firm and decided with an undertone of apology. "But I'm doing this for myself and for Dan."

Peter's lungs tightened, fearing her next response.

"Dan?" Molly said, taking a step towards him. "You talked this over with him, didn't you?"

Peter's chest ached. "Yes."

"I am going to be your wife. Shouldn't I come first?"

"Dan is my brother. You are both my family. I should have given you the same courtesy."

"Your brother!" Molly's round, sapphire eyes narrowed into cat-like slits. "He is as black as tar. He isn't your brother. I'm going to be your real family."

Peter swallowed the heated response that made his mouth burn. Any racist comment lit a fire in his stomach, but words against Dan… He watched as her eyes filled with regret and she bit her lip, apparently too ashamed to voice her apology.

Peter's timbre softened and when he spoke there was sadness in each word, "Aunt Ruth, his mother, our mother, is the only mother I know." He wiped his sweaty palms on his black pants. "Please don't make me choose between the two of you," Peter said. "Dan has been with me every day of my life."

"Then how can you bear to leave him?" she asked in a harsh tone, throwing her arms in the air.

Peter's left eye twitched. He ignored the sarcasm in her voice. This was the anger and shock and pain talking. It wasn't the Molly he loved.

"Dan understands my need to enlist. I had hoped you would, too."

She responded with a steely glare. "I understand. You're proving something to yourself and your father. But that doesn't mean I like it."

"I know." Peter paused and ran his tongue around his dry mouth. "I am leaving tomorrow afternoon at one. Will you see me off?"

Molly rocked back on her heels, her lips pursed. "No."

A lump rose in his throat. "No?" Molly's stern expression didn't lessen. "Will you at least think about it?"

Molly exhaled loudly. "Yes. I can do that."

☆　　☆　　☆

Peter hurried to the train station, searching for Molly. Coal smoke mingled with the crisp autumn air. Soldiers, their family, and friends arrived in slow waves. The loved ones broke into small groups feigning some privacy.

Dan shortened his stride to walk beside Peter.

A couple railroad workers walked the length of the platform. One of them slapped the side of the train. The clunk made Dan wince.

Peter put a hand on Dan's bicep for a second. Dan always seemed strong for him, but Peter knew he had hidden scars as well.

"I wish you could go with me," Peter said. "But it helps me to know you'll take care of Molly while I'm gone."

Dan nodded. "Belle said she wouldn't let me go even if I could."

Peter's stomach turned. Molly had tried to prevent him and failed.

An ensemble of horns, violins, and flutes had gathered to see the boys off in style, striking up "Wait for the Wagon." The band, in military-inspired uniforms, were in good spirits, feet tapping in time.

The upbeat tune made Peter more uneasy. He faked a smile—the tight kind that he knew Dan could see through.

He drummed his fingers on his thigh mimicking the telegraph taps. Impatience and worry crept into his voice. "Thanks for packing my knapsack. I couldn't ask Molly after our fight last night, and I wasn't in the mood to do it myself." He continued searching the crowd. *Would she come or not?*

"I know. You were brooding," Dan said, rubbing his stubbly cheek.

Peter's stomach felt hollow, anxiety rising from his toes. "I don't want to part with her on strained terms."

"She loves you, Peter. War is hard for women to understand."

Peter gritted his teeth. "If she loves me, she'll support me. If she doesn't…" His facial muscles tightened.

Peter felt soft hands over his eyes. His voice rose in pitch, relief rose from the depths of his heart and happiness untied the knots in his chest. "You came."

He turned around and Molly removed her hands. She tilted her neck and gave him her best puppy eyes. "I feel bad about our fight last night. Your news caught me by surprise. I had to think it through."

Peter pulled her close, his pulse threatening to skid out of control. "It was my fault. Do you forgive me?"

In lieu of a response, Molly gave him a sugary inviting smile. Peter felt her stiffly boned corset and worked his hands up to the soft skin of her arms. Her eyes twinkled; he lowered his head, inching closer to her lips.

"I will come back," he promised. He kissed her long and hard. Adrenaline charged through his veins, and he longed to kiss her again, but he held back for the sake of propriety.

"Peter, I will miss you so," Molly said, resting her head on his shoulder.

Peter fingered her hair. For a moment, they breathed in harmony. Her eyes spoke to his soul, filled with unsaid words and unfulfilled promises. Her quivering lip gave way to sobs.

Peter pulled back from her embrace. He couldn't handle her fragile emotions. He hated to see her hurt. Hated that his decision had stabbed her heart, leaving a wound he could not mend. He looked away at three soldiers passing their little group. Would he soon be serving with one of them?

She brushed away her tears. "I'm sorry," she said, taking a deep breath. "I told myself I wasn't going to cry."

He brushed her cheek. "You have many things to keep you busy, with the building of our house and planning the wedding for when I return."

"I'll never get busy enough not to worry." Her shaky voice sped up, making her words run together. "I'll worry that you're cold. I'll worry that you're hungry. I'll worry that you're ill. I'll worry that—"

Peter put a finger to her lips. "I know," he breathed. "I know."

"I really don't believe you'll be home in ninety days," she said.

A tense silence hung between them.

He gave her a long look from head to toe. Her red lawn dress trimmed with white rosettes looked strikingly patriotic against his new wool uniform: navy coat and sky blue pants. Hopefully, she approved of her solider.

Peter pulled a tintype out of his pocket and thrust it into Molly's hand. "Something to remember me by. I was afraid I'd have to leave it with Dan."

She kissed the picture of him in full Union uniform, standing proudly by an American flag, knapsack on his back, musket in hand. "I packed a surprise for you—"

"You packed?" He shot an accusing look at Dan.

The six-foot man shrugged his large shoulders, failing to hold back a smile.

"The surprise is at the bottom," Molly said.

Peter unslung his knapsack, opened it and gently rummaged through. Socks, underwear, shaving tools, blankets, and carefully wrapped provisions. The lead balls reminded him he wasn't going on a trip to Philadelphia.

"Look in *Romeo and Juliet*," Molly said, her eagerness palpable.

Peter lifted out the book of Shakespeare and turned to the first page of his favorite play. There rested a tintype of Molly in her best silk dress with lacy sleeves and a watch fob made of a lock of her golden hair.

"I wish you could say it was a picture of your wife, but mother wouldn't hear of it. She wants us to have a grand wedding."

Peter nodded. Despite her mother's attempt to prolong their courtship, in his mind he and Molly were already one. He repositioned some of the goods in his knapsack, hoisted it onto his back, and checked the time.

"Train will be leaving soon."

The platform became crowded with soldiers and friends and family saying their farewells. Peter looked over his shoulder at the throng of people filling the station. He searched the crowd for familiar faces. He recognized members of the Abolitionist Society enlisting with him.

Where were the Kane brothers? Dan had been his crutch. Now he'd have to rely on them to control his nostalgia. His friends Jim, Eli, and Nathan knew how to help him handle and control his chilling memories.

The train roared to life, coal smoke billowing from the chimney. A whistle blew clear and shrill.

"All aboard," a deep voice shouted.

Peter gave Molly a kiss on the cheek. Her eyes brimmed with tears and she clutched the sides of her dress, her fingers digging into the material. He sensed she was resisting an attempt to stop him. Peter gripped Dan's arm in a silent parting. Dan's round chin dipped to him, his face full of fierce pride. Peter's heart stumbled forward along with his feet as he climbed on the train. Other soldiers followed. It was a short ride to Concord where they'd be officially mustered in.

Peter took a seat; it was hard and uncomfortable just like his parting. He hadn't been separated from Dan for more than a day at a time. Being torn from his brother was as painful as being torn from Molly, but he hoped that didn't show.

He shifted in the seat he wished to have all to himself. His skin crawled with a combination of excitement and apprehension. He listened to the band, his eyes closed, trying to catch every note.

Jacob, the attorney, boarded the train and pushed his way down the aisle as if the world owed him. His jaw was tense, eyes threatening. Farm boys, laborers, and shopkeepers meant nothing to him. The other soldiers, not wanting to brave his anger, parted and let him pass.

Jacob inched closer. His brassy brown hair and heavy footsteps announced his presence. Dread settled in Peter's throat. If Jacob sat next to him, he knew the ride to Concord would be filled with silent misery. The two barely talked to each other and Peter wanted to keep it that way.

Nathan refused to get out of Jacob's way. For a minute they faced off like two wolves.

With farm boy defiance, Nathan took a step towards Jacob, the muscles on his arms flexing.

Jacob's dark green eyes shifted to the men around him, then his gaze locked with Nathan.

Peter's stomach tightened. *Don't fight*, screamed through his head. With a sly, determined twist of the mouth, Nathan sat next to Peter.

"Thank you," Peter whispered.

Nathan's lips twitched. "You'd think it was *his father* who owned a plantation."

Peter laughed softly, without feeling. Smiling and laughing were mechanical actions. He knew when they were expected. They seldom came freely.

Peter stuck his head out the window and inhaled hometown air. His eyes widened and his heart stirred inside his chest. Molly ran up and reached her hand through the open glass.

"I want to soak up every last second of your presence," she said.

Peter etched her gorgeous, gleaming eyes into his mind. Her full, delicate lips. The dignified way she held her head. The way a stray wisp of hair hung in front of her ear. He'd recall them on all those nights ahead.

"I'm just going to Washington after training," Peter said. "Won't be on the battlefield yet."

Their fingers brushed a final time. "My love be with you," she said.

A sharp jerk pitched the passengers in their seats. The train lumbered out of the station, carrying the men into the army. He glanced back and did not see Molly or Dan. His stomach rolled like the train at the thought he'd never see them again.

CHAPTER 2

December 5, 1862
Bank of the Rappahannock River, Virginia

UNDER THE BRIGHT, yellow moon, Peter stared down the Confederate picket on the opposite riverbank—his eyes burning with disgust, burning with pain, burning with hate.

The rebel met his glare with a cold, stony eyes and spat a stream of tobacco juice.

Peter blinked. The rebel's appearance, tall and muscular with a full brown beard, triggered rapid breathing. The rebel resembled his father. Peter's insides clenched—preparing for a fight.

He'd make the gray viper suffer for forcing him as a boy to witness the cruelest evils of slavery.

Not moving, the rebel stared back with a defiant coolness.

Peter shook his head. His father had black hair not brown. Peter scratched the back of his neck. Of course that man wasn't his father. Cold, fatigue, and tension were getting to him.

"Damn my father." His words fell on the wind. He was imagining things again—didn't need to start that while on duty.

He didn't need to provoke the enemy into showing off his firing skills. He took a deep breath and exhaled through his nose forcing his lungs to expand.

Peter's fingers were clumsy and frozen as if weighted with lead. He rubbed them vigorously against his thigh and felt a twinge of pain, but other than that they had no feeling.

He wished the rest of him was numb, too. His cold, wet uniform felt like ice against his skin. A chill, spreading down his exposed neck, made him shiver. He shifted the musket to his left hand and brushed the icicles off his short, black beard. The 12th New Hampshire – the Mountaineers – would likely freeze to death before facing the Rebs.

His eyelids felt heavy. He yawned and they began to close. "Blasted," he mumbled. He kicked the back of his left leg to keep himself lucid.

Footsteps.

"Halt," Peter said, his head snapping around.

"Just your relief, Sergeant," the man replied.

Peter barely smiled, his lips too fatigued to stretch far. He stumbled to his hut, his legs unsteady from exhaustion.

Stirring the fire back to life, he walked over to the pit and blew on the dying embers, hoping it would thaw his fingers. He cupped his hands over his cheeks. His teeth chattered.

The fire wasn't much, but it was better than none at all. He had learned to be grateful for the small, crackling flames. Many slaves did not have such comfort.

Years ago, his father had struck a slave boy, about his age, across the head with a shovel for taking a piece of wood out of the yard without permission. Struck him so hard he'd left mute. At first, his father thought the boy was playing dumb, so he had the overseer whip him for being so stubborn. The boy opened his mouth to scream when the lash descended upon his skin but no sound came out.

Those and many similar horrors haunted Peter. There hadn't been a single carefree day in his childhood.

Peter didn't know why he couldn't control those memories, couldn't keep them at bay for long.

Staring into the flames, he imagined his father trapped in hell for all eternity. It helped somehow. Picturing his father sweating, thirsty, his flesh burning, melted the past away. The thought boiled his memories until they evaporated as steam.

With trembling hands, he opened his book of Shakespeare and turned to *Romeo and Juliet*. Picking up Molly's tintype, he gazed at her fair face. Perhaps at this exact moment she was also thinking of him.

Memories and dreams were all he had to hold on to. Would this picture be the last he ever saw of her? Would the day he enlisted be the last he felt her embrace? Two tears escaped, freezing on his cheeks.

"Haven't you read that whole book yet?" Nathan asked in a quivering voice.

Peter raised his head. Nathan was wrapped in blankets, only his copper hair and brown eyes visible. He looked like a mole peering out of his hole.

"Many times," Peter said. His longing gaze returned to Molly's picture. It was in God's hands whether or not he lived long enough for their happily-ever-after.

At least it wasn't in his father's hands. His father's hands had already left enough of his life in ruins.

Covering his eyes with his palm, he willed himself to shed no more tears, willed strength back into his muscles.

Willed the past to stop torturing him.

Peter forced himself to at least act calm and in control. *Damn my inherent weakness. I was elected sergeant for God's sake.*

"Want to play cards?" Nathan asked.

"You're too young to play cards."

"I am not." Nathan's face flushed. "If sixteen is old enough to make me a soldier, then it ought to make me old enough to play cards."

Peter repressed a laugh, though Nathan's serious face made it difficult. Sixteen was old enough to fight with his father's permission, but Peter was not about to point that out.

"You're only four years older than me. I wish you and my brothers would quit treating me like a boy. I'm a *man*."

"All right, all right. I'm just giving you a hard time. I know you're a man, Nathan. But I don't want to play cards right now. Maybe later."

"You want a cup of coffee then?" Nathan's voice softened, resuming its friendly farm boy tone. "There's some left in the pot."

Peter poured the last of the coffee into his tin cup. He sipped it and grimaced. The dregs were bitter and gritty. Still, it helped warm his insides.

He pulled out his pocket watch and lovingly fingered the fob, a braided lock of Molly's golden hair. It was as soft and silky as he remembered; strong like her will and her love. He felt close to her, and at the same time he realized how far apart they were.

He ran his hand across one of the hut's walls, admiring his handiwork. Molly would have been impressed. Well, maybe not. It didn't compare to her father's mansion.

☆ ☆ ☆

Two loud knocks drew Peter's attention to the door.

"Come in," Peter said, as if the two words were all he could manage. He put the watch back in his pocket and rolled his neck.

Andrew Silas stuck his head inside the hut. The soldier looked like a shaggy buffalo with a thick brown beard and mustache.

"Sergeant Warren, Lieutenant French wants to see you."

Peter nodded, with a groan.

He put Molly's picture back into the Shakespeare book for safekeeping and stepped outside. The cold air took his breath away, like his father's hands gripping his throat. Peter opened his mouth and gasped. He carefully walked and in some places skidded on the slick sheet of ice over to where the lanky blond-headed lieutenant was standing.

"You wanted to see me, sir?" he asked.

"No." Surprised, Peter turned to go, but Lieutenant French stopped him. The slender officer stared out across the Rappahannock at the shadow of Fredericksburg. "The rebels are watching us. We're watching them, and they're watching us."

"Yes, sir."

Licking his bottom lip, Lieutenant French continued, "General Burnside requested pontoons to cross the river. Building bridges seems like the only way to cross."

"It is a large river," Peter said.

Peter's muscles tensed. The awkward conversation made him feel like a stone had settled in his gullet.

Lieutenant French ran his thumb across the nails of his left hand and glanced at him with one eye.

Peter sensed there was something else on the officer's mind.

"It's taking forever for him to get around to building the bridges. The element of surprise will be lost. Lee will be ready for us."

"I know. Maybe he's decided against taking Fredericksburg."

The lieutenant shook his head. "No. He's just acting like McClellan, too blasted slow and cautious. It'll be a hellish fight."

Peter held his breath to restrain a shiver. He tried not to think about the piles of dead bodies and pools of blood. But, images of wounded soldiers being treated on the battlefield, losing limbs, and being left at the mercy of the enemy invaded his mind.

Peter nodded. A moment of eerie silence followed. "Is that all, Lieutenant?"

"What? Oh … yes … you are excused."

Returning to his hut, Peter found it packed with soldiers wanting to keep warm. There was barely enough room for him to stand. The body heat generated from the crowded conditions was more warming than the small fire.

"Lieutenant French didn't want to see me. Funny how you tricked me out into the cold so you could get warm in my hut. Now if you would have listened to me you would have your own instead of crowding mine!" Peter snapped.

Some of the soldiers nodded while others ignored him.

"You deserve to freeze for being lazy. I built this hut with my hands and sweat to keep myself warm, not for the rest of you."

"How were we supposed to know the weather would turn cold all of a sudden?" Andrew said, wrapping his blanket tighter around him.

"You'd think all your hair would keep you warm like a dog," one of the soldiers said.

Andrew glared at him.

Peter gripped the sides of his thighs. A fight in his hut. That's just what he needed. He shot Nathan a wary look, his lips tight. He wanted to be alone.

"They're not trying to bother you," Nathan said. "They're just trying to stay warm."

Peter gritted his teeth. For his sanity, he set a limit to how many men could be in his hut, and a rotation so that they left after they had warmed; so more men could come in.

Sitting down, Peter pulled out Molly's latest letter. He ignored the idle chatter of his comrades and focused on her poetic words. Her words, the delicate pressure of each pen stroke reminded him of her grace, her concern, her love.

Being private with his own thoughts and feelings, he was not about to share Molly's words with the men. They were far more precious to him than anything. He sighed, putting down her letter.

He wanted to write her, but the bottle of ink was frozen.

The cold snap passed as quickly as it had set in. The warmer temperature gave the soldiers the opportunity to thaw. The opportunity to enjoy themselves and briefly forget the danger lurking on the other side of the river.

Peter watched Nathan's older brothers Jim and Eli race each other. Eli's walnut-colored hair was long enough to cover his ears. Peter wished he hadn't cut his hair. Under his breath, Peter urged Jim on. Jim was his age – twenty-two – and could almost have been his twin: they had the same black hair, hazel eyes, and thin lips. Peter silently cheered when Jim touched the Virginia pine first. The warm weather had lifted everyone's spirits. Peering back across the river, he saw rebels enjoying themselves with a baseball game.

Jim walked over to Peter, still trying to catch his breath.

"That was a close call," Peter said.

"I won. That's all that matters." Jim flashed a smile. "I've beaten everyone who has challenged me. You up for a race?"

"No. I've never won a foot race in my life."

Jim cocked his head to the right, his eyes squinted, concentrating. "I can see why. Growing up, you were racing Dan."

Peter nodded, his face fading back to its usual soberness. "Unfortunately, my father can run fast too…" His quiet voice faded.

Jim gave him a look of understanding. "Looks like you need a smoke."

"I'm fresh out of tobacco, but I'll be sergeant of the guard in a few hours." He winked. "You know what that means?"

Peter opened his mouth again to say more but had a hard time forming the words. A sinister thought swam in his head, gray and bleak like the pewter sky. "You know my face is well-known around here."

Jim bobbed his head.

"And since we look so much alike, I am afraid you might be in danger."

Jim grabbed Peter's shoulder. "Wouldn't be the first time," he said with a playfulness that made Peter cringe.

"I'm serious. It won't be like before. In New Hampshire we were surrounded by friends. New Hampshire is your home, but here—"

"I can take care of myself, Peter. You have enough to worry about as it is."

Peter felt like protesting. Felt like drilling home his point, but he knew Jim would brush it off. Jim had faced down the devil's henchman before, on Peter's behalf. Perhaps he could face down the devil as well.

Peter admired Jim's steel nerve and brassy, carefree demeanor. Those were qualities he didn't possess.

He thought too much, his father often told him, as if thinking was a crime. Weren't men supposed to think to get ahead in the world? Growing up, he tried to plan out every encounter with his father like a chess piece. One move to avoid him, another to appear busy.

Just like the poor slaves, the slaves who weren't supposed to think. Who were supposed to bend their backs to his father's will.

Peter ran his fingers through his hair, digging his nails into his scalp. Maybe his father thought of him more as a slave than a son. He had no value in his father's eyes.

☆ ☆ ☆

The following hours passed quickly, and soon Peter found himself standing post on the riverbank, again looking warily at his gray-clad adversary. He didn't trust any of them. He didn't trust the implicit agreement for the pickets not to shoot at one another unless one side attempted to cross the river.

His comrades didn't understand Southerners, didn't understand their deviousness. Even the southern belles used their charms to the best of their advantage. His comrades were easily taken in. The Union soldiers trusted the rebels and seemed to view them as equals unless facing them on the field.

The double standard made Peter sick to his stomach. Everything was black and white to him. There was not room for gray. Gray was dangerous.

Peter walked his beat and watched Union soldiers patching up their small sailboat. The trading vessel needed a tight hull to carry coffee grounds to the Rebs.

One of the soldiers looked at Peter as he passed. "'Bout ready to set sail."

Peter turned his head so he didn't see the boat enter the water. He kept his back to the soldiers until the Union soldier whistled, and then resumed walking his beat. Peter tapped his fingers against his thigh. *Come on!* He willed the wind to switch directions. He craved the sweet taste of tobacco almost as badly as the touch of Molly's lips.

One of the Union soldiers let out a soft hoot. Peter looked out at the water and saw the sailboat coming back carrying precious cargo.

The soldier lifted the boat out of the water and divided the cargo of tobacco among his companions. He took some of the leaves, rolled a cigarette and handed it to Peter. "Thanks, Sergeant."

"I need a light," Peter said.

The soldier nodded and dug a match out of his coat pocket.

Peter took the match and wetted his bottom lip. He put the cigarette and match in his own coat pocket. He'd have to wait until after his shift was over. Something to look forward to.

As he walked his remaining time on the picket line, he resisted the urge to light the cigarette. The Union Army had been here too long. They needed to cross or leave camp. They had to go somewhere. Everyone was getting restless, on edge. The more he thought about it the more agitated he became.

When his relief finally came, he rolled the cigarette between his fingers, took a deep puff and exhaled. The smoke curled upward lazily.

He hated being in the South. He hated being this close to Fredericksburg—too close to the Springdale Plantation. He was more afraid of being recognized than charging the battlefield. Anyone who had seen his father could guess their relationship. He had his father's rectangular face, coal black hair, and wide nose.

If news spread to his old man that he had joined the Yankee army… Peter's heart constricted, strength drained from his legs.

Nathan put a caring hand on his shoulder. "Are you all right?"

Peter's stomach churned. Nathan knew his past—all of it.

Peter swallowed and nodded. The youth returned to cleaning his musket. Peter exhaled, relieved that Nathan had understood him.

All the men seemed stressed. Peter ran his tongue across the bottom of his teeth taking comfort from the gentle roughness. Still, his isolation, his Southern roots, made him more anxious. And, he didn't want to air his personal problems like old blankets out a window.

He concentrated on watching Nathan. That boy treated his musket as gently as he treated a woman. His lips curved upward. Nathan had yet to know what war was like—or a woman for that matter.

With his finger, Peter absentmindedly drew pictures in the dirt floor. He didn't really know what war was like either, but he already knew the bloody mess a lead ball made tearing through flesh. He knew that all too well.

☆　☆　☆

The bedtime smoke wasn't strong enough to ease his nerves. All the tobacco in Dixie wouldn't have been strong enough. He awoke on edge. A feeling all too familiar.

Peter stepped out of his hut, a heavy sigh working its way up his throat. The rays of sun did nothing to ease the tension out of his body through the brisk morning air. Icy pricks stabbed his heart. He had lived under daily stress with his father, but this was different. Different because he never felt his own life was in danger.

After breakfast, he walked over and watched Andrew whittle a piece of wood. "What are you making?"

"Buffalo if I can manage it. Since that's become my nickname."

Peter grasped the man on the shoulder, and then sat next to him.

"You know how to whittle?" Andrew asked.

"My father did not think gentlemen should learn the art," Peter replied, his voice flat.

"Ah. Forgot. Too bad. Whittling is a good way to work out stress. Anything that involves working with your hands is. At least for a farm boy."

The sound of music drew Peter's attention. A stocky soldier with lightning-fast fingers played the banjo. The upbeat song seemed to catch hold of his company. Soon most of the men were dancing.

Peter pretended to dance the reel with an invisible partner, wishing Molly was in his arms, wishing she was wearing the burgundy dress she had worn to the mayor's ball. He smiled. Jacob had escorted her to the dance, but Molly had spent more time with him.

Peter shook his head. God had dealt him a strange hand. He had a horrible upbringing by his father, but once he reached Pittsfield, things seemed to fall into place. Molly and her father had both overlooked the fact he was eking out a living as a stable boy. He was grateful that they were able to look past his circumstances and see him for the person that he was.

The banjo music slowed and Peter's steps did the same. He needed a slow dance to catch his breath. He closed his eyes and focused on Molly's image.

Someone tapped his shoulder. "I'll dance with you in a minute," Peter said.

"I don't want to dance with you," a deep voice responded.

A burning sensation sped down his neck. Peter snapped to attention. "Sorry. I was daydreaming, Captain."

Captain Morton grunted. "I figured that. That's one thing that keeps us sane in the God-forsaken South." He gazed into the distance, a blank look on his face, his eyes following the soldiers who were still dancing. He nodded to the man playing the banjo then returned his attention to Peter. "I need to talk to you, Sergeant. Or rather *we* need to talk to you."

"Yes, sir." He followed Captain Morton to a hut, curious as to what the captain meant by *we*.

When Peter stepped inside, his breathing slowed to a halt, and he forgot to salute. Colonel Palmer sat at the desk. Lieutenant French sat on the campstool to the left of him.

"I think I have the man you've been looking for," Captain Morton said. "Sergeant Warren was born and bred in Fredericksburg, Virginia."

"What am I the man for, sir?"

"General Whipple is recruiting scouts," Colonel Palmer said.

Peter's heart knotted inside his chest. "Isn't scout a fancy word for spy, sir?" he asked, unable to keep the nervous twinge out of his voice.

"You've a southern accent and you know the area. You are the only soldier in General Whipple's command with both those requirements."

Peter's legs quivered and the rhythm of his pulse surpassed the quickstep. Sweat coated his palms in a sticky, wet film.

"Are you okay? You seem a bit pale," Captain Morton said.

"A bit?" he shouted. "Sorry, sirs. I shouldn't have raised my voice." He paused to regain control of his emotions. "I don't want to be a spy. I-I can't. I'm wanted in the South."

"What do you mean you're wanted?" Lieutenant French said.

"I thought you knew," Peter spoke slowly, a drop at the end of his words, "I was a conductor on the Underground Railroad."

"So you're wanted for helping slaves escape?" Colonel Palmer asked.

"Yes, sir. Not just any slaves—my manservant, Dan."

All the officers looked at each other. In the moment of silence that followed, Peter rubbed his tongue across his teeth. He tried to swallow, but his throat was too dry.

"I'm sure you're not the only conductor on the Underground Railroad serving in the Union ranks," Colonel Palmer said.

Peter's flesh goose pimpled. *Espionage.* He didn't enlist to spend the war in a secret network. He had spent enough time underground already, spent enough time under a fake name.

"It's not just that I was involved in the Underground Railroad..." Peter attempted to explain.

He shifted his weight and glanced at the corner. Unfortunately, no answers were hiding there. He felt the officers staring at him, burning with anticipation.

"I can't be a spy. My family and I are well known in the region," he said in a soft mumble.

An icy chill swept across his shoulders and down his back. He resisted the urge to wrap his hands around his arms lest it be seen as a sign of weakness. If he was turned in for running slaves, it would be worse than death. His father would make sure of that—he'd pay the guards to torture him, cook up reasons to send him to the hole, whip him, not feed him.

He looked back at the officers and took a deep breath. They had to understand.

"Sirs, pardon my impudent speech, but this is a crazy idea. My father is well-known in the South. I'm well-known in the South. Most conductors don't have their faces on posters all over the southern states like I do."

Colonel Palmer rubbed his chin. "I see," he said in a tone that made Peter fear he didn't believe him.

He couldn't blame the colonel. Only a few conductors were unlucky enough to be in his position. He was probably the most publicized of the group, next to Harriet Tubman. Likely, they just thought he was trying to talk his way out of the assignment.

The officers exchanged glances. "We're getting desperate," Captain Morton said. "We don't have much time either."

"What would happen if you were turned in for the reward?" Lieutenant French asked.

"The case would go to trial."

"What would happen if you were caught spying?" Captain Morton spoke, fast and strong.

Peter's heart rattled against his rib cage. "I'd be killed."

Captain Morton nodded slightly, clearly satisfied.

Peter stiffened. Apparently being wanted wasn't a greater risk—to them anyway. The colonel's stony expression weakened Peter's knees.

Palmer's face softened, and his eyes turned sorrowful, with a hint of regret. "I guess it was too much to ask for you to volunteer. I don't know what we are going to do. We don't have another option. We can't send a Connecticut storekeeper across the river; they'd kill him the first time he opened his mouth."

Damn. Peter's stomach turned and turned, his breakfast mixing with guilt.

"Sirs, you might be willing to risk my life for precious information, but it is my life." His chest felt heavy making it hard to breathe. He knew he was letting them down.

He wanted to do his part to fight the Confederacy and free the slaves. Wasn't fighting in the ranks enough?

"Sergeant, it would take much courage to be a spy with a price on your head," Palmer said. "I understand your reluctance."

"It has nothing to do with courage, sir," Peter said, though he wondered if he was lying. "My father holds sway over people, especially around Fredericksburg. I wouldn't live long enough to bring back the information you need. It would be a lose-lose situation."

"Think about it," Captain Morton said. "I don't believe in lose-lose situations. There is always a chance.

Peter gulped air.

"We hope that you will change your mind," Captain Morton continued. "You could help end this war. You could save the lives of your comrades."

"We'll talk again," Colonel Palmer said.

CHAPTER 3

PETER STOOD AS straight and still as a post driven deep into the ground. At last, the officers dismissed him. Relief poured into his bones and muscles and blood, only to vanish in an instant. His fitful stomach filled with criticism and doubt. Biting his lip, he walked to his hut and sensed the dull, familiar ache in his chest. He hadn't even had the courage to reply.

Peter's hands folded into fists. His actions disgusted him. Feeling that his father was right disgusted him. Realizing he was spineless disgusted him.

How could he be a soldier? He never did anything right. Fear was a natural instinct, but he reeked of it.

He scrunched up his nose trying to block out the smell. How had Jack Selah ever persuaded him to become an Underground Railroad conductor in the first place? It hadn't seemed like such a risk. Jack and his network of friends throughout the South had taken him under their tutelage. Made sure he knew how to conduct business safely. They looked out for each other ... but the dangers over the past two years had dissolved his courage like butter in a hot frying pan.

Peter ground his teeth. *Posters.* It all had to do with those damn posters. He was wanted.

The three Kane boys' laughter grated on his anger, shredding the last of his nerves. How could they be so carefree? So happy at a time like this? They were in his hut sitting around the fire, and playing poker on a hardtack crate. Hoping to get his mind off things, Peter joined them, slumping into his seat.

"Something bothering you?" Eli asked. "It's your turn to deal."

Peter picked up the deck and began shuffling it. He shoved the cards into the palm of his hand. He was just asked to become a spy. He opened his mouth, tempted to share the bit of intimate information, but changed his mind. Instead, he said, "Yeah. Something's always bothering me. Let's just play."

He dealt the cards and stared at his hand. Nothing. Of course. Just his luck. It had been his luck since the day he was born, and his mother died.

He quickly folded and watched the three brothers continue the game. He almost wished Aunt Ruth was there to give him a tongue lashing for playing cards. They weren't betting anything, not even pennies. But she didn't even like the *idea* of gambling.

"You cheated, Jim," Eli said. "That card came from the bottom of the deck."

"Not so," Jim said, giving his brother a gentle push in the chest. Eli pushed him back.

"Don't knock over the table," Nathan warned, "or all the cards will go flying."

Peter shook his head. Brothers. He already missed his. The only difference between the Kanes and him and Dan, was Dan's dusky skin. Dan always knew how to cheer him up, though. If only the big colored man would have been allowed to enlist with him.

"You gonna say something, Sergeant?" Jim asked. "You've been quiet all evening."

"Glad you got your disagreement settled," Peter said, feigning a laugh. He picked up his new hand. The hearts and diamonds blurred together. He threw them at Nathan, the dealer. This had been his idea. This game.

Nathan's eyes doubled in size.

"I'm sorry," Peter mumbled. "I'm just tired. I'll turn in early."

He straightened out his bedroll near the left wall, smoothing it with both hands before lying down. "Dear Lord," he whispered. "How much must we suffer? How much do you ask of me to atone for my father's sins? I pray that I live through the war to wed Molly. Let her feel my love even though she is thousands of miles away. Keep her safe and comfort her fears. Your will be done. Amen."

Peter closed his eyes and pictured Molly standing in front of him, wearing a blue dress and carrying a cream parasol. She twirled the parasol in her hands and hummed. Her image gave him strength. He pulled himself out of his melancholy.

He could be a good soldier. He'd prove it.

Molly believed in him. With her support, he could do anything.

He wasn't a scared boy any more. He was a man. A man who had learned from his past.

☆　☆　☆

Reveille jolted Peter awake. His heart sagged, dragging the corners of his lips with it. Damnit. He was in his hut, not with Molly. He had been dreaming of a pleasant afternoon in New Hampshire. Basking in the remnants of Molly's image, he sat up, still dazed with sleep.

The smell of coffee, fried salt pork, and beans finally drew him out of his hut. He was the last to join his mess.

Andrew pushed the leftover breakfast onto Peter's tin plate. The soldiers ate with sober faces. The campfire glowed amber against the gray sky, the flames dancing with the breeze.

"I wish we were still back in Washington," Nathan said.

Andrew nodded. "It was safe in the capitol."

Peter stretched out, lying on his side, while the rest of the men sat around the fire. He remembered the city which seemed too big for its buildings. They were spread apart at such distances that walking from one to another was a chore. There were blue-clad soldiers everywhere, constantly passing one another with salutes, nods, and smiles. Trains came into the city daily. The passengers were monitored closely, each one required to carry a pass.

Peter rubbed his forehead. So much had happened since he enlisted in the infantry and was elected sergeant. Their regiment had been ordered to defend the capitol after training.

"I still remember hearing enemy fire in Maryland back in October," Andrew said. "I was sure we were going to be in a fight then."

Henry Jackson bobbed his head. The lad, in his early twenties, rarely spoke. His almond eyes were as lively as his mouth.

Thinking of the incident, Peter laughed. "Before that the Mountaineers actually thought they knew what they were doing. Guess that's what should be expected from raw recruits."

Though the gunshots had rung far off in the distance, it caused great excitement amid the ranks of the 12th New Hampshire. With danger near, Peter gripped his musket tightly, thirsting to kill like the plague. But the foe didn't come. Deeply disheartened, he had helped the officers calm down the men and restore order.

But they weren't in Maryland any more. They were in Virginia.

Nathan stared into the flames. "We still don't know what we're doing," he said.

The men fell silent. Peter opened his mouth, then shut it again. He glanced at the faces of his friends. They all had distant ghost-like gazes.

Peter looked at his empty plate. He didn't want to disturb them. They could be thinking about home—or the coming battle.

At the thought of battle, his insides tangled tighter and tighter. He stood and walked to a clump of snow to wash his tin plate. He dug into the icy crust with his fingernails and pulled out a wet handful of snow. The coldness slowly calmed him. He scrubbed his plate until he could look at it and see his reflection.

When he got up again, he instantly tensed, his body rigid from his jaw to his toes. Colonel Palmer was watching him. Peter stood there like a gravestone, not knowing what to do. Since the officer did not motion him to come over, he decided he could leave. Self-conscious of each step, he walked back to his messmates.

"Are we ever going to cross the river?" Andrew asked.

"Yes," Peter said. "The pontoons will get here eventually—the engineers are going to build bridges across the river."

"It's already been six damn weeks!" Jim spat.

"Likely, they'll get here any day now," Peter said. "We should all prepare to face the enemy."

When pontoons arrived two days later, the pickets tensed and tightened the grip on their muskets, now taking their beats seriously.

The rebels dared them to cross—dared them to invade Fredericksburg.

Dared them to prove their courage.

Peter headed towards the river, musket at his side. He exhaled, his breath lingering in the air. It seemed all they had done for six weeks was polish their brass, freeze, and stand guard. Now the pontoons had arrived, and little had changed.

Jacob turned around and pointed his musket at Peter's chest and shouted. "Halt!"

Peter's eyes narrowed and his voice sharpened, adding force to the beginning of each word. "Private Vickery, you are supposed to be threatening to shoot them." Grabbing Jacob's shoulder, Peter pointed at the rebels on the opposite bank.

Jacob lowered his musket. "You surprised me, Sergeant," he mumbled.

Peter stared for a long minute at the Confederate camp. "We've been here so long we're all getting jumpy." He took a deep breath. "I'm here to relieve you."

Jacob nodded and walked away.

Peter resumed his post. He watched Jacob enter his tent, pleased that he didn't have to exchange more words with him. He might have won Molly's hand, but he still didn't cotton to her other suitor.

☆　☆　☆

A loud crack-thump rang through the air. Startled, Peter jumped to his feet. His heart twisted in his chest, and dread settled in his stomach. Was that cannon fire?

The noise came again. He didn't hear screaming or smell black powder. His eyes darted across the riverbank. In the predawn darkness, small, distant shadows moved towards the river. Squinting, Peter saw Union engineers moving pontoon boats on wagons to the river's bluffs, unloading and manhandling them down the steep slope to the river's edge. He bit his lip so hard it bled.

A hand gripped his shoulder, and he jerked it away. "Take it easy," Eli said.

Anger bubbled inside Peter's stomach and surged up his throat. His voice rose with a rough edge. "How can I take it easy in the middle of a damn war?"

With a thumb, Eli pointed at the engineers. "They're just starting. We have plenty of time."

"The battle is going to happen. It doesn't matter when."

The two of them watched the engineers tie the first pontoon to the shore. When the next was anchored, the pontoons were planked together.

A dense fog shielded their comrades from the foe with long, wispy fingers. "Thank God for small favors," Peter breathed.

Not long after his prayer, a southern battery fired two shots.

Jim joined them and watched the spectacle. "Were those shots? What are those for?"

"Warning signal," Peter said in a monotone. Hands fisted, his voice became more animated. "The rebels know we're crossing. Likely they heard the crack of the pontoons breaking through the ice."

Jim's face turned grave, lips firm, jaw tight. "Son of a bitch! I was afraid of that."

The fog cleared and Peter saw a long line of Confederates rapidly ramming cartridges. He doubted it was for target practice. As the fog returned, they could hear the enemy firing into the mist.

Peter's stomach twisted and tossed. Lead rained down on the unfinished bridges, boats, and engineers. Overcome with nausea, he looked over his shoulder, searching for Nathan. The boy wasn't in sight. Good. He didn't need to witness this.

The engineers frantically raced towards shore, throwing themselves face down in the mud to escape the shower of lead. Crimson blood stained the bridges. The battle hadn't even started and there were dead bodies.

Swallowing hard, Peter felt warm tears pushing on his eyelids. He turned away from the bridges, bile burning his throat. The sight tore his heart, sucked the breath from his lungs.

He couldn't help them. If he raced onto the bridge, he'd just get himself killed.

When the sharpshooter fire eased, Union engineers made a second attempt under the protection of cannon fire.

"What are they doing?" Eli said loudly, his voice rising in pitch. "They're plumb crazy!"

Peter shifted his weight upon the balls of his feet. "They're not the crazy ones. They're just obeying orders."

"They're working faster this time," Jim said.

Peter grunted. What good would that do? His voice dropped so soft it was barely audible. "If the brass knew what they were doing, they'd cancel this whole operation."

No one responded. Perhaps they didn't hear him. Perhaps that was a good thing.

Seeking to lighten the mood; Peter cracked a smile and consciously forced his voice to soften. "You think we'll end up swimming to the other side?"

Jim was the only one to laugh.

Eli's face tensed. "They wouldn't have us do that, would they?" His words were rushed, airy.

Jim put a hand on his brother's shoulder. "No. That's even beyond Burnside's stupidity."

The bridge-building effort continued for an hour with no progress, but heavy casualties. Some engineers were shot dead and fell into the boats, while others fell into the river.

Corpses littered the bridges. The wounded crawled off the bridge, leaving their fallen comrades behind. Unarmed and undaunted, the engineers went back into the water a third and fourth time, continuing to build the bridges under ceaseless fire from rebel sharpshooters.

☆　　☆　　☆

Despite the late hour, Peter was unable to sleep. He wrapped his blanket tighter around his body, delighting in the false comfort. It took great effort to push the impending battle out of his thoughts. Whenever he closed his eyes, the bleeding engineers came to mind. How could he sleep when the engineers couldn't? How could he sleep with the Confederates waiting to shoot, wound, and kill him?

At the first rays of sun, Peter paced. He rubbed the bottom of his coat between his fingers. This was wrong, dead wrong.

The bridges remained more than one hundred feet from the Confederate shore. Peter shook his head. The engineers had labored all night in vain—many to their graves.

The rising sun burned through the curtain of fog. Peter's eyes widened, and he gasped. Artillery had been transported to the water's edge where they blasted the town at direct range. The thunder of bursting shells couldn't drown out the occasional screams piercing the air.

Peter clamped his hands over his ears. Down there were civilians. War wasn't supposed to involve civilians.

Though he couldn't see it, Peter knew shells were flying though houses. At that range, that must have been Burnside's objective. He bared his teeth, his heart punching his rib cage. "God, let my sister and niece be safe." They lived in the countryside out of range of the cannons. Hopefully, they'd remained near Springdale.

"That is quite a shelling," Jim said.

"There's no need for this destruction." Peter kept his voice a coarse whisper for Jim's ears only.

"True," Jim said, his shoulders tense, "but war is, well, war. I think Burnside's just retaliating because the Rebs are preventing the building of his bridges."

"War should be confined to battles between soldiers, not enforce hardship on civilians. They don't deserve cannonballs crashing through their houses. Still, I don't mind the bombardment destroying the shops and factories."

Jim nodded.

The buildings, in full view, lined the waterfront like a battle line, creating a fortress to protect Fredericksburg. The brass seemed determined to strike a saber though the heart of the city. Flames, shooting from rooftops, proudly displayed the Union's presence.

"As if there was no doubt, we were here," Peter said, rolling his eyes.

"We might not cross after all." Jim pointed to the bridges; little progress had been made in their construction. His voice carried a little hope.

After all this death, Peter doubted that General Burnside would give up. Not that easily.

A few hours later, an officer Peter did not recognize, rode into camp. "We're looking for volunteers," he said loudly, spacing his words.

"Volunteers for what, sir?" Eli asked.

Don't speak! Peter willed the Kane brothers to read his mind. The last thing he needed was for one of the Kanes to get into something all-fired foolish. Get the 12th New Hampshire into something they'd regret.

The officer's lips thinned into a grim line. He spoke, frank and serious. "We need to get across the river. We're looking for volunteers to row the pontoons and drive the Confederates from the waterfront."

Peter's chest bunched. He had been right about Burnside. Scary how he knew the commander of the army so well, especially since how he had only seen him once on parade. His father would have done the same thing. Were all academy graduates that determined?

"Volunteers," the officer said again. "I'm looking for a valiant regiment."

By damn, Peter wasn't going to volunteer. He clamped his mouth shut. Only fools would go first.

The 7th Michigan ended up volunteering.

Peter held his breath, blood pulsing in his ears. This was a shipwreck about to happen. A pontoon raced across the muddy water under the cover of heavy cannon fire. Lead balls flew by the soldiers in the pontoons landing in the water. Others splintered off bits of wood from the boats.

The Michiganders touched the shore, jumped out of the boats, and hastily assembled into a skirmish line. They charged from the shelter of the river bluff into Fredericksburg, entering the houses that lined the river and rooting out the sharpshooters.

"Huzzah!" a chorus of Federals shouted as each new boatload of troops reached the contested shore. After such a grueling trial to cross the river, the completion in itself seemed like a victory.

Soldiers rowed across the river all day. The rhythmic splash in the water became commonplace. When night came, the 12th New Hampshire remained on the Stafford side. The Confederates fell back and left Fredericksburg in Burnside's hands.

Sitting around their campfires, the Mountaineers whispered their opinions of their commanders and thoughts about the rebels. General Whipple rode up on his chestnut horse interrupting their conversations. He was a handsome man with a thick beard and mustache. His black hair touched his blouse collar. The general took a moment to survey the soldiers before speaking to them.

"Men, we're going into battle in the morning. We're crossing the bridge and entering Fredericksburg. It's going to be a hard fight to keep the city. We're trying to defeat the rebels on their home ground. Remember your fallen comrades. Let that inspire your actions and spur your courage. If we take Fredericksburg, we will cripple the South. When we are victorious, it's on to Richmond!"

The men cheered. Peter remained silent, overlooked in the sea of men. Him a starry-eyed, glory-seeking volunteer? Far from it.

The general motioned for everyone to be quiet. "Don't fire until you're given the order. Have courage, men. A soldier is trained to fight, not run scared." With his speech done, he rode off.

Scared? The word stung. The men searched the faces of their comrades to see if they could find a coward. Everyone was sober.

"Back in training, they told us that few men died in battle in proportion to all those who fought," a thin, bony lad said to no one in particular. "The odds of us dying are slim. The odds are slim," he repeated.

Everyone ignored him, lost in their own thoughts. Some had their heads bowed in prayer, while others cussed the rebels, whipping themselves up so they'd be angry enough to fight.

Half-amused, half-inspired, Peter overheard bits and pieces of their conversations.

"What do the Rebs look like?" a young boy from another company asked. Peter's ears strained to hear every word.

Andrew chuckled. "Well, son, they all have horns like the devil and pointy tails to match."

"Either leave the boy alone or quit telling him lies like that!" Peter scolded. "The Rebs are ungodly sons of bitches, but we're all human."

"You drawl like a Johnny Reb," the boy blurted.

"That's because I'm originally from Virginia. Unfortunately, after two years in the North, my accent hasn't weakened one bit."

"You're from Virginia, Sergeant?" the boy asked.

"Right around here, as a matter-of-fact. And, as you can see, I'm not a Reb."

Speechless, the redheaded boy's eyes widened, lips pressed together. Even the freckles on his face paled.

Peter walked back to the campfire with a that-was-a-good-joke smile. It was better for the boy to have the shock now, than in battle.

Anticipation of the battle made it hard for the men to sleep. Peter tossed and turned, fighting with his blanket. That night he dreamed another horrible nightmare.

His father sat in a leather armchair ridiculing him between nips of whiskey. He'd caught him, and now Peter was going to pay the ultimate price for betraying his family. His father set his whiskey bottle down and picked up his 1848 Colt dragoon revolver.

"This helped me get rid of enemies during the Mexican-American War," he said, spinning the chamber. "It will help me again."

He pulled the trigger and Peter flinched.

His father roared with laughter and pulled the trigger again. "Am I getting to you, boy? A lot of war is in your head. You have about four more minutes to live, depending on where the bullet is. You better start praying."

Peter didn't say a word.

"Did the North make you an atheist? Pray."

Peter recited the whole "Our Father." He breathed "amen."

His father pulled the trigger. "I'm impressed. You didn't even flinch that time. You're showing courage for once in your life."

Peter glared at him, silently asking God to forgive the anger in his own heart. "How can you kill your own son?"

"You're not my son. You're a traitor! You knew when you left I'd never welcome you back." Once more, he pulled the trigger. Again, it was empty. "All your friends in Yankee uniforms are shelling Fredericksburg. I'll be lucky if Springdale is still standing when this war is over. The blue devils vandalize southern property and steal everything they can get their hands on. You would know the latter. You stole Dan." He pulled the trigger again.

"Just because I don't agree with you, means I don't have the right to live?"

"You're a threat. You made the mistake of coming back. I've been waiting to do this ever since you ran."

This would be the sixth shot. It was guaranteed to have lead. His father raised the revolver and pointed it at his Peter's head.

"No!"

Peter didn't hear himself shout over the roar of his heart.

"Sergeant?" Jim said, shaking Peter's shoulder.

Peter swallowed and his ears popped.

"Sergeant?" Jim said again, worry in his voice. He propped himself up on his arms.

Peter felt weak; sweat rolled off his forehead. He put a hand on his chest, trying to force his lungs to take in more air.

He cupped his hands over his flushed face. Peter hadn't acted out his nightmares about his father since he had quit living above the livery stable in Pittsfield years ago. It had seemed so real.

"Are you ill? You look pale."

Peter did not reply. Jim's words did not make sense to him, sounding garbled.

"Are you afraid of the battle tomorrow? It will be our first one."

"Thanks, Jim," Peter said, his voice weak.

The concern in Jim's eyes didn't lessen. "I'm here for you. What was that all about?"

Peter looked off to the side. "I'm afraid. But not of the battle."

"Your father?"

Peter nodded.

Jim sat next to Peter. His strong presence stilled Peter's racing heart, just as Dan's presence had done back at home.

"You're not going to see him," Jim said.

"You don't know that. He could be commanding a Confederate regiment."

"Even if he was, the odds of him being in Fredericksburg, the odds of him being close enough for you to recognize each other are slim."

Peter folded his right hand into a fist and tapped it on Jim's knee. "Thanks for talking me down."

Jim gave him a crooked smile. "Farm boy reasoning. Sometimes good common sense is all it takes."

"My father said I lacked all common sense."

"Rubbish. You had common sense enough to leave Springdale and settle in Pittsfield."

"That wasn't common sense; that was desperation." He paused, switching subjects back to the present. "How can I be a model for the men when…?" His voice trailed off.

"You'll be all right when morning comes. It'll just be reaction. Try to go back to sleep."

Peter rolled over and closed his eyes, but sleep was impossible.

☆　　☆　　☆

In the early morning hours, the sun brawled with the thick fog giving the haze an orange cast. Peter performed his battle preparations in a blur. Eat. Clean musket. Pack. The Mountaineers moved from their camp to one mile from the Rappahannock River. Closer to the crossing. Closer to the enemy. His stomach convulsed, making it hard to concentrate.

Peter pulled himself together with sheer determination. The men were counting on him.

The 12th New Hampshire marched over the hill and rested near the river in front of the lower pontoon bridge. They'd barely stopped walking when the enemy spotted them. Shots disrupted the silence. Peter froze.

There was a reason why men didn't charge into a bear's den. Running into danger went against every fiber of his nature.

Officers shouting and the staccato of musket fire pierced his thoughts.

"Onward, men!" Lieutenant French's voice roared over the racket.

As they drew closer, the rate of fire quickened. Some soldiers, stunned, walked forward without a word before collapsing to the ground. The sight caused the men to waver.

Peter swallowed hard and got over his shock, remembering his job. He started yelling at his men continually. "Dress those ranks! Keep it tight boys. Form smart lines on the other side. Remember, there's safety in numbers—keep sight of the man beside you."

The gears in the military machine began to turn. Obediently, the men closed ranks and kept plodding forward. The bridge swayed beneath the heavy tread of feet. Cannon shells flew overhead.

An undertaker stood at the foot of the bridges handing out cards. Peter shook his head at the depressing sight.

"Get out of here, or you'll need to find an undertaker yourself," a big Irishman threatened, in a thick accent.

"I have every right to be here," the undertaker protested coolly.

The Irishman cussed the coffin peddler, and after giving him two strong jabs, pushed him into the water. Death was on the minds of all the soldiers. They didn't need an undertaker to point out the possibility that this battle would be their last one.

Scores of playing card decks were discarded on the bridge. Many cards fell out of their boxes and fluttered to the water. Men didn't want to be carrying a deck when it was their time to be judged by their Maker.

Jacob clasped both hands across his stomach, doubled in pain. "Private Vickery," Peter snapped, his voice harsh, rebuking. "You're going across the bridge if I have to drag you."

"I'm ill, Sergeant," Jacob said in a pitiful whine. "I feel like there's a knife in my stomach."

"You have a bellyful of cowardice," Peter said, pulling him to his feet. "Now keep your place in line. I have my eye on you."

Even in the moments before battle, Peter enjoyed prodding Jacob. He looked down the line at the poor private. His knees were quivering, his pale face tinted green. Peter forced his lips not to smile but allowed a minute of enjoyment to show in his eyes. Now, with sergeant chevrons on his sleeves, he was the superior one in their private quarrel.

He approached the crossing and looked out across the bridge. The rebels had commenced shelling the head of the column. Crossing the bridge, Peter felt helpless. The trek seemed to take hours, though in reality, it was mere minutes.

Once on the other side, Peter ran for the shelter of a large Virginia pine. He had hardly gotten behind it and congratulated himself when a shell struck the tree next to him and exploded. He quickly found another place to take cover.

Peter observed the rest of the company advancing. Jacob seemed to be pointing his musket at him. He shook his head, convinced he was seeing things. All the soldiers had their muskets raised, ready to fire.

Peter shouted at his comrades. "Come on men."

He waited until the Kanes were by his side before continuing. His regiment moved forward until it was sheltered by the bluffs of the river. They stayed until they were ordered to retire to a position near the railroad.

Knowing the area, Peter guessed the Confederates were hunkered down in the sunken road behind a stone wall at the rear of the city. Peter rubbed his jaw with his thumb and forefinger. The Union would have to root them out. Trying to capture the strong defensible position could cost thousands of lives.

A thousand was just a number.

He couldn't imagine what a thousand corpses actually looked like.

He didn't want to.

"I have n-never k-killed anyone b-before, Sergeant," a boy with a slender face said.

Peter looked at him and it turned his stomach. The lad was barely big enough to shoulder the heavy musket. Surely he had lied about his age.

Peter didn't offer comforting words. He knew what it was like to kill someone. The horror never left him. Her stiff body, still warm, covered in blood, haunted him. His entire past haunted him. It followed him like his shadow.

☆　☆　☆

"Let's go," Peter said.

"Go where?" Eli asked.

Peter saw smoke rising from the buildings in Fredericksburg, swirling into a dense net. There were people in those buildings, people caught in the chaos. "Anywhere I can't see this destruction."

He'd been sergeant long enough to know that men figured they didn't need to use their muskets; plundering and destroying property were safer ways for them to punish the enemy. Not to mention, mirrors, pianos, paintings and the like were symbols of the slave-sweat wealth that was despised in the North.

Yankees from other regiments came back with their arms loaded with clocks, tobacco, blankets, anything small enough to carry that would be useful or valuable. Some had even donned southern finery over their uniforms. The soldiers looked strange in top hats, white gloves, frock coats, silk cravats—some even sported tails.

Peter witnessed his old city, a place of rich history and tradition, undergo the transformation of war. He knew the Confederates defending Marye's Heights also looked on in horror.

The Confederate Army had not set foot on northern soil. They were being invaded. To most southerners the word Yankee already tasted bitter.

Destroying Fredericksburg would just enflame their hatred. It made Peter feel both vindicated and sad. Fredericksburg was home to people—generous and evil—people who had helped him and hurt him. He wished the innocent could be spared the pain of war. He wished the slaveholders would get so caught up in fighting to save their slaves that they'd forget about him.

Invisible. Peter yearned to be invisible. To just be another nameless, faceless soldier.

CHAPTER 4

EARLY IN THE morning, the 12th New Hampshire was ordered forward to the sloping open field. Fog settled in like angels' wings above them. Peter dropped to his stomach in the dirt. He breathed in the earthiness.

Cannon shells burst all around them. One shell flew long over the lines and landed in the river. Others tossed clods of dirt and shrapnel in their direction. Many men around him quietly praying, making peace with God.

Smoke stung their eyes and obscured their view. It looked like a dust cloud had settled on the field. They didn't need to see. They knew they were helpless targets. Peter didn't know whether advancing from this position would be better or worse. The Union soldiers were unable to reach the cannoneers with rifle fire, allowing them to continue the onslaught from relative safety. Time ticked by and the battle loomed closer. The Mountaineers waited for the order to advance on Marye's Heights.

Peter took deliberate, deep breaths, trying not to let his fear show. He had to appear strong. Dan had taught him how to hide his emotions. Still, acting brave around his father was one thing; acting brave in the middle of the war, another.

The panicked faces of his friends told him they were thinking they were about to die. To distract them, Peter began singing the "Battle Hymn of the Republic." Nathan and then Jim and Eli joined in. By the last verse, most of the men sang loud and strong.

They watched as column after column of Union soldiers charged Marye's Heights. Hunched forward, the men struggled up the hill like fish fighting against a strong current. Each time they were cut down by a dreadful storm of lead.

"I wish I had married Molly before I left," Peter said to Eli.

"You'll marry her when you get back," Eli replied. "Mr. Canton's having your house built right now."

"I wish he didn't have to pay for everything," Peter said under his breath. Out of the corner of Peter's eye, he could tell Eli hadn't heard his complaint over the cannon fire. "Why couldn't she marry me before we had a place to live? Why couldn't her mother understand we needed to make our union legal?"

The next line of men charging the heights fell. It seemed more like the destruction from a volcanic blast than a battle. Still, men marched towards the Heights in steady ranks.

Eli offered an eerily distant smile. "Molly's a proper lady. What'd you expect? Don't worry; you two *will* get married."

Peter nodded. Focusing on his wedding kept his mind from the present.

The next regiment sent onto the field was cut down in rows, wave after wave. Bloody corpses lined the path towards the long stone wall.

Nathan gritted his teeth and his eyes glossed with tears. He squeezed Peter's arm.

"Hang in there. No one said war was pretty," Peter said.

The stench of urine and vomit floated down the line. With his left hand, Peter covered his mouth. The shrieks of the wounded were agonizing, desperate. He shut his eyes to block out the mangled corpses. The images remained in his mind as clear as on the field.

If his company participated in this battle, likely, he wouldn't have to worry about being recognized in Fredericksburg; he knew he'd be buried right here on this field. His body would be stacked with the rest in a massive trench like cordwood.

Peter's legs trembled. His heart twisted in his chest, sweat oozing out of every pore in his body. He slapped his cheek. The sting made the dark thought fade, made the adrenaline pump harder, made his focus sharpen.

It wasn't how he had imagined his first battle. Peter thought he'd be charging across an open field as a scale in a gigantic blue snake with the gray snake advancing towards him. Each time they got too close to each other, there'd be a clash. But this was suicide.

Peter shifted his weight and prayed while he stood in line with his regiment. After each wave of men attempted to gain the Heights, the line got shorter and shorter. His heart clenched for a second and then pounded so hard his chest hurt. Next would be their turn to charge the Heights. It was some comfort that he'd die with his friends around him. They'd march into heaven, side by side, just as they'd charged in battle.

Jim was ghostly pale, every muscle tense. Eli, beside him, chewed on his bottom lip, staring at his shoes. Peter looked to his other side. Henry Jackson's cheeks were puffed out but slowly deflating. On the other side of Henry, Andrew tugged at his beard, his eyes scanning the open field.

The stench of death slithered its way into Peter's gut, made him hesitate. He held his breath, waiting for the order to charge.

A murmur echoed down the line. The assault was cancelled. The madness of war temporarily over.

Peter's legs grew weak and he dropped to his knees. Jim grabbed his shoulder and pulled him to his feet. Peter exhaled numerous times. His heartbeat slowed from racing to jogging to normal. Strength slowly rejuvenated his numb limbs. His muscles remained tense and ready for action. "Thank you, Lord," he said.

He ripped off the paper pinned to his coat; on it, he had written his name and regiment. He crumpled it into a ball and threw it on the ground. Molly wasn't going to claim his corpse. Not yet, anyway. But then again, today wasn't over.

Now assigned burial duty, nausea punched Peter in the stomach. In the dim morning light, Fredericksburg transformed into a Union cemetery; lawns and fields were dug up to hide the dead. Peter helped cart the bodies to their graves. They were disassembled in every way imaginable, resembling meat on a butcher's table more than men. He'd never forget their corpses.

Some of the bodies were stripped of their clothing and shoes, a couple completely naked. Peter shook his head. The rebels had scavenged the dead.

"All this bloodshed just to keep the country together," Peter said, shaking his head.

Eli rested his hand on Peter's back. "When we start winning this war, Lincoln will free the slaves. That'll show 'em."

Peter sighed. He had grown weary of such talk. In the face of so much death and pain it was cold comfort.

Jacob's glare grew icier with each shovelful of dirt he tossed into the trenches.

Peter's insides knotted tighter, the constriction bringing on another wave of bile. He gripped his stomach. He didn't need to put up with his rival at the moment. He didn't have the cool head and patience it required, so he ignored him.

"I doubt we'll stay here long," Andrew said, "if that'll make you feel any better."

"Nothing will make me feel better except going home and marrying Molly," Peter said in a heavy voice.

Jacob's face reddened, but he didn't say a word.

"I know," Eli said, "but we're fighting for what we believe in."

Andrew grunted. "Patriotism doesn't stop lead."

After that, all the men continued their chores silently.

Andrew was right about not staying in Fredericksburg long. After four days, General Burnside ordered a retreat. The assault had cost him more men than he could afford. He needed to save the remnants of his ragged army.

"We fought like cornered cats to capture this city and now we're giving it back," Jacob grumbled.

For once Peter had to agree with his rival. This quick retreat seemed to make all the bloodshed pointless.

That night, the 12th New Hampshire took position near the canal. Peter lay on the ground with a blanket over him. Even with a small fire burning, he shivered. He folded his arms across his chest and held still, trying to retain his body heat.

Sleep did not come. Peace did not come. Finally, in the wee hours of the morning, his eyelids were so heavy, they closed—and the nightmares came.

"You look like a corpse," he dreamed his father saying, "pale and stiff. You will be a corpse, soon. Very soon."

"You can't see into the future," Peter fired back.

His father smiled wide and menacing and laughed. "Are you sure about that, boy? Traitors always get their due."

Peter bit his lip, not dignifying that with a response. If his father couldn't win an argument with words, he resorted to using his fists and, if necessary, throwing chairs or striking someone over the head with whatever was handy.

"You tongue-tied, boy? You've always been a coward. You've never once thrown a punch at me."

Peter's ears burned. His hands folded into fists, but he couldn't bring himself to confront his tormenter. Perhaps he was a coward. How could he keep enduring this abuse day after day?

Because of what his father might do to the others he loved. Yes, that was why he took it all on his shoulders.

"You going to do something with those fists or just stand there?"

Peter didn't move a muscle.

"I hope that's not what you do tomorrow. Then again, if you just freeze up on the field and can't fire, you'll prove me right. Prove that you're worthless. A true Southerner is going to lay you in your grave. Maybe tomorrow. I wish I could do it myself."

☆　☆　☆

A man shouted. "Wake up!"

Peter sprang to his feet. Darkness enveloped camp. A group of fires illuminated Lieutenant French's grim face.

Peter's comrades woke each other until all the men stood, ready for orders.

"Get something to eat and then get ready to be deployed as skirmishers," the officer ordered.

Fear clamped Peter's teeth together. He nodded instead of saying, 'yes, sir'.

He went about his business slowly, trying hard not to think about facing the enemy in advance of the army. Charging the field with a whole brigade was bad enough—skirmishing something worse.

Peter took deep, calming breaths. He heard his comrades crossing the Rappahannock. Footsteps echoed on the pontoon bridge. Soft voices caught his ears and the occasional moan or curse. He wished he was retreating with them.

He stood his ground, rifle in hand, the dream he'd had playing in his mind. *You look like a corpse. A true Southerner is going to lay you in your grave. You were born a coward.*

Peter shook his head to make his father's voice stop. His eyes narrowed. He focused on the approaching Confederates. This *was* life or death. This was not a dream.

His heart barely kept time with his lungs. His head felt fuzzy, but his judgment remained clear. He forced his feet to remain planted.

Forced himself to listen to the officers.

Forced himself to follow orders.

Lieutenant French spoke, sharp, and booming. "Hold your position."

The skirmishers formed a hasty battle line. He'd give all his pay for an ounce of cover. Fully focused on loading and firing, he ignored the crackling volleys, lead tearing into flesh, and chilling screams.

The Confederates were fifty yards away and closing fast.

Pulling a cartridge out, he bit the top off. Poured in the acrid powder. Pushed the wad and bullet on top. Shoved it down the barrel with his ramrod. He grabbed a percussion cap out of his pouch. Cocking the hammer, he put the percussion cap on the nipple. He nearly fired without removing his ramrod.

"Damn." His arms trembled. He held his breath to steady his actions and fired. He saw his target fall to the ground, gripping his chest. Peter exhaled. They were targets. Not men.

One of the Kane brothers moaned. Peter's head jerked to his right expecting to see one of them wounded. Instead, Jim rubbed his swollen eyes. Standing shoulder to shoulder, their faces black from biting numerous cartridges, they looked like miners. With his tongue, Peter tried to wipe the grime off his teeth. The bitterness soured his mouth and when he swallowed, the powder stuck like glue in his throat.

The trees screamed at him. The ground bled. His whole body smelled like gunpowder. Henry Jackson grabbed his shoulder and crumpled to the ground. Andrew Silas lay beside him.

Lifeless bodies. Glossy eyes. Peter blinked. Another man went into convulsions. Peter sucked on his bottom lip. The vein on his neck pulsed. He loaded his rifle again. It seemed they were taking on the entire Confederate Army.

A wounded Federal kept crying out, "Mother! Mother! Mother!"

The wrenching plea brought tears to Peter's irritated eyes, splintered his nerves. It was the redheaded boy who had been shocked to find out he talked like a Johnny Reb.

"Shut up," Peter said, then cringed at his heartlessness.

A burning pain seared his right arm. He touched the wound and the sting it brought overpowered his senses. He pulled his hand away as if he had touched a hot stove, his fingers dripping blood.

A rebel raised his rifle and fired at the redheaded boy's skull. Peter clutched his rifle tighter.

His eyes darted from one panic-stricken comrade to another. His chest felt hollow. His emotions went numb, no longer able to register grief or pain.

"Damn the brass!" Peter's words were drowned by the next volley.

Either send in reinforcements or let us retreat. Neither happened.

His scalp, hands, forehead, chest were soaked with sweat—as if it had been raining sweat.

The Confederates advanced towards them. The dwindling line of fire his friends provided offered little hindrance.

A clattering noise clipped the air. Bayonets. As if the blood and bullets weren't enough. A sour taste rose in Peter's throat. Realizing they had the upper-hand, the rebels let out a horrendous "Yyyeeeaaaa!"

Peter froze. The rebel yell rang in his ears, turning his heart to stone. He swallowed his fear in a big gulp and grabbed his leather pouch. His ammunition was running low—everyone was running out. He felt his coat pocket. It contained a handful of bullets. Soon, they'd be surrounded.

His stomach clenched; his lungs seemed to shut down. He struggled to breathe, struggled to stand, struggled to think. The darkness of death drifted towards him, ready to devour him in seconds. The scope of his thoughts narrowed to the point of a bayonet. The bayonet gleaming in the hands of his enemy. He could surrender and end up in prison. He could stay on the field and die. Or he could make a run for it and have a chance to live.

He glanced back at the pontoon bridge. With the Confederates in pursuit, crossing it would be a death trap. If he could escape the battlefield, he'd be forgotten.

He took to his heels. *Must keep moving. Must get off the field. Must get to the city.*

A Confederate soldier lay on his side, his eyes glassy. As he ran past he took the soldier for dead, but a hand reached out and grabbed his ankle. Iciness spread up his leg and he fell headlong onto the ground.

"Peter," the rebel whispered hoarsely.

Peter sat up and blinked at the soldier. He had taken a ball to the gut and gripped his middle with both hands.

"Amos?" Peter said. "Amos Dawson?" He had never expected to run into an old school friend like this.

"Help me," Amos said. "Water." Amos reached his arm out.

Peter glanced at his canteen and then at the wounded man. He didn't have time to talk and tend the man's wounds.

"I'm dying, Peter." His skin was white and waxy and he labored to breathe. "My throat is dry."

Peter passed him his canteen. His heart beat erratically as he waited for the man to finish. Amos took a long drink, and then grimaced and moaned when he pulled the canteen from his lips.

"Thank you."

Peter nodded. He wanted to say more, wanted to help, but he couldn't stay.

Amos' green eyes registered understanding. "Take care of yourself, Peter," Amos lay down on his back and moaned again. "I will speak to your mother for you."

Peter's throat tightened and he struggled to hold back tears.

"Go," Amos said. "Or we'll both by lying here."

Peter slung the canteen over his shoulder and resumed running. Once inside the limits of Fredericksburg, he moved deeper into the city, using the trees and buildings as cover.

A burning sensation spread up his arm, blood dripping down his sleeve. "Blasted!" His pulse pounded in his ears in time to his throbbing arm. He kneeled and pulled a bandanna out of his haversack and tied it above the elbow, pulling it taut with his free hand and teeth.

He got to his feet and stumbled forward. Don't stay in one place long. The familiar warning echoed through his mind. He wasn't safe. He could be discovered. He could be pursued. He could be captured.

Adrenaline propelled him onward through the battle-scarred city. He felt numb seeing most houses in town scathed by the Union bombardment. The artillery had blown holes as big as barrels through the structures. The town lay deserted and pillaged.

Peter's feet pounded the ground in a swift, steady motion. He held his rifle across his chest, his right hand on the butt and his left gripping the hot muzzle. He didn't dare get any closer to the trigger, for fear his taut nerves would cause him to fire by accident.

The Confederate soldiers drifted farther and farther and farther away. He ran to the countryside heaving for breath, his lungs burning, his sides aching.

At first he was running blindly, but then the path became familiar. He felt pulled towards a certain mansion. He could only hope that it would provide him refuge.

CHAPTER 5

PETER STAGGERED UP the walkway and grasped the gate. He eyed the whitewashed house with apprehension. His past and future lay behind that door. A future in the Union Army or in prison.

Taking a deep breath, he pounded on the door. All he heard was the blood rushing in his ears.

At last, the knob slowly turned. The door opened to reveal a young woman swollen with child. Her hand flew to her mouth, stifling a scream. Her knees buckled, and she grabbed the doorframe to steady herself.

This wasn't the same innocent woman from his childhood. Was she carrying her second child? Third? So much had happened in the past two years. "You remember me, don't you, Abigail?"

She visibly relaxed. "Peter? What are you doing here? You were the last person I had expected to see."

"I know. I don't have anywhere else to go."

Her sharp eyes looked him over—searching his soul to see how Yankee he had become, he was sure.

"I'm glad you're well," Peter said, breaking the uneasy silence. "I was worried about you."

Abigail opened her mouth, but hesitated as if searching for the right words. She turned her head and flicked a glance inside the house. When she spoke her voice was soft. "General Lee urged everyone to leave the city. He even sent army wagons and ambulances to transport people to safer ground." She paused and shifted her weight, taking long pauses between her words. "Many women and children fled to the safety of my house. I am hosting them until it's safe for them to return."

Peter nodded, a deep frown etched across his face. "You needn't say more. I'm not welcome here. I'll be on my way."

"Wait," Abigail called just as he reached the white picket fence. Peter stopped. "Your arm is bleeding. Where are you going?"

"I don't know."

"There are Confederate soldiers everywhere in town; others are roaming the countryside."

Peter pinched his lips together. Anxiety wormed its way into the pit of his stomach. He shrugged, tightening his voice. "I figured that."

"It isn't safe for you to go anywhere. You can stay here, sir." She took his hand and helped him into her home, ushering him to a door. "You can stay in the cellar."

"Thank you, ma'am," Peter said, bobbing his head.

His nose wrinkled at the stench of the onions and turnips. They hung in bunches from the ceiling.

Creeaak. Peter's heart sank like a rock thrown in the river. Abigail had shut the door, but he understood. His world had been turned on its head, not by the war, but by his actions on his eighteenth birthday. He was putting her in danger by being here. An uncomfortable feeling crawled up his neck. He shook his head and it fell away. She'd never stood up for him when they were children. She owed him.

Peter felt his way around the cellar with his left arm, waiting for his eyes to adjust to the darkness. He found an empty barrel, turned it over and sat, cradling his right arm in his lap. He untied the bandanna and tried to examine his wound. All he saw was coagulating blood. Poking at it made it hurt worse, made the pain pulsate through his body.

His heart raced. He closed his eyes and took a deep, ragged breath.

"You're safe here," Peter whispered. "You're safe."

The floor stared back at him. He imagined he was a boy again, playing hide and seek. It was no use. He couldn't fool himself. He was a wanted man. Whether he would be turned in or not was up to his sister.

☆　☆　☆

The cellar door opened, revealing a light at the top of the stairs. Peter darted behind some crates. He knew someone could easily find him by following his trail of blood. Still, his musket was within reach.

"Peter," Abigail called out, her voice hushed. "Peter, we have to talk."

He came out from hiding and turned over another barrel for her to sit on. This was not how he'd envisioned a reunion with his sister.

The lantern she held illuminated her face. Her hair still the color of tanned leather was worn parted in the middle and poofed over the ears, then braided and pinned into a low bun at the back of the neck. In some ways she looked like she hadn't aged a day. Her beauty stood in sharp contrast to her sour demeanor.

"You're one of them. I never thought you'd wear a blue uniform," Abigail said in a tone of disgust.

"Why?"

"Because your home is in Virginia," she replied. "For eighteen years, you lived in Virginia. Goodness sakes, Peter, your mother is buried here, and Father would die if he saw you dressed like that."

The thought cheered him. "Yes," Peter said, "I'm sure Father would. But you're wrong, Abigail; my home is in New Hampshire. I've made a new life there, new friends. I'm going to marry soon."

"Are you in the cavalry?"

Abigail's glare was out of place with her sweet tone. Still, Peter appreciated her pretending to care.

"No, I'm in the infantry."

"You're a foot soldier? How disgraceful." Abigail turned her nose in the air.

"It's no secret that the infantry does most of the work. I figured that's where I'd do the most good."

"You were always good mounted."

"Yes, but recruiters came to Pittsfield to raise an infantry company. Most of the men I knew in town were joining, so I signed up, too."

"Gentlemen ride horses," Abigail said, her voice curt and sharp.

"Sis, let's try to have a decent conversation. Where's little Sarah?"

"Sarah is now five. Mrs. Scott is taking care of her for me."

"You mean her nurse Deborah is taking care of her."

"Eeerrr." Abigail made a growling noise. "The North sure has filled your head with nonsense. Servants help, but we do take care of our children, Peter."

"To a point, yes. But you can't deny that Aunt Ruth raised us."

"No, but that's different. Father didn't know what to do after Mother died. Aunt Ruth had to raise you when you were a baby. She had given birth to Dan a couple months before Mother died, so she had to wet-nurse you. Maybe that destroyed your mind."

Peter gritted his teeth, trying to overlook the racist comment. "Father still didn't raise me when I was older, though he assisted in your upbringing."

"He tried to guide you, Peter. You refused to listen to him."

Peter shook his head. "The only thing he tried hard at was staying drunk." Abigail did not respond. Peter decided to change the subject. "I regret that I've been unable to see my niece. I remember that she's a spitting image of you."

"She's fine."

Peter shifted in his seat. Abigail clearly did not want to discuss her family, but he decided to press a little harder. "I'm happy your family is about to grow. I knew you and John wanted more children."

Abigail's eyes twinkled. She rubbed her bulging belly. "It is a blessing."

"You said Mrs. Scott was taking care of Sarah. Maybe I could go over and see her. I'd love to see Mrs. Scott too. She always—"

"I don't think that is a good idea," Abigail interrupted. Her voice grew richer, rounded with pride. "Mr. Scott is a colonel in J. E. B. Stuart's cavalry. John serves under him. He's a first lieutenant."

"I'm not surprised."

"I see my little brother hasn't become brass yet." Her words carried a heavy slight.

"I wouldn't want a commission even if it was offered. I was elected sergeant and that's where I want to stay. I know your husband had his epaulettes handed to him on a silver platter."

"How dare you say that, Peter Joshua Warren!" Her voice was icy. "My husband is a gentleman, like you used to be before you ran off. You're the one betraying your heritage."

Peter shook his head. "I'm trying to make a new name for myself. I want to distance myself as far as possible from the evils of my past."

"I've been told that you still have Dan," Abigail said, her words rushed, forceful.

Peter's breath hitched. Had she talked to the bounty hunters? Who else knew about his life in New Hampshire? "Dan has a job and it *isn't* working for me."

"Friends aren't normally glued to each other for two years."

Peter's eyes sharpened into daggers. They were more than friends; they were brothers. She'd continue to argue her point, so he remained silent.

☆　☆　☆

"So why'd you come here?" Abigail asked. "After two years, it couldn't have been a social call. You know this house isn't safe."

"I'm a coward," Peter said, his face now contorted with suffering. His voice sounded raspy and rough. "Forgotten, in the line of fire, my company fought as long and as hard as we could. The Confederates killed many of my comrades. Is that what you want to hear? We were nearly surrounded and I deserted."

"So you're not ready to face up to your responsibilities. You ran."

The pain in his arm flared as if an invisible hand rubbed salt in his wound. "Yes, I ran. Yes, it was disgraceful. But with the way the fight was going, there might only be a handful of my company left. Your husband would've done the same in my situation."

"Then I should be thankful it was a Confederate victory."

"Forgive me if I can't cheer the loss of so many good men. Friends, no less."

"We are at war, you know."

Peter straightened. "Yes, I've heard that."

"Then you can understand my reason for being cold."

Peter noticed the determined tone in her voice, but the way she kept playing with the heart-shaped locket around her neck gave her up. She was really worried about him.

"So it's just the fact that I'm a Yankee?"

"Peter, you ran away at eighteen. Sure, you had grown into a man, but I still saw you as my little brother. I felt like my heart had been ripped out of my chest when you left."

Peter opened his mouth to object, and closed it when he found no words to adequately express his regrets. He hated the way he had slipped silently into the night without once looking back. He should have at least told Abigail goodbye.

"Father ranted about you endlessly," Abigail continued. "He had me so worked up my heart hardened and his bitterness became intertwined in my blood. If you had told me you were leaving—"

"If I had told you, you would have snitched on me."

"I might have. Or talked you out of it. But you never even thought I deserved the chance, did you?"

"No. I didn't." Peter paused, wincing when a movement caused the pain in his arm to radiate to his fingertips. "I needed to leave and was afraid you'd stop me. Stop my adventure."

Abigail's face turned scarlet. "*Adventure.* You wanted to leave your family for an adventure!"

"Adventure wasn't the right word, but that's what it turned out to be—a glorious adventure. I needed to get away from here. I needed to get away from Father."

"Peter, you know how childish that sounds? You had responsibilities, which apparently did not factor into your decision."

"I'm sorry if the right choice for me happened to disgrace my family."

"You've outdone yourself, now—my brother, a Yankee!"

Pain hit Peter with a right hook. Sweat blanketed his forehead and he ground his teeth. But when he spoke his voice remained strong and steady. "I gave my heart and hand to the Union, and I'm proud of it."

"Proud! Sure, rub it in." Her voice was as harsh as the winter wind.

"I had to put up with Father for eighteen years. You never once stepped in to help, never came to my aid."

"Is that what you think, Peter?" Abigail's hands fidgeted in her lap. "I couldn't break up a fight when Father began swinging. God, I wanted to. But I wasn't capable. I did tend your bruises on numerous occasions."

Peter nodded. She did try to ease his misery afterward, but he needed her to try to prevent it.

As if reading his mind, Abigail continued, "And I tried watering down Father's whiskey. That helped at times."

"I didn't realize that you had tried…"

"I tried more than you know. But it is impossible to reason with a drunk."

"Father's drinking caused me so much pain. Striking Dan was the last straw. I had responsibilities to myself, too. I couldn't live with myself if I had stayed. I couldn't endure it anymore."

"So you could have left Fredericksburg. You didn't have to move *halfway across the country*." Abigail said, her timbre inching closer to a screech.

"You'd never understand," Peter said, his words sagging under the sadness of his heart. "Father loves you. He treats you like an angel."

"I think I reminded him of mother, but he loved you, too."

Peter's fingers folded into fists. The movement sent a jarring shot of agony to his core. In a second he straightened his hands. "I was completely neglected. If I hadn't had Dan as my playmate…" Peter's lips kept moving but the words were inaudible.

Abigail's leaned forward as if trying to hear his private thoughts. She wanted to know more; well then, he'd get something off his chest. "Why didn't you try to calm Father down when he had worked himself into a fury? You always fled when he started pounding me with his fists."

Abigail's eyes turned a darker shade of green and she briefly lowered her gaze to her lap. "I tried, Peter. I talked to him when you weren't around. I tried to step into our mother's shoes and failed."

Peter humphed.

"Love comes in different forms. I tried to be there for you, but I didn't understand you, Peter. I still don't. Father and I struggled to accept your differences."

"Continue to stand up for Father, Sis, but he never once said a kind word to me."

"He was trying to teach you, Peter."

"Teach me to be a man. I know." Peter did not try to contain his sarcasm.

"Father did the best he could."

"His best! It wasn't even a tenth of what I needed. His love came with too many strings attached."

"If you had listened to *some* of what he said…"

"Like how to be stricter with the help?" Peter's timbre carried knife-like sharpness.

Abigail folded her arms across her chest. She gave Peter a disapproving glare, one he had imagined his mother would give if she were alive. "Peter, you hold on to your hate, your blind hate, so tightly that you have forgotten all the good times."

"What good times?"

Abigail looked smug, a determined twist to her mouth. "Singing. You remember when Mrs. Scott would come over and play the piano? Father and Mr. Scott would sing. All of us would sing. Your remember that?"

"I remember. What does that prove?"

"Those were happy times, weren't they?"

"Yes," Peter conceded. They would have been happier if Dan and Hattie had been invited to sing, too. Dan had a deep voice that would have added richness to every song.

Abigail rubbed her cheek. The conversation seemed to tire her. Her shoulders rolled in, the rosiness in her face fading. Peter had really hurt her because he'd never seen his sweet and caring sister so annoyed with him.

"Father loves the holidays," Abigail said. "Even without Mother, Father threw lavish Christmas parties. In the fall, we went on hayrides. We spent Thanksgiving with our friends at the Scotts' house."

"Yes." He grew up surrounded by people, but he always felt alone. He spent his time going to social events and studying, but he was always uneasy in a crowd. It was Abigail's scene, not his.

Abigail continued with more energy. "Father attended all our special events at school. When I sang for charity, he was there. When you entered Hamlet in a horse race, he was there."

"I know." Peter clawed the front of his legs, nailed his mouth shut, and kept himself from saying something he'd regret. His father had to put in those appearances or people would talk.

"It wasn't all bad, Peter. You have to realize that."

"I do, Abigail…" His voice dropped off.

Abigail's face softened. She inclined her head forward, her words quiet, as if divulging a secret. "You know Father's been drinking like a fish ever since you left."

"I'm not surprised. I expected his guilt to eat at him eventually." Peter spoke in a casual manner.

"What about your guilt, Peter?" Abigail's words were sharp and staccato. "Do you have guilt?"

Peter looked away, staring down at a crate. "I carry a lot of guilt, Abigail." He paused and more bricks of shame piled on his chest. "It is a heavy burden for any man to bear. And I do not have broad shoulders like Father."

Peter swayed in his seat, his face scrunched like he had just taken castor oil. "Are you through with your lecture, Abigail? My arm hurts real bad."

"Very bad."

"*Abigail.* I'm doing all I can to keep from weeping and howling in pain, and you're correcting my grammar… Do you want me to suffer, or are you going to clean and dress my wound?"

☆　☆　☆

Abigail gripped her thighs. "Well, I can't operate in the cellar. Follow me."

They climbed the stairs. Abigail cracked open the door and peeked out. It was clear. She put her hand up for Peter to stop and she walked out of the room.

"How is everyone doing?" he heard her ask.

"We're fine, Abigail, thanks to your hospitality," a woman said. A chorus of other women agreed.

"Are you sure you don't need anything?"

"No. You've done all you possibly can, dear."

"It just doesn't seem enough. The poor children are so frightened."

"We're all strong Southern folk. We'll manage. It's better for the Yankees to destroy the town than for us to surrender it without a fight."

"I know."

"The Yankees will leave. As soon as we hear word that they have, we can stop burdening you."

"You're no burden."

"You look exhausted. You better lie down."

"You're right, Jane. Ladies, if you will excuse me, I am going into the back parlor. I don't feel up to climbing the stairs to my room."

Abigail returned and motioned for Peter to follow her. "You won't be hard to spot being the only man in blue," she whispered. "I'm going back out there and will fake labor pain. That will get everyone's attention, and then you sneak into the parlor."

Peter nodded. She made it sound so easy. So many eyes. So many chances to be seen. So many chances to be recognized.

Abigail walked back into the front parlor. With one eye, Peter peeked around the wall. Abigail gripped the table, grimaced, and moaned.

"Oh my!" one of the women exclaimed. Quickly, the ladies rushed to her aid.

Abigail turned so that the hallway was out of sight. Before apprehension could stall his steps, Peter scurried into the parlor. He leaned against the far wall, watching the door. The throb in his arm kept time with the hammering of his heart.

It seemed like a lifetime before Abigail came into the room. A lifetime of unbearable pain. She carried a bowl of water, pressed against her chest. Melting into a burgundy armchair, she sloshed some of the water on her olive-green dress. Her face, a sickly pale, showed more of the wrinkles on her forehead and around her mouth. She acted like all the strength had drained from her body.

"I didn't think it would be so difficult to convince them it was a false alarm," she said in a low voice, her eyes closed.

Peter realized the strain his presence was taking on her and wished he hadn't imposed. But he couldn't change that now. His sister had to help him. "Damn, the ball is still in there. I can feel it."

Abigail didn't respond.

"Sis, you better get to work on my arm."

Abigail didn't move.

"Sis, it feels like my arm is on fire." He increased the whine in his voice.

Abigail's eyes popped open. She rubbed a fold in her dress, twisting the fabric tighter around her fingers.

"What's wrong?" Peter asked.

"I can't take it out. You need a real surgeon. I'm afraid something could go wrong." Her words were high-pitched, but hushed.

Silently pleading, Peter locked eyes with his sister. He spoke slow and forceful. "I can't have a surgeon. All I have is *you*."

Abigail pressed her lips together and cocked her head to the side, clearly considering this. "I could make it worse. If I dug into your arm I might sever a nerve."

"That is a chance I'm willing to take."

"I'm not sure if it is a chance *I'm* willing to take." Abigail massaged her eyelids. "I don't want that on my conscience, Peter."

"Do you want my bleeding to death on your conscience?"

"No." She said the word with a resigned sigh. Walking over to the ornate fireplace mantel, she picked up a pocketknife. "This will have to do."

"That's fine," Peter said, encouraging her with his eyes. "You can dig it out."

Much to his surprise, Abigail pulled a small bottle of laudanum out of her dress pocket. "I don't know what I'm doing. You better have some of this."

Peter took a sip straight out of the bottle.

"Lie on the sofa," Abigail said her voice shaky.

Peter shook his head. He looked at the large, round mahogany table in the middle of the room, assessing its usefulness. With his left hand, he took off his belt before lying on the floor next to the table.

"Get something you can wrap around my wrist and tie to the table leg, so I can't move my arm," he said.

Abigail's eyes darted around the room, searching. She returned her attention to him, a look of exasperation on her face. She threw up her arms. "What do you suggest?"

"Take one of the curtains off the window. It will do. Now pour the laudanum on my arm."

Peter grimaced as she let drops of the medicine cover the wound. "Now pour some on the knife." He put the belt in his mouth and nodded to her that he was ready.

With her large belly, Abigail kneeled awkwardly beside Peter, her hands trembling. She held her breath and began by cutting his sleeve, folding the fabric back. She dug into the wound with the pocketknife.

Peter bit the leather hard.

"I can't get it out," Abigail said, her words dripping with despair. Peter stared at her through tear-filled eyes.

He pressed words through his gritted teeth, "Go deeper."

The knife slid further into his arm, the pain winding into every cell, every nerve, every synapse. His eyes rolled back in his head. Tears of anguish flooded his cheeks. A soft moan escaped his gag.

"I found it. Hang in there."

Peter bit the belt so hard he was sure he'd chew it in two. Abigail's fingers reached into the hole in his flesh. His head felt fuzzy, but he willed himself to stay lucid.

"I have it," she said, holding the lead ball in the palm of her bloody hand for him to see.

"Good," he breathed. His arm burned as if hot coals smoldered under his skin.

Through all the blood, Peter saw a ribbon of white bone. Luckily the minie ball hadn't shattered it.

His words came short, raspy. "I can't keep bleeding like this if I'm going to make it back to camp alive."

"You talked me through getting the lead out, but I don't know if I can sew you up." She stretched out her hands, her fingers trembling like the legs of a newborn colt.

Someone had to sew him up. Panic tightened his chest, sent his heart thundering. A warmness spread across his cheeks and he thought he might pass out.

"I hurt you," Abigail said. "I couldn't bear to cause you more pain." Her eyes glossed with tears. "I hope applying pressure will help."

Peter's heart sunk to the bottom of his chest. Applying pressure wasn't enough. Still, he kept his mouth shut. She wasn't in a state to be pushed.

She pulled gauze out of her pocket and applied it to the wound. "I will get the bleeding to stop." She tore a cloth and tied it tightly around his arm. Not quite tight enough for a tourniquet. Warm drops of blood oozed through.

"Can you get Hattie to sew my arm?" She had the strength and skill to rise to the task.

A little color rushed back into Abigail's cheeks. "Yes. I will get her."

Dogs barked, loud, shrill, excited. Abigail peered out the window. "Soldiers!" She hurriedly untied Peter from the table and rinsed her hands in the bowl of water, turning it a shade of pink.

"Here, take the water and knife." She handed them to him. "Hold them while you hide behind the piano," she said, pushing him in that direction.

She moved the rug to hide the blood on the floor. It wasn't long before a man entered the parlor.

Peter kneeled behind the piano, afraid the sound of his pounding heart would give him away. He held his breath, and when forced to, exhaled with caution.

"It's time to celebrate, Abigail. We achieved another victory. God is smiling on us."

"That's wonderful, John." Abigail said with little enthusiasm.

"What's wrong, my dear?"

"I-I d-didn't know if you w-were c-coming home," Abigail stammered.

"Now you can feel that I am alive and well. Is that better?"

"Oh, John." She sobbed. "I never thought I'd be in your arms again."

"What's the matter?"

"This awful war."

"I've been in battles before."

"I'm also worried about the baby."

"Do you want me to send for the doctor?"

Doctor! They couldn't send for a doctor! Peter's pulse pounded faster sending more blood rushing to his wound and a dizzying pain to his head. They needed to hurry.

"No. What can he do to calm my worries?"

"He can assure you that you're all right."

"I've been through this before. I know I'm fine. I'm just going to be nervous until the baby comes."

Dang. A rotten feeling slithered into Peter's gut. He had no right to be so callous. After all, his sister's remarks weren't just to cover her anxiety about his presence, but also because she was genuinely worried about her husband and her baby.

"I'm going to have Hattie prepare the officers something to eat. Everyone will understand if you need to lie down."

"Honestly I'm fine. I will sit with you."

☆　　☆　　☆

Peter couldn't figure his sister out. Not all the pieces of the puzzle fit. One minute she gave him a tongue-lashing for being a Yankee, and the next she protected him from becoming a prisoner of war.

He wished he knew whether Abigail would be willing, after the war, to welcome him back into the family. There was still a glimmer of hope for him to make amends with his sister, to see his niece, Sarah, to have an open invitation even if he was unable to visit again.

Peter knew little about his brother-in-law, John Raleigh. Abigail had been married three years before he left, but the man kept to himself.

Peter strained to hear the soldiers' distant voices. He caught a few words. They didn't make any sense. One voice he recognized: Mr. Scott. His commanding baritone was unmistakable.

Peter's legs began to hurt, and his arm bled at a steady drip. He pressed one hand on the wound as hard as he could to stop the bleeding. Not working, He took his hand off and wedged the bowl between his stomach and piano. With both hands free he ripped his sleeve. The noise made him grimace.

No one came running into the room to investigate. Of course, they couldn't hear him from the other room. He wrapped more fabric around his bloody arm and using his good hand and his teeth managed to pull it tight. It finally stopped the rest of the bleeding. He closed his eyes, and his head dropped, his forehead resting against the piano.

CHAPTER 6

ABIGAIL WALKED TO the piano and whispered for Peter to come out. He didn't move. She gave him a good shake, and he forced his head up.

"Go sit at the dining room table. The men brought wagons and took the women and children back into town."

Peter sat in a high-backed wooden chair and rubbed his sore legs. A man was not meant to be on his knees for hours. "Thank you for hiding me."

"I didn't have much time to think about it," Abigail said, unwinding a ball of cloth to bandage his arm.

"Does that mean you wish you'd turned me in?"

"No. You're my brother. I don't want to see you in prison." She reached up and pulled the curtains, then lit a candle on the table. "I wouldn't want the wrong person to see you," she said in a tight whisper.

Peter licked his lips and shifted in his seat. He paused between his words, hoping the sincerity in his voice would strike a chord on Abigail's heartstrings. "After this war is over, I don't care which side wins, I'd like to be your brother again. I mean, I'd like to be an uncle to Sarah. You're the only sister I have."

"So?"

"So," Peter dragged out the word. Softening his response, he spoke in a smooth whisper, "Is there any chance you could welcome me back?"

"Things will never be the way they were when we were children, Peter. I don't know why it matters if I welcomed you back or not now that six states separate us."

"What if I chose to move back to Virginia after the war?" His voice cracked.

"Why would you want to do that? You've worked hard enough to make a living in New Hampshire."

"I don't know. It was just a thought." Peter looked away and swallowed his tears. "There have been days when I missed Virginia so much I would stare out the window and wish the scenery would change to something familiar."

Abigail touched his shoulder and the softness eased the pain in his heart. "Hattie will be here in a minute to sew your arm. You must be starving." She bustled out of the room and returned with a plate of ham, a couple of biscuits, and a glass of milk.

"I appreciate everything, Abby."

Her hand jerked, causing some milk to spill out of the glass. "Abby? No one's called me Abby for a long time."

"Likely not since I left. People thought you'd outgrown it."

There was a moment of silence, happy childhood moments brightening the darkness of Peter's mind. Abigail reached over, picked up the fork and knife, and cut his meat.

Peter offered a small smile, touched by the simple act of kindness. He surveyed the room as he ate. It was decorated in floral bouquet wallpaper. Ten chairs surrounded the long, rectangular, mahogany table. There was a sideboard with oversized serving pieces and candelabras. It looked similar to his father's house, but his sister's feminine touch was evident.

Abigail's house and plantation were more welcoming than Springdale. It felt cozy, yet uncomfortable.

☆　　☆　　☆

"Miss Abigail would you like me to…" The negress stopped talking when she saw Peter.

Peter nodded once to Hattie. She looked pretty in her pale yellow dress, a basket on her arm. He stood and took her left hand in his. "It's nice to see you again, Hattie."

"Marse Peter," Hattie said, not looking him in the eye.

"How is your mother?"

"She's fine, sir." Her voice was hollow.

Peter let go of her hand, disappointed at her lack of feeling. "Dan is well, too. He thinks about you often."

Hattie's eyes filled with sadness. "I miss my brother."

"I know."

"Hattie, you will not tell anyone about Peter, will you?" Abigail asked.

"Of course not, ma'am."

"Keep the other servants away from here."

"Yes, ma'am. I already told them to stay are upstairs." She browsed through the contents of her basket. "I have my sewing needles in here." Her voice was deep and dull. "I'll heat the needle over a candle flame." She fingered a few different strands of thread. "I need something heavier. I wouldn't want the thread to break."

Peter watched Hattie disappear. She was a stocky woman like her mother, but handsome in her own right. Her wide hips evened out her figure.

Peter leaned forward to catch a final sight of her as she headed up the stairs. This all seemed unreal. Hattie sounded like a ghost.

He swallowed, pushing down his raw emotions. He rubbed the heel of his hand against his chest. Every heartbeat brought a flood of pain, insecurity, regret, and sorrow.

He'd give anything to see Aunt Ruth again.

Peter returned his attention to his sister. If she hadn't been so pregnant he would have begged Abigail to fetch his surrogate mother. But it was the sibling bond he now had a chance to mend. They'd been so close. Would they ever be like that again?

For a moment, Peter pondered old memories, happy memories. He remembered sitting in the parlor, listening to her play the piano, or reading a book while she did her needlework beside him. Peter laughed softly. Before she found John, he would escort her to town and they'd enter every store in Fredericksburg. Abigail even took him to his first ball.

Peter's voice regained a brotherly tone and softness. "You don't need to be taking care of me. You need to take care of yourself, Sis."

Abigail screamed, loud and shrill.

Peter's eyes widened and his heart gave a resounding thud. "What's the matter? Is it the baby?"

☆   ☆   ☆

"No. I'm afraid I'm the cause. I walked in unannounced. Forgive me, Abigail, but I didn't want to disturb you if you were resting."

The voice, a booming bass, made Peter's skin goose pimple with dread. Dread that paralyzed him like a helpless child. It was Mr. Scott's voice.

"Nice to see you again, Peter. It's been a long time," the officer said. His bushy blond hair protruded under his cavalry hat, though his beard and mustache were neatly trimmed.

"It has, sir." Peter stood at attention and held a salute, despite the agony it brought his injured arm. To his surprise, Scott returned the courtesy.

"This is a pleasant surprise. Abigail, you should have told me your brother was here. So we find ourselves on opposite sides of the war," Scott continued, not allowing Abigail to reply.

"We do, Colonel."

"War makes our circumstances awkward, but I hope it in no way affects our friendship."

"That greatly relieves me, sir."

"I've thought about it and decided that it isn't your fault," Scott said. "You fell in love with Molly, not her family. It wasn't your fault that her father is an abolitionist. I can't imagine he'd let his daughter court a slaveholder. New Hampshire was a free state. You were forced to convert to that ideology."

"I made the choice of my own free will," Peter said. His heart palpitated and nervous energy shot through his legs. How did Scott know he lived in New Hampshire?

The colonel's mouth twisted. "You see, Peter, I've paid quite a few people not to pursue you." He paused, and the sly sheen in his eyes faded. "I hope it wasn't a waste of money."

That was not what I expected. Peter took a deep breath to calm himself. "Thank you for protecting me, sir, but nothing will change my morals. I've always hated that peculiar institution. Now I can do something about it."

"Your father raised you better than that," Scott said. "You should appreciate states' rights and realize that the Christian thing to do is to take care of the black race. Ephesians 6: 'Servants, be obedient to them that are your masters according to the flesh, with fear and trembling, in singleness of your heart, as unto Christ; not with eye-service as men-pleasers, but as the servants of Christ, doing the will of God from the heart.'"

"Christian to care for them? But you do *more* than care for them. You exploit the black race for free labor. So you can reap profits from your plantation. And as far as Ephesians goes, you're ignoring verse 9: 'And, ye masters, do the same things unto them, forbearing threatening: knowing that your Master also is in heaven.'" Peter's voice rose, and he inflated his chest. "God views blacks and whites as equals. I do, too."

"The institution of slavery existed since the beginning of time. It is all throughout the Bible. If the Lord saw it as wrong, the prophets would have preached against it. Instead, the Apostle Paul instructs Christian slaves in Ephesus how to act. Slavery upheld the economy of Rome as it does the economy of the South. Romans 13: 'Let every soul be subject to the governing authorities. For there is no authority except from God, and the authorities that exist are appointed by God.'"

"Then why does Exodus say, 'Whoever steals a man and sells him, and anyone found in possession of him, shall be put to death'?"

Not missing a beat, Scott switched the subject back to the war. "If your father hadn't injured his foot during the Mexican-American War, I'd be proudly serving under him right now."

Peter exhaled slowly, trying to quell the spark the Biblical debate had lit. At least, Scott had confined their argument to religious grounds. "A *drunkard* isn't fit to command," Peter said.

"Your father hasn't always been a drunk."

"So I've been told. I don't recall him sober. He raised a southern boy, but he couldn't change my northern heart."

"Northern heart." A mocking tone undercut Scott's voice. "You've always been soft. I'm surprised you can stomach war."

"Those are biting words coming from a friend."

"Nothing's changed. I've always told you what I think."

"I'll tell you what I think. A man can stomach war if he's fighting for his family, for his beliefs, and he knows that God is on his side."

"I couldn't have said it better myself. Now time will only tell which one of us is right."

Peter had finished eating. The fresh bandages on his arm were bloody. He glanced over at Abigail. Her face was blanched and her muscles tight.

"What's to become of me now, Colonel?" Peter asked, unable to keep the worried twinge from his voice.

"Abigail, I'm sorry to have caused you trouble."

Peter held his breath.

Scott continued, "I left my hat and that's why I came back. Now that I have it, I will see myself out."

"Thank you, sir," Peter said. *A graduate of the Virginia Military Institute and trained in law is willing to let me go… Scott didn't go by the book as much as Father. What a blessing!*

Colonel Scott nodded and walked towards the door.

"Colonel," Peter called, stopping him in his tracks. The man turned around, his eyebrows silently questioning. "Before you go, I'd sure appreciate if you could help me with my arm."

"You'll have to come with me if you want a surgeon, and you know what that means."

"If this bleeding continues, I won't have the strength to make it back."

"Hattie was going to stitch his arm," Abigail said, her voice barely above a whisper. "But I suppose when she heard your voice she thought it was safer not to get involved."

Colonel Scott squeezed both of his cheeks with his left hand.

"I don't like the idea of the needle threading through my flesh, just to have the stitches taken out later. Could you cauterize it?"

Scott took his army saber out of its sheath and stared at the blade.

Minutes passed by, but it seemed like a decade. The roar in Peter's ears muted the bong of the clock. Finally, Scott looked up and nodded.

"Abigail you'll have to do it because I have to hold him still. This is going to hurt like hell." A light flush washed over his face. "Pardon my language."

"I can't do it," Abigail said in an ear-grating squeak.

"You can't hold him down. We need you to do this," Scott said, enunciating every word for emphasis. He held out the saber for her to take, but she hesitated. "Peter's right, Abigail, his arm has to stop bleeding."

"You can do it, Sis," Peter encouraged through gritted teeth.

Abigail pressed her lips together, her eyes hard-set, determined. She walked to the kitchen, opened the stove door, and put the saber in the coals.

Peter stood and a rush of lightheadedness made him sit down. When he stood again Colonel Scott was by his side steadying him. Together they walked into the parlor. Peter looked at the rug and his stomach revolted. The bile burned his throat. Colonel Scott moved the rug and Peter crumpled to the floor.

"More than one person should be holding you still," Scott said. "It's going to be torture."

"You're a big man. You can handle me."

Why was he putting himself through this torture just to spare the needle? This was going to be much more painful. *Quick and painful though*. Before he could think of his burning flesh Abigail walked over, the tip of the saber red hot.

Peter glanced at the glowing iron and his stomach pitched. He turned his head away and closed his eyes.

Colonel Scott held both his arms down and placed his right knee on Peter's chest.

Peter gasped for breath. He felt the tip of the saber on his arm. He tried to scream curses, but could not push the sound through his tightened throat. His arm was on fire. He smelled the burnt tissue and wanted to vomit. He willed his stomach to keep his food where it belonged.

Abigail pulled the iron away, tears rolling down her cheeks. "I'm so sorry, Peter. So sorry." Her voice choked with sobs.

His arm hurt a million times worse than it had with the lead ball inside. Colonel Scott continued to press his knee on Peter's chest.

"I know this is uncomfortable, but I'm staying here until you work past more of the pain," Scott said.

Peter opened his eyes, but he couldn't see through his torrent of tears.

Abigail gently brushed the drops away.

Peter strained his neck to look at his arm, but Colonel Scott wouldn't let him. "You're not moving, and that means your neck, too. You really don't want to look at your arm—trust me. Abigail, get some bandages and wrap the wound." Once Peter's arm was tightly wrapped, Colonel Scott finally let him go. "Does your father know you're in the Union Army?"

"No, sir."

"I don't plan on telling him, then. Did Abigail tell you he's ill?"

"No, sir."

"I wish you could go see him, but if he saw you dressed like that, he'd either have you killed or die of a heart attack. If you plan on escaping back to Union lines, I recommend you get into some of John's clothes. You won't make it otherwise. We have men everywhere."

"Thank you." Peter's pulse sped and he watched his friend walk away. "Abigail, what's wrong with Father?"

"Consumption." Her voice stretched so thin it threatened to break.

The thought of his father slowly dying sent a frisson of excitement through his body, muted by the heavy thud of his heart. Peter didn't know what to say, so he just gave his sister a gentle hug with his good arm. He couldn't imagine his father, a tall man, as strong as an ox and as mean as a rattlesnake, dying from the cough.

Abigail wrung her hands. "He's not himself, Peter. He's a different man, now."

"That may be so, but he still doesn't want to see me."

"Do you want to see him?"

"I would see him. I'd be lying if I said I wanted to."

Abigail nodded. "Well, that's something. Come on. I'll help you get some of John's clothes."

Pain clouded Peter's vision. He staggered into the bedroom. The room began spinning, and then everything went dark.

☆   ☆   ☆

Peter came to hours later. Abigail pressed a cool cloth to his forehead. "How are you feeling?"

Peter groaned. "Like Father just gave me a working-over."

Abigail pulled the cloth away and shot him a sharp stare. "That's not funny."

The edge in her words bruised him. Their relationship was made of eggshells. "I wasn't being funny…" Peter's voice trailed off. He searched for the words to mend the growing rift between them. "I shouldn't have said that, Abigail. Words against Father spill too easily out of my mouth. I am sorry."

Abigail rubbed the back of her neck and gave Peter a tight look. "Can you walk?" she said at last.

Peter sat up and gritted his teeth. "Have to."

Abigail helped him get out of his uniform and into John's clothes. For the first time in over two years, he was dressed like a southern gentleman: black frock coat over his white wingtip shirt, gray dress pants, emerald-green vest and black cravat.

Abigail completed his outfit with a black derby hat and kissed his forehead. "You look handsome."

"I feel like a fool. Where are you taking my uniform?"

Abigail stopped. "I was going to burn it. It's dangerous to take it with you. If you get caught, they'll think you're a spy."

"I don't plan to get caught. You're not burning it."

She threw the uniform on the bed. "You're stubborn."

That was one thing we have in common. Peter stuffed the uniform into his haversack. "It's dark. It's time for me to leave."

Abigail walked him to the door. "Take one of the horses, Peter. That's the only way you'll get across the river."

She grabbed her coat, followed him out to the barn, and silently watched him saddle a gray mare. After he mounted, she reached up and softly touched his hand.

"Her name's Cloudy. We had a big thunderstorm the day she was born."

"Well, Cloudy, I hope you're a good swimmer," Peter said, stroking her nose.

"Godspeed," Abigail whispered.

"Thank you." He rode away, his musket slung around his neck. Fighting the urge to look back at his sister, his heart pained him as much as his arm. His hatred was only for his father. He hadn't realized how much leaving home had hurt his sister.

Fleeing with Dan had seemed his only option at the time. Now, he wished he had made another choice. Freedom was never carefree in the North. And not one day went by that he didn't pine for Aunt Ruth and Abigail.

But staying one step ahead of the bounty hunters had kept him occupied, and it was all he could manage until Lincoln had called for soldiers.

☆   ☆   ☆

Peter cautiously approached the river, watching for signs of the rebel camp and listening for a patrol. He saw a small raccoon, but no rebels. He heard a dog barking, but no rebels. It appeared the

Confederates had left a section of the river unoccupied. Peter ran a finger across his brow. Colonel Scott probably had something to do with that.

Peter pushed Cloudy into the Rappahannock. The water rose until it hit above his waist. Cloudy swam hard to fight the swift current. The iciness took Peter's breath away. Numbed his lower body. Unfortunately, his wound still burned with the power of Hades.

Once on land, Peter headed to where his regiment had camped the night before. He shifted in his saddle, too numb to feel his legs. His arm rested stiffly below his breast.

"Halt and give the countersign," a sentry challenged him.

"Sergeant Warren, Company F of the 12th New Hampshire." Peter paused, and then quickly added, "I've been lost since the battle earlier today."

"Dismount and come forward slowly with your hands raised." The sentry's words were short and gruff.

Raise his hands? *God, don't make me do that.* "I was shot in the arm," Peter said, his voice hoarse. "I can only raise one arm. I promise I do not pose a threat." He pleaded with great sincerity.

He raised his left arm and stood still for a long minute, waiting for the blood to warm in his legs.

The sentry had his musket pointed at Peter's chest as he approached. "Why are you dressed like that?"

Peter lowered his left arm, opened his haversack, and showed him his uniform. "Like I said, I was lost all day and I figured I was safer in the South dressed like this. It wasn't hard to get a change of clothes with the town deserted."

"Colonel Palmer will want to talk with you."

Peter's chest bunched. What was he going to say to him? "At this hour?"

"He's still awake. Corporal of the guard!"

Peter picked up Cloudy's reins and followed the corporal. He tried to think of the best way to phrase his actions. Nothing he'd rehearsed seemed sufficient. He was still mulling over what to say when they reached Palmer's tent.

Peter looked around in vain for somewhere to tie his horse. One of the colonel's aides, a young lieutenant, saw his dilemma and took the reins.

The lieutenant spoke in just above a whisper. "The battle has rattled him." He paused, and lowered his eyes to the ground. "I hope you have good news."

"I don't know if I have any news at all, sir."

"Either way, you can go on in; Palmer's not doing anything but frettin'."

Colonel Palmer looked up from the map on his desk. In the candlelight, Peter saw the dark circles under the man's eyes. Exhaustion weighed heavily on the officer.

"Have a seat, Sergeant Warren."

Peter licked his bottom lip repeatedly and sat on the campstool. Colonel Palmer remembered who he was. He didn't know why, but he wasn't expecting that.

The colonel's eyes widened, making Peter uneasy. He did not want to be charged with cowardice or desertion. "I know your company was forgotten." Palmer spoke slow, pausing long between words. "It was an unfortunate error. You don't need to tell me about the battle. I know what happened."

He was quiet for a moment. A frown creased his lips and an apology flashed in his brown eyes, tears welling in the edges. "Tell me what happened after the battle."

"I thought it would be safer to run to my sister's house instead of crossing the pontoon bridge. I stayed there until dark, she gave me a horse, and I crossed back over the river."

"Why'd you leave Fredericksburg? Why'd you move to New Hampshire?"

"Excuse me, sir?" Was the man questioning his loyalty?

Colonel Palmer spoke louder. "I want to know why you moved to New Hampshire. It is a valid question."

Peter took a deep breath and threw a rope around his voice to rein in his jitters. "I had a disagreement with my father, sir, on my eighteenth birthday. I had had enough of taking his abuse, and watching him abuse others. I followed a map my friend gave me, which marked abolitionist towns. I stopped at Pittsfield because I ran out of money."

The colonel shook his head. "I see…"

A cold silence caused Peter's teeth to chatter.

"I have to confess, Sergeant, I had given you all up as lost. Against my orders, Colonel Marsh crawled onto the field and motioned the men to fall back. Everyone hurried over the bridge, expecting the enemy to fire upon them, but the rebels went in another direction."

Peter let out a quiet whistle.

"I know. I'm glad your company had a little luck." Colonel Palmer spoke soft and low. "Otherwise, it would've been easy murder." He ran a hand down the front of his throat. "Your conduct could be questioned," he said, getting back to business, "but I will take the circumstances into consideration."

"Thank you, sir." The invisible vice gripping Peter's heart let go and relief flooded his body. He breathed normally, his stomach settling.

Colonel Palmer nodded. "It's late. We'll talk more about this in the morning. I have a few more questions for you."

☆   ☆   ☆

Reveille sounded—obnoxiously loud and upbeat. With his left hand, Peter threw off his blankets. It took more effort than he expected. He bit his tongue to keep from voicing pain. "Damn my arm," he mumbled. The slightest movement reminded him of yesterday, of his sister and father and this rotten war. After changing into his uniform pants last night, his arm had burned so bad that he didn't bother changing out of the rest of his clothes.

He shoved his feet into his brogans. Slowly, he buttoned his uniform jacket over his fancy shirt, vest, and cravat. The long notes of reveille continued to sound. He headed outside, kepi in hand.

An armed soldier, a foot outside his door, raised a flexed palm.

"Sergeant Warren?" the brown-haired man asked, twirling a pistol in his right hand.

Peter eyed the sergeant-major. He was a stocky man, perhaps in his early thirties. "Yes?"

"Come with me, please. The brass wishes to speak with you."

"Now?" The complaint in his voice surprised him.

The sergeant-major's eyes turned into blue flames. He rocked backward and pointed to the extra half circle at the top of his chevrons. "*Now.*"

Peter nodded, once, and followed the sergeant-major to where the horses were tied. He mounted Cloudy and rode beside the sergeant-major as they headed out of camp.

"At least we're not going to Whipple's hut," Peter said under his breath.

Peter dismounted and followed the sergeant-major down a row of tents. Bits of a muffled conversation floated to his ears.

"Sergeant Warren," a deep voice said.

The sergeant-major pointed with his thumb to the wall tent. "It came from there."

Peter's face contorted with a pinch of panic. He blinked at the officer's tent, belonging to the regiment's commander. He slowed his steps, trying to delay the inevitable.

The corporal, sitting outside the tent door, motioned with his head for Peter to go inside.

He stepped into the tent. Instantly, there was dead silence. Six officers turned to look at him—Captain Morton and Colonel Palmer among them. His prior conversation rushed to mind, crushing his chest and speeding his pulse. *Oh shit. This is not good. Not good at all.*

CHAPTER 7

COLONEL PALMER EXTENDED his hand, pointing to the gentlemen at the table. "Sergeant Warren, this is General Whipple, Colonel Marsh, Captains Van Horn, Morton, and Hall, and Lieutenant Nevin."

Peter saluted. His mouth was as dry as cured tobacco. He ran his tongue against the sides of his cheeks, unable to generate any saliva.

His eyes darted around the room. All the seats were taken. Standing felt awkward.

Lieutenant Nevin stood. "I'll find a couple more chairs," he said, excusing himself.

Nevin had been the officer who had held Cloudy's reins the night before. One friendly face was better than none.

"Considering the circumstances, we need to ask you a few questions," Captain Van Horn explained.

Peter's heart skipped several beats. He glanced over at Colonel Palmer. The man could've had the decency to warn him about the nature of this meeting. Damn. He wanted to forget yesterday.

With a slightly shaky voice, he said, "What kind of questions, sir?"

General Whipple sat as ramrod straight, his eyes heavy with the weight of command. His fingers steepled. "Sergeant Warren, you're being charged with desertion and cowardice." He enunciated each word.

Peter's lungs ached. He gripped the table and sputtered, "Colonel, you said that you understood my actions under the circumstances."

"I don't think you remember correctly." Palmer drilled him with a smug smile. "I said I would take that into consideration. Many of your comrades died yesterday. You are a sergeant. You are meant to set an example for the enlisted men. We plan to make an example out of you."

Peter swallowed hard. All the strength left his body as if oozing from an unseen wound. He sank into the chair Lieutenant Nevin had brought him. For several seconds, he sat there in silence with his head in his hands.

Finally, he looked up, light-headed. "Exactly what does that mean?"

"Well," General Whipple said, "if you are found guilty of either charge, you will be shot."

Peter's eyes bulged. "Shot..." He paused, digesting his situation.

"After the battle, General Hooker is tightening his belt. Tightening his rein on command. We have your confession and we have witnesses. It doesn't look good." Whipple's voice sliced through his self-pity like a sharpened saber.

Peter stared at his palms—waxy, streaked with perspiration, hot with worry. "B-b-but," he stammered.

A shade of concern flashed in Lieutenant Nevin's eyes. "I think he's in shock. We better give him a minute."

Peter's heart rumbled as load as a cannon. He sat in silence, trying hard to form his mangled thoughts into words. They whirled in his head. Cowardice. Desertion. Confession. Death.

He shifted his weight and slumped forward. Caught in the current, it threatened to pull him under, threatened to drown him.

General Whipple cleared his throat. His raised eyebrows and pinched mouth left no doubt that he was tired of waiting. Peter had to respond.

"Is there is a way out?" Peter asked meekly, digging his fingers into his scalp as he ran them through his hair.

Whipple smiled tight and malicious, his eyes sparkled sly and intense.

"Just one: you become a scout."

Peter closed his eyes, trying to process what the general had proposed. He didn't like being the center of attention—though that was the least of his worries. He rubbed the back of his neck, but the feeling remained.

"I should have known," he finally mumbled, forgetting his bred-in respect. "I guess I don't have a choice, since you're blackmailing me into it. What do you need to know?"

General Whipple's eyes grew colder, and darker; his voice grew stronger, and harsher. "I do not appreciate you saying I'm involved in blackmail. *You.* You got yourself in this position."

Peter choked back an apology. An icy gust of guilt caused him to shiver. He scooted to the edge of his seat to get closer to the wood stove. "Yes, sir."

Colonel Palmer shot a quick glance at General Whipple. The general nodded. Colonel Palmer tugged on his earlobe before speaking.

"Normally we'd have had you study up on military matters before becoming a spy, but we don't have the time. We'd like to ask you some basic questions just the same. And we better like your answers."

Dread rose from Peter's feet, increasing with each minute, making him unable to concentrate, unable to sit still. He jumped up and began pacing the confines of the tent. His steps trained to march, his posture purposefully strong. He had to make a good impression. They fired questions at him, volley after volley.

Peter responded carefully, realizing the weight of each answer.

"Why did you enlist? What is your take on the war? How good are you on horseback? How much do you know about firearms? What would you do if you were captured?"

Peter took an especially long pause before answering the last question. Perhaps they were concerned about his loyalty. If they didn't think he was trustworthy, they'd court-marshal him. They'd kill him. He had to convince them his heart was with the Union, convince them he could rise to the challenge, convince them he was a damn good soldier.

Peter ran his tongue across his teeth, willing his heart to dislodge from his Adam's apple so he could speak.

In a measured tone, he answered, "My father disowned me for being an abolitionist. The wicked South is dead to me. I know spies—if captured—are executed, but I could just as easily die in battle for our cause. They could do nothing to me that would make me betray the Union. I believe in the power of a man's word, even to his own destruction.

"I realize I deserted in the last battle, sirs, but that was my first battle. I was unprepared to watch my comrades die all around me. Fear took hold of my senses. Now that I know what to expect it will never happen again. My desertion had nothing to do with loyalty. Thoughts of dying blinded me to my duties on the field. I am not blind to my duties any more. And if I must die for our cause I will do so."

General Whipple stood and clapped.

The rest of the officers followed.

"That was elegantly put," Whipple said. "That satisfies me. Gentlemen, do you have any more questions?"

"No," they all replied.

Peter's fingers folded into fists. This couldn't be happening. A current of acid surged up his throat, turning his mouth sour.

Whipple nodded, clearly pleased. They all sat down.

Peter sat, too. Silence followed. Unable to sit still, Peter crossed and uncrossed his ankles. The tent began spinning the officer's faces whirling around him. Peter blinked and forced himself to focus.

"I need information about the enemy, and I need it *now*," Whipple said. "I needed it yesterday, in fact. If we're going to make a last attempt at taking Fredericksburg, we must know the softest targets in the city. You will cross back over the river and talk with civilians, soldiers, anyone you can find."

"And what am I looking for, sir?"

Whipple's nostrils flared. "Think, Sergeant, think. I need to know how well the bank is manned and how well the soldiers are equipped. I need to know if there are any weaknesses along the bank and where the pieces of artillery are located."

Peter nodded.

General Whipple made his right hand into a fist and hit the table. "We keep losing these battles! By being my eyes and ears, you'll be my edge. Winter's setting in and General Burnside is talking about setting up winter quarters and delaying any further action until spring."

Peter swallowed. "Sir, why can't we wait till spring?"

Whipple's eyes narrowed and he leaned across the table towards Peter. Peter could feel the man's warm breath laced with tobacco.

"More Union soldiers than I can fathom died charging that wall. None of them even laid their hands on it. Northerners will be outraged. We've been at this war for a year now and have yet to win a decisive victory over Lee. I'm losing my patience; so is Congress.

"You will cross the river tomorrow night. If you get any good information, maybe we can take them by surprise. The *fact* winter's setting in will work in our favor. They won't expect us to attack now."

Goose pimples sprang up on Peter's arms. "Am I going alone, sir?"

"It only takes one man to talk to people," Colonel Palmer said. "You will go dressed as a civilian. If you run into trouble, you can enlist as a Confederate."

"I understand, sir."

"I have full confidence in *you*," Whipple added.

The quiver in the way Whipple emphasized the last word did not increase Peter's spirits.

Colonel Marsh had remained silent during the meeting. That increased the nervous energy roiling his stomach. Did Marsh think he was a poor choice for the assignment? Or was mute because of the horrors of the battle?

"This should be easy," Captain Hall said. "The rebels are still basking in their victory, and I wager they're loose-lipped."

Peter's muscles tensed, his face sober. They had it all planned to the letter. But nothing ever went as planned.

His marriage to Molly hadn't gone as planned.

His peaceful life in the North hadn't gone as planned.

His first battle hadn't gone as planned.

"General, the fact that you judge me worthy of this mission is an honor," Peter said with a catch in his voice, "but I don't know if I'm as confident in my abilities as you are." *They don't think I should be a spy, but they don't have any Southerners volunteering.* Peter bit the inside of his cheek. If he kept questioning this assignment he'd get himself killed.

Colonel Palmer slapped Peter on the back. "The first mission is always the hardest, because you're naturally nervous. But after you return safely, the next ones will be easier."

Peter's chest bunched. *Next ones?* "May I be dismissed, sirs? I need to get ready."

"Certainly," General Whipple said.

☆　　☆　　☆

Peter walked back to his hut in a daze, his feet heavy as if he was wading through mud. Inside he felt numb. He struck his cheek with his left hand. It stung. Damn. That meant he wasn't dreaming.

Sitting on a boulder, he pulled out a piece of paper and his pen. He tapped the pen on his leg. Should he tell her he was becoming a spy? He could disguise it and say he was involved in secret maneuvers, or something like that, to explain why he might not be able to write for a while.

He took a deep breath. Every fiber of his being resisted telling her he was involved in espionage. Still, he had promised never to keep secrets from her.

He was a man of his word. He had to tell her. And if the letter fell into the wrong hands, it didn't matter—he was already branded for dead. He gritted his teeth and forced his right hand to write the words despite the pain that shot up his arm. With loving patience he carefully formed each letter. If Molly read uneven script she'd know something was wrong, and he didn't want her to worry.

Fredericksburg, VA,
December 16, 1862.
Dearest Maiden,

It's impossible to express how much I miss you. My heart aches each day we're apart. Let it comfort you that I have survived my first battle. I took a minie ball in my right arm, but I am well.

Please do not worry about me. God is with me as He is with you. Tell Dan that I saw Abigail, Hattie, and Mr. Scott. Abigail is about to have another baby. She is doing well. Hattie told me that Aunt Ruth is in good health.

Also inform my brother that he owes me a letter. I miss him almost as much as I miss you. It is torture to be separated from the ones I love. I want to know more about Rebecca. She's getting bigger now. Dan and Belle should start looking for another place to live. I know the loft above the livery stable has held many pleasant memories, but it just isn't practical anymore.

I can't wait until we have children, Molly. I know you'll be a gentle, caring mother. I want to be a father. Taking care of Rebecca has shown me that.

Let me know when our house is finished. If you have questions, don't hesitate to ask. Unfortunately, it might take longer for my letters to reach you. I have been recruited as a scout. I know the South like the back of my hand. I feel this is a better use of my services. We are not making much progress on the battlefield. I hope my scouting will help the Union.

I look forward to the day that we are wed.

Your loving beau,
Peter Joshua Warren
Sergeant, Volunteer Infantry

Peter read over the letter, put it in an envelope and addressed it. He wrote New Hampshire and wished he could transport himself there. Transport himself to the safety of Molly's arms, to the safety of friends, to the safety of peace.

But they weren't at peace. And he'd just got himself between a rock and a hard place—no, a rock and a coffin.

Walking outside into the brisk air, Peter set his pocket mirror in the hollow of an oak tree. He tried to shave with his off hand, but cut himself. Damnit.

Jim stepped in front of him and rested his hand on the tree trunk. "You ran." His tone carried a heavy accusation.

Peter's cheeks burned. He looked away, scuffed the dirt with his right foot. "I know," he mumbled.

"Men are talking. I understand, but some of the others…" his voice faded. "Nathan is really hurt. He looked up to you."

"Sorry." It was all he could say.

Jim's eyes bulged, his gaze locked on Peter's coat. "I see you tried to dye your clothes red."

"A ball hit me in the arm. I'm fine," Peter said quickly.

"By the looks of your uniform, you're far from fine. Did you see a surgeon?"

"I don't need to."

"You don't need to," Jim snapped, his tone sharp as a razor. "I know you have more learnin' than I do, but you're not a doctor."

Peter stomped, raising dust. He hated to have his judgment questioned. His father was a first class fault-finder; criticizing every decision Peter ever made. His father would criticize the archangel Gabriel if he visited with a message from heaven.

Peter bit back a reply he'd regret. Jim was merely concerned.

"I got the minie ball out. The wound has been cauterized. It just hurts."

Jim nodded, although his frown remained. "All right."

Peter exhaled loudly. "I'm glad all of you made it through the battle."

"It was a miracle. I wouldn't want to go through that again."

Peter glanced at the razor and then back up at Jim. "I hate to ask this, but can you help me?"

"Yes, but you wouldn't want to ask my brothers. They might accidentally cut your throat." He lathered soap in the tin cup. "But their anger will eventually drop to a simmer."

Jim brushed the soap on Peter's short black beard. He picked up his razor and shaved while there was still enough light to see.

Peter examined his face in the looking glass. Clean-cut definitely made him look younger. Still, the sorrow and pain lurking in his hazel eyes showed that he had seen too much for his years. Could he pull off being a boy?

"Why are you getting cleaned up?" Jim asked, after he had finished.

"I have to prove my courage—to everyone."

Jim opened his mouth, and then shut it.

"I can't tell you more."

"I understand."

Peter attempted to pull off his jacket one-handed.

"Here." Jim helped Peter take off the jacket and put on the black frock coat.

Captain Morton came by, his arms full of clothes and accoutrements. He looked Peter over. "Not bad. Those are fancier clothes than we would have provided."

"They are my brother-in-law's. I'd feel more comfortable in a different outfit, sir."

Jim flashed him an encouraging smile and then walked away.

"Being comfortable isn't part of the assignment," Morton replied dryly. "The townspeople will respect you more—looking like that. It is very important to win them over."

Peter nodded.

Morton set his bundle on the ground and examined it. He took a Confederate flag pin off a gray broad-brimmed hat. "Put it on your collar."

Peter stared at the little pin in his hand, wondering if it made any difference.

"Put it on," Morton repeated.

Peter did so reluctantly. "Can I switch to that gray hat, sir?" Peter asked, taking off his derby hat. "It has a wider brim and I need to hide my face."

Morton handed him the gray hat. "Here are some riding boots. And here's your haversack."

All it contained was a banded stack of Confederate bills and several rounds of ammunition.

"There's enough for you to buy food and a little extra in case some other need arises."

"Thank you, sir." Peter picked up his Shakespeare book and stuck it in the sack. He wasn't going anywhere without Molly's picture safely tucked inside the pages. He also threw in his pipe and a few sheets of paper.

Peter handed the officer Molly's letter. "Please mail this for me, sir. It is a letter home in case…" His voice trailed off—unsure, shaky.

Captain Morton smiled as if willing him strength. "Will do." He mounted a black stallion and escorted Peter to the river. "Acting the part of a southern gentleman, the only firearm you need is a pistol." He handed one to Peter.

I have to do this, Peter mouthed. *I was a coward when I ran away from my father. I was a coward to desert my men on the battlefield and flee to my sister's house. I have to do this to prove I'm not yellow.* Fear slid down his throat and pricked his stomach like a piece of ice. He couldn't block out the fact facing the firing squad had been his alternative.

"Do you have an alias?" Morton asked. "It needs to be a name you'll easily remember."

"Jeff Burnett. I won't forget it. It's been my alias on the Underground Railroad for years."

"Good. Remember: If you run into trouble, you can always enlist in the Confederate Army."

"Yes, sir."

"Good luck!" Morton called as he rode away. The hoofbeats grew fainter and fainter.

Peter grasped his breast and gasped for breath.

Being a spy wasn't any more dangerous than going into battle. Either way, he'd be facing down death.

But he'd be doing this alone.

CHAPTER 8

THE RAPPAHANNOCK CRESTED. One more inch and it would slide into camp, saturating the dirt and sleeping soldiers. Peter sat, pulled off his boots, and tied them on his saddle. He took off all his clothes, pressing the bundle against his chest with his left hand.

The gray mare's ears flattened against her head as he urged her into the ice river, and Peter's heart thumped wildly. The water numbed his naked body.

Peter strained to stay in the saddle and keep his clothes dry. The water rose higher and higher.

Cloudy's long, gentle movements in the water were soothing. Peter allowed them to drown his thoughts. The bank loomed just out of reach. The crossing seemed slower than it had the previous night.

This time he was entering danger instead of fleeing.

His stomach tangled; anxiety slid through his insides and lodged in his gut like a piece of driftwood.

Once firmly footed on the rebel side, he dressed, pants first then shirt, and boots. His cold fingers refused to work fast—not to mention his struggle to do it mostly one-handed. It felt like he was standing half naked for hours.

A realization struck him, bringing on a violent tremor. His spirits shriveled in horror. He could not lie with a straight-face.

His father could lie.

Politicians could lie.

The brass could lie.

Perhaps lying was a trait of successful men.

He had to be successful. He had to lie. Best keep his conversations with people to a minimum. Get information without seeming nosy or getting too friendly.

A surge of primal fear threatened to drive him back across the river—drive him back to the Union side. But that would prove his father was right. He couldn't let his father win.

He couldn't let the Union officers win. If he had to face death it wasn't going to be in disgrace. He owed Molly that ... and Dan.

He curled his toes in his boots. There was nothing to this. He'd get the information and get out.

Peter tugged on Cloudy's reins and led her through the pine trees. When he met the rebels, it had to appear he was coming from the south. After he got turned in the right direction, he mounted and spurred Cloudy with his heels, galloping full bore.

"Halt!"

Peter managed to pull Cloudy to a stop just in time—merely inches from knocking the sentry down.

"What's gotten into you, boy? You can't ride into our camp like that!" The man's voice thundered, his face red.

Peter's throat tightened. He backed up Cloudy, his eyes locked with the musket barrel pointed at his neck.

He wanted to make a bold entrance. He had succeeded. Perhaps a little too well.

"What regiment are you with?" Peter asked, out of breath.

"The 14th Virginia Infantry. Why?"

The shiny musket made the lines he had rehearsed spill out of his mouth with more urgency. "My mother's dying." Guilt from the past brought tears to his eyes. "I have to find my brother. He has to see her," Peter said between gasps.

"What outfit's your brother with?"

"J. E. B Stuart's cavalry."

The sentry's face softened. "I'm sorry to tell you this, boy, but they rode out towards Chancellorsville."

"Chancellorsville," Peter said with a catch in his voice that he didn't understand.

The man lowered his voice, softened it to just above a whisper. "Sorry. We'll let you through camp, you better ride home."

Peter spurred Cloudy on. "Thank you."

Once in Fredericksburg, he relaxed. He wasn't going to talk to anyone else till morning, if he could help it. He dismounted Cloudy, hid her in a thicket, hobbled her, and sunk to the ground. She'd be able to graze all night. Locking his fingers behind his head, he lay in the grass looking up at the stars.

Aunt Ruth loved to look at the stars. She knew the names of the constellations and would point them out. Later, Peter learned them in school, but Aunt Ruth had taught them to him first. Often she would stare at the North Star for a long time before going to bed. Stare and pray.

Peter located the North Star and let out a silent prayer of his own. God be with him. He rested his arms across his chest and closed his eyes.

Thankfully, Stuart's cavalry was out of the city. He needed to steer clear of Colonel Scott and his brother-in-law. For a moment, he felt that this could all work as planned: sneak and snoop around the city for bits of information that could help the Federals cross the Rappahannock and take the city again. This time for good. A sliver of hope eased him into a deep, pleasant sleep.

"Get your paper! We whipped the Yanks! Read accounts of the battle!"

Peter bolted upright. The shrill, excited cries of newsboys seemed out of place.

Peter stood, brushing blades of grass off his shoulder. Mounting Cloudy, he returned to the river to get her some water, and then they walked into the city. Newsboys hurried up and down the street shoving papers in people's faces.

Peter held a coin in his outstretched hand and a newsboy handed him a paper. The bold, black headlines boasted of the Confederate victory. He folded and stuffed it in his haversack. General Whipple would read it.

How would he maneuver his way through the city? How would he explain his presence if recognized?

Emotions still worn from last night, he felt raw, vulnerable. He could make up a story. He was back to see his sister. He heard she was having a baby. He decided to become a southern gentleman again and see if he could hunt down a commission in the Confederate Army. That wasn't too hard to believe. He was dressed the part.

Or he could say that he wanted to make amends with his father. It was the truth. He just didn't know how to go about it. His father was the one who needed to make things right. Of course, likely no matter what reason he gave for being in the city, he'd wind up in jail. His father was still offering a hefty reward for his capture.

☆   ☆   ☆

Peter tied Cloudy to the hitching post outside the mercantile. With a powerful hunger he cautiously stepped into Dandy's restaurant. His lungs tightened and he slowly exhaled through his nose. There were more empty tables than occupied ones. A sign that the South was hurting. No one turned to look at him—they were all engrossed in their food and conversations.

A small-framed negro man was waiting on the tables; Peter recognized Lawrence, one of his father's slaves. Lawrence saw him and his eyes bulged, shock registering in every muscle. He walked over and escorted Peter to the table in the darkest corner. "Name's Jeff Burnett," Peter said, quick and quiet.

Lawrence nodded. "What would you like to eat, Mr. Burnett? Seems I remember you like dumplings."

"That will do."

He waited for Lawrence to return with his meal, each second punctuated by a pronounced thud of his heart. He scanned the room. A few rich ladies, their small children and a couple old men caught his eye. The ladies proudly wore the patriotic colors of the South— red and gray. One of the children, a boy about seven, wore a miniature version of a Confederate uniform. Though none of the faces looked familiar, he didn't feel safe. Someone could walk through the door any time.

Lawrence brought Peter a plate of chicken and dumplings.

"Are you still with…?" Peter asked.

"Yes. Hired out, thank God," the man whispered. "You?"

"Damn Yankees!" Peter exclaimed.

Lawrence nodded. His eyes registering the truth. "If you need anything, Mr. Burnett, please let me know."

"Information," Peter said, his voice scarcely audible. "About the Rebs along the river."

"Apple pie for dessert, it is."

Peter bowed his head. "Dear Lord, bless this food that it may nourish my body and please watch over the Confederacy and bring us victory," he said loud and clear. "Amen."

"Amen," an old man echoed and raised his glass in Peter's direction.

Peter ate in silence. He shoveled spoonfuls into his mouth as fast as polite manners would allow. Warm and pillowy and gooey and soft, the dumplings made his stomach rejoice. At least being in life-threatening peril brought the reward of a good meal.

Lawrence set a plate with a slice of apple pie on the table. Peter moved the plate closer to him and saw that there was a piece of paper underneath it. He stuffed the piece of paper into his inner coat pocket.

"Mr. Smalls still runs the place. He'll recognize you. Just set the money on the table and leave. I'll take care of it," Lawrence said, his voice hushed.

Peter rubbed his left eye. He appreciated Lawrence's offer but feared not going up to the counter would spark suspicion. It would prove he had something to hide. Mr. Smalls might even follow him out of the restaurant and that would be worse.

Peter would have to outmaneuver Mr. Smalls somehow, fool the man into believing he was someone else.

"Can't do that, boy," Peter said. Guilt warmed his face. He hated calling Lawrence a boy, the man was almost as old as his father, but he had to make an impression on the patrons.

With a reverent expression, Lawrence fingered his beard. He took a concerned glance over at Mr. Smalls, manning the till. He more mouthed than spoke, "You're still wanted."

Peter pulled the bundle of Confederate bills out of his pocket. He wrapped three five dollar bills into his napkin and placed it on his plate. "Just take my plate and leave," Peter ordered.

Lawrence offered a tight smile and dipped his chin. "Yes, sir. You know what's best."

Walking across the floor, Peter's pulse pounded a rhythm in time with his steps. His forced swallow failed to bring relief. Overcome with the sensation that everyone's eyes were on him, he held his breath. Pointing his chin down, a hot wave washed over his cheeks. At least his broad-brimmed hat hid most of his face.

Mr. Smalls eyed him and Peter's heart rammed his rib cage, the lump of worry in his throat souring his mouth. His life depended on convincing Mr. Smalls he was someone else. Peter handed Mr. Smalls a twenty dollar note along with his bill.

Perhaps all those Shakespeare readings in school would pay off. He needed Tybalt's bravado.

Mr. Smalls' beady blue eyes continued to scrutinize him. "You know, you remind me of someone."

Peter's heart teetered in his chest. He reached out and put a hand on the counter. He paused a half-second to level his voice. "Who would that be?" His tone was so natural it surprised himself.

"Peter Warren."

Peter laughed a little too shrill. "If only I was that lucky. Name's Jeff Burnett, sir," Peter said, extending his hand. "I'm from Charleston. My father was the overseer at the Purcell Plantation. I worked for the old man, too. Had to scrape pennies together all my life. Finally got a stake together."

"Is that so," Mr. Smalls said.

Peter grinned as devilishly as he could. "Been thinking I could get a similar job myself. No age requirement to being an overseer, sir. You just have to keep the slaves in line."

"Suppose you're right. None of the plantations around here are looking for help though."

A line of perspiration wetted his hairline.

Mr. Smalls continued sizing him up. "Why'd you lose your job?" he asked.

Peter squinted one eye, inclined his head, and cracked a lewd smile. "I started eying Mr. Purcell's daughter."

Mr. Smalls laughed.

"By chance are you interested in selling your restaurant?"

"Sorry. I've been running it for years and don't plan on stopping anytime soon."

"My change, sir?"

"Oh." Mr. Smalls finally took his eyes off Peter and counted out the change. "I'm sorry, Mr. Burnett, for comparing you to Peter Warren. A true southerner shouldn't be demeaned by being taken for an abolitionist bastard."

Peter struggled to find a comfortable grin. "Thank you, sir. If you change your mind about selling your restaurant let me know. I'll be back. You have good service and good food."

Peter strode outside and down the street. He had to consciously slow his steps. It was relatively easy to be inconspicuous on foot, but not at a run.

Cloudy tossed her head in his direction as if begging to go with him. He bowed his head, staring at his shoes. Hopefully, he could work his way back to her later.

The farther he distanced himself from the restaurant the slower he breathed; until finally his lungs regained a normal rhythm.

☆ ☆ ☆

Peter carefully wound his way through Fredericksburg, keeping in the shadows and off the main streets. He kept his eyes and ears wide open for signs of people he knew. Sticking his head around the corner, he saw his old headmaster talking with Reverend Hoffman. He quickly pulled his head back.

Even though they couldn't see him in the alley, he pushed his back up against the side of the building. The hand he pressed on his chest failed to quiet his heart's thunderous pounding. He took several deep breaths. How could the brass expect him to spy in the city where he was raised? If he made it through this without being recognized, it would be a miracle.

It was several minutes before he checked around the corner again. Both men were gone. He looked down the other end of the street. He didn't recognize anyone. He ventured out into the open.

An eerie feeling came over him as he walked closer to the jail. Staring at him was a familiar face—his own.

The sight of the wanted poster made him bite his tongue. When he got close enough to read it, he folded his hands into fists and held his breath to keep from making a scene. His heart stumbled as he silently mouthed the words.

$5,000 REWARD!

Peter Joshua Warren
For helping slaves escape on the Underground Railroad and the murder of the colored woman, Sally.
Description:
Height: 5 feet, 7 inches; weight: 150 pounds; wiry build; hair: jet black, straight, medium length; eyes: dark brown; when talking, inclines his head forward.

Peter shook his head. He didn't incline his head forward when talking, did he?

"It wasn't murder," he mumbled, "and it was just as much Father's doing as mine."

Gruesome images assaulted him. He put a hand to his forehead, willing for the scene to stop. His head ached, throbbed with the concentration of pushing the pictures away. His defenses, shredded by the attack, gave way. Images, scents, and sounds snuck through cracks in the wall of his mind. His father reeking of whiskey. Pistol in hand. Sally.

A shot pierced the darkness. Then a blood-curdling scream. Dan came running from the barn.

"You killed your father!" he blurted in alarm. The burly man lay motionless.

"No," Peter said with regret. "He's just stone drunk, but Sally is dead," he said, pointing to her lifeless body. "To Father, she was just an object for pleasure."

Dan's eyes followed Peter's finger. He could only see through his right eye. His left was swollen shut from Mr. Warren's earlier punch. The girl lay on her stomach, her dress torn off. Blood soaked her back.

He blinked with disbelief at his little sister, Sally. Immediately, Dan's eyes blurred through his tears.

"That's Father's doing," Peter lamented in a shaky voice, revolver in hand. "She was beautiful. He couldn't keep his paws off her." Peter's left hand tightened into a fist. "I caught him. He threatened to shoot me! His own son! It went off when I tried to wrestle it away from him." Peter paused and glanced at his grief-stricken friend. "I'm so sorry."

"I should have protected her," Dan said.

Peter shook with rage.

His father groaned, drawing his attention. Peter pointed the revolver at his father's head. As far as his old man was concerned, he may as well dye his skin black. Dan's mother, Ruth, had raised both of them together. He pulled the trigger. The bullet struck the ground next to his father's ear.

"It's not my fault my mother died birthing me," Peter said, his voice a shaky roar. "It's not my fault I don't share your twisted values! It's not my fault I have a heart, a soul, a conscience!"

Peter's upper body shook as the memory faded. He looked down and realized his hands were folded into fists. The trembles continued despite his attempt to control them.

"Are you all right?" an elderly woman asked. Her soft touch on his shoulder startled him, making him feel like an edgy, wild animal.

Peter took a deep breath and nodded, not trusting himself to speak. He was in Fredericksburg, not at Springdale. He blinked at the wanted poster and bit his tongue, hoping the woman wouldn't notice it.

"Are you sure, young man?" the woman asked in a shaky voice. "You don't look well."

"I just had a seizure, ma'am. It has passed. I'm fine. Thank you for your concern."

The white-haired woman smiled weakly. "That was a bad one. You should see a doctor."

Peter was touched by her concern. "Thank you, ma'am. I have medicine at home."

"Do you need help getting home?"

Peter's pulse increased. He needed to get rid of this kind, old woman immediately. "No, ma'am. That is not necessary."

The woman bobbed her head. "If you insist. Perhaps you should start carrying the medicine with you."

Peter sucked in his breath. "Yes, ma'am. That is an excellent suggestion. I will start doing that."

The woman's eyes brightened, clearly happy that she had helped in a small way. "Good day, sir."

She tottered down the street. As soon as she was a good distance away, Peter glanced around, taking in his surroundings.

No one was near the jail.

He ripped the wanted poster of himself off the board and wadded it into a ball. Quickening his pace, he headed down the street. Last thing he needed was for a police officer to see him. The thought turned his palms clammy.

He wiped them once on his pants. Hopefully, he didn't look as nervous as he felt. He couldn't draw attention to himself.

Blend in. Act like a southern gentleman. Blend in. Act like a southern gentleman. Blend in. Act like a southern gentleman. He mentally chanted the phrase like a litany.

He had to embrace his past. He had to embrace every dark, bigoted corner. No matter what it cost his soul.

Because his life depended on it.

CHAPTER 9

PETER KNOCKED ON Jack Selah's door.

The man answered in his usual gray pin-striped suit with a genteel smile and an outstretched hand. Nothing seemed out of place, except for the hint of shock in his walnut eyes. Jack paused as if words were just out of reach.

"Come in, Mr. Burnett," he said, his voice normal, casual, friendly. "Forgive me, I completely forgot about our business meeting."

"Business meeting?" a feminine voice questioned.

Peter's stomach lurched, and he put a hand on the wall to steady himself.

A short, slender woman stepped into the room, her auburn hair pulled back in a bun.

Jack introduced them. "Miss Tabitha Edmunds, this is Jeff Burnett."

Peter didn't recognize her. Relief soothed his fear, washing over his raw vulnerability. He took off his hat, his cheeks warming. "I did not know that there was a lady present. It's a pleasure to make your acquaintance, ma'am."

The woman smiled with closed lips. "It is always a pleasure to meet one of Jack's friends."

"Tabitha, I apologize about the interruption, but this is important. Shall I call on you later?"

"I'll be looking forward to it. Good day, Mr. Burnett."

"Good day, ma'am." The door shut behind her.

Peter switched his attention to his friend. Grabbing Jack's shoulder, he laughed softly. "I never thought you'd find yourself a lady."

Jack lowered his head and looked away, his ears fiery red. "She didn't want to be a spinster and just happened to snag me."

Peter chuckled louder. "Wait till Dan finds this out. You have been known as the unmatched matchmaker."

Jack took a step back, jaw tightening, eyes narrowed.

"Hey, I didn't coin the term."

"I don't care who came up with it. I don't want to hear it."

The no-questions-asked voice took Peter by surprise. He recognized it well, but hadn't heard it since he became involved in the Underground Railroad. "All right, all right. You don't have to get sore."

Pleasant memories of spending time with Jack soaked up his tension like a sponge. Everything seemed the way it was before the war. For a moment, he expected to ride Hamlet to Springdale, where Aunt Ruth would have dinner waiting.

"What are you doing back in Virginia, Jeff?"

"Soldiering."

"Dressed like that?"

"The brass thought I'd do more good snooping around than firing a musket."

"And you've come to me for answers?"

"Yes. The Union needs every advantage it can get. Things haven't been going well."

Jack motioned for Peter to have a seat in a leather armchair. He sat in the matching one across from him.

"I know all about that," Jack said with a weary undertone. "I've had to put on masked patriotism ever since the war began."

A box of cigars rested on the small square table next to Jack's chair. He pulled out two cigars and handed one to Peter. Peter used the oil lamp on a table next to his chair to light the cigar and then he passed the lamp to Jack.

"So," Peter dragged out the word, "is Miss Edmunds Union or Confederate?"

Jack cradled his chin in his right hand and closed his eyes. "Confederate," he said, as if uttering the word was painful. "She helps me keep my patriotism believable."

"I guess there are two sides to every coin," Peter said, trying hard not to judge.

"After this war is over, it won't matter what side she's on, and we'll get married." Jack swallowed, ill at ease. He shifted in his seat. "How are Dan, Belle, and little Rebecca? I always like to stay informed on the negroes I helped escape to the North."

"They are well. Belle wanted me to thank you again for reuniting her with Dan." Peter looked out the window. "It seems like forever since I saw them. They're fine. Belle's decorated their small room with light blue curtains and pictures. It looks real homey. Now that I am not around people won't have to ask if I am Rebecca's father."

"That must be hard on you."

"Pittsfield is a town always bustling with new faces. I'm uneasy every time I take Rebecca anywhere without Dan, especially when Belle's with me. I love that little girl, but I can't forget..." His voice trailed off as he remembered the day Rebecca was born.

When he saw the baby's copper skin, his heart had constricted. He knew before asking Belle that Rebecca was actually his sister. His father went after all the good-looking colored gals. Likely he had other half-siblings he didn't know about.

He had made peace with that. Made peace with his brothers and sisters in bondage. But his father raping Dan's girl...

"How is Molly?"

Peter turned his head and met Jack's gentle eyes. Grateful at Jack's attempt to change the subject to something more cheerful. Slowly, his chilling thoughts dissipated. "Molly is still picking out furniture and such to go in our house, I suspect. It's been a while since I got her last letter."

☆　☆　☆

Peter took the piece of paper Lawrence had given him out of his pocket. He squinted, struggling to make out the script.

"What do you have there?"

"Information Lawrence gave me."

"I talk to him frequently. Without shipping tobacco north, your father has hired out more of his slaves to make up lost income. Those are the lucky ones."

"By the number of regiments, it looks like Lawrence thinks the whole Confederate Army is along the bank of the Rappahannock and there's Confederate cavalry at Chancellorsville."

Jack nodded with a rueful shrug. "That's about right. Any other reinforcements farther away could quickly arrive by rail."

"Apparently there are quite a number of cannon, too."

"I've never gotten close enough to see many of them, but I think they've gotten the bank pretty much blockaded. They brag about it all the time."

"Are there any weaknesses?"

Jack's deep-seated frown gave an answer before his words. "None I can think of. It'd be a turkey shoot if the Union tried to cross the river again."

"Are they planning on spending the winter near Fredericksburg?"

"If the bluecoats break camp, the Rebs will follow them like a pack of bloodhounds; otherwise, they're staying to protect the city. They'll entrench themselves if they think it's necessary. Too many influential people want Fredericksburg protected. Taking Richmond by Fredericksburg is no longer feasible."

Peter rubbed his forehead. "I figured it'd be that way." Jack had been a bachelor for many years but he kept a tidy house. Everything from the large painting of his parents on the wall to the wood rack by the small brick fireplace seemed to be perfectly positioned.

"How well equipped are the Rebs?"

"They have high spirits and plenty of ammunition."

Peter interlocked his fingers behind his head. A contemplative silence settled on the room. "Do you have any suggestions?"

Jack laughed in a melancholy tone. "Suggestions? As much as your brass wants another crack at the Rebs, its best to stay put till spring. Right now the Confederacy has manpower, but little food or other necessities. Virginia's resources are nearly exhausted, and the food supply line is in shambles. They'll be forced to break camp early and forage for food on the march. It could be possible to catch them unprepared—or at least a handful of them."

Peter nodded. "I guess that's as much information as I could hope to obtain. General Whipple was grasping at straws when he sent me into Fredericksburg."

"You know they're going to protect the capitol with every ounce of fight they have. It's going to be a hard road to travel."

Peter rested his cheek in his left hand. "The North's expecting results and it's getting difficult to explain our lack of progress."

"I expect disease to set in heavy on the rebs."

Peter remembered all the histories of war he had read. Disease could thin the ranks faster than a battle. "Likely it will take a toll on both sides."

Jack tilted his head back and looked up at the ceiling. "True." His voice strained. "I wish I had better news. Wish I could help you more."

"You could be our eyes and ears if you joined me as a spy." A plea invaded Peter's voice. He didn't want to continue this mission alone.

Jack stroked his chin. He stood and added another log to the fire. When he spoke, his tone was reflective. "I reckon that's as good a way as any to help the Union."

Peter hesitated before speaking, "Well, how about I give you your first assignment?"

Jack leaned forward. "What would that be?"

"Get my horse and bring her here. I don't feel safe walking down the middle of town in broad daylight."

"I can do that."

"She's tied in front of the mercantile. A gray mare. She has Abigail's brand."

"All right."

Peter watched the clock on the mantle and shifted in his seat. How long did it take to walk to the restaurant and ride back? Jack must have run into someone he knew. Peter tapped his foot on the floor. The sooner he got out of the city, the better.

Jack walked in. "Horse is tied up outside."

"Thank you." Peter gave Jack's hand a hearty shake, and then gripped his shoulder.

☆   ☆   ☆

Peter walked his horse on the road towards Falmouth. He stopped, bent over, and inspected Cloudy's hooves, placing a small stone under one of the horseshoes. Examining the riverbank, he got a better idea of the strength of the soldiers and artillery.

"Where are you going, sir?" a soldier called out.

"Falmouth. I have business there," Peter replied. He forced a cordial smile.

"Something wrong with your horse?"

"She's favoring her right forelimb. I don't mind walking. It's a sunny day."

The Confederate soldier nodded, and Peter continued without further delay. Golden rays spilled across the land, reflecting on patches of snow. Peter squinted. His heart thumped harder with each step. He hung his hope on crossing unseen at Falmouth.

In the distance, the gray-clad sentries seemed nothing but deciduous trees—until the sun struck their muskets, making them visible.

Peter patted Cloudy's flank a little rougher than he meant to. "Damn." He scanned the line of sentries. All were carefully placed, spaced evenly. "Damn. Damn. Damn." His soft curses died with his hope.

Most of the rebels were concentrated closer to Fredericksburg. Still, the odds of him crossing the river undetected were slim.

Peter rolled the pistol in his hand. He could shoot the pickets and cross, but he didn't know if a larger force would come running.

No. He had to come up with a story and talk his way across the river. He pulled the rock out from under Cloudy's horseshoe. "Sorry I had to leave it in for so long, girl," he whispered. He took the newspaper out of his haversack and thumbed through the pages.

THREE HUNDRED DOLLARS. Ran away from the subscriber on the 10th inst., negro man JONAS ADAMS, 30 years old, about six feet tall, weighs about 180 lbs, brown black, good looking, round face, straight hair. Clothes not known other than that he wore away a black silk hat. I will give the above reward if secured in Fredericksburg jail so that I can get him again.

Peter tore it out. "I don't know about this, girl," he whispered to Cloudy, "but it's the only thing I can come up with." He decided to wait until dark. Slaves were harder to track in the dark.

He lay in the thicket, cradling the back of his head with his left hand. A few moments of sleep would do him good. He closed his eyes and felt a soft coldness land on his lids. He batted it away hoping he was dreaming. The coldness continued to land on him, slowly wetting his face.

He opened his eyes and glared at the falling snow. Normally he liked snow. Growing up, he and Dan had many a snowball fight. But snow just made his life miserable as a soldier. And he was in enough discomfort already. Didn't God understand that?

His heartbeat rang in his ears. Hopefully, that wasn't a sign he'd soon be listening to drums beat the death march. He rubbed his sweaty palms on his pants. If he kept acting like this, they'd know something was up for sure.

Peter had sworn he would never do this, but he was desperate. Desperate enough that for a moment he would have to turn into his father. He could do it. Faced with no alternative, he had survived the day by telling lie after lie.

The sky was black, except for pinpricks of light coming from the stars. Peter mounted Cloudy, ran his fingers through her mane. "Wish me luck, girl."

He rode towards the sentry. Not waiting to be challenged, he spoke in a rough roar. "Soldier, have you seen a runaway slave?" Peter showed him the newspaper clipping, but it was too dark for him to read it. "I'm offering three hundred dollars for his capture. I'm looking for a negro man, brownish in color. He goes by the name of Jonas Adams. He's in his early thirties, my height, muscular."

"I haven't seen anyone matching that description," the soldier said.

"I've been tracking him since the day before the battle, but then the Yankees came. A little earlier, I was told he was seen running in this direction. Most expensive slave I ever bought. That's why I'm offering such a high reward."

"That's a lot of money. I'd sure love to have it."

"If you catch him, you get the reward. This is the second time he's run away!" Peter's voice increased in volume. "I'm beginning to think I didn't get anything for my money but trouble. But he's worth the time and money to get him back. I have to teach him a lesson, set an example for the others."

He had worked himself up so much that his words rushed together. "I can't have all my slaves running to the Yankees, I'd be broke!" Peter's face heated. He pulled out his revolver. "And if he won't come any other way, I'll kill him," Peter said, and then spat on the ground.

"If I find him, I'll take him into custody," the sentry said.

Peter scowled at the soldier and lowered his voice. "You better," he said, slowly, force behind each word. "If I find out you've let him cross the river, I'll have you tried as a traitor! By law, my property is to be returned."

"I know," the soldier replied, exasperation written on his face.

Peter pointed and yelled. "The bush on the opposite bank is moving!"

"What bush? I don't see anything moving."

"He probably heard me yelling and stopped. I can't lose my property to those damn Yankees." Peter's voice cut through the darkness. "If he's that close to their camp, it won't be long, and they'll be protecting him."

Peter charged into the river, not giving the man a chance to respond. Urging with Peter's kicks, Cloudy swam as fast as she could. Peter wanted to get across before the bewildered soldier came to his senses. He had a painful death grip on the reins with his right hand.

Fire from the wound burned up his arm, while he wildly waved his revolver in the left hand.

"Come on out, Jonas! I know you're over there!" Peter shouted, wishing the anger was directed at his father. "If you surrender, I won't kill you."

Cloudy carried Peter to the Union bank and crawled onto the dry land, exhausted. Peter felt sorry for the horse, but he knew it wasn't safe to stop. The rebel picket still had a clear shot at him. Peter dismounted and ran into the bushes and fired his revolver a couple times. He crawled on his stomach along the bushes. Then he stopped, turned his head around, and clicked his teeth.

Cloudy's ears perked up. She stared at him.

Peter locked eyes with the mare. *Follow me. Come on, you're a smart horse.* He clicked his teeth again.

She slowly clopped in his direction.

Peter resumed crawling until he made it to the road. He stood and brushed himself off. Cloudy was behind him. He mounted and pushed her hard. She lathered from the exertion. Her tongue hung out as she paid close attention to his commands.

"Halt!" a man ordered.

☆　☆　☆

The moonlight revealed the sentry's blue uniform and streaked across the man's alarmed eyes. Peter's lungs heaved and he was unable to speak. He put a hand on his chest and waited till he regained his bearings. Gradually his heart rate slowed.

"I'm Sergeant Warren," he gasped, breathless. "I need to see General Whipple."

The sentry smiled. "So I'm the lucky one. I'm glad to see you made it. His headquarters hasn't moved. Pass on through."

Peter nodded.

He took his time getting to headquarters. Cloudy had worked hard enough. He wanted his sister's horse to live through the war, if at all possible.

His drenched clothes clung to his skin. A shrill wind blew right through them, chilling him to the marrow.

Peter shivered, thinking about how he had yelled at the rebel sentry. Those words had spilled out of his mouth so easily, almost too easily. Every man had a dark side. He had a bit of his father in him after all. His stomach churned, a sour taste rising up his throat.

He rode towards headquarters, looking forward to a hot cup of coffee and a wool blanket. Captain Morton sat outside the tent, smoking a cigar. He pulled out his cigar, and a relieved grin erupted. "Boy am I glad to see you."

Morton returned Peter's shaky salute. "I see you weren't recognized. I've been waiting for you. Go inside the tent and change into your uniform. It's on the desk."

Peter gladly became Sergeant Warren again. He hoped Jeff Burnett had disappeared from the face of the earth.

"I bet it feels good to be in dry clothes," Morton said. He handed him a navy blue blanket. "Wrap up in this."

Peter's teeth chattered. He sat in the chair, bundled in a thick wool blanket. Being cold, his wounded arm felt even stiffer than before. He pressed it to his body to generate more warmth.

"Do you feel like telling me what happened?"

"May I have a cup of coffee, sir?"

Captain Morton nodded, stepped outside the tent, and returned with a steaming cup of coffee. "I could spike it if you like," he said, taking a flask from his desk.

"No, thank you." Peter took the cup of coffee and sipped it slowly, letting the hot liquid warm his throat, warm his insides, warm him down to his toes.

Finally, he set the coffee down. "There's not much to tell, sir, but if you give me paper and a pen, I'll write it down." He took the pen with his left hand and transferred it to his right, his injured arm pressed tight around his shoulder and against his chest. His hand shook, but he steadied it by grasping his wrist. In slow, careful strokes he struggled to make his words legible.

Captain Morton's head bobbed as he read the wobbly script. "You got much of the information we were hoping for, though I figured it would point to the conclusion that we shouldn't attack until spring." Morton's eyes grew wide when he reached the last line. He spoke with pauses long enough to drive a wagon through. "You met a man who wants to be a spy for us?"

"Being from Fredericksburg, I have friends around here, some with Union loyalty."

"I'm sure the general will be elated to hear that. How'd you get back across the river?"

Peter dug into his haversack and pulled out the Fredericksburg newspaper. He showed him where he had torn out the ad on the runaway slave. "I crossed the river to get my property back."

"You do know how to think fast," Morton said. "Good work. Now get some sleep. You deserve it. I'll have someone take care of your horse."

"Thank you, sir."

Peter thought he'd never get back to his tent; his steps were shaky and slow. The more he walked, the more the blood circulated in his limbs.

He tried not to wake the Kanes as he stepped over them to his bedroll. "Lord, thanks for protecting me," he whispered.

He sat on his bedroll tremors rippling through his body. Shaking from the crazy escape he just managed. He must have been half out of his mind! The shivers continued and they weren't due to the cold. *But it had worked.* Unable to rein in his fear, Peter debated slapping himself.

Instead, he took a deep breath, closed his eyes, remembered why he had enlisted. Vivid images refortified his determination to fight. Aunt Ruth crying at night when she thought no one could hear her. Dan's face—his eye swollen shut. The body of Dan's little sister Sally. The night they buried Dan's father.

Dan was counting on him to secure his freedom. And the freedom of his family. He didn't want to live a fugitive forever with the threat of being hauled back South hanging over his head.

Jack and his other Underground Railroad conductor friends didn't want to live with the threat of fines and jail sentences.

And Molly needed to be proud of him. If he was unable to stand up for his beliefs then he didn't deserve her hand.

If this was the only way he could help crush the gray vipers then he would do it. Slavery was a blight that all this bloodletting would cure.

CHAPTER 10

PETER LAY WITH his eyes closed trying to cling to the remnants of sleep when a hand shook his shoulder. He tossed his head fighting the interruption.

"Sergeant, wake up!"

Peter opened his eyes. They widened when he realized that Lieutenant Nevin was shaking him.

"You slept through reveille. I never thought that was possible. The dang drum beats for five minutes."

"I'm sorry, sir," Peter said in the midst of a yawn. Truthfully, he hadn't slept much at all, but the officer didn't care.

Nevin ushered him outside and Peter fumbled with the buttons on his coat. He glanced at his bloodstained uniform and sighed—remembering his sister, and Colonel Scott and their tender care.

"We have to go see General Whipple."

Peter yawned again which he cut short to be polite. "I know."

The lieutenant got Peter a cup of coffee to drink on the walk over. "I hope this helps wake you up. How's your arm?"

"It's sore and stiff, sir," Peter said, keeping the arm still against his chest. Peter's voice stayed formal, businesslike. What did the lieutenant expect him to say? It hurt like hell?

"Good, that's not too serious."

This time when he sat across from General Whipple he wasn't intimidated, wasn't concerned, wasn't nervous.

The man needed him. That gave him some power.

General Whipple leaned back in his chair. "So how was your first mission?"

"Better than I expected," Peter replied in a monotone.

The general steepled his fingers, his elbows on the table. "What did you learn?"

Peter explained their situation. He mentioned all the details he'd learned, including how close he had come to being recognized, to make certain the brass wouldn't send him across the river again this winter.

Throughout the report Whipple nodded periodically. His face remained relaxed. He seemed pleased even though the information amounted to nothing they could use to their advantage.

Once Peter finished, there was a long pause.

The light in Whipple's eye made Peter shift in his seat. The general had plans—plans that included him. Whipple tapped his fingers on the table, his head tilted slightly to the left.

"So you have a contact in Fredericksburg?" he asked, a lift to his last word.

"Yes, sir."

"You're sure he's reliable?"

"I trust him with my life, sir. He's been involved in the Underground Railroad for years."

"Is he well-respected in town?"

"Yes, sir, with most people who are also respectable. Mr. Selah's a writer and has worked for several Southern newspapers."

"That's a decent answer. We have to end this stalemate. We have to take Richmond. Future information this Mr. Selah could provide could help us greatly." Whipple paused. "Are you up to crossing the river again?"

"No." Peter's voice was firmer than he expected. "I'm not crossing the river again."

"You *will* cross the river again," Whipple said with authority. "I can still charge you with cowardice and desertion."

"You're trying to get me killed," Peter said unable to keep the anger out of his voice.

"Your friend Mr. Selah could help us win the war. Don't you want that?"

"Yes, sir, of course."

"Don't you want to return home to your loved ones?"

"Yes, sir."

"Don't you want the slaves to be freed?"

"Yes, sir."

"Don't you want to fulfill your duty by spying?"

"Yes, sir," Peter said. Once he realized what he had agreed to his ears burned. He shifted in his chair. He hated his beliefs being used against him, being used to manipulate him.

"Sacrifices are made in wartime," General Whipple said. "Soldiers have to sacrifice a good diet, have to sacrifice their personal goals, their professions, have to sacrifice being with their loved ones.

"And men. Men have to be sacrificed for the good of the army." Whipple's grim face was stern, his lips tight, eyes determined. "If I have to sacrifice you, I will." He paused, scanned the other officers with a single glance. "It is a dirty, regrettable business, war."

"Why do I have to be the lamb?" Peter asked, irritated but unsteady.

"In the Bible it was an honor for the lamb to be offered to God," Captain Hall said.

Peter grunted. "I'm not living during the Old Testament. I don't feel honored. I feel bullied." *Bullied just like my father bullied me for years.*

The general ignored Peter's complaint and asked, "How's your arm, Sergeant?"

"It is fine, sir," Lieutenant Nevin responded before Peter could open his mouth. "He's well enough to cross again tonight."

"Tonight?" Peter said. "Can't I have a little break, sir?"

Whipple shook his head. "The river could ice over any time now."

Peter hung his head. He rubbed the back of his neck. He didn't have a choice. If he was going to live through the war to wed Molly he'd have to live through the war as a spy.

He took a deep breath and raised his head. "I'll be ready, sir."

"Since he knows you as Jeff Burnett, tell him he can safely contact us by asking a sentry for Jeff Burnett."

"I will, sir."

"Now what does Mr. Selah look like?" Captain Hall asked. "We wouldn't want to exchange information with the wrong person."

"He's a stout man, five-foot-four, in his early forties with short light-brown hair and brown eyes. He has a small mustache. He also has a red oval-shaped birthmark on the back of his left hand."

General Whipple's lips transformed into a satisfied smile. "I think I could recognize him." He put a hand on his chest and belched softy.

"You'll cross at a different point tonight. I wouldn't want you to run into the same men. Try to see if you can find where their cannons are placed."

Peter crunched through unbroken snow forging a winding path on his way back to his tent. Walking helped him think.

Jack's service would aid the Union. Together they'd make a difference in this war. Together they'd help protect each other—just like on the Underground Railroad. He would no longer be spying alone.

Peter awoke to the drum of dinner call. He couldn't believe he'd slept till noon. He hadn't even had breakfast. He stepped outside his tent, yawned, and tipped his head back. Jim, Eli, and Nathan approached carrying plates.

Peter spoke, a bounce to his voice. "Private Kane, Private Kane, and Private Kane," he said.

Jim laughed. "You love to say that."

"You're the three musketeers."

Eli looked at his older brother then at his younger brother. "I don't know about that."

He handed Peter a plate and the four of them sat to eat. Peter looked down at the hardtack, beans, and vegetable slices fried in fat. "Army fare," he mumbled. "And no meat."

"It's nothing like home cooking or Mrs. Cox's restaurant," Jim said. "There's meat if you want it, but it's rancid."

Peter shook his head. "No, thanks." He ate with his left hand. He knew that if he used it too much it would never heal properly.

Sacrifices are made in wartime, General Whipple had said.

Jacob Vickery walked up to them. "Where were you this morning?" he asked, his voice an accusing jab.

Peter didn't feel like dealing with him. "Special assignment," he replied, looking down at his food.

Jacob smirked. "They make sleeping a special assignment now?"

Nathan jumped to his feet and took a fighting stance, but Peter motioned for him to sit. If he was willing to stand up for him that must mean he was over Peter's battlefield indiscretion.

"That was part of the assignment," Peter said. With a cold, calculating stare he asked, "Do you care to join us, Private Vickery?"

Jacob glared at Peter. "No." He walked away and found a place to eat alone, stabbing the meat with his fork.

☆　☆　☆

Peter moved off by himself, too. Not to sulk like Jacob, but to reflect, to put words on paper. He sat on a boulder, stationary and ink bottle in hand. He set the ink bottle down and rubbed his forehead. What should he write Dan and Belle? When Molly got the letter he sent her it would be shared with them.

Still, private words with his brother seemed necessary. Especially considering the danger of his new assignment. He wished he could say more about Aunt Ruth but he had not seen her. He had barely spoken to Hattie.

Peter picked up his pen and wrote what came to mind—his letters a little shaky. Why couldn't he be shot in his off arm?

Fredericksburg, VA,
December 17, 1862.
Dear Dan,

It is with pleasure that I have this opportunity to write you a few lines to let you know that I am well and if ever these lines reach you, may they find you the same.

I have become acquainted with many residents of Pittsfield that before I only knew by name. With winter approaching, I expect to see hard times. Now that I have survived the horror of the battlefield, I know the closest enemy is disease. Army meals sure make me miss Belle's cooking. Consider yourself lucky to be married to such a cook.

Brother, miles separate us from each other, but you must not think that I have forgotten you. I know my letters have been scarce. I have not and I do not want you to worry yourself about me for I am invested in a good cause.

I must bring this to a close. Write as soon as you get this letter and let me know how you are. Kiss your gals for me. I hope Rebecca will have a brother or sister soon. Keep trying and do not lose heart. God will provide.

No more to write at the present, but ever remains your brother,

Peter Joshua Warren
Sergeant, Volunteer Infantry

Peter folded the letter as he walked back to his hut. He stopped and handed it to Nathan. "Mail this for me."

"Why can't you do it?"

"Mail it," Peter ordered. "It is important."

"It's as good as done," Nathan promised.

"Thank you."

Peter sat next to Jim and Eli. He hunched over and stared at the ground. He had been lucky on the first trip. He had a sickening feeling in his gut that he wouldn't be lucky again.

Peter's latest dream kept replaying in his mind. His father had said that his time was drawing near. Peter bit his lip. That was his overactive imagination. He had to wrestle with his fears … and win. He had to be strong in mind and body to enter Fredericksburg again.

He silently prayed for extra courage. In the background, Eli and Jim swapped jokes. Sometimes Peter would crack a smile—just for appearances.

☆　☆　☆

At dark, Peter applied spirit gum and pressed wool crepe hair to his chin and upper lip. He looked in the mirror and had to keep from laughing at appearance. Although facial hair was in style he'd never much cared for it.

Peter no longer blamed General Whipple for blackmailing him into espionage. He always knew in the back of his mind that his own actions had caused his reassignment. He couldn't accept that until now. Accepting it meant admitting his guilt, admitting the punishment was just, and enduring it.

His face warmed with shame. The heat didn't last long. His feet felt the ice-cold water of the Rappahannock again and his chest tightened and the breath left his lungs.

Peter and his partner in espionage Cloudy crossed the river without incident. Peter was able to talk his way through the sentries into town with another sob story. He rode through the crowded streets hoping not to draw attention to himself. He stopped in front of Dandy's Restaurant, tied Cloudy to the hitching post, and went inside.

This time Lawrence's shock only registered in his eyes. He led Peter to same table in the dark corner he had eaten at before.

"What would you like to order, sir?"

Peter rubbed the small beard glued to his chin trying to get used to the feel. "A bowl of stew and a glass of milk."

"Yes, sir."

Peter didn't observe the other patrons this time. If he stared at the table top as if studying the grain of the wood maybe they'd not even realize he was there. He inhaled deeply and the scent of bread and beef and salt mingled together made saliva pool in his mouth. It took longer than expected for his food to arrive and his stomach protested with grumbling noises.

A man cleared his throat and Peter looked up expecting Lawrence to be standing there holding his meal. Instead Mr. Smalls set the bowl of stew and glass of milk in front of him. "You must really like the food to be back so soon, Mr. Burnett."

Peter's vocal chords thickened and all he could manage to say was "Yes."

Mr. Smalls chuckled. "Eat hardy. I appreciate repeat customers." His gaze flicked to the left and then returned to Peter. "Maybe you'll become a regular."

"Maybe."

After Mr. Smalls returned to the till, Peter took a long swallow of milk. The creaminess coated his raw throat. It just occurred to him he was wearing more than a day's worth of beard. Would Mr. Smalls notice?

Peter did enjoy the food here, but Mr. Smalls had taken too much interest in him. The man seldom greeted customers at their table. What would he have done if Mr. Smalls had decided to sell him the restaurant?

After eating, Peter nodded to Lawrence, paid for the meal, and left the restaurant. Men and women passed him on the street. Peter searched for someone to question, and chose an old man with a bushy, white beard.

He rode up beside him and bobbed his head. "Excuse me sir, do you know where the 18th Georgia Infantry is camped?"

"Our boys are occupying the whole riverbank. Here let me draw you a map or you'll never find it.

The old man ripped out a piece of the newspaper he was holding and drew a map. He marked Longstreet's headquarters. From there, he drew an X representing the Georgia regiment.

"They're camped there."

"Thank you, sir."

A burst of adrenaline made Peter grip Cloudy's flanks a little tighter. For once he felt the thrill of the hunt instead of the fear of the hunted. He couldn't believe he had got the information that easily. He pressed his lips together, suppressing a smile.

Map in hand, he rode towards the river. Confederate infantry stretched as far as he could see, just as the man had said. General Burnside and General Lee were staring down each other with the Rappahannock between them.

Peter followed directions until he was certain he was in Longstreet's division. The easiest way to find out about the enemy was to pay them a visit. He rode out to the nearest camp.

"State your business," the sentry said.

Peter took stock of the man. He looked a little older than himself, five-foot-nine with short black hair and sideburns. His stature mirrored the Kanes, muscles rippled along his thin arms. Definitely a farmer.

"My name's Jeff Burnett. I came to ask if you were in need of any supplies. I'd send them over," Peter said.

The man flashed a wide grin showing all his teeth. "Something to drink."

Peter nodded. "After whipping the Yanks like that you deserve to celebrate." Peter forced a small laugh. "You'd think that Burnside would have more sense than to keep sending those poor blue-bellies to their deaths."

"He was sure doing us a favor. We hardly had to fight atall. We were sheltered comfortably behind the stone wall and all we had to do was fire. A chicken couldn't have survived the barrage."

"It was a job well done." Peter looked past the sentry trying to see their camp. He returned his gaze to the man before he could spark suspicion. Cocking his head, he gave the sentry a probing look. "Surely I can bring you something besides liquor. Surely the boys need more."

The man scrutinized Peter with gray-blue eyes, then spat a wad of tobacco on the ground. He wiped the sticky juice off his mouth with the back of his hand.

"No offense friend, but all you rich people want to do is send us aid. If you really wanted to help you'd enlist. It was a hollow victory, though the paper you're carrying fails to mention that. Word is we lost over 5,000 men. We need men to fill the thinning ranks."

"I'll be back," Peter said.

"You going to enlist?" the sentry prodded.

"Liquor and bandages first, then maybe … we'll see what happens," Peter said. He turned Cloudy around and headed for his sister's house.

Peter thought better of knocking on the door. Instead, he rode to the barn. A negro boy around twelve years old looked up from cleaning to the stalls. His raggedy brown trousers showed both his knees.

"Go tell Mrs. Raleigh to come out to the barn," Peter instructed.

"Missus is havin' a baby," the boy said.

"Now?" Peter half-shouted. He had been counting on her help.

"Dat's what I heared."

"Is Mr. Raleigh here?"

"Nosuh. He's off wid de army."

Peter nodded. Of course. "What about Mr. Warren?"

"Yessuh. He's here. He's in a wheelchair now."

Peter's flesh goose pimpled. He considered waiting in the barn until his father left and then visiting Abigail. But he knew he couldn't now. Maybe later.

He looked at the kegs realizing he couldn't pick them up one-handed. "Boy," Peter said, "put two of those kegs in the wagon bed."

It took all his muscle but the bony boy managed. Peter bit his tongue and hitched Cloudy and a bay horse to the wagon. He should have had the boy do that too, but hated ordering him around.

"What yuh doin', mistah?" the boy asked.

"Don't worry. I'm Abigail's kin."

"I ain't saw yuh 'fore."

"Abigail's having a baby. With all the commotion they won't know anything's missing."

"What if dey does?"

"Then you tell Abigail the gray mare got thirsty."

The boy's eyes bulged, but he didn't say a word. With a flick of the eyes he noticed the pistol on Peter's hip.

"I'm not crazy. Really. You won't get in trouble. She'll know what I mean," Peter assured him.

"Y-y-yessah."

Peter held his breath, aware the boy would be whipped if they thought he had lied. Still, it needed to be done. "Do you know where you can get me some blankets?"

The boy nodded. "I can sneak into de Big House." He ran off. A few minutes later he returned with his arms full.

"They will miss the blankets," Peter said, "but you can tell Abigail that the gray mare needed something to keep her warm. Be sure you tell this to *Abigail*."

Peter drove the wagon down the picket line and stopped in front of the man he had talked to earlier. The sentry's eyes lit up when he saw the blankets and he licked his lips when he saw the kegs. He took a break from his post and unloaded the wagon.

"Do you think the Yankees will be foolish enough to attack again?" Peter asked.

"They better do it quick. The weather won't hold off much longer." The soldier flashed a confident smile "We're ready for 'em. They've got to rebuild the pontoon bridges and even if they do, the cannons are in place to stop 'em just like before."

Peter squinted and saw the pieces of artillery placed along the bank—sunshine gleamed off the metal. "Those cannons did a nasty job the first time. They can do it again. A lot of men seem occupied staring at the Yanks. Any of them sharpshooters?"

"Whole mess of 'em are."

"That makes me feel mighty safe. I'm afraid if they invaded Fredericksburg again they'd make it out to the country."

The sentry glared at him and spoke in an irritated tone. "Don't worry—your plantation's safe." The man paused. "You going to enlist?"

"No. I'm going to take the wagon back."

"You'll never enlist. Even with the Confederacy enacting the draft, you'd just pay someone to take your place. Or better yet, you'd become brass." The sentry's voice dripped with disdain.

"I resent that," Peter said.

The sentry shrugged. "No skin off my nose."

Peter eyed the Confederate soldier. Such a comment would have brought a challenge in some hot-headed circles.

The vein on Peter's neck pulsed and a blaze of anger burned in his chest. He replied, his voice chilly and formal, "I introduced myself but I never got your name."

"Elbert Eaton."

"Well, I might surprise you, Mr. Eaton." Peter climbed into the wagon. "I might come back to join the ranks."

Peter rode away. "You do that," Eaton yelled.

Peter headed back to Abigail's house. He stopped the wagon beside the barn, unhitched the bay horse and led him back to his stall, trying to move his right arm as little as possible.

"Missus had anuder girl," the negro boy said.

"Have they named her yet?"

"Hannah."

The corners of Peter's lips twitched upward. "She named her after our mother."

"Yuh Missus' bruddah," the boy blurted, his eyes as big as full moons.

Peter slapped his thigh. He pulled out his pistol, pointed it on the boy's head, and took a couple steps towards him.

The boy trembled and backed against the wall. He looked like a fawn, knees wobbly, eager to skitter away.

"Sit," Peter commanded.

Promptly, the boy sat. Peter paced the barn, the whole time keeping a watchful eye on the boy. He didn't stir, didn't speak. Peter tapped the pistol against his thigh. Now that he had gotten himself into this mess he might as well use it to his advantage.

"When Mr. Warren leaves, you will hitch up his carriage, right?"

"Yessuh."

"Good."

Peter clenched his teeth, agitation making his temples throb.

"You will tell me when Mr. Warren has disappeared out of sight, out of earshot. Understand?"

"Yessuh."

Peter sat across from the boy, gun in hand, the scent of hay, dung, and horses flooding his nostrils. Now they had to wait.

☆　　☆　　☆

"Moses," Hattie called, her voice high-pitched but rich. "Moses, get out here."

The boy drew a sharp breath and looked at Peter. "Dat's me. I's Moses."

Peter motioned with his head to the door. "Go on. But I'll be watching you. You tell no one you saw me. You hear?"

"Nosuh. I mean yessuh, I won't suh," the boy blubbered. He ran outside.

Peter lay with his ear to the barn wall so he could hear the conversation.

"Master Warren is ready to go home. Hitch up his carriage."

"Yes'm."

"And be quick about it," Hattie said with an edge in her voice.

"Yes'm."

Moses hurried back into the barn and over to a stall with a sleek black stallion. "Massa Warren, he's leavin'," the boy said, breathless.

Peter motioned with his head. "Go on about your business as usual. Don't make any moves that would tip them off. They find out I'm here…" Peter's voice trailed off.

Fear flashed in the boy's eyes like a streak of lightning. Moses hitched up the carriage and stayed outside a long, long time.

Peter shifted on the balls of his feet. It had been too long. Had the boy reported him? Still, he couldn't just leave. He couldn't glance out and look for the boy. Someone might see him.

At last Moses returned to the barn. His face, tense, serious, that of a man twice his age. "I done watch him, suh. I walked all de way to de end of de plantation. Dat's why I took so long, suh," he said, an apology creeping into his eyes.

"Good. Good work."

Peter holstered his pistol and walked around to the back of the house. He bit his bottom lip, tore off his mustache and beard, stuffed them in his pocket, and walked through the servant's entrance. He almost expected to see Aunt Ruth standing there.

She wasn't. His heart dropped a little lower in his chest.

Perhaps she was upstairs with Abigail. He climbed the rounded staircase on his tiptoes avoiding every creaking board he could remember. He stopped outside Abigail's door. It was closed. Could she be sleeping? Even if she was, he could take a peek at the baby.

He pushed the door open and walked in. Abigail's eyes were glued to her newborn. She didn't notice his presence until he squatted down next to her.

"Sis," he whispered.

"I didn't expect you to return, Peter," she said, her voice even, measured. "What are you doing here?"

Peter stuck the tip of tongue out his mouth. He hadn't thought of a response to that question. "I deserted for good," he said.

Abigail nodded, smug, confident. "I thought so."

Peter sucked in his breath, hurt that she would believe that without a second thought. "I wanted to see the baby, to see Hannah. I heard the slaves saying you named her Hannah."

Abigail nodded. "It was the least I could do for father. It pleased him so."

"It pleased me, too, Abigail, you honoring our mother. I risked my life coming here. I risked my life to see my niece."

Abigail met Peter's gaze, her tired eyes dazzling, joyful. "You did, didn't you?"

Peter noticed the smile in her voice though her lips were a weary line. Perhaps his presence would help mend their relationship.

"May I hold her?" he asked.

Abigail pushed the blanket down so Peter could see Hannah's face. Peter marveled at the angelic image of his new niece. Her dark eyelashes stood in stark contrast to her bald pink scalp. Unlike her big sister Sarah, she took more after her father. She had the cutest button nose and was sucking on a corner of the blanket, sleeping soundly.

"I don't want you to wake her."

"Of course." Peter backed up awkwardly, suddenly feeling out of place, wrong-footed. "Well…" He glanced around expecting someone to enter the room any minute. "I should go now."

Abigail reached out and touched his hand. "Thank you for coming."

Peter nodded and left without a word.

He stepped outside and slapped his face to work up his anger. His skin tightened and his gut ached. With heavy strides he headed to the barn. Now all he had to worry about was Moses.

The boy leaned against the barn wall, drawing lines in the dirt with his bare feet. When he heard Peter, his head jerked up.

Peter met his eyes with a stony glare, and bared his teeth.

"What'd I does?" Moses choked out.

"You're the only one who knows about me. I don't know if I can trust you."

"Yuh can trust me, suh. I won't tell." He clamped his lips together with his thumb and forefinger.

Peter advanced towards him, not convinced. There was still a fortune for his capture, after all. Enough to buy his freedom. He pointed his pistol at the boy's head. "The only way to make sure you don't tell anyone you saw me is if I kill you," Peter said, cocking his pistol.

"I woan tell no one, suh. I promise," the boy said, his voice cracking, turning into a dry sob. "Yuh neber here. Yuh a stranga. I doan know yuh."

The guilt Peter felt was almost overwhelming. He stormed out of the barn leaving the boy alone with his tears.

Still holding his pistol, Peter mounted Cloudy and galloped as fast as he could back to Fredericksburg.

☆   ☆   ☆

Peter had to talk to Jack and get back to safety.

Hopefully, Tabitha Edmunds would not be there. It would be terrible to interrupt his friend's courting twice.

"I didn't expect you back so soon," Jack said.

Peter nodded. With caution he looked around the house.

"Don't worry. I'm alone," Jack assured him.

"General Whipple said that he welcomes your help in espionage. You can contact the Yankees by asking a Union sentry for Jeff Burnett."

Jack offered him a half-smile. "You've become quite popular, haven't you?"

Peter grunted. "I'm not too happy about it."

"How long can you stay? Care to join me for supper?"

"I would like that." Peter sat at the polished oak table and shifted in his seat. The saliva felt thick in his mouth. Jack handed him a glass of water and Peter took a long drink. What did two spies say to each other? It seemed like their friendship had changed somehow. He needed to forget about the war for a minute and have a normal conversation with his friend.

"By the way, Abigail just had a baby girl. They named her Hannah."

"That was thoughtful of her."

"I snuck in and saw her. Hannah was sleeping. She's chubby."

"Babies often are." Jack's fatherly smile grew wider.

"Can you take care of Cloudy for me? I'm sure that poor horse needs some food and water as bad as I do."

"Sure thing. And then I'll fix you something."

The table was only big enough to comfortably seat four and the close quarters seemed to make their meal more private. Jack's cooking wasn't near as good as Aunt Ruth's, but it was a million times better than army fare, and his stomach was grateful. It had been a long time since he last had roasted rabbit.

Peter chewed his last piece of buttered bread, gazed out the large window and watched the sun fade, the light slowly disappearing, blocked by the buildings. He pushed his chair back from the table. "Jack, it's time for me to leave."

Jack nodded. He lifted his glass, which only had a swallow of water left. "God save the Union."

Peter clinked his friend's glass. "God save the Union."

Filled with encouragement, Peter didn't feel nervous as he headed out of town. He took slow breaths to maintain a steady heart rate. He had to appear casual or he could spark alarm. A task not easily accomplished with his white-knuckle grip he had on the reins. Still, he couldn't prevent being on edge.

Being this comfortable in Fredericksburg meant his guard was down. The high stress he'd been under struck him with a right hook. Exhaustion made him slump in the saddle. God would have to watch out for him.

He headed for the bushes and trees on the outskirts of the city. Now he just had to lay low until dark.

☆　　☆　　☆

Peter dismounted, reeling in pain as soon as his feet touched the ground. His left hand gripped the reins while his right hand gripped his stomach. It felt like a mule had kicked him in the gut.

With fuzzy vision, a dry mouth, and a rapid, irregular pulse, he stretched out his left hand to catch himself as he half-sat, half-fell backward, landing hard on the frozen ground.

The jarring motion aggravated his cramps. Moaning, he blinked longingly at the ice floating down river. His tongue rolled around his parched mouth, longing for any drop of moisture. But, even if he managed to drag himself to the river, he couldn't get there unnoticed.

He closed his eyes, and Molly's face filled his thoughts, his dreams. Her loving eyes warmed him, encouraged him. With renewed strength, he staggered forward into the bushes and lay on his stomach, only half-lucid. He felt her arms embrace him and he succumbed to their warmth.

"Molly," he murmured. Stretching to caress her tender cheek, he touched only dirt. An intense stomach cramp broke his illusion and he clenched his teeth to keep from yelling in pain. "God," he groaned, "make it stop…"

Dirt. Bushes. Rebel sentries. That was reality.

The mustache and small beard were still in his pocket. They wouldn't do him any good now. They'd never stick to his sweat-soaked face. And if they were found on him, how could he possibly explain them? Pawing feebly at the frozen ground, he buried them.

Licking his cracked lips, he tasted only salt. With the winter breeze catching the moisture on his skin to cool him, he rested his head on a pile of pine cones and needles and drifted off again into fitful sleep.

As the hours ticked by, Peter convinced himself he was getting better. The city was fully enveloped in darkness. This was his chance—maybe his only chance.

Pushing himself to his feet, he called softly to Cloudy. "Come here, girl." When the mare appeared dutifully at this side, he mounted her on the second attempt, his strength fleeting.

The stench of death hung in the air. Possibly exuding from his skin. Clenching his teeth, he spurred Cloudy to a gallop, despite his rattling insides. The treacherous moon filled the night sky, the icy river creaked and cracked, and the rebels stood resolutely at their posts.

"Eleven o'clock and all's well," the sing-song call of the sentry rang out.

Peter rode towards him. He was going to use this illness to his advantage. It would give them a reason to let him pass. He must pass.

He must get to a doctor. He must deliver what he had learned.

CHAPTER 11

THE COOL TOUCH of a hand on Peter's forehead awakened him. He blinked at the man leaning over his bed—was he wearing a Confederate private's coat? Peter's head felt stuffed with cotton. He tried to sit up, but the weight of illness pinned him to the bed. Pain lanced his head as he tried to figure out his surroundings.

"Good afternoon. I'm Charles Taylor, the surgeon around here, but everyone just calls me Doc." His voice rolled softly in a rich Southern drawl.

"Afternoon?" Peter croaked. "How long have I been here?"

"Two weeks, son. You've been passing in and out of fever. Delirious. It's been quite a ride…"

Peter's heart clutched in alarm. Groaning weakly, he whispered, "What day is it?"

"Happy New Year, Mr. Burnett! Welcome to 1863."

"I slept through Christmas?"

"You're lucky to have lived through Christmas." The sepia-haired man stroked his thin mustache thoughtfully. "Don't worry. It wasn't much of a celebration. The only thing that marked the day as 'special' was suspension of drill."

Doc's sharp green eyes scanned Peter's face intently. "I never thought your fever would break… Wish I could take credit for it though…" A crooked smile tweaked the surgeon's lips. "You mumbled a lot. I believe your wife's name is 'Molly' and you have a brother named 'Dan'…"

"Yes," Peter whispered, desperation flooding his veins. The hammering of his heart made his headache pound even worse. Was that all he'd divulged in his fever? Hand clutching his hair, he thrashed, his eyes darting to find some indicator of place. Wait—no handcuffs—no guards... "Where am I?"

"Your mind's still cloudy from the fever, but it will improve. We're near Guiney's Station."

"Guiney's Station," Peter repeated. That was only fourteen miles southeast of the city. Too close to Fredericksburg for comfort.

"One of the sentries found you and carried you here. You'd been poisoned Mr. Burnett."

Peter's heart pounded hard against his rib cage and his breathing increased to keep time. The rush of air brought on a coughing fit. *Poisoned? Someone tried to kill me? Who?*

Doc put a hand on his shoulder. "Calm down. You are so weak it is not good for you to get upset."

"How do you expect me not to get upset!"

"I know. I know. It is a lot to ask of a man, but please try."

Peter rolled his head around on the pillow in slow turns and gradually his burst of adrenaline faded. He caught his breath and the coughing stopped.

"Do you have any enemies? You really should get the authorities involved."

Peter coughed deep, once. Authorities? *They'd take one look at me, lock me up, and bury the key.* "I didn't do anything out of the ordinary before... How long was the poison in my system?"

"There is no way to know exactly what you were poisoned with, sir. Some slow acting poisons take several days to manifest such illness, and some only a few hours."

"I see." Peter closed his eyes and two faces came to mind: Jacob Vickery and Mr. Smalls.

Did Jacob really want him dead? Did he have the stomach for murder? Mr. Smalls sure did. Of course someone else could have recognized him, and decided to take matters into his own hands, too.

"Perhaps it was one of your slaves. It has been known to happen."

Peter forced himself to swallow. "Yes. Thank you for letting me know. I will deal with it when I get home." He took a deep breath, but his chest remained heavy. He coughed again. "If I was poisoned why am I in this hospital for so long?"

"Well," Doc drew out the word, "because after you were in the hospital you developed a severe case of pneumonia. Too much cold air and not enough medicine to go around, I'm afraid."

Peter drew another raspy breath. That explained the dull ache in his chest.

"Would you like something to eat?"

Peter shook his head.

"You've almost wasted away," Doc said, taking on a fatherly tone.

It took all of Peter's strength to roll over onto his stomach. Two weeks on a pine slab had made his back sore—all of his muscles sore. All day Peter heard the continual sound of saws and axes. He'd be stuck wintering on the wrong side of the river.

In the morning, Doc brought Peter some stew. He stared at the unappealing broth and ate very little. He pulled his blanket off and was startled to see his emaciated legs. He hadn't realized how close he'd come to dying from disease. The next time he was brought food he forced himself to eat.

Peter swung his legs over the edge of the bunk and tried to sit up. After teetering for a moment he fell backward. He resigned himself to lying down.

"You're on the top bunk. If you fell forward it would be a drop," the orderly warned.

"I'm not the kind of man who can lie still." Peter groaned. He put his hands to his face. His cheeks felt sunken, his flesh withered and worn.

The orderly gave him an understanding nod and handed Peter an old copy of the Fredericksburg newspaper. "Read this. It will help."

"Thank you."

During the next few days, Peter read that paper front to back so many times he'd memorized what it said. Memorized the fact that the South was winning the war.

☆　☆　☆

Peter woke to find a solider about his age, with short black hair and bushy eyebrows, going bed to bed visiting with all the men in the hospital. He was the first clean-shaven man he'd seen in a long time.

"I see that one of my prayers was answered," the man said, approaching Peter. "Tyler Frazier, chaplain."

"Jeff Burnett," Peter said, shaking his hand.

"Are you a Christian, Mr. Burnett?"

"Yes."

"I'm glad to hear it."

"Pardon the fact that it's none of my business," Peter said, "but you're a private."

"That's quite all right," the chaplain said, his gentle smile reaching his eyes. "Yes, I am. A committee of soldiers tried to get me commissioned, but the colonel wouldn't have it. He said no good soldier could be spared from the ranks. I'm a soldier both in this army and in the army of the Lord."

Peter's eyebrows rose and inched together. "Don't they conflict?"

The chaplain's brown eyes turned serious and his spine straightened. "I suppose you mean killing?"

Peter nodded.

"God forgives us of all our sins no matter how great." He paused. "Can I do something for you? Would you like to pray?"

"No, but I've enjoyed our conversation."

"I'm afraid I did most of the talking," the chaplain said. "Next time, I come around you'll have to tell me about yourself."

After trying each day, Peter could sit up for an extended period. The hospital orderly helped him get off the bunk. That first day it took all his strength to stand, legs trembling like a newborn colt.

Once able to stand without fear of falling, he wrapped one arm around the orderly's shoulder and walked unsteadily around the building. That became his daily exercise. He lay on the plank exhausted and frustrated. He was improving, but not as quickly as he would've liked.

Peter began passing time playing checkers with the hospital orderlies and Doc. The checkerboard was crudely made and the checker pieces were kernels of corn.

"Crown me," Peter said.

Doc added another kernel to the square, a playful glint in his eye. "I think you might actually win this game."

"It's only right that you let the patient win once."

Doc let out a deep laugh. "Wish I had a chess set." A man moaned loudly and he excused himself to check on him. Peter sighed and lay down. He didn't realize boredom could be so painful.

Some of the other patients were playing a game of cards. Peter debated whether he should join in. They'd probably expect him to have good money to bet and that was not the case. Other patients were reading books or writing letters home.

A sob or a laugh broke the silence from time to time. Peter lay on his side to give his back a break. He kept still, feigning sleep, but trying to catch bits of their conversations. Footsteps from the hospital orderlies. A man begged for some whiskey. Another man folded a letter, taking deep breaths as if he was trying to hold back tears.

"Mr. Burnett?"

Peter rolled over and saw the chaplain at his bedside. "So you made it back around."

"I did. Tell me about your family."

"I've been married to my wife, Molly, for two years." Peter pulled her tintype out of his pocket. "Isn't she beautiful?"

Frazier nodded. "Where do you live?"

"I have a plantation outside of Fredericksburg," Peter answered, hoping the chaplain wouldn't want him to be more specific.

"You'll be happy to know that the 7th raised $776 to aid the citizens of Fredericksburg."

"That's wonderful news but by the looks of the soldiers the needy are donating to the less fortunate. Half the men I've seen don't have shoes."

"We are lacking in many things," the chaplain agreed, "but God will provide for us. Our spirit, valor, faith, and determination aren't lacking."

"I'm glad to hear it. I usually ride into town every Sunday to go to the Fredericksburg Baptist Church. Have you been there?"

"No. I'm not from this area. I saw the poor church after the battle though. It was shot in at least fifteen places."

"That's a shame. When I'm able to leave, I probably won't recognize the town."

"Hopefully, you can get back to your family soon. I could get a message to your wife," he offered. "I'm surprised no one's come looking for you."

"Don't bother. I won't be here much longer. Molly wouldn't be worried about me yet; I've been gone for weeks before."

The chaplain pressed his lips together. "I see."

"Don't judge me," Peter spoke with an icy edge.

"I'm not judging you, Mr. Burnett," the chaplain said, and walked away.

Peter sighed as he looked at Molly's picture. If only what he had said was true.

He wished he had been married to her for two years. Love at first sight had seemed like the work of writers. But when he saw her smile and felt her soft, pale skin he understood its power. The power to melt his heart and send warm tingles through his body.

☆　　☆　　☆

"Your color is much better today," Doc said.

"I feel stronger." Peter ate his last bite of stew.

Doc rubbed his chin between his thumb and forefinger. "Perhaps today's the day."

"Day for what?"

"For you to leave the hospital."

A burst of excitement barreled through Peter's body. After it passed, anxiety crept in. He finished his meal and got out of bed. He was finally able to walk unaided without becoming winded.

"That just proved to me that you're well enough to go home," Doc said. "I'm sure you'll be well cared for there."

Peter forced a smile, though his heart was shuddering. "I am happy to leave. Thanks for taking care of me."

The doctor gave him a strong handshake. "You're welcome, Mr. Burnett. This time of year I take care of sick patients instead of wounded ones. I like it better that way."

Peter walked Cloudy through Fredericksburg in the dark, looking all around him like a prowling cat. Paranoid. He knew he was paranoid, but he couldn't stop feeling that someone was watching. Faint moonlight slid across the destroyed city. The shadows cast by the burnt, broken buildings were strange, eerie.

An owl hooted. The hair on the back of Peter's neck stood at attention. He expected ghosts to join him in the street. Expected them to escort him to his destination.

Not that he needed an escort. He knew every road in Fredericksburg, every house, every shed. His pulse echoed in his ears. He quickened his stride, made it to the door, and struck it with a balled fist.

"Who in God's name comes at this hour," Jack said in a soft grumble. He answered the door, in his nightshirt, a revolver in his hand.

Peter burst into the house and held his right hand over his heart. He took several deep breaths.

Jack's eyes filled with concern. "What's wrong, Jeff?" He lit a lamp. It cast a flickering orange glow. "Sit down."

"I'm stuck on the wrong side of the river. I got pneumonia. A Confederate sentry picked me up off the ground, near the river, and took me to the camp hospital." The words spilled out of his mouth.

"I understand your concerns. Given the late hour, perhaps it would be best if we discussed this in the morning." Jack gestured to the sofa. "I am sure you are tired, too. I'm going back to bed."

Peter pulled the tintype of Molly out of his pocket. He kissed her picture. "I love you," he whispered to her image.

Jack stopped in front of his bedroom door and turned around. "I can hide you here, but not for long."

CHAPTER 12

A LOUD THUMPING sounded outside. A rush of adrenaline penetrated his muscles. He sprang off the sofa, reached for his haversack, and pulled out his pistol. Was it man or animal?

Jack Selah hurried into the room, barefoot, brown pants under his wrinkled nightshirt. "Two Confederate soldiers," he whispered. "Just enough sunlight. I saw them from my bedroom window."

Peter's insides tightened constricting his air flow. There was a bulge on Jack's waist not well disguised by the thin cotton. His revolver. This was serious.

"What do I do, Jack?" Peter said, panic flooding his veins, rushing his words together.

"Hide under my bed. Quick."

Fear and frailty caused Peter's steps to wobble. He staggered towards the white door, hands flung in front of him, groping in the dark for something to grab on to. Hopefully, he wouldn't fall headlong into the room.

He grabbed for the nearest poster of the bed and miscalculated, falling to his knees with a handful of blanket. A vibrating twinge of pain shot to his thigh. He winced. His legs, nothing more than skin covered bones, had little padding to soften the blow.

Well, he had to get to the floor anyway. He pressed his stomach against the floor, clawing the carpet like a cat scaling a downed tree. He stretched his arms above his head and sank his fingernails into the thick carpet again, slowly pulling himself further under. His arms ached as he pulled a third time. Peter was only half in hiding when a friendly, boyish voice asked Jack, "Do you have any food or money you can donate to the Confederate cause?"

Peter's heart contorted inside his chest as he squeezed his body further out of sight. Thankfully the blanket he had torn off the bed covered his feet.

"I donate to the hospitals to help the wounded," Jack said. "I am sorry I have nothing else to spare."

"It is the able bodied soldiers who are continuing to defend Fredericksburg. To protect you. You should be helping us," another soldier growled.

"I'm sorry. I'm just a writer. I don't have much. You should visit some of the plantations and beg from them to fill your stomachs."

"We should go check your barn. We'll take whatever we find."

"There are only a couple horses in there. Both mounts have been overworked and underfed. I doubt the tough meat will be appetizing."

One of the soldiers grunted. "We could still kill them. Then where would you be?"

Cloudy. They couldn't kill Cloudy. "The food—it is not just for us," the boy said, possibly implying there were more soldiers hidden by darkness.

"I see." Jack's voice remained calm and level. "Well, I still say you'd have better luck in the country."

An aggravated stomp. "I'd be starving by the time I reached those plantations," the other soldier complained, gruff, forceful.

Peter's lungs constricted, squeezing out the breath he had been holding. He shut his eyes tightly and began to pray.

"Well, if you don't get any food in town you'll still be starving. Good day gentleman."

Slow and threatening the older soldier said, "We're not leaving here without breakfast."

"Hey," the boy said. "No need to shove that pistol in our faces, mister."

"Go ahead and draw your own," Jack said in a baiting timbre. "Just give me a reason to kill you legal."

Silence followed.

"You are both ruffians. You don't even have the decency to beg at a decent hour. As you can see by my clothes I was still in bed. Now if you don't leave this minute I will start shooting."

The door slammed shut. Peter exhaled loudly. Still, he didn't move. The soldiers could come back. They had sounded determined to fill their bellies. It seemed like hours before the sound of footsteps caught his ears. "Come on out, Peter," Jack whispered.

Peter did so. He saw the concern sliding into his friend's eyes.

"It is not safe for you to be out in the open. They could have pushed their way into the house. We need to find a safe place for you."

"Where? The doctor at the camp hospital expected my family and servants to tend to me."

Jack nodded, his head slightly lowered, lips pursed together. He straightened and waved for Peter to follow him. Haversack slung over his shoulder, Peter headed into Jack's office.

The oak desk, scattered with stationary and newspapers, made Peter smile. Jack kept a copy of every article he wrote, even the ones he'd penned when he was Peter's age.

Jack walked up to a bookshelf. It stood floor to ceiling and sat back against the far wall. Each book, meticulously placed according to topic. Jack pushed roughly with both hands on the right side of the bookshelf and it slid a foot. "Squeeze in there."

Peter's mouth parted, surprise and relief registering at once. So this was the secret room. He would never have guessed that there was a false wall. It didn't show from the outside.

Bile burned Peter's throat threatening to reach his mouth. He swallowed forcing it into retreat. Small spaces. He hated small spaces.

"The space is tight, but it has been hiding people for years."

Peter didn't move.

"It isn't exactly a warm hut." Jack's hand rested on his shoulder. "But it isn't that bad for one person, really. There are several blankets. Get some sleep."

Peter turned sideways and inched his way through into the opening. A stale smell and particles of disturbed dust mixed in the stagnant air. Overcome with a coughing fit, Peter covered his mouth.

He lowered himself to the hard-packed dirt floor and unfolded a tattered patchwork blanket. Rough and itchy, he didn't mind that it didn't reach his chin. He wadded up another blanket and used it as a pillow.

Without another word, Jack moved the bookshelf back in place.

The room turned as black as a tomb.

Peter's heart shrunk with his plummeting spirits.

Lice welcomed his company by throwing a party in his honor. The microscopic pests crawled from the blanket infesting his clothes, his hair, irritating his skin.

Just great. This was worse than the hospital. Slowly his eyes grew accustomed to the darkness. He began making out colors not just shadowy shapes.

He took stock of his surroundings: A lamp sat in the middle of the room with a half-full book of matches. There was a chamber pot in the far corner emanating a faint urine stench. A Bible and a deck of cards rested next to it.

He shook his head wondering if he'd be playing cards with himself or using them to wipe.

Exhaustion washed over him, the hot air seeming to press down on his chest. Beads of sweat popped on his forehead, the heat lulling him into false relaxation.

☆　　☆　　☆

Peter paced the confines of the small room. He fidgeted with the bottom of his coat, crinkling and rubbing the fabric between his fingers, unable to keep still. It was a constant struggle to maintain his sanity. Since his voice echoed, he sang the negro spirituals Aunt Ruth had taught him in his mind.

"Molly," he said, "Molly I wish you were here." He lit the lamp and then dug her picture out of his haversack. He studied her image until he went to sleep with the tintype resting against his breast.

A few hours later, the grinding sound of the bookshelf moving woke him.

"Noon meal," Jack said, "hopping John."

"That sounds good. You're a far better cook than I am."

"I've had more practice at it than you have. If Aunt Ruth had been cooking all my meals I wouldn't have had the need to learn at such an early age."

Peter pressed his lips together and stared at the floor.

Jack put a hand on his shoulder. "I didn't mean to make you sad. How are you doing?"

"I'm going stir crazy."

"Already? I'll get you a book to read. Shakespeare?"

Peter shook his head. "Would make me think too much of Molly."

"*Moby Dick?*"

Peter laughed softly. "That will do and a rag for when I need to…"

Jack shook his head with a grin. "You should have told me there wasn't one a long time ago."

"It was a fleeting thought. I had more important things on my mind. After all, being in the army, I've gotten used to scratchy leaves."

Peter cleaned the bowl of black-eyed peas, salt pork, rice, and onions. Then he began reading to pass the time. Bloodied corpses from the skirmish line haunted him; making it impossible to focus on the story.

His friends Henry Jackson and Andrew Silas were dead. The lad crying for his mother, dead.

His eyes widened when he heard a gunshot, not a ghostly echo of one in his mind, but a real gunshot close by.

Jack! He yelled in his head. The words wouldn't come out of his mouth.

If men were sacking the house they'd surely kill him. Peter's heart raced trying to rush out of his chest. If Jack was killed—he was trapped.

He couldn't push the bookshelf over.

He looked down at his empty bowl. Although he had eaten hours only before, his stomach gurgled. He'd starve to death in here or die from lack of water. He'd rot in this dark hole.

His hands trembled. Tears rolled down his cheeks. He felt a wet coolness trickle down his leg.

Damn my father. Damn the war. Damn the whole South.

He lay back down, in the fetal position, and curled up in the blanket. He closed his eyes tightly. "Lord," he whispered, "don't let this hidden room be my grave."

Peter cried himself into a lull. He wanted to sleep but it remained elusive.

Hours later, a scratching sound jolted him. He sat up and stared at the bookcase. Slowly it moved and light passed through the crack.

Peter bit his lip. His heart constricted and sweat coated his palms. He exhaled loudly when he saw Jack.

"I heard a gunshot. I thought maybe you..."

Jack shook his head and spoke in a low voice. "You'll hear a gunshot once in a while. People are shooting rabbits and birds, and eating them. Even in the city. With the price of food in the shops."

"I thought the soldiers from this morning had come back."

Jack shook his head. "They won't come back unless they get drunk. They're not the brave, reckless sort."

Peter let his chin drop to his chest as he contemplated his friend's words. "You've gotten good at reading people."

"You carry secrets for as long as I have you *better* learn how to read people."

A sluggish, sly smile spread across Peter's lips. "You'll make a good spy."

Jack rolled his shoulders, his posture tight. "I hope so. Since you didn't manage to get word to the Federals I'll have to."

"Ask a Union soldier with the Army of the Potomac for Jeff Burnett and they'll sort it out."

"That's the least of my worries." Jack stroked one of his eyebrows, his posture stooped. "I can't hide you here all winter. Tabitha comes over regularly and if she found out about you—"

"Let's not discuss this now."

Jack pinched his throat. "I've only hid people here for a few days at a time..." He looked around the room. "I'll empty your chamber pot and take away your dishes."

Peter handed him both. After Jack left, Peter peeked his head into his friend's office and inhaled the fresh air. The natural light from the window was much brighter than the pool of light from his lamp. He snuck out of his room, with the thrill of child who was up past his bedtime.

When Jack returned he gave Peter a stern look.

Peter's feet stuck to the floor. Stubbornly they refused to move.

Jack gave him a gentle shove back into the secret room. Peter cringed and the bookshelf slide back to its usual place.

Once again, locking him in.

☆ ☆ ☆

Peter returned to staring at the shadows dancing on the wall. He didn't know how much of this he could take—being isolated, alone.

He wished he had his pocket watch so he could check the time. Of course, Aunt Ruth always said a watched pot never boiled. A watched timepiece would not make the hours tick by faster.

He lay down again. Sleep would help him get stronger. The sooner he got stronger the sooner he could get out of hiding—at least hiding here.

A week had passed. Peter relished the hushed conversations he had with Jack while the man worked in his office and the occasional game of cards. Jack was the closest thing he had to father figure.

Strange his father still living and yet long ago replaced. Of course, as a boy, he'd clung to the first man who took an interest in him, offered to teach him things. Thankfully, he'd found a man with a strong moral code and a generous heart. He molded himself in Jack's image.

That night when Jack brought him his dinner he motioned for Peter to come out of the room. Before this he was only allowed out of the room for a few hours during the dead of night when no light shone through the windows.

Jack blew out the lamp on his desk. The room darkened instantly. "Take a quick glance out the window," Jack said, inclining his head in that direction.

Peter's pulse pounded loudly, uncertainty and fear turning his stomach as he approached the glass. He had no idea what he was about to see. Were Confederate soldiers now camped *in* the town? Was his father out there?

His back pressed up against the wall, he rubbed his clammy hands on his pants, and took a few deep breaths building up the nerve to look.

He peeked for a mere second before returning out of sight. "There is an old negress across the street hanging a blanket out the window."

"Exactly."

"Airing a blanket? What does that mean?"

Jack frowned, his whole demeanor sagging.

Peter knew from his eyes, his silence, his tense features, that he had disappointed him. He hated letting him down. He thought about it for a moment but couldn't figure out what was so significant.

Jack looked him in the eye. "That means that you are going to have company tomorrow."

Peter mentally kicked himself for not putting this together on his own. It would make since that not every house would use a lantern signal. Peter blushed but remained silent, letting his thoughts turn to his soon to be roommates.

CHAPTER 13

THE SOUND OF wood grinding against wood jolted Peter upright. How could Jack keep this small room a secret if he made such a loud noise unblocking the entrance? The bookshelf moved a little at a time Peter fidgeted with nervous curiosity. He ran his fingers through his hair hoping he looked more presentable than he felt.

A negro man was the first to enter the small room. When he saw Peter his eyes widened.

"I'm a friend," Peter said.

The slender man's lips thinned and looked at him suspiciously. Finally, he sat on the ground as far away from Peter as he could get. He sat stiff and straight on alert.

Next a negress entered the room. She was several years younger than the man, perhaps seventeen.

She accepted Peter right off, offering a tired smile. "My name's Linda," she said. "This is my husband George."

Peter nodded. "My name's Jeff."

"Yuh runnin' too, Jeff?" Linda asked.

Peter was silent for a long time, evading her probing gaze. "I'm not a yellow man. I'm white."

Linda's mouth parted.

"I am running though," Peter continued, his eyes shifting from the man to the woman. "I'm running from the gray soldiers."

"Yuh in deir army and yuh doan want to be a soldier no more?" Linda said.

Peter shook his head. "No. I was in the blue army – the Northern Army – the Union."

"Yuh helpin' to make us free," George said. His face softened, and his eyes brightened.

Peter smiled. Lincoln hadn't made that the objective yet, but it was better to give them hope.

"Yes I am. How did you know that the Northern Army was fighting to free you?"

George reached into the pocket of his brown trousers and pulled out a small torn piece of paper. "Dat's what dis says. At least dat's what we's done been told."

Peter reached out his hand and took the piece of paper. He lit the lamp and held it close so he could read the small print. "The war is to make the Southern states come into line with the North and that emancipation was a part of the fighting," he whispered.

"Doan dat mean dey goin' to free us?" Linda asked.

Peter nodded. "Where did you get this? This was written by an abolitionist up North."

"I done steal it from ma massah," George said. "He was cussin' as he read dat paper so I done know dat dere had to be somethin' in dere worth knowin'."

Peter laughed softly. George and Linda were both thin, in tattered clothes of coarse negro cloth, and had trouble keeping their eyes open.

"We're safe here. Lay down and rest."

Linda lay down with her head in George's lap.

Peter draped the patchwork blanket over her and handed George the rolled up blanket he had been using as a pillow.

"Dat leave nothin' for yuh," he said.

"I'm fine. You need to get some good sleep. You have many long nights ahead of you."

"Yessuh, we does." George wrapped up in the blanket. "But we's goin' to be free. We can't wait for de blue army to free us. Nosuh. Not now dat Linda's wid chile."

Peter bit his tongue. He had many questions for them, but Linda was already asleep, and George rested next to her, an arm draped over her side. They'd wait till morning.

☆　☆　☆

Jack handed them each a plate of ham and beans for breakfast. Linda ate hers quickly like she hadn't had a meal in days.

George gave her half of his ham. "Yuh eatin' for two," he said.

Peter felt guilty as he nibbled on his ham. He hadn't experienced the true pain of hunger since he fled his father's plantation and made the long migration to New Hampshire. The guilt ate at him until handed Linda the other half of his ham, too. "Ma'am, you need this more than I do."

"Thankyuh."

"Why are you running now?" Peter asked.

"Massa says he goin' to sell me," George said. "Say I was weak-minded just 'cause I doan talk much."

"He wants to sell you because you don't talk?" Peter asked his nose wrinkled.

"Not really," George replied. "It's 'cause he needs the money and I fetch a good price. But he done say dat I's hexed and dat was why he goin' to sell me."

"You a tobacco hand?"

George nodded. "We both was." George took off his holey white shirt.

Even in the dim light of the lamp Peter could see a maze of old scars and a mess of fresh scabs covering the man's back. It soured his stomach leaving a bitter taste in his mouth.

"What did you do to get that?" Peter asked.

George bowed his head and spoke barely above a whisper. "Tried to stop him from beating Linda."

Linda sucked in her breath and stared at the ground.

Peter felt the anger boiling inside him. His neck burned and slowly his whole face grew hot.

"How dare he," Peter said in a loud growl.

Peter shut his eyes tightly trying hard to repress a dark memory, but it was no use. The horror of that day rushed back and he shook with rage remembering every sickening detail.

His father ordered the gardener to dig a shallow hole in the backyard. He walked out of the barn holding the arm of a naked negress, and a whip in the other.

The woman struggled, but was unable to break away.

"I don't care that you're in the family way. You work if you want to eat around here," his father had said gruffly. He let her go with a rough push. "Lay in that hole," he ordered.

Trembling, the woman shot Peter a pleading look then obeyed, tears streaming down her face. She screamed as the whip bloodied her back.

Peter tried walking towards the house but his father locked eyes with him.

"You will watch this," he shouted.

"I don't want to," Peter fired back, too foolish and too angry to be scared.

His father waved the bloody whip in front of his face. "You will do as I say, boy, or I will lay you bare, too."

Peter looked at Linda, glad she was running with her husband. She wasn't showing yet. She'd be able to make the trip without much difficultly—hopefully.

"Yuh all right, suh?" Linda asked. "Yuh's cryin'."

Peter brushed the salty tears out of his eyes and off his cheeks. "I'm fine. I just remembered something terrible."

All three of them exchanged knowing looks. Peter took a deep breath. Of course they'd understand.

☆　☆　☆

Peter ran out of things to say. He picked up the Bible and flipped to the story of Moses. That was Aunt Ruth's favorite, Moses leading his people out of Egypt. In a low voice he began reading.

Linda tilted her ear towards Peter. "Speak up a little. I doan want to miss a word."

George rested his hand on her shoulder. He closed his eyes focusing on the scripture.

A slight smile curled Peter's lips. He felt useful for the first time in days. As he got to the good part his voice grew to a normal pitch. "By strength of hand the Lord brought us out of Egypt, out of the house of bondage…"

The bookshelf moved. Jack's wrinkles were deeper around his eyes and across his forehead. He looked like he had aged in the past hour. He had never seen his friend so frayed.

"What's wrong?" Peter asked.

Jack looked past Peter to George and Linda. "I just finished talking with Mr. Hays."

Linda and George's eyes widened. Linda grabbed her husband's hand and squeezed. Mr. Hays was clearly their master.

Jack repeatedly smoothed his shirt with his left hand. "I also talked to a couple bounty hunters. Would you believe that he's already circulated posters?"

"He needs money powerful bad," Linda said. "He's not goin' to give up till he drags us back and den—" She stopped talking, tears dripping onto her cheeks.

"You're safe here," Jack said. "They didn't have dogs with them. Tonight you'll have to go to the next safe house."

"Thankyuh, suh," George said.

Jack lips twitched as if they didn't know whether to smile or frown. "I'm sure you're hungry. I will make you a hearty stew," he said, moving the bookshelf back.

"You have to be strong," Peter said. "It is going to be a *long* journey. Be strong for your baby."

Linda nodded. "Dat's not what I's worry 'bout, suh. I's worry 'bout gettin' caught."

"More and more southerners are being occupied with the war. Surely that will aid in your escape."

"Or make it mo' dangerous to get North. We could wind up in de middle of a battle."

Peter swallowed hard, thinking about his first battle. That had only been a skirmish. He hadn't thought of all the negroes that this war was affecting.

☆   ☆   ☆

Jack motioned for Linda and George to come out. The house was as dark as the secret room. Even the moon seemed to be hiding.

Peter followed them, searching for light. He saw the worry in Linda's eyes even though she didn't speak. Her steps were timid.

"You'll be safer out of town. Too many people around here," Jack said. "Just stay in the shadows, head out of town and keep on going. Hide in the daylight. Walk in water when you can. Dogs have a hard time tracking in water."

George nodded. "Yessuh."

"Thankyuh," Linda whispered.

"Look for the hanging quilts or two lanterns."

Peter shook George's hand. The man was stone-faced but his eyes were friendly. Next, Peter gave Linda a quick hug. Spending so much time with them Peter felt like he had known them for years even though it had just been a couple days.

Before they left Jack gave them a blanket with food wrapped inside. "More roast beef and bread," he said.

"God be with you," Peter said as George and Linda slipped out of the house into the night. "Follow the North Star." Then he whispered more to himself then to anyone else, "I wish I was going North with you."

Jack stood staring into the darkness. He took several deep breaths.

"Are they going to make it?" Peter asked.

Jack shrugged. "If they're not recognized. So many slaves have run off since the start of the war…"

When Peter had been a boy just starting to get involved in the Underground Railroad Jack always sounded sure of himself. Of course later he learned that the rosy picture was just for his benefit, not the truth.

'If they were not recognized' was a sensible answer. He looked at Jack out of the corner of his eye hoping his friend would sense he needed reassurance. He wanted Jack to say they'd have safe passage like he had promised years ago.

"You know," Jack said finally, "the same goes for you."

Peter nodded absentmindedly and then jerked to an abrupt stop. "What do you mean?"

"I didn't tell you this earlier because I didn't want to worry you, but you *have* been recognized."

Peter's heart slowed and then froze.

CHAPTER 14

CONTINUING TO STARE out the window, Peter turned rigid. "What do you mean I've been recognized?"

"An old woman swears she saw you a couple of weeks ago standing as bold as brass in front of the jail. Her name is Mrs. Collier. You're lucky though. Most people think she's crazy. She's been touched in the head for years—ever since all her children died with fever."

Peter exhaled softly, fear slicing his thoughts. "Should I get out of sight? I am enjoying being in the house."

Jack shook his head. "It's pitch black outside and no lamps are lit. Enjoy your freedom. But," he paused, "you know you can't stay in that room forever."

Peter's pulse increased and he curled his toes. He'd knew the time was coming, but he hadn't expected it to come so soon. It always seemed to be in the future.

"How are you feeling? Do you have all your strength back yet?"

Peter wanted to say no, but that would have been a lie. His friend would be able to see right through him so there was no use in trying. "Yes. I've spent many hours pacing."

"Then you're well enough to leave."

Where was he going to go now? "Should I go back to Abigail's?"

"She'll be entertaining Confederate soldiers all winter. Not to mention the fact that your father is a frequent visitor. That would be asking for trouble. There is one more option."

"What?"

"Go back and enlist with the Rebs."

"Are you crazy?" Peter's voice came out in a breathy screech. "Jack, I don't want to be a spy. I just want to be back with my friends. I can't be a Confederate soldier. I'd strangle one of them the first time I heard them slander Lincoln."

Jack stroked his mustache, the hand over his mouth stifling a laugh. "You'll have to keep your anger under control. I wasn't suggesting that you would transform into a Confederate permanently. They're diligently watching for attempts to cross the frozen river. You'll have to wait it out. The safest way to do that is with the Rebs."

"Then what?"

"You wait for the right time to join your army again. I'll come visit you when the weather permits. I visit the soldiers frequently."

"If I enlist, I expect your help."

"I know, I know. I'll do what I can to get you back with the Army of the Potomac."

Jack grabbed Peter by the arm and dragged him over to the mirror in the modest parlor. "You don't look like a soldier at the moment. I'll heat some water for a bath. Get out of those filthy clothes. We need you enlisting with class."

Peter gladly shed his dirty, sweaty, lice infested clothes and sat in the tub. Jack dumped hot water on his head and Peter yelled. Jack washed Peter's hair, combed out the lice, and then handed Peter a bar of soap and cloth. By the time Peter was done, the smell of lye and stale water wafted from his skin. He stepped out of the tub and Jack had a clean nightshirt waiting for him.

In the middle of the night, Jack washed and pressed Peter's suit. Peter had wanted to do it himself, but Jack insisted he save his strength. After breakfast the next morning, Peter dressed in his suit. Unable to resist his fatherly instinct, Jack straightened Peter's cravat.

Afterward, Jack left to saddle Cloudy. He led her out and handed Peter the reins. Peter mounted the mare, and the men exchanged silent nods. Peter rode Cloudy back to the camp near Guiney's Station. His chest tightened and he tied her up at the picket line.

With unsteady steps and a quivering heart, Peter returned to the camp hospital. He couldn't believe his options had dwindled to this.

"Doc?"

The man turned around, a question in his eyebrows.

"If you think I'm fit for duty, I'd like to enlist."

The surgeon rocked back on his heels. "The infantry is a rough life." His serious expression emphasized the warning in his voice. "Rank and file infantry is not fit for gentlemen."

Peter's eye's burned. One more comment like that and he'd catch Doc's coat on fire.

"Gentlemen are not china dolls." His tone had more of a bite than he intended. He inhaled deeply, but calm eluded him and his heart beat faster. "Serving my country is the least I can do to repay you for saving my life."

Doc smiled though his eyes looked doubtful. "That is a nice thought, but I don't think you should."

"Last night I discussed it with my family."

Doc cocked his head. "Did you inform them you'd be a private?"

Peter gritted his teeth. The man was just trying to get his goat. "That's none of your business."

"Suppose you're right."

"My mind is made up and no one can persuade me otherwise. I want to be a soldier. A soldier with no special treatment."

"All right, go ahead, but remember I warned you. I don't understand why anyone would want to join this war."

"Where's your southern patriotism?"

"I patch up men wounded by minie balls, shrapnel, and cannon shot. I've seen so many men die in my care that it haunts me. This war just gives me more gruesome work. I want it to end."

"Hopefully, I can help it end. Besides, I've gotten fond of being here."

Doc laughed. "You must be the only one." He rubbed his chin with his thumb and forefinger. "Since you're so determined, I'll take you to see Colonel Kemper. I need some fresh air."

Peter walked outside and the unseasonably cold weather nearly took his breath away. His hands felt frozen by the time he stepped into the colonel's hut.

"This man wants to enlist," Doc said.

Kemper's appearance was not professional like the Union officers of his regiment. He looked unkempt; his uniform was soiled and discolored.

The colonel looked up from his paperwork with the enthusiasm of someone approaching the gallows. "Have you had any formal military training?"

"I served three months in the Virginia militia, sir," Peter said. "I left when my wife had a baby."

The colonel grunted. He pulled a newspaper out from his traveling desk and pointed to the map drawn on it. "Why'd you have this?"

Peter had forgotten about his map and he sucked in his breath. "How'd you get it?" he blurted.

"Doc figured you were no longer in need of it."

Peter bobbed his head. "My friend is serving with Longstreet. I wanted to visit him. With Confederate regiments everywhere I never would have found him without some direction."

"There's no need to question him. He's been in the hospital for weeks," Doc said.

Kemper gave Peter a probing look, suspicion written into every line on his face. "That doesn't mean anything. Why in tarnation would a gentleman choose the ranks?" The question was posed to Doc, but Peter knew he had to answer.

"I was born and raised in Fredericksburg," Peter said. "The war hadn't directly affected me until just recently. The damn Yankees destroyed my city. They frightened my wife and child. I have a right to serve my country. If you don't want my help fighting the Yanks I'm sure I can find another regiment that will appreciate my patriotism."

"Just swear him in, Colonel," Doc insisted. "We could use an extra man. I warned him about what he was getting into."

Kemper rubbed the back of his neck. "Is there some reason why you haven't been offered a commission? Have you spent time in jail?"

Peter smoothed a wrinkle in his coat. "No, sir. I've never been in jail."

"Doc's right. We're short men. What's your full name?"

"Jefferson Peter Burnett." Peter forced a smile as his new name was added to the muster roll.

"Welcome to company D of the 7th Virginia," Kemper said. "I'll have to hunt you up a uniform."

Peter felt as if he was committing a sin as he dressed in gray. In his weeks at the hospital he'd already gotten used to saying his name was Jeff Burnett—now it was Private Burnett.

Private Burnett a soldier in Kemper's brigade assigned to Pickett's division of Beauregard's army. The thought made bile rise up his throat, sour his mouth, burn his tongue.

Peter examined his Confederate uniform: sweat stained under the arms and the knees on his pants were wearing thin. He put on his brown frock coat to keep him warmer, put his boots back on, and stuffed the rest of his civilian clothes in his knapsack, and then ran his fingers through his hair. He wasn't given a cap. Half of the Rebs didn't have one either.

Peter couldn't help but notice that his new regiment was missing more than just caps.

Many were suffering in the cold without coats or blankets and their worn uniforms were patched in several places. As a partial remedy, those barefoot made themselves rawhide moccasins.

If all the Confederate Army was in such shoddy shape the end of the war would be near. But he soon realized cold feet did little to dampen their spirits. They were still eager to fight.

☆   ☆   ☆

Private Eaton accepted Peter as a comrade when no one else seemed interested in his friendship. Peter reckoned that was because he had taken the man's dare and enlisted. In return Eaton tried to make Peter's transition into the Confederate Army as smooth as possible. A small, welcome favor.

"I think you should know more about the Mountain Boomers. That's what we call ourselves in this company," Eaton explained.

"I would like that," Peter said. "From the looks of things you've been through a lot."

"We've been through it *all*," Eaton said. "The first year of the war, we tasted victory. We tasted it twice in July, first at Blackburn's Ford and then at the First battle of Manassas. We got accustomed to victory." Eaton's chest puffed out and slowly deflated.

"Our next battle was Williamsburg. It was officially a draw as was Seven Pines after it. Then we fought at Frayser's Farm and at Second battle of Manassas.

"The Yankees beat us at South Mountain and Antietam. That not only diminished our numbers but crushed our spirit. It wasn't until then that we could say we were truly battle hardened veterans. Of course you know of our glorious victory at Fredericksburg and here we are."

Peter nodded. "That's quite a history."

"We've come to the conclusion that beating the Yanks isn't going to be easy. We have to make sacrifices and are willing to do so. You'll be accepted once you prove that you're as dedicated to the cause as we are."

Peter's Adam's apple jumped. *That would be a challenge.*

Soldiers swapped jokes, cleaned their muskets, and played cards in an attempt to amuse themselves. They looked like they didn't have a care in the world. He pushed his shoulders to his ears then brought them back down. He had to relax.

Out of the corner of his eye he saw that Eaton was patiently waiting for him to talk.

In the silence Peter's heart thudded. He voiced the only question that entered his mind. "Where does everyone in Company D hail from?"

"Giles County, Virginia," Eaton said. "We didn't have it as easy as you. We're poor farmers. We sweat in the field every day to eke out an existence for ourselves and our families."

That explained why the men disliked me.

The first day he drilled with his new company, Sergeant Snidow was in charge. In his early twenties, the thin man of average height with a ruddy complexion was by no means imposing. However, his steely blue eyes watched Peter closely.

Self-conscious of every motion, Peter felt his cheeks flush hot. He breathed erratically as he performed the maneuvers, though he still did them with mechanical precision.

Snidow repositioned his cap on dark brown hair. "I'm glad you know what you're doing," he told Peter afterward.

"I know how to march, use a musket and bayonet, but I'm sure I still have lots to learn."

"In the future, when you talk to me address me by rank, Private."

Peter pressed his lips together and blinked. He hadn't cared if the Mountaineers called him sergeant or not. "Yes, Sergeant."

Snidow laughed, deep, loud, mocking. A laugh that would have made Peter's father proud.

Peter stood there confused and annoyed. He didn't know what was so funny. He knew better than to ask.

"You don't belong here, Burnett," Snidow snapped, adding force to each word.

"I disagree, Sergeant. It's my responsibility to fight for the Confederacy and protect my home state."

"Then you should do it as an officer. It's clear you were born with a silver spoon in your mouth. If you think it's manlier to be in the ranks, you're wrong. Giving up your privileges doesn't make a lick of sense."

Peter started to protest but Snidow walked away. Staring at his back, Peter felt caught somewhere between dumbfounded and irritated.

Peter walked with Eaton towards the row of huts. A tall, negro man in coarse gray trousers and a black frock coat passed them. A young negro boy was running to catch up with the man. The young boy was dressed in brown trousers and a gray coat that were two sizes too big. Despite that, he was well dressed for his young age.

"Who are they?" Peter asked.

"Both named James. They belong to the captain."

Peter's eyebrows lifted along with the end of his words. "A captain with two slaves?"

"And a horse," Eaton said. "Tried to take all the property he could with him so the Yanks wouldn't get it."

Both of Peter's hands folded into fists. He willed his tongue to remain silent. He was a southern gentleman now. Human chattel was the backbone of the South. He had to appear to accept it.

"I thought you said everyone in this company were poor farmers."

"We are. Captain Bane just has a little help."

Peter kicked a rock.

"I can see you didn't get along with Sergeant Snidow," Eaton said, changing the subject.

Peter nodded, relieved by the new discussion. "But I didn't do anything."

"You didn't have to. He already had his mind made up not to like you because you're wealthy. If you think *he's* bad, watch out for Lieutenant Mullins. He's a stickler for military procedure and is mean enough to spit nails.

"If Sergeant Fry ever gets loose from those damned Yankees, then you would have to watch for him, too. We keep hoping for a prisoner exchange. He's a good man, but he was bucking to become brass so he doesn't let much slide."

Peter rolled his eyes. "This sure is a friendly company."

Eaton offered a brotherly smile and gave Peter hearty pat on the back. "For the most part the ranks are friendly. Us common soldiers stick together."

☆　☆　☆

Peter walked up to his log hut. A painted wooden sign affixed to the roof proclaimed the building Mountain Lake Hotel. The humble abode being named after a famous hotel in Giles County, Virginia.

Peter was sure their hotel was nothing compared to the actual establishment but it was a decent, well-constructed building.

For a minute he admired his comrades' craftsmanship. It was much nicer and warmer than the shelter he had hastily constructed before the late battle. The logs were laid out on stones underneath the bottom log, in a rectangle and notched to fit tight at the corners. Mud-covered logs were formed into a small fireplace in one end. Mud filled the gap between the logs and inside of the chimney over the fireplace. The hut had a sawn board roof.

He walked across the dirt floor to the fire. The fire had been built on the opposite wall across from the door. The heat warmed his cold, aching limbs. Suddenly he was overwhelmed with the desire to feel Molly's kisses once more.

He noticed the wood rack and his dreamy smile vanished. It was empty. Again. His three hut-mates, John Crawford, Joseph Lewry, and George Johnson decided since he had been unable to help construct the hut he could bring in the firewood. Did they mean to stick him with the chore all winter? If so, he'd raise a fuss.

"Lewry," Peter muttered under his breath. He yawned and stepped outside. After standing by the fire it brought an instant chill.

Lewry fed the fire in the cabin constantly. He was the most cold-blooded man Peter had ever seen. It wouldn't have surprised him if Lewry was part reptile. He wore all the clothing the army had given him at once. Peter laughed thinking of how awkwardly Lewry moved in his overcoat, dress-coat, blouse, and flannels.

The Confederate Army had a shortage of clothes, but Lewry didn't.

Peter carried a few logs inside. He didn't want to encourage Lewry's behavior. He'd make Lewry fetch more if he wanted them. Make *him* venture out into the cold.

The hut had two sets of bunks one on each of the short walls. His hut-mates gave him the top bunk to the left. Peter rifled through his belongings, in the knapsack, at the head of his bunk. He didn't have much to speak of: his civilian clothes, pocket watch, pipe, Shakespeare book, and the tintype of Molly. From the bottom of the bag he pulled out a couple sheets of wrinkled stationary.

He sat on the crude, three-footed stool and hunched over the improvised table, a wooden box turned upside down. Peter lit the candle held in his bayonet shank. It cast a small pool of light. He pulled Molly's picture out of his Shakespeare book and gazed at her image lovingly.

Peter began his letter with the greeting: Dearest maiden. He had written Molly a love letter with that salutation and every letter to her since began the same way. Peter core warmed thinking of the love letter that had brought them together. That letter had been rewarded with an invitation to dinner with Molly's family and permission to escort her to church.

Peter closed his eyes, he imagined Molly's fingers wrapped around his arms. He sighed longingly as he looked out the window at the bare trees and snow covered ground. He wouldn't be escorting Molly to church this Sunday.

He returned his attention to writing the letter he could not mail. Still, it helped just getting the words on paper.

Dearest Maiden,

My body yearns for your touch. Time creeps by slowly without you by my side. I have now settled into winter camp. There will be no more battles for a while. You have no reason to fear for my safety.

I am happy that you will spend the winter in our house. I expect Dan and Belle and Rebecca will keep you company. If you get lonely do not feel bad about moving back in with your parents. These lonely nights without you are hard to bear.

Pray that the war will end soon.

Peter folded the letter and tucked it into his knapsack, blew out the candle, and threw himself onto his wooden plank. Peter sighed. He throbbed with the need for Molly to lie beside him. If her mother had allowed a quick marriage before he left then he could have had one hour of pleasure to replay in his mind. Now he just had his dreams.

None of his hut-mates had returned. Until fully healed he didn't plan on spending extra time outside. He heard men grunting, cracked the door, and saw men playing a game to test their mettle. Two men would face off a birch in hand, and take turns striking each other's ankles. The man who yelled first lost.

Torture was not a game.

Thankfully, gentlemen did not participate in such tom foolery. Company D was filled with brawn not brains. And it was young—the average age perhaps nineteen.

Peter slipped his shoes off and pulled the blanket Doc had given him up over his shoulders. He didn't have the energy to undress. He'd pay for it in the middle of the night when the hut turned into a sweatbox.

Conscious of the need to make a good impression, he didn't want to fall asleep so quickly after his first day of drill. But his body demanded rest. He forced himself to wait a while longer by praying but with "Amen," he surrendered to sleep.

Peter dreamed he could barely move. He lifted his head and saw chains around his ankles. He tried to move his hands and could feel rope digging into his wrists. Footsteps. Approaching.

Beads of sweat ran down his forehead. On the far wall he saw the shadow of a tall, large man. The man walked closer, with a distinguishable limp. Now illuminated by the fire, Peter saw his father's face.

Peter's blood turned to ice water. His heart thumped faster and faster and faster. He struggled once more to get free, but expended the energy in vein.

Out of the corner of his eye, he saw a Bowie knife in his father's right hand. He swallowed.

His father loomed over him. His voice dripped with maliciousness. "I have you now, Yankee spy." He held the broadside of the knife against Peter's throat. Hate blazed in his father's eyes. The cold metal pressed into his flesh.

Why don't you just get it over with? Peter mouthed silently.

His father grinned, wide, malicious. "With pleasure."

The blade began to turn, the sharpness slicing his flesh.

Peter screamed. He awoke drenching wet and freezing. Crawford, Lewry, and Johnson roared with laughter.

"You've been 'Haled!'" a young man with mischievous blue eyes, sandy-colored hair, and a stubbly beard said, his words dripping with self-importance.

"What?" Peter shouted, his thoughts a mixture of anger and confusion.

The man frowned. "You haven't heard about me? I thought my reputation was better than that. I guess my comrades didn't have time to get around to it. I'm John Hale," he said, extending his hand. Peter glared at him as he shook it. "Welcome to the Mountain Boomers, Mr. Burnett. You should beware of my practical jokes."

"Sshh," Lewry whispered, "we need to keep it down. We don't need to get arrested for turbulence after taps."

"Your joke was throwing a bucket of water on me?" Peter said slowly, disappointment weighing down his words. "I hope you can do better."

"Don't worry," Hale said, his lips cracking into a just-you-wait smile. "Next time, I will."

"You got me tonight," Peter said, wringing out his coat. The water created a muddy puddle on the floor. "But I'll be ready next time."

"You might be expectin' it but you won't be able to stop it," said Hale. "Well, now that I've officially welcomed you into the company, in my own special way, I must be getting back to my hut. Be glad you don't live with me," he said, with a wink as he left.

Peter's hut-mates commenced laughing again. "I didn't think you'd scream like a wildcat," Crawford said.

He was a homely looking fellow. His dull, gray eyes brightened a bit as he laughed. He brushed his long fingers through his shaggy copper-colored hair.

"I think that was his first joke of the winter. Consider that an honor, Jeff," Lewry said.

Peter ventured a guess, "I suppose he's soaked you with water, too?"

"Yes. That's how he got to know all of us," Johnson, a tall, thin fellow with blond hair, explained.

"Care to tell me what you think he's going to do next?" Peter continued to carry the conversation in a hushed voice.

"No. You can't predict what Hale will do," Johnson said, rubbing his ribs. "He sure got you good."

"Yes," Peter admitted. "It was a unique way to meet someone. That's for sure. Good thing Lewry keeps this hut so hot. I'll dry in minutes."

"You'll get used to the army life eventually," Crawford said.

"And us," Lewry added.

Peter gave a quick nod. How could he get used to living in close quarters with the enemy? To working with the enemy? To breaking bread with the enemy?

A chill penetrated Peter to the bone.

CHAPTER 15

"YOU LOOK LIKE you didn't sleep much. You miss your feather bed, Burnett?" A tall, skinny lad taunted. He shook his head grinning like a dog that had cornered a cat. "The army's going to age you something awful." His three friends laughed deep and hearty.

Peter's insides tensed, but he maintained a calm outward appearance. Dan had taught how to control his emotions.

He turned his back on the group. Chewing on a piece of raw bacon, his face wrinkled in silent disapproval.

"That bacon you're having for breakfast isn't the three course meal you're used to," another soldier said. "Don't know if you'll last the winter."

"You'll be tired of soldiering before the snow melts."

"You'll die from lack of luxuries."

Peter's heart drummed in his ears, the vein on his neck pulsing. He swallowed the squishy meat and downed it with the last of his bitter chicory coffee.

A pound of flour and five slices of bacon a week didn't keep weight on his bones. In his hand-me-down uniform and with his protruding bones he looked more like a plow boy than a gentleman. Still, they judged him by his upbringing.

His hands balled into fists, he walked over to a poker game set up outside East's hut. Most of the men playing cards were smoking. The strong stench drifted in his direction.

Elisha East, a mahogany-haired lad with bright green eyes studied his cards. Peter stood behind him, watching the exchange of cards.

East looked over his shoulder. "Hey, Jeff, why don't you join in?"

"Thanks for the invitation, but I don't play cards," Peter said.

"You don't play cards," East said. "I thought poker was a gentleman's game."

"I suppose it's a game for everyone," Peter replied. "I just choose not to participate."

"You a preacher?"

Peter shifted upon the balls of his feet. "No." The dull ache of regret overcame him as soon as he said it. Perhaps it would have been in his best interest to say yes.

"Good, 'cause I figure Frazier's enough for this comp'ny."

"Guess I'm not your typical gentleman."

"You can say that again," Eaton said. "You're the only one with enough guts to join the ranks."

"I'll take that as a compliment."

A twinge of a headache throbbed above his right eye. The men sneered at him and admired him at the same time. Even among fellow southerners he didn't belong.

As much as he didn't like it he had to fit in. "I changed my mind," he said. "Deal me in on the next hand."

Lewry gestured to the empty chair beside him. "Take a seat by me. Maybe you'll change my luck."

As he played poker, Peter joined friendly conversations about issues pertaining to the war, its conduct, and prospects for peace.

Out of nowhere, East asked, "What are your slaves going to do without you, Jeff?"

Peter's heart tripped and stumbled. "My wife can manage them. They like living at my place."

"Really?" East said.

Peter's stomach turned as if he was tossed at sea. He fanned and bunched up his cards repeatedly. He consciously kept his face casual. Somehow his upset stomach didn't sour his voice, "I don't tolerate bad behavior. I sell the troublemakers down south."

East nodded. "I see." His eyes slyly focused on Peter.

Peter swallowed hard, his rate of breathing increasing. Did East know something?

"Too bad the North has to stick their nose in our business."

Peter blew on his aching cold fingers then finally resorted to putting his free hand on his cheek. Too bad the eight of them couldn't fit in the small hut.

An hour later, Lewry got up from the table. He shook his head. "Jeff, you didn't change my luck. I think it is time to leave."

Peter debated whether he could use this as a polite exit, too. "I'm ready for the warm fire. Freezing isn't good for your health."

The men, still playing poker, smiled and laughed softly.

"You're a well-educated man," Lewry said to Peter, as they walked back to their hut. "Can I ask you a political question?"

"Well, I ... uh ... I'm not sure if I can answer it. But what do you want to know?"

"According to all the founding documents, does the South have the legal right to leave the Union?"

The question felt like a knife to Peter's insides, attempting to gut his beliefs from his roots. He wanted to say no. He didn't want to justify the rebels killing to protect the peculiar institution, but his conscience wouldn't let him lie.

"Ratification of the Constitution implied that states are subject to Federal laws, however, the Constitution did not explicitly prohibit states from leaving the Union. Yes, I believe it's legal."

Lewry's lips curled with a satisfied smile. "Good. Not that I wouldn't fight if we didn't, but I like to know it's legal." He licked his bottom lip, scanning the unfortunate lot now on duty guarding the riverbank. Many gripped their musket with one hand and kept their other hand warm under their arm pit.

"Fine bunch of soldiers."

Peter restrained a laugh by rubbing a hand across his mouth. Perhaps. But Lewry wasn't one of them. He only worked under pain of death.

"So," Lewry dragged out the word, "so what are our chances of winning?"

Peter pursed his lips, carefully contemplating each word before speaking. "The North's enlisting immigrants, from the Old World, right off the boats and into the Union Army. We have limited manpower. It's going to be a hard victory but not altogether impossible."

"What'd you think about the possibility of foreign intervention, Jeff?"

"I think foreign intervention will be needed if the Confederacy stands a chance."

Lewry pulled his head back, a roll of fat forming on his neck, his eyes bulging. "Why'd you join if you were so convinced we were going to lose?"

"I couldn't live with my shame if I failed to come to the aid of my state," Peter replied. "President Davis can still get England and France involved. After all, it's our cotton they've been buying cheap for years. This war will all come down to resources."

"I figure it has more to do with good generals and His divine will."

Peter nodded. "I'm religious but…" his voice trailed off.

He knew Lee was a brilliant general. However, he would have to perform a miracle to prevent the tide from turning to the North. The men had so much confidence in their leader that they expected him to perform that miracle.

Peter sensed they were ready to follow him wherever he led them, even into the depths of hell.

"God," Peter mumbled under his breath, "is being evoked on both sides of this damned war."

Peter walked to Frazier's tent. He stuck his head inside and saw the chaplain thumbing through the pages of his Bible. He cleared his throat to get Frazier's attention. "I heard you have devotional every night."

The chaplain smiled, pleasant and brotherly, an inviting warmness in his eyes. "Yes. You're a little early. Please come in."

Peter sat. He silently watched the chaplain read over the passage he was going to talk about.

Ten minutes later, several more soldiers stepped inside and found a chair. Frazier looked at his pocket watch then at the crowd that had gathered.

"Let's begin in prayer," he said. Everyone bowed their heads.

The prayer eased Peter's fear and calmness grasped him like Aunt Ruth's caring hands. For a little while he didn't feel so alone in his mission.

☆   ☆   ☆

Captain Bane shouted, "Fall in!" Lieutenant Mullins echoed the command until the entire company was in formation.

Peter shot a questioning look at the Lieutenant. He was a built as solid as a stack or bricks and thankfully Peter had not tangled with him yet. According to the men, Mullins was close to a model soldier: serious, strong, stout, faithful, duty-minded, and had a thirst that would make all of Ireland proud.

The lieutenant didn't seem to be enjoying this outing any more than Peter did. His grim face was riddled with deep wrinkles. Were they headed into danger? Where in the world were they going? It was January 20, still the dead of winter. Why were they being called to arms?

Peter's fingers were red and cold and numb. He marched along frozen roads in the direction of Banks Ford. It was reported the Union Army was threatening to cross the river.

Surely the rumor couldn't be true.

But it was.

Peter allowed himself to frown as he stood sentry in the downpour, rain bouncing off the ground, stinging any exposed skin. "Damn Burnside for being an idiot!"

Sublett laughed. "If he comes our way he'll be doing us a favor."

"I doubt he's going very far in the rain." Peter knew that his comrades in blue, who were marching in the rain, were worse off. It was easy to guess that their wagons were getting stuck in mud and the venture was doomed to fail.

Burnside was just bringing them all misery.

Peter sighed, but disguised it with a loud yawn. If the Yanks succeeded in crossing the Rappahannock it might give him an opportunity to rejoin them. Peter shook his head.

In this weather, there was no way the Union Army would make it across.

As the night lingered on the temperature plummeted, dropping like a stone in a stream. The freezing sensation spread throughout Peter's body. He looked down the line at his shivering hut-mates. An inch of snow had accumulated on top of their caps. Peter brushed the flakes off his eyelashes.

His warm hut and fire seemed years away.

Despite the unrelenting snowstorm, the Virginians remained in good spirits. Men in Company D erected a giant signboard within rebel lines, visible to the Union Army, inscribed, "This way to Richmond," making fun of Burnside's progress. A laugh bubbled up and tickled Peter's throat. He couldn't contain it much longer and finally let out a hearty, side-aching chuckle. He felt guilty for doing so. The shamefulness of mocking his superior erased his pleasure.

Still, Burnside should have known better. Just like his father, being an academy graduate did not ensure a decent helping of brains.

Lieutenant Mullins walked over, blowing on his gloved hands, a canteen slung over his shoulder. He was a stocky man with broad shoulders. His black hair and neatly trimmed mustaches were as thick as a beaver pelt. All the soldiers gave him a shaky salute which he returned. Mullins stepped back and examined the signboard.

"Now that I like," he said, with a grin. He took the canteen off his shoulder and unscrewed the cap. "I know a soldier's life isn't the most pleasant, but at least this will warm your insides," he said, passing it to Eaton.

Eaton took a drink and his eyes widened. "That will melt the ice right off the river," he said, passing it to Johnson. Slowly the canteen made its way around the group. When it was Peter's turn, he declined.

"Don't think you can handle the hard stuff, Burnett?" Mullins said with a heavy taunt in his voice. His eyes narrowed slightly to accentuate the tone of his voice.

"Considering I haven't tasted a drop of spirits in my life, I know I can't."

Mullins slate gray eyes darkened to black. He gave Peter a halfhearted warning, "I don't cotton to men who refuse to drink out of my canteen."

"If it was water or coffee I would, sir," Peter said.

Mullins took his canteen back and finished it off with a long swig. "I don't drink those till I run out of this."

Trudging through eight inches of snow, the rebels returned to camp. Peter's legs ached, his energy drained. It felt like there was an invisible boulder resting on his shoulders, making each step painfully heavy. His hut seemed miles away instead of in front of him.

A soldier yelled from outside his hut. "Hey, the camp followers stole my shaving kit."

"Damnit. Looks like I'll be eating with my fingers."

Hearing other soldiers grumble and curse, Johnson, Lewry, and Crawford raced into their hut to see if they'd fallen victim too, Peter followed at a distance. Crawford blinked at his bare bunk. His blanket was gone.

Lewry walked over to the burned out fire. The frying pan he had left on the floor was missing.

"What a wonderful way to treat soldiers fightin' for your country," Lewry grumbled.

Straight-faced and mute, Peter took off his shoes and reclined on his bunk. He had carried everything he owned with him. He might have enlisted under the guise of a southern gentleman, but he was one of the poorest soldiers in camp.

"Quit complaining," Peter said finally, his voice a reprimand. "They wouldn't have taken your belongings if they weren't in desperate need."

"We're in desperate need," Johnson said in an irritated whine. "My coat's threadbare."

Peter nodded. "I know. I just want to remind you that those thieves, you're calling names, likely have family serving in the Confederate Army."

His hut-mates were silent, their faces pinched in reflection.

Peter ran his fingers through his hair. If a peddler came by he'd probably sell all the goods on his wagon. Take the Rebs for every cent they had. He could use a few things, too. But money was more precious than water in a desert.

Peter dried off his musket with a piece of oil cloth. He'd have to clean and polish it to keep it from rusting. He created a paste from water and ashes from the fire and rubbed it onto the barrel. He continued rubbing until the metal shined.

Crawford opened the door revealing a full-scale snowball battle in progress. He grinned with boyish mischief. "Time for some fun, boys!" He ran to join in.

Peter followed. He hadn't gone very far before he felt the iciness of a splattered snowball right between his shoulder blades. He turned around to find Elbert Eaton and another soldier grinning.

"I'd like you to meet my brother, John Sublett," Eaton said.

"Your brother?" Peter said, slowly, struggling to make the connection.

They looked nothing alike. The blond-haired stranger was five-foot-seven, clean-shaven, with dark brown eyes. Peter smiled realizing the one thing Eaton and Sublett had in common; they both had butternut colored patches on their trousers and coat-sleeves.

"We're not blood related," Eaton explained. "My father took John in when he was eight."

"Glad to be fighting with you," Peter said. He shook Sublett's hand.

"I know what you're up to," Sublett said, laughing softly, "but I'm not the culprit. Bert's the one with wet hands."

"I'm not surprised, but I have a feeling you're just as capable of mischief," Peter said.

"That would be correct. I've taught my little brother everything I know," Eaton said.

"Then I'm in for lots of fun," Peter replied, with a relaxed smile. He was glad to now have two friends in the company.

"Eaton tell you he has four sisters?" Sublett asked. "Only reason his pa took me in was 'cause he needed another boy to help run the farm."

"That's not true!"

Peter laughed easily and freely for the first time in several weeks. "So how long ..." He stopped what he was saying as he, Eaton, and Sublett were pelted with snowballs.

Sublett yelled. "Let's get them!"

The three men made as many snowballs as they could carry and ran after the offenders. The guilty soldiers took off running. Peter tackled a lad with straggly blond hair.

"What's your name?" Peter demanded.

"David Dulaney," the lad answered, while struggling to get away.

Peter didn't see a single whisker on Dulaney's face. The boy's brown eyes showed panic as if he guessed what was coming. Eaton and Sublett overcame his accomplices. Then the three of them were quickly sentenced and got soaking wet.

Snowballs flew everywhere, the soldiers well-stocked with ammunition. Peter ducked and crouched and swerved, but it was impossible to dodge them all. He grabbed another handful and molded it in his numb fingers. The tip of his tongue stuck out between his teeth, he scanned the soldiers for Sergeant Snidow. Finding him, he pulled back his arm and let it fly. It hit the man across the side of his neck. Snidow snapped around, but Peter was safely out of sight.

Peter grinned. A combination of relief and delight lightened his heavy heart, and a warmness spread through his chest.

Little James watched the soldiers having fun. The negro boy, perhaps five or six years old, looked up at his pa with eager eyes. Big James shook his head.

Seeing that the boy wanted to join in, Peter rolled a snowball and threw it at him. It hit the boy's chest and crumbled.

Little James' eyes got big and his jaw dropped open from the shock of the icy coldness. He picked up a handful of snow and motioned as if to throw it at Peter when his pa grabbed his arm and made him drop it.

"Yuh wanna cause trouble?" Big James scolded in a low growl.

"No. I just wanna get'm back."

"Dat's causin' trouble. Yuh doan throw snowballs at white folks."

"Dat ain't fair! Why can't I play, too?"

Big James put a hand on his son's shoulder. "Not everyone's as friendly as cap'n Bane. Life just ain't fair, boy," he said, low and airy.

"Why not?"

Big James sighed and rubbed his forehead. "Bane's spoiled yuh too much. Yuh got it so easy yuh doan understand how things wuk."

"Dat ain't true!" Little James stuck out his bottom lip and it began to quiver.

Big James firmly gripped his son's arm and led him away from the action. Out of curiosity, Peter followed at a distance.

"It's 'bout time yuh act like what yuh is—a colored boy," Big James said, his deep voice carrying a ragged edge. "Remember yuh be respec'ful to white folks or yuh goin' to be hurt mighty bad." He cuffed his son's right ear to make his point. Finally, he stopped and let go of his son. "Does yuh understand, boy?"

Little James hung his head. "I understand, Pa."

Big James sighed. "Make yo' snowballs and I's make mine. No one say you can't play."

Little James grinned and his eyes brightened. He bent down and rolled a mound of snowballs until his hands were deep red. Big James picked up one of his snowballs and his son did the same.

"On de count of three—one ... two ... three," Big James said. His snowball fell short, but he was hit in the stomach and let out a booming laugh. "Yuh got me," he exclaimed, gripping his middle, reeling backward and slowly crumpling to the ground.

Little James ran over to him and his pa pulled him down. The two rolled in the snow giggling so hard they'd tears in their eyes.

Peter laughed softly, the tender image warming the icy wall around his heart.

With a playful smile and a boyish eagerness in his eyes, Bane walked over to them, a snowball in each hand. He let both of them have it. Soon the three were throwing snow back and forth.

Peter pressed his lips together, matching the curvature of the line across his forehead. He was making friends in the company very slowly. He needed to gain the captain's confidence, if he had any hope of making progress in gaining popularity in the ranks. Increased safety would come with popularity ... and perhaps more valuable information.

☆ ☆ ☆

That night the soldiers sat around the campfire, smoking tobacco, as usual. Peter turned his head around searching for the captain. He was nowhere in sight. Probably in his quarters again. A twitchy feeling infected his feet, and he fought the urge to curse the captain's private nature.

Peter rubbed his cheeks and yawned. The soldiers argued between puffs. Wisps of smoke floated in the air along with an occasional curse. Peter stayed and listened, hoping to catch something interesting, something important.

Sergeant Snidow was eyeing him. What had he done now?

"You know you can't keep that horse of yours," he said. "Privates in the infantry don't have mounts."

"Yes, sir. I plan to give her to the Confederate Army. I've heard they're low on horses." Peter's carefree response seemed to take the words out of the sergeant's mouth. Peter wasn't allowing him to have any fun.

"Good," the sergeant said at last. "I just wanted you to know. When we break winter camp Cloudy goes."

Lieutenant Mullins joined them smoking a strong cigar. He nodded to Sergeant Snidow and then Peter got the brunt of his attention.

"You don't smoke either, Burnett?" he asked.

"Some," Peter said.

Mullins grunted.

The wind picked up. Peter wrapped his arms tightly across his chest sealing in the warmth. Smoke from the fire and from Mullin's cigar blew in Peter's direction. His eyes stung. He squinted and endured it. It was worth it to catch a whiff of tobacco. The strong scent overwhelmed his senses, blurring past and present.

His father flashed into his mind. He tried to push it away, but like usual his father won the argument. His stomach twisted. His fingers folded and he slammed a fist into the dirt.

Peter felt haunted by the bringer of death. He had been running away from the dark feeling for years. His breath hitched and he rubbed the coldness out of his arms. One day it was bound to catch up with him.

CHAPTER 16

ONCE LEE WAS confident that the Yankees had given up fighting for the winter he allowed soldiers to leave on furlough. To Peter's surprise, he was given a three day pass.

"Doc," he said. It had to be him. He shouldn't have been placed ahead of the veterans in the company. But he wasn't about to turn it down. Perhaps he could get more information.

"Whatcha you going to do?" Johnson asked. "Going home to your wife? Going to stay in your bedroom the rest of the day?"

"I'm going home," Peter said, not looking at him. "But I'm also going to buy some supplies. The South isn't supplying its soldiers well."

Johnson grunted. "We're not all rich like you."

"The government is letting us down. Jefferson Davis and his cabinet."

Johnson shrugged, clearly not the slightest bit interested in politics.

Peter considered taking Cloudy and leaving her at Abigail's, but decided against it. He might need the mare later.

It was a hard walk to his sister's house. With every step he sank knee-deep in mud. By the time he got there he was breathing hard, heart working overtime, cursing his decision to go on foot.

Peter knocked on the door of the Raleigh Plantation. He had to have some luck. Surely Mr. Raleigh wouldn't be on leave, too. The knob turned and food turned in his stomach.

A plump, negro woman opened the door, her graying hair up in a bun.

"Aunt Ruth!"

The woman smiled, revealing a row of teeth like ivory piano keys. Her eyes lit up. "Marse Peter! I always knew you done come back. Come inside before you catch cold."

Peter stepped inside, his face aching with a jaw-busting grin. Her rich voice was music to his ears.

She looked him up and down. "Why, you've grown into a fine figure of a man. I never thought I'd see the day that you'd have a beard." She cackled. "I do declare you look just like yo' father," she said, and then burst into tears.

He touched her arm. "What's wrong?"

"What am I thinking? You've got to get over to your father's house right now. I have no business occupying your time when the good Lord could call him up any minute." Her words rushed together. "Saddle up one of the horses and ride over there, hurry now."

"So it is true? Father is really dying? *Now?*"

"It will heal your father's heart to see you again. Now ride over there, make haste, boy," she said, giving him a gentle nudge.

Reflex took over. Peter sprinted to the stables. He saddled a palomino horse and rode to his father's house. The stately white mansion loomed over him and he walked up the columned entry porch. Peter knocked on the door and no one answered. He opened it, looked around and walked in.

None of this was part of his plan. He wanted to get supplies at his sister's house and get out. What was he doing? This was a good way to get arrested for working on the Underground Railroad—or shot.

He fingered the buttons on his Confederate jacket. If Abigail was there she would know he was a spy.

Damn Aunt Ruth's persuasive influence. He could be walking into a trap. Colonel Scott had said that if his father saw him, he'd either kill him or die of a heart attack. Of course being hauled off to prison was the third option. Anxiety ate at Peter, devouring his nerve.

His heart sped and sputtered. He crept to his father's room, put his ear to the door. Hushed, muffled voices... No crying. So the bastard was still alive. His hands balled. After several deep breaths, he entered, prepared for the yelling that was sure to come.

Abigail's mouth dropped open. "Welcome home," she said, half-hearted, fake, failing to disguise her shock. Prominent dark circles under her eyes told him she hadn't slept well.

Peter blinked. His father looked so frail. His emaciated frame was buried under a pile of blankets. Once fiery eyes seemed distant, as if he was looking past Peter instead of at him. His pale face lacked emotion.

Does he even know who I am?

Instinct took over. Peter hurried to his father's bedside and took his hand. His touch was weak, his skin wrinkled. The opposite of the circulation-stopping grip he was known for. Still, contact with his father filled him with equal parts sorrow, anger, and a numbing iciness.

"Peter, they let you come home," his father said, his words feeble and raspy.

Peter had to continue his cover. He opened his mouth but it took a second for the words to come. "The 7th Virginia Infantry is camped nearby and when I heard you were ill, there was no way they could stop me."

"Infantry." His father spat out the word.

It triggered a coughing fit. His whole body seemed to retract and expand with each cough. He was coughing with such force Peter was sure bones were rattling inside the frail body.

His father let go of Peter's hand and held a handkerchief over his mouth.

When he removed the handkerchief it was speckled with blood. So was the collar on his shirt and there were drops on the blanket.

Peter blinked. His father was actually ill, weak, clearly out of his head. It didn't seem real before he had witnessed it firsthand.

"What's gotten into you, boy? Joining the infantry." His father snapped, his usual disgust lining every word.

"That's where the Virginia Military Institute assigned me. I didn't have a choice."

His father smiled with more warmth than he had ever seen. "You look handsome in gray. I wish I was fighting with you, but you're doing the family proud, son."

A strange euphoria made Peter's fingers tingle and a lightness made his head fuzzy.

Peter folded his fingers into tight fists. After years of waiting, this was not how he wanted to hear those words. He bit his cheek. His father was proud of an illusion. Peter's chest felt empty as if his heart had shut down.

His father's eyes narrowed into razor sharp slits. "Why are you wearing a private's coat?"

Peter shrugged. "It's comfortable."

"Comfortable! It's unbecoming of an officer." His father began coughing again.

"Yes, Father. I'll take it off when I get back to camp."

"Doctor," his father called, "I want you to write out my will."

Peter's lungs constricted. He did not realize at first a doctor was present, but there the man stood in the far corner, arms loosely at his sides.

At least his posture wasn't threatening—he didn't look like he was going to turn him in.

"Considering the circumstances, that would be wise," the doctor said, pulling a chair up to the bed. Peter stepped out of the way and pressed his back against the wall. Abigail walked to the other side of the bed, reached into the desk drawer and handed the doctor a pen and paper. Abigail's olive-colored dress rustled when she moved.

"I, Joshua Warren, being of sound mind but considering my mortality do make and declare this my last will and testament. Upon my death the negress Aunt Ruth is to be free."

Peter's mouth parted. He did not think his father had it in him to free anyone. Perhaps he did have a heart.

His father continued, "To my daughter Abigail, my personal effects. After my debts and burial expenses are paid, the entire Springdale estate passes to my son Peter."

The doctor wrote it out and Mr. Warren signed it. Peter felt a laugh bubbling in his stomach and had to restrain himself from making a scene. *I am being willed Springdale.* Abigail, Peter, and the doctor signed as witnesses.

After Father died I could free all of the slaves at Springdale.

An awkward joy spread throughout his body. God would make something good come from Mr. Warren's death.

"I'm going to leave it in the desk drawer," the doctor said. "You can rest and regain your strength. You're a tough, old soldier, Mr. Warren. Don't give up on life yet. We haven't whipped the Yanks."

"When the war ends with the Confederacy victorious, then I can die a happy man." Father's voice gained some strength and roughness. "Now that the examination is over, give me back my pistol."

"Father," Abigail said, her voice dripping with exasperation.

The doctor patted the air. "Nothing to worry about, Mrs. Raleigh. It keeps him calm."

The doctor took the pistol out of the drawer and pressed it into Father's right hand, folding his bony fingers around the handle.

"I'll be ready for the Yanks now," Father said, looking Peter in the eye.

Seeing the anger etched into every inch of his father's face, Peter gulped, his hands hot. Did his father remember?

His father's eyes became distant as if clouded by some vision. He stared at the door, focused, as if he expected the Union Army to march through.

Peter realized that his father was in his own world. Fighting his own demons.

He yearned to tell his father all the things that he had been rehearsing for years, night after night in New Hampshire. He wanted to unload all the pain and fear that he had been caring all these years. If he didn't unload his feelings would continue to eat him from the inside out.

Peter's breathing quickened, speeding the adrenaline through his blood. He felt a hot blush working its way from his cheeks to his neck. He screamed the speech in his head. *I'm not afraid of you any more, you son of a bitch! Look at me. Look at your abolitionist son. I'm going to spend the rest of my life undoing your devil's work.*

Peter saw the warning in his sister's eyes, her mouth twisted as if she was holding back her own thoughts. Peter's chest bunched, making his exhaling painful. If he laid into his father with all his hatred, the fragile bond with his sister would be broken.

Peter shook his head. He had thought it would have been impossible for his father to be so sick that he had forgotten his son had become an abolitionist. The gears in his mind struggled to turn fast enough to bring him clarity. Was that really the man he had been frightened of, the man who had terrorized him for so many years?

Damnit! God could at least let him unbottle the anger that had been building for years. His father could not have the last word. Peter needed vindication.

God could not do this to him. His father needed to know the pain he had caused. He needed to feel an ounce of the wrath Peter endured as a boy.

It was too much for him. He had to leave.

"Father, I have to get back to camp. I wish I could stay longer."

"I understand son, duty calls. I'm not giving up until the North is defeated."

"The family will need you even after the North is defeated."

"Don't fool yourself son, people can't live forever. My time's coming. I'm looking forward to being with your mother again. She was a lovely, gentle-hearted woman." His voice trailed off, a smile on his lips. His eyes closed.

"Father…" An eerie feeling swept over him, his pulse quickening, His muscles froze. Even his breath had stilled. *Had my father died?*

"You'll be the man of the family," Father said. "Springdale isn't doing well right now but it will be prosperous again once the war's over."

Peter didn't know how to reply. He felt himself being pulled back, an invisible hand dragging him away from his father.

He hurried but his feet didn't keep time with his thoughts. He left the house, mounted the palomino horse, spurred him hard. Galloping down the familiar road this all seemed a dream.

Surely, his father wasn't as frail as he appeared.

But he had to have been frail to call him a man, call him his son. To forget he had disowned him. To forget the reason he had disowned him. To forget Peter's work on the Underground Railroad, running with Dan, killing Sally, the reward on his head. The reward his father offered. None of this made a speck of sense.

He headed back to his sister's house. Aunt Ruth would set him straight.

☆ ☆ ☆

"Did you mend things with your father?" Aunt Ruth asked the minute Peter appeared in the parlor.

Peter sat in the burgundy arm chair and fingered the golden tassels. "Yes. He said I was part of the family."

Aunt Ruth's shoulders lifted. "I knew he would. Deep down he's a good man."

"I didn't have as much faith as you." Peter paused, uncomfortable with all this talk about his father. "By the way, Dan is well."

"I know." Aunt Ruth's voice threatened to crack. "A mamma always knows about her own even when they are far away."

Peter could talk to Aunt Ruth for hours but he didn't have hours. He had to get what he came for. He forced himself to his feet. "The army's short on supplies and I need a few things," he paused, "but I have no right to take any of Mr. Raleigh's possessions."

"Nonsense. You are family and you are fighting for the same cause." Her eyes gleamed like someone keeping a secret. A secret heartwarming and thrilling. "He'll understand."

Peter nodded. That was half right anyway and she knew what half. "Do you live here now?"

"No." Aunt Ruth dragged out the word. It carried an undertone of sorrow. "But your sister hasn't left your father's side these past few days and she wanted me to mind the house. What supplies do you need?"

"A blanket, some matches, enough food for a few days. And I don't need tobacco but I would sure appreciate it."

"Tobacco? Why, you know we have a whole store of tobacco!" Aunt Ruth let out a shrill laugh and she filled up a large pouch with leaves. "That is one thing that Mr. Raleigh won't be missing." Then she found a blanket and began filling it with all kinds of food.

Peter shifted his weight. "There's one more thing I need..." His dry throat made his voice scratchy. He forced saliva down his windpipe. "But I'm afraid I won't be able to get it—money."

The old woman cocked her head back as if she was trying to read him. "You haven't taken to drinking like your father, have you? Or gambling?"

Her teasing tone brought on another smile. "I haven't. I promise."

"I believe you, Marse Peter. I always could catch you in a lie. What'd you need money for then?"

"Basic needs. The army's slow about paying its soldiers."

"Come with me to your father's house."

"No," Peter replied quickly, hoping she didn't notice the nervousness in his voice.

Aunt Ruth didn't argue. "All right. I'll be right back."

☆   ☆   ☆

"Mamma," a woman's voice called. When there was no response, Hattie walked into the room. Her voluptuous frame filled the doorway in a bright yellow dress. Unlike last time, she smiled at Peter. "You sure do know how to surprise a person, Marse Peter."

"Your mother should be back soon."

"It's been nice having her here the past few days. I always could go over and see her," she scuffed her shoe against the floor, "but I didn't like being around your father."

"You know that's why Dan left," Peter said.

"I know. I don't hold it against him."

His heart tripped. A question rose in his throat. "Do you hold it against me?"

Hattie looked away, silent for what felt like several minutes. "No, sir. We all do what we've got to do."

Peter rubbed a hand across his mouth, his heart resuming a normal beat. He knew Hattie noticed the relief in his eyes.

Hattie had a lot of her mother in her: strong intuition and the wisdom to know what to say.

Peter reached out and touched her shoulder. "You will see Dan again."

Hattie's nod seemed to be a reflex rather than a response. She didn't believe him.

"Excuse me, Marse Peter, I've got sewing to do." She stopped just before she was out of the room and turned around. "Miss Abigail ain't as bitter towards you as she was before, sir."

Peter's heart lightened. That was a welcome improvement.

He waited a few minutes then peeked around the corner. He didn't see Hattie or any of the other servants. He hurried down the hall to the library. He pulled open a drawer in one of the small tables. The pistol was still there. He shoved it into the front of his belt, covered it up with his shirt and uniform coat. He didn't like the idea of stealing, but he might need it if he was going to escape.

Would Aunt Ruth call him on it? He knew he couldn't hide it from her eagle eyes.

His mind raced. He needed rope. Bullets for the pistol. A knife. He bit his lip.

He had never seen his brother-in-law with a Bowie knife before—well he could get everything else. The rope was in the barn. He reached back into the desk drawer and his fingers felt some bullets. He pulled them out and shoved them in his coat pocket. He patted the bulge and hoped Aunt Ruth wouldn't ask him any questions.

The door to the house creaked open and he hurried into the parlor.

Aunt Ruth returned carrying a small mahogany box and set it on the table. "I keep special things in here."

Peter sucked in his breath. He had never seen the box before. A pang of irritation struck him. He thought they had shared everything. Was the fact he was the young master of the house the cause for her secrets? Didn't she trust him?

It felt like he had been punched in the stomach.

"Something wrong, honey?" Aunt Ruth placed a soft, firm hand on his arm.

He kept his words short. "The box. How long have you had the box?"

Aunt Ruth's eyes registered understanding. "Your mother gave me the box when we were girls. Sometimes I run my hand across the polished wood and think of her. Sometimes I tell her 'bout you and Abigail."

"Oh."

Aunt Ruth raised the lid. She took out a stack of Confederate bills and handed them to Peter.

He counted out the money, his eyes widening. "You have fifty dollars?"

She smiled, but the corners of her lips did not stretch far. A mixture of happiness and grief swirled in her eyes. "I'm an old woman, been saving a long time. I never had reason to spend it. Your father always took care of me."

She smoothed her white apron. "I was always worried he was going to get hard up for money and sell one of my children. I was keeping the money for that. But the good Lord kept my family together. I used to have Yankee money," she said then laughed, "but as soon as the war began your father hated everything Yankee. He didn't want anything Yankee in his house so Miss Abigail exchanged all my money for Confederate bills—just in case."

"I am touched that you want to give me your money, but I can't accept it. You earned it. God knows you earned it."

"Since your mamma died, I felt like you was my own. You needed a mamma, both you and Miss Abigail. I'm just being your mamma now."

"But I can't," Peter persisted. "I just can't."

"Yes, you can," Aunt Ruth said, folding his fingers around the money with her gentle hands. "I'd never use it."

Peter put the money in his pocket and flung his arms around Aunt Ruth.

Aunt Ruth cupped the back of his head and pressed it on her shoulder. "You're too young for this war," she whispered in his ear.

Peter knew their embrace had given his pistol away. Aunt Ruth took a step back and her eyes flicked to his belt and then back to his face.

He didn't say a word. She didn't either.

Aunt Ruth was teary-eyed as Peter prepared to leave, sorrow accentuating the wrinkles around her mouth. "I haven't seen you for two years and now you're going again."

"I'll be back," Peter said, strong and firm, though he wondered if he would keep his promise.

Aunt Ruth gave a ragged sigh. "I know. I had faith before. I waited and waited and you came."

Before leaving, he entered the barn and wrapped some rope around his shoulder.

Aunt Ruth stood outside the door, the breeze blowing the bottom of her gray dress. She watched Peter walk down the road.

When she was almost out of sight, he stopped, turned around and waved. She waved back. He committed her image to memory fearful he'd never see her again.

His reunion with his father had not gone as expected. Being willed Springdale had not entered his mind. He slapped his thigh. He should have told Aunt Ruth that her freedom was near. Dangit. Why didn't he?

CHAPTER 17

DRESSED IN HIS Confederate uniform, Peter walked boldly through the city. A mulatto couple yielded him the sidewalk.

Peter bit his tongue. The attitudes and customs of the South … had to change. He knew emancipating all the slaves would not get the job done. It would be a start though, would be the first step.

His shoulders shook and he swallowed, on the verge of a breakdown. Hot tears stung his eyes. He knocked on Jack's door.

Miss Edmunds answered. "Jack," she called. "Come quickly."

Jack's face wrinkled, concern clouding his eyes. "Peter, what's the matter?"

"Peter? I-I thought his name was Jeff," Miss Edmunds said.

"It's both, ma'am," Peter said. "My full name's Jefferson Peter Burnett. My close friends call me Peter."

Peter collapsed into a navy blue chair and dropped his supplies on the floor. He probably looked strange carrying rope around his shoulder. Oh well. That was the least of his worries.

"Oh," Tabitha said. She sat in a chair and closely watched him. "That's an interesting name."

"It is?" Peter asked as casually as possible. "You see my father wanted to name me Jeff after his father and my mother wanted to name me after someone in the Bible so they compromised."

"Sit down and collect yourself," Jack said, his eyes flashed an apology and he rubbed his forehead. "Would you like something to drink?"

"Yes."

Jack nodded and left the room.

Miss Tabitha's worried eyes made his stomach ribbon with worry. Peter wanted to reflect the attention off him so he boldly asked, "Have you and Jack set a date yet?"

Miss Edmunds blushed. "Did he talk to you about that? We haven't been courting that long."

"No, but he doesn't have to say anything. I've known Jack a long time and I've never seen him this happy. So I just figured, naturally, you two would be getting married."

Miss Edmunds grinned and wiggled in her seat. "He is a gentle soul. I'm surprised he remained a bachelor for so long. Me. I never expected to marry. I've been teaching at a girl's school for years."

"Then Jack won't have to correct your English."

Miss Edmunds giggled like a child. "No. I know grammar extremely well." The teacher was acting like a school girl. It warmed Peter's heart.

"How long have you known him?" Miss Edmunds asked.

The question took Peter by surprise. Of course it was a basic question, but answering was tricky considering the circumstances. "Five years ... I think."

"What do you do?"

Damn. More personal questions. Peter arched his back, stretching. "Nothing since my brother bought out my shares in the tobacco factory. I'm looking for another venture."

"How do you know Jack?"

"He didn't tell you?"

"No."

Peter shifted his weight. If she was lying and trying to catch him in a wrong answer... He ignored the sudden clamminess of his palms. Swiping them on his pants would make him seem too nervous.

He took slow deep breaths forcing his heartbeat to pound a normal rhythm. "We started out doing business together. He used to buy slaves for people and bought several for my brother and me to work in our factory. I won't go near the market."

"What are you two talking about?" Jack asked. He slowly walked into the room, a glass in each hand, trying not to spill the drinks.

"I was just explaining to Miss Edmunds that you used to buy slaves for me."

"Oh yes," Jack said and quickly took a gulp of brandy.

"Where are your manners? Hand him his glass first," Miss Edmunds scolded.

Peter laughed. "That's quite all right."

"I like to see you smiling but you're still not yourself. What's wrong? You didn't desert did you?" Jack asked.

"Of course not. I got a letter a couple days ago and found out that my father's ill, so I was granted a day pass."

"Oh? Really? Sorry to hear that. He's a good man." Jack took another gulp of brandy.

"It was just very unexpected," Peter said, looking at the floor.

"Have you heard from your sister?"

"She was the one who wrote me about father. Now she's busy taking care of him. I'm homesick and I haven't been away that long. Have you talked to any of my friends recently?"

"No. I haven't had a chance. What's your outfit so I can tell them?"

"The 7th Virginia Infantry. I'm in company D."

"Why don't you enlist, Jack?" Miss Edmunds suggested. "I'm sure we could get you in his company."

"I'm a writer not a fighter." Jack met her gaze, his eyes small, serious. "You've already lost a brother to this war. Do you want to lose me, too?"

Miss Edmunds' face turned ashen. She did not say another word on the subject.

"I better get back to camp. I only have a day pass," Peter said, standing.

"But you just got here, Mr. Burnett. You haven't even touched your drink," Tabitha protested.

Peter looked at the glass of brandy in front of him and willed his stomach to stop churning. "I don't mean to be rude, ma'am but I should be going." He slipped the rope around his arm and picked up his blanket of goods.

"I understand. Thanks for stopping by to tell me the news," Jack said.

"I wish it was happier news. Until we meet again." Peter nodded towards Miss Edmunds. "It was a pleasure to see you again."

"Perhaps I'll make it out to your camp soon. I've been meaning to visit the soldiers."

Peter wanted to smile, but the heaviness in chest made feigning any happiness impossible. "I would like that, Jack."

Jack shook his hand. "Take care, my friend. I wish the war was over."

With nowhere safe to go, Peter reported back to camp. He couldn't believe that had been his father lying in that bed. He felt pity for the frail, confused man. Pity for his father? He kicked himself and then laughed.

He was now going to inherit Springdale. A Yankee in possession of a southern plantation! How much longer would the old buzzard live? What would happen to all the slaves after he died? Peter sunk to the ground under a tall white ash tree.

"Are you all right, Private Burnett?" Frazier asked, approaching Peter.

Peter glanced up and nodded.

"Normally a man enjoys every hour of his furlough and you came back before the end of the first day. There has to be something wrong."

"I'm fine, Chaplain."

"Uh huh," Frazier replied, clearly unconvinced. "As a chaplain, I've listened to many confessions and the woes of the masses. I sense you are distracted by mental turmoil. Is there something you would like to discuss?" he pressed.

"No, sir. I just need to be alone."

Frazier continued looking at him, clearly hoping he would change his mind or share more. He took a deep breath and relented. "Well," he dragged out the word, "find me if you ever want to talk."

"I will. Thank you."

Peter watched the chaplain walk to his hut. He was a good man. And a sensitive one, likely because of his profession. He'd have to keep his emotion in check, especially when around him. If only Peter could share what was on his mind. He'd gladly get the burden off his chest if it wouldn't land him in jail or worse.

In the morning, Peter was found Joseph Lewry bundled in his bunk under a pile of blankets—his own, Johnson's and Crawford's. Only Lewry's dark brown hair, sleepy eyes, and nose were visible. He had appeared well last night and wasn't pale. Perhaps he was just tuckered out.

There was a knock on the door. Peter didn't bother looking at Lewry. The man wasn't about to move.

Peter got up and answered the door.

"Is Lewry here?" Sergeant Snidow's voice barreled through the silence.

"He is. Come in."

Sergeant Snidow saw Lewry buried under the mountain of blankets and roared with laughter. "Get up. It's your turn for fatigue duty."

"I can't. I'm ill," Lewry said in an insistent whine.

"Well, Burnett, is he sick?"

"His illness came on suddenly. I know nothing about it, Sergeant."

"Procuring wood for camp is a necessity in winter," Snidow growled. "There are worst things I could have you do."

"I'm too weak to haul wood," Lewry persisted in a raspy voice.

"You'll have to improve on your act for next time. You're not convincing me. But if you need me to utter some fiery language to give you energy I'll happily oblige." Snidow grinned.

Lewry peeled off the layers of blankets and crawled off his bunk. "It's not fair that I'm getting stuck with this. Burnett's new to the company. He should have to do it."

"You're on my list," Snidow said. He impatiently waited for Lewry to get his shoes on and gather his gear.

"Burnett must be your pet, then."

"His pet!" Peter snapped. "After the countless times he's cussed at me—how can you say that?"

Snidow laughed loudly with a hint of disdain. "I couldn't have said it better myself, but you're actually on my list too, Burnett, since one of the other boys is really in the hospital."

Peter nodded. "I expected my name would come around soon, Sergeant. Unlike Lewry here, I won't try to con you to shirk my duty."

Snidow smiled like a cat handed a mouse. "Glad to hear it. I was expecting you to be a beat. I thought gentlemen despised manual labor."

"Some do, some don't. I don't."

Lewry glared at Peter hard enough to leave a bruise. "Thanks for nothing."

"You're welcome for nothing."

The detail was sent with the wagons for wood. "Hey, the recruit's here," Elijah East mocked.

Peter ignored the comment. He pulled an ax out of the wagon and set to work chopping a good sized tree. Once it fell, East went over and clasped Peter shoulder. "Good job. Now we can lift it into the wagon. You get the bottom end and I'll get the top."

Peter held back a sigh. He'd expected as much.

The base of the tree was three feet in diameter. He grunted as he lifted it off the ground. Carrying it, he slowly waddled over to the wagon. With a good heave it landed in the bed. Sweat already ran down his neck. The day dragged on and on and on. Peter was an Underground Railroad conductor, a soldier, a spy, a man who homesick and lovesick, but he wasn't a logger.

"Not used to sweating like us poor farmers," East said an unmistakable taunt to his voice.

☆　☆　☆

Later that week, Peter was "Haled" again. While he was absent, all his belongings were taken outside the hut. None of his hut-mates were there when he returned to discover the joke. But soldiers passing by laughed at the wet, muddy mix of clothes, blankets, and knickknacks.

Peter cursed under his breath. Just his luck—Hale waited for the thaw. The snow had melted to create such a mess. How many more times he'd be Hale's target?

It took Peter time to move everything back in, wash off the mud, and dry them by the fire. His blanket dried a nasty brown color. He ran his hand across the fabric and felt the grit ground deep into the fibers.

"Damnit, Hale," Peter said. He couldn't believe he'd be sleeping in such filth.

Peter sat on his bunk, his arms ached from all the scrubbing. Scrubbing that didn't do much good.

He drummed his fingers on his thigh. This couldn't go unnoticed. Now he had to think of a way to get Hale back. Maybe he could get Johnson, Crawford or Lewry to help him.

A horrible thought stabbed him. Peter sprang off the bed and opened his Shakespeare book, frantically flipping through the pages. "Son of a …!"

His money was gone. *Aunt Ruth's money.*

Crawford entered the hut in time to see him throw the book on the floor. The sound made him jump. "What's wrong, Jeff?"

"He stole my money!" Peter's voice roared like thunder.

"Who did?"

"Hale. He moved all my belongings outside and in the process he stole all my money."

"I just don't believe it. Hale's mischievous, but I don't think he's a thief."

Peter charged outside to search for the rat. Behind him the door slammed shut.

CHAPTER 18

PETER FOUND HALE outside his hut, sitting on a tree stump, whistling "The Valiant Conscript." He cocked his head to the left and gave Peter a tricky smile. "You've been 'Haled' again."

"'Haled!' I've been more than 'Haled'," his voice a rumbling roar. "You stole my money!"

Hale stood his eyes bulging. "What are you talking about?"

Peter glared at him. "Don't play dumb with me. I want it back!"

Hale took a couple steps. "I moved all your belongings outside but I never saw any money. Where was it?"

"It was in the pages of my Shakespeare book."

"Maybe the bills fell out," Hale said.

"If they fell out then you would have seen them!" Peter fumed. He raised his hand to throw a punch but stopped himself. He opened the door to Hale's hut and began rifling through his knapsack and other belongings.

"You're not going to find it. I didn't take your money. Why would I steal from a comrade?" Peter didn't find the money, but he wasn't satisfied that Hale wasn't a thief. "Maybe one of your hut-mates took it," Hale suggested.

Peter shot a look at Crawford. "I didn't do it," Crawford said quickly.

Peter took a deep breath. Money wasn't important. But it wasn't just any money it was Aunt Ruth's life savings! All her work was only worth fifty dollars! A Union private made thirteen dollars a month so that was less than five months wages.

His heart twisted tighter in his chest and his blood increased in temperature until his skin burned. Still, there was nothing he could do about it now, and he needed John to be a friend. He didn't need to start a fight. A fight would likely diminish the last of his likeability.

"I believe both of you," Peter lied. "I'm sorry I acted irrationally, John."

Peter yawned as he stepped outside into the brisk winter breeze. Morning came too quickly. He hadn't slept well. He rubbed the sleep out of his eyes, rolling the grit between his thumb and forefinger before blowing it off. He took a sip of hot chicory water. He couldn't call it coffee. It tasted nothing like coffee.

It burned his throat on the way down. He didn't care.

"Aunt Ruth's money," he grumbled. He sighed loudly and shook his head. He had to let it go. Or he wouldn't sleep tonight either. All he could do to make amends was to be more careful in the future.

Men shouting and exchanging angry curses drew Peter's attention. Musket in hand, he ran towards the disturbance. Elisha East was fighting with another soldier. East, skinny and wiry was easy prey for his opponent a stocky man with muscular arms.

"Beat him in to a pulp, Fortner," one of the soldiers shouted.

Peter ground his teeth together. East was not liked by most of the men. This could end badly.

East came at Fortner in a rush, his arms swinging. Fortner caught one of his fists, spun East around and flipped him to the ground. East landed with a thud and groaned. He quickly staggered to his feet to avoid Fortner's large shoes.

With his left fist, East did an upper cut and connected under Fortner's chin, sending Fortner's teeth crashing into each other with such force that he shattered his tooth. Fortner gagged bits of his blood soaked tooth.

Fortner blocked another blow with his forearm, and then struck him across the side of the head.

East wheeled backward, recovered, lowered his head, and then charged at the man's mid-section. Fortner lost his footing and fell into the large crowd.

"Get him, Fortner," a soldier in the crowd said, pushing him back into the circle.

Fortner lunged at East and his right fist connected with East's nose. East nose heaved for breath and a hand flew up to cover his bloody nose. For a second the two men glared at each other.

East recovered and swung at Fortner again. Fortner stepped to the side dodging it. His maul-like fists delivered two blows to East's stomach. The man dropped to his knees. While in that vulnerable position Fortner lunged on top of him.

The crowd cheered.

Sergeant Snidow stepped in and broke it up before East was seriously injured. East and the other man were both arrested.

"What was that all about?" Peter asked Sublett.

"East stole Fortner's clothes, pocket watch, and knife and Fortner caught him red-handed. His belongings were in East's hut."

Peter whistled. "That's something."

"That's nothing new for him. He's always turning up after battle with a full haversack, good blanket, overcoat and shoes he'd likely scavenged off corpses. Haven't you heard about him?"

Peter shook his head. "I've drilled with him and worked with him but that's all. He keeps to himself."

"East has never been in a battle and never intends to be. However, he seems to know more about the battles than anyone who's actually experienced them. He's in this war only to make a profit."

"Has he stolen from other comrades?"

"Likely, but this was the first time he's gotten caught. There's no way he can get out of it. We have undeniable proof of his guilt."

Peter's stomach knotted and his eyes narrowed. East was being led out for trial and Peter ran after him. "Did you steal my money?" he demanded.

"You're wealthy. Why does fifty dollars matter to you?" East responded.

Peter's face turned hot and both his hands folded into fists. "You took it you bastard!"

"Gotta plead guilty to that."

"I want it back."

"Sorry, I gambled it away."

"Gambled all fifty dollars?" It took every ounce of restraint for Peter not to throw a punch. If Aunt Ruth knew her money had been gambled away he'd never hear the last of it.

East was sentenced. Ordered to be drummed out of the army. Blushing, his head already shaved, East stood at attention while Lieutenant Mullins ripped all the brass buttons off his uniform and the insignia off his hat.

Peter watched engrossed in the scene as if watching a cockfight. He wasn't normally a grim person, but he couldn't restrain his joy at East getting his due.

East bowed his head. Having stripped off all the markings of a soldier, Mullins placed a placard around East's neck proclaiming he stole from comrades. East was led out of camp by guards holding their muskets in the reversed arms position. The drummers beat the disgraceful Rogue's March.

"Don't go back to Giles County," Eaton's voice rang out in a rough rumble. "We'll tar and feather you if you show your face!"

"And ride you out of town on a rail!" Sublett said.

"You're not only a disgrace to the army you're a disgrace to the South! You best move to the protection of the Yanks because you'll need it!" Fortner bellowed. "I can't wait to get my hands on you someday."

"You thieving bastard." Peter's hands shook. "Stealing from comrades you don't even have the guts to charge the field with!"

Once East was gone tempers remained high. Seeing that the men now had energy to burn Captain Bane ordered them into drill formation. Peter groaned and guessed what was coming. Leg aching exercise. Bane put them through maneuvers ignoring the chorus of complaints. By suppertime everyone was exhausted—so exhausted that they cared for nothing but sleep.

Peter crumpled to the ground and closed his eyes.

☆　☆　☆

"Mr. Burnett, I've been looking all over camp for you."

Peter turned around when he heard Jack's voice. For the first time he could remember his friend wasn't wearing gray. He was dressed in a stylish butternut pinstriped suit with a coffee-colored vest, red cravat, and he was wearing his reading glasses. The new outfit went better with his light brown hair than the gray suits he was used to seeing his friend wear. Jack looked years younger.

"Why don't you introduce me to your friends?" Jack said.

Peter nodded. "Elbert Eaton and John Sublett this is Jack Selah." The three men shook hands.

"You a professor or something?" Eaton asked.

Jack laughed. "No. I write for the *Staunton Spectator*."

"A newspaper man, huh?" Sublett said. "I guess you're getting pretty desperate for a story if you're coming out here. Though, I figure, there really isn't much to report lately."

"This isn't actually a business visit. I just found out Jeff enlisted and thought we could talk before he wound up someplace else. However, if you have a story idea I'm all ears."

Sublett shook his head. "Afraid not, unless you want to report how cold and hungry the Confederate soldiers are."

"Or the fact that one of our comrades Elisha East was caught stealing from us and drummed out of the army," Eaton said.

"How terrible," Jack said. "I do think I could write a few lines on that. We need to discourage that behavior."

"Indeed. Come on, Bert; let's let them talk in private."

"Those seem like nice fellows," Jack said after they'd left.

"Yes," Peter said drawing out the word, "probably the only two friends I have around here."

"I did tell your other friends that you enlisted. So how are you enjoying army life?"

"Being a Confederate soldier isn't exactly what I had expected." Peter shrugged when he saw all the Rebs watching him. "But no sacrifice is too great to ensure Virginia keeps her rights."

"I thought you would've found yourself a commission a long time ago, Jeff."

Peter nodded. "I'm proud to be a secesh but I had to warm up to the idea of being shot at."

"Apparently, you also have to warm up to the idea that you're not going to be warm for a long time."

Peter rubbed his arms vigorously. "This uniform isn't very thick. Shall we step inside my hut? It has a roaring fire."

"That sounds like a good plan."

Thankfully, the hut was deserted. Peter stood by the door so he'd know if someone wanted to come in. His ears heightened "I suppose we've a few minutes to talk freely."

"I won't actually meet your friends until they break winter camp," Jack explained.

"That won't be too long from now."

"They have big plans for me, but I'll help you if I can."

Peter didn't know how much more Jack could do. Jack had been helping him for years without much in return. Peter remembered the day that Jack brought Belle to Pittsfield. Dan hadn't said it but Peter knew that he didn't expect to see his love again.

He had chosen a life with Peter instead of a life with his sweetheart. Peter licked his lips and swallowed. Dan's devotion, his caring nature. He would have been lost if he had been forced to flee the plantation alone—likely wouldn't have made it.

Peter sighed. If Dan could be with him now he would make it through this war. He didn't know if he had it in him to carry on this charade much longer. His chest bunched and a thick sorrow slid down his throat and settled uncomfortably in his stomach.

He pulled the letter he had written Molly out of his knapsack, rubbed his hand across the first page, hoping to infuse his scent into the paper. Finally, he handed the letter to Jack. "Can you see Molly gets this? The last page is really important."

"Sure." Jack glanced at the back page and saw it had information meant for Union headquarters. "I'll add to it and explain things."

"I'd be grateful," Peter said. Sorrow sat uneasy in his gut like a fist-sized clump of dirt, and when he spoke he spaced his words with train-length pauses. "I wouldn't want Molly to think I was buried."

"It would take a long time before she'd think that."

"I'm useless here. It being winter…"

"Keep your eyes and ears open nonetheless. I know this isn't what you had planned, but you have to remember you're still serving your country."

Peter grunted. "I didn't choose to be a spy…"

One of Jack's eyebrows slanted. "What do you mean?"

Peter's neck tingled and then burned. He forced himself not to bow his head. "Cowardice. I ran during the last battle. Fled to Abigail's." Peter spoke so softly it grated his throat. "They gave me this assignment as a way to keep breathing."

Jack's facial muscles tightened, but he didn't give away any emotion. It felt like the silence lasted for years. Peter's heartbeat grew louder until it was all he heard.

Finally, Jack spoke. "You've been running all your life. Fear is engrained into you, beat into you. Here is your chance to stand and fight."

Peter straightened his posture and thrust his shoulders back. He couldn't fight his father, but Jack was right. This was the next best thing. "I will."

Jack put his hand on Peter's shoulder. "Have anything to eat?"

"I don't have much to offer, but you are welcome to some army food."

"A spoonful of beans is a feast when you're dining with friends."

After the meal Jack pulled a small bag out of his coat pocket. "This is for you. I wish I could help more."

Peter took the bag and untied it. Inside rested several gold coins. "Where did you get this?"

"I have my ways," Jack said cryptically.

Peter knew not to press him further. "How much?"

"One hundred dollars. Use it wisely," he said. The familiar fatherly tone returned to Jack's voice.

"I will." He had to guard it closely so that these precious coins, possibly the key to a tolerable life in a gray uniform, or even better, a chance to escape wouldn't be stolen. Losing Aunt Ruth's money had taught him a valuable lesson. He vowed to always carry it with him. "Thank you."

Jack nodded. "Would you like me to take Cloudy back with me?"

"No. I've already agreed to give her to the Confederate Army. I need to make friends."

"True. I hadn't thought of that." The two men stood in uneasy silence. Peter willed Jack to speak because he didn't know how to end the visit. The visit he didn't want to end.

"I will see you around," Jack said at last. "Maybe next time I stop by you'll have a story worth me writing up for the newspaper."

Peter just hoped he would have something of value to share with Jack next time they met whether it was newsworthy or not. The Union Army was counting on him to make a difference.

☆　☆　☆

When a peddler came by offering the soldiers everything from pans to blankets they emptied out their pockets trying their best to replace all the items that had been stolen. The redheaded peddler grinned and pocketed more bills. "I didn't expect to do so much business," he said.

"I'm sure. Some of our camp followers robbed us," Crawford said through gritted teeth.

The peddler frowned. "Sorry to hear that. I guess I traveled by at the right time." He pulled out a gold-colored pocket watch and checked the time.

Hale let out a rebel yell and then lunged at the short peddler knocking him flat on his back. "That is my watch! You stole all of this from us and now you are trying to sell it back, you son of a bitch."

Hale stiffened two of his fingers and attempted to jab the peddler's eyes.

The soldiers froze—their faces a mixture of shock, anger, and eagerness. The peddler struggled, kicking his legs and squirming with all his strength. Hale grabbed his throat and squeezed. The peddler's face turned red.

Peter rushed in and pulled Hale off. "You don't need to kill the man," Peter said.

"Why not? Let me at him!"

Peter gripped tighter to Hale's arm. "No. It isn't worth it."

The peddler hurried towards his wagon. A soldier thrust out his foot sending the man face first into the ground. "You're not leaving with all our money," he said in a low growl. "Give it back."

The peddler got to his feet and swallowed hard. He dug all the money out of his pockets and handed it to Peter.

"I'll make sure this gets to the right people," Peter said.

"And we better not see you in our camp again!" another soldier yelled.

The peddler scrambled into his seat, slapped the reins and soon had his cart rolling at a fast pace.

Peter shook his head. Desperate times made men do desperate things. That peddler was lucky to still have his life. Hungry men seldom thought clearly.

The Confederate soldiers hadn't had a round meal in several months. The government cut soldiers' rations until they weren't eating a decent meal once a day.

Peter stared glumly at the piece of cornbread. He gratefully chewed the dry lump hoping he wouldn't go stretches without food in the future.

There was talk that some of the regiments would be disbanded because of the government's inability to feed them. Peter hoped that the 7th Virginia would be one of them. That would give him an easy ticket out. But would he be so lucky?

On February 16, the 7th Virginia was ordered to strike their winter encampment. Peter lined up with the rest of the Mountain Boomers in the midst of a snowstorm. Did the generals know what a harebrained idea it was to start campaigning this early? He glanced ahead at

Lieutenant Mullins and Captain Bane. They were muttering complaints along with everyone else.

Peter pulled his coat collar up higher on his neck. The cold air stung his exposed skin. Head bowed, he marched with the rest of Pickett's division. The longer they walked the harder Peter breathed. When he exhaled puffs lingered in front of his mouth. His ears ached first and soon his whole face was painfully cold. It was going to be a long trek to North Carolina.

At Hanover Junction, Sergeant Fry, whom the Yankees had released from prison, rejoined the company. The thin man stood five-foot-six, wisps of his fiery red hair protruded under his forage cap. He looked Irish to the bone.

"Welcome back, Sarge," Dulaney said.

Fry nodded to the lad. "Good to be back."

"You mean you missed us?" Crawford asked.

"Yes. Believe it or not I did."

"Looks like you lost some weight," Johnson said.

"Prison fare is even worse than the slop we get here."

"We haven't even been getting slop lately. You might want to go back to the Yanks!" Lewry complained.

Lieutenant Mullins grabbed Fry by both his shoulders and shook him playfully. "Took long enough for a prisoner exchange, didn't it?" Mullins said. "I really appreciate you coming to my aid after Second Manassas. I owe you."

"No, you don't. I didn't do anything special. I'm sure any man here would have done the same thing."

"And know they could be taken prisoner? No. You went above and beyond the call of duty."

Fry grinned, a blush in his cheeks. "Looks like you're faring well."

Mullins laughed. "Wound healed. When we stop I will make you a large plate of vitals. That's the least I can do."

Later, Peter was formally introduced to Sergeant Fry and the man's steely, blue eyes seemed to probe his soul. Fry was constantly alert, watching, listening. It could have been due to his time as a prisoner of war, but Peter got the impression that Fry naturally suspicious sort. Peter's chest tightened and his toes curled in his brogans. The man made his skin crawl. He instantly knew that he would have to be very careful around him.

The crisp, cool weather made their arrival to Chester Station pleasant. There wasn't a cloud in the sky and the sun shone brightly, gently warming Peter's cheeks. It was another slice of Virginia paradise. Something worthy of a painting. A picture Molly could hang in the parlor.

After spending over two years in New Hampshire Peter's mind had begun to diminish the beauty of the South. His anger and bitterness towards his father had begun to seep through to everything Southern, marring his memory. That had been wrong. If only the beauty didn't have to be marred by slavery or war.

That night, the stars shone like diamonds on the wall of a dark cave. Peter stood in awe, gazing at their beauty. Molly and Dan and his comrades in blue were all sleeping under the same stars.

A star streaked across the sky taking a piece of Peter's heart with it. *I wish upon this star that I will survive this war to wed Molly.*

Molly. Thoughts of her kept him going.

CHAPTER 19

WINTER HAD ENDED according to the Confederate brass. But it snowed intermittently proving God disagreed.

After a gusty storm, the row of tents looked like tombstones in a cemetery. Men emerged from the foot and half of powder like dead rising from their graves. They built roaring fires to warm themselves, but it did little to relieve their discomfort.

Peter ate a handful of cornmeal for breakfast and looked forlornly at his boots. They were soaked with icy water, numbing his feet. It wouldn't be long before the bottoms of his pant legs were frozen stiff. He gathered some sticks and set to work making snowshoes.

In order to survive, the soldiers were forced to forage for their meals. Eaton and Sublett would often come into camp with a turkey speared on their bayonets or carrying a pig in a bag. On most occasions, Peter was invited to share in their spoils. In this manner Peter subsisted for as long as possible, but eventually the charity ended.

Finally, his stomach pains got the best of him. Peter resigned himself to the deplorable task.

That evening, he and Dulaney walked two miles to a rundown farm. "They have a hen house," Dulaney said.

Peter shook his head. "I'm not stealing, David."

Dulaney's brown eyes widened. "Then why'd we walk all the way down here! I'm hungry, Jeff. How'd you expect us to eat?"

"This isn't enemy territory," Peter said. He shifted his musket to his left hand so he could knock on the door.

An older woman in a patched black dress with graying hair answered. Her bottom lip trembled and fear flashed in her eyes. "Don't hurt me," she said, backing up a couple steps.

Peter, surprised by the woman's reaction, quickly pointed his musket at the ground. "We're not here to harm you, ma'am," he explained. He looked back at Dulaney. "My friend and I haven't eaten much in several days and we were hoping you could spare some food."

The woman looked at Peter and blinked her gray eyes. "Why didn't you take what you want? Everyone else does."

Peter sighed. Likely, the soldiers had already taken everything, leaving the poor woman little for herself. "Stealing is against God's commandments. Begging is deplorable, but it's not a sin." The woman blinked at Peter again and then looked past him to Dulaney. "Ma'am," Peter continued, "we understand if you have nothing to give. We'll just go to the next house."

"Come inside, both of you, I'll fix you something to eat."

Peter quickly took off his kepi. He flashed a smile at Dulaney and they entered the house. They were directed to a small roughhewn table.

"I've seen lots of soldiers," the woman said, heating water on the stove, "but you're the first with manners."

Peter blushed. "My name's Jeff Burnett, ma'am."

Dulaney's mouth watered as he watched the woman put a small chicken in the pot and he wiped his mouth.

"And who's your quiet friend?" she asked, stirring the broth.

"David Dulaney," the boy replied in a meek voice.

Later, the woman dished them both a bowl of soup, and then sat the table with them. "My name is Mrs. Lannum. My husband died long before this war started. Last December, my two boys, Ambrose and Daniel, died of pneumonia while serving the Confederacy." The woman paused. She looked over at Dulaney. "You remind me of Ambrose. He was your height with golden hair and it was nearly impossible for him to speak a complete sentence. What are you, fifteen?"

Dulaney didn't answer.

Mrs. Lannum offered a tight, weary smile. "Your secret's safe."

"Thank you for the soup, Mrs. Lannum. It was delicious," Peter said.

"I know my cooking isn't that good. I haven't had anyone to cook for since I lost my boys."

"You're just being modest. Your cooking is much better than mine," Peter said. Truth was the chicken was stringy and a little too salty, but the meat settled well in his empty stomach.

"Here. You boys need to keep up your strength. I'll pour the rest of the soup in a glass jar for you to take."

"Thank you, ma'am."

"You've thanked me enough. It is my pleasure."

She handed Peter the jar and walked outside to see them off. If Peter still had Cloudy he would have given her to the kind woman. She looked like she had drawn a hard lot in life, and Peter knew she would have given his mount a good home. But Cloudy now had CS branded on her flank and Peter doubted he'd see her again.

Almost to the road, Peter stopped, turned around and waved at Mrs. Lannum. Even from the distance he could see the dim light in the woman's eyes brighten. She waved back.

"I would like to think my mother was like her," Peter said, and they made their way back to camp.

"Jeff, you didn't know your mother?"

"No. She died giving birth to me."

Dulaney stopped and looked at Peter puzzled. "Then where'd you learn your manners?"

"I'd like to think a man can get what he wants from charm as equally as he can from force."

The lad pondered that bit of wisdom for a moment then nodded. "Perhaps you're right. Too bad we can't charm our way out of this war."

Given free rein to leave camp and find food, Peter's pulse quickened. It had been easy to walk the miles to Mrs. Lannum's house. Perhaps he could go foraging for food and just keep walking.

But men seldom scoured the countryside alone. If he tried it would they get suspicious?

He bit his lip. He had to think on that some more.

When not foraging for their meals, the 7th Virginia guarded the Wilmington, Weldon and Petersburg Railroad. The line carried supplies to Lee's army. The soldiers set up camp near Hanover Junction. They stayed there for three weeks resting and recuperating from the fatiguing march. The local people expressed appreciation for their service by bringing the soldiers hams, pies, and other delicious food. For once, Peter did not mind wearing a Confederate uniform.

With a full stomach, Peter sat back, propping himself up on his elbows, listening to a banjoist and violinist play negro melodies. The two musicians were sent by their master to provide entertainment. The twangs of the strings lightened Peter's heart. The negroes were dressed in black suits, their white shirts in stark contrast to their dark skin. Most of the soldiers were sitting on the ground around, all enjoying themselves, some half asleep. The company stretched out in a loose circle around the entertainers.

Peter's mouth dropped open when Dulaney joined them on the bones. The violinist stood, not losing time and allowed the young white man to set on his overturned barrel. At first Dulaney still seemed a little shy. However, after the violinist gave him a drink from a small jug, he was clicking the bones like a regular minstrel.

A little voice, coming from behind Peter, sang out the words in a sweet tenor. Peter looked over his shoulder and smiled when he saw Captain Bane's negro boy.

The banjoist stopped playing, went over and grabbed the boy's hand, and dragged him out in front of where they were playing so he could perform for everyone. The boy's eyes got big as he looked at the crowd who had gathered to hear the music.

"Go on Little James, sing. You'll do fine," the banjoist encouraged, sitting back down on a barrel and resuming the song.

When the song ended everyone clapped. Little James, had a big smile on his face. When the next song began he sang out even louder and began to jig. The boy dancing in his ragged trousers and baggy coat looked like a marionette.

His pa caught the end of the song, charged in, and grabbed his hand. "How dast you drag my son into dis!" he bellowed, at the musicians.

Peter couldn't believe the man was bold enough to take that tone. Still, the man had the presence of mind not to look the soldiers in the eye.

"He was just singin'," the banjoist replied.

"When dat's no longer fun de tricks start," Big James said.

"We wouldn't do that to him. He's just a child," Lewry said.

"Yuh not do dat. He's just a chile," Big James mumbled, as he led his son away from the crowd.

"I likes singin'," Little James whined.

Big James put a hand on his son's shoulder. "I knows. I just can't bear seein' yuh heartbroken when dey starts makin' fun of yuh."

"But de soldiers is my friends."

"No, dey ain't," Big James said, shaking his head.

The boy tilted his head and looked at his pa. "Cap'n Bane's a soldier and he's a friend, right?"

Big James looked into his son's big, brown eyes, ruffled his black curls, and nodded. "He's a friend."

Peter smiled at the boy's innocence. Often it was taken from the colored youths too early.

Peter took advantage of the soldiers' relaxed afternoon and asked them questions about the state of the Confederate Army, if they'd heard of any coming battles, and anything else useful he could think of that wouldn't sound too nosy. At night he wrote what he had learned on a small strip of paper and sewed it into the hem of his left pant leg.

☆   ☆   ☆

Standing on the train platform, Peter shifted his weight, impatiently waiting for the order to board. The train would take him further south so that they could get supplies and rejoin General Hood's division. He was testing fate being in the Confederate Army so long. Any day he could be recognized. His posters were not just confined to Fredericksburg.

But he had yet to find an easy way out of Captain Bane's command.

His irritation grew the more he dwelled on his situation.

Sublett stepped up behind him and slapped him on the back. "Getting antsy? You should have a drink."

"No, thanks." Peter turned his head, Sublett's hot, whisky breath lingered on his cheek. The stench made his insides coil.

Many of the soldiers had imbibed freely to pass the time. The group of soldiers grew louder and more animated. Peter chewed his lip. The company was on the brink of chaos. Captain Bane and the other officers didn't seem eager to step up and restore order. In fact, Lieutenant Mullins was among the drunk and most boisterous.

Wearing officer's bars didn't automatically make someone a gentleman. Peter had learned that the hard way. He didn't want the power to control men's lives, but he wished he had the power to control the present situation.

It was on the verge of spiraling out of hand. Could a whole company of soldiers be thrown in jail?

Women from town had gathered to see the soldiers off—some respectable ladies, others of questionable repute. Many talked to the soldiers starry-eyed and flirted shamelessly.

One woman in a patriotic red dress toyed with the lieutenant. She twirled one of the black curls that fell to her shoulders.

The lieutenant grabbed her by the arm, pulled her close, and gave her a long kiss on the lips. While holding her still with one large hand, cupping the back of her head, his other hand worked down the front of her dress until he was feeling her breast.

Peter clenched his teeth and fisted his hands. Would he get in trouble for punching the lieutenant? No. He couldn't start a fight, couldn't interfere. He couldn't possibly fight the stocky lieutenant. It would be like fighting his father.

Peter eyed the officer with a threatening glare. Mullins hadn't tried to migrate his attentions lower. Mullins could kiss a long time! His face flushed a light shade of red and he finally pulled back.

The woman shrieked and slapped him across the face. Before she ran she kicked him in the shins, hatred shooting from her eyes. The other ladies fled, uttering things like, "The soldiers are brutes! They do not know how to treat a lady. The fun's all over. Let's get out of here."

Many of the soldiers roared with laughter, enjoying the spectacle the officer was making of himself. Peter couldn't help but feel sorry for the poor woman. Would she report him to the police?

When Mullins started looking to cause more trouble the Mountain Boomers locked him in a boxcar to sober up. The lieutenant's hollering became progressively louder until he kicked off one of the doors to escape.

The police, alerted to the disturbance, came running.

"Time to board," one of the officers said. "Now!"

The Mountain Boomers filed on board quickly. With a squeaky turn of gears and a lurch the train pulled out of the station and the lieutenant avoided arrest.

The next morning, they arrived at Weldon and were again crowded into boxcars like cattle. There weren't enough cars for the soldiers to travel comfortably. Still, even Peter agreed that a stuffy ride was better than a hard, long walk. They were grateful for the chance to sit or stand as opposed to walking. Temperatures hovered at the bottom of the thermometer. Peter wrapped his hands around his arms and pushed his arms tightly against his chest.

"Hang on," Johnson said. He smiled at Peter. "We'll have you warm in a minute."

"What are you going to do?" Peter asked.

"Build a fire. Common folk have ingenuity, too." Johnson's words were a jab, but his voice was friendly. So this was how it was going to be.

Johnson and some of the others covered the floor of each car with sand. On this, fires fed with North Carolina pine kept them warm.

"Thank you," Peter said.

"Didn't do it just for you," Johnson said, a bite to his voice.

Peter huddled close to the fire, putting his hands over the flames, his teeth chattering. He tried in vain to divert the smoke away from his face. Unable to vent, the thick, acrid smoke settled upon Peter's skin and clothes. His eyes burned. His stomach grew uneasy. When they reached Goldsboro the Mountain Boomers could have passed for the colored brigade.

Peter groaned once he learned of the march ahead. It was a long twenty-five miles before they camped in Kingston on the Neuse River. Too tired to fix a meal, he reclined on the ground with fevered, blistered bare feet and aching limbs. His head rested on his blanket roll. He closed his eyes and silently prayed that God would deliver him from the Confederate Army, before he ventured too much further south.

The men conducted picket duty on the roads leading to New Bern. Union troops were in the city not far away. While the commissariat gathered provisions the Mountain Boomers watched for the enemy. They walked stiffly, alert, expecting a raid.

During his turn scouting, Peter hoped a Union patrol would advance and find them. He planned to shoot his companions and join them. A sick feeling settled in the pit of his stomach. Could he really shoot these men after getting to know them? Maybe if he just struck them on the head with his rifle, knocked them out so he could escape. His fingers trembled and he gripped his sides. Could he do even that?

He was spared this moral dilemma. No Yankees appeared.

Peter held back tears of frustration. His raw emotions lurked too close to the surface.

Peter no longer blamed General Whipple for blackmailing him into espionage. He always knew in the back of his mind that his own actions had caused his reassignment. He couldn't accept that until now. Accepting it meant admitting his guilt, admitting the punishment was just, and enduring it.

An icy ball formed behind Peter's ribs, chilling him. If only he could take it all back. If only he had stood his ground a little longer. If only he could blink and transport himself back to the Union Army. How he longed to rejoin the Kane brothers in a friendly game of cards.

Still, suffering was better than death. If he hadn't been blinded by anger at his own foolish actions he should have thanked the officers for sparing his life and giving him this assignment. At least now he had a chance to see Dan and Molly again. And a chance to clear his name.

He wasn't going to squander the opportunity.

Wide-eyed, like children at Christmas, the ragged rebels accepted new caps, coats, trousers, blouses, socks, shoes, and blankets. Peter took his share of the desperately needed supplies.

Finally, Kemper's brigade left the deserted town of Kingston and reunited with General Hood's division. They continued to advance deeper and deeper and deeper south.

A little voice in the back of Peter's mind warned him he was going in the wrong direction. It made the hair on his neck prickle and goose pimples blanket his arms. It nagged him all day, unrelenting like a plaguing headache. But unlike a headache this misery could not be cured with medicine. At night, Peter was overcome with a wave of anxiety. He gripped his stomach, bent over and vomited.

He could not ignore the warning about going deeper south. Over the past two years it had saved his skin many times.

Hopefully, it would save him again.

CHAPTER 20

PETER'S UNCERTAINTY WITH his situation continued to grow, leaving him frustrated. He desperately wanted to make a break for it and return to his comrades in blue. Fear made his inner voice louder. Escape. Don't escape. His heart said run now! His head said, examine the situation first.

An escape didn't seem feasible. Damn. Too much time in a gray uniform increased his sense of vulnerability. His nerves were frayed like an overused rope. If they snapped...

He needed to do something so that he didn't feel powerless. In an attempt to test the boundaries, he decided to see how far he could lag behind while on the move. With any luck they might not notice the space that began to grow between him and the brood of vipers that seemed to have him tethered on a leash. For a minute he thought he was going to get away with it, but before he could make his break, Sergeant Fry noticed him.

"Got something wrong with your legs there, Burnett?" he hollered, approaching Peter with long and purposeful strides. "Or do you think that just because you were born with a silver spoon in your mouth, you can set the pace for the rest of the ranks?"

Peter flushed. "No sir," he mumbled and his shoulders dropped. *Damned viper!* He kicked the dust.

Sergeant Fry drilled him mercilessly with a long line of Irish laced swear words, in step beside him. Peter increased his pace and finally caught up. Fry kept an annoyingly close eye on Peter after that, reprimanded him for the slightest break of formation.

Peter rolled his eyes skyward. Why? Why wasn't anything going his way?

As hard as it was he had to wait. Wait until Sergeant Fry's guard dropped. Peter decided it was best to hold off until they were camped in one place for more than a day or two. He just hoped that he wouldn't have to continue this charade much longer.

Peter took a deep breath. He had to get a hold of himself. He had a job to do; a job for the Union Army. He still had to get information. One of his father's sayings came to mind: Make the best of things—take sour grapes and make wine.

He didn't know what information to dig for and he didn't want to raise suspicion. However, if caught he'd face the same fate whether he passed important information to the Federal lines or not.

At least he hadn't been in an engagement yet, but he had a sickening feeling that he would be unable to avoid it much longer. It wasn't very often that a company avoided going to the front. They were all young, rested, and able-bodied.

And ready for action.

As they continued to move on. Kemper's brigade brought up the rear of the 7th Virginia. The long gray and butternut column marched down the Somerton Road and joined Longstreet's men.

"Where are we going?" Peter asked Sergeant Snidow.

"Suffolk. Yankee fort is there."

Fort? They were going to take a fort?

Peter marched the last few miles in silence. His chest bunched tighter with each step.

Peter's close proximity to Union soldiers sucked the breath from his lungs. The agony in his heart radiated pain to all his limbs. Musket shots from the skirmishers at times erupted into a battle. It seemed to grow closer. He winced.

Peter shielded his eyes with his hand and watched the Union garrison in the distance.

"Form a battle line!" an officer bellowed.

Peter inhaled sharply and joined the others in his regiment. There was a cold, hard, choking lump in his throat. He chugged water from his canteen wishing for once it was whiskey. Whiskey so he could numb himself to this war, numb himself to the danger, numb to his inner turmoil. *I can't do this. I can't battle fellow Yankees.*

The breeze carried the scent of gunpowder towards them. Peter shifted upon the balls of his feet afraid he'd be ordered to charge the fort. Charging the fort would be as bad a place to overtake as the stone wall at Marye's Heights. It could cost another thousand lives.

Peter desperately tried to come up with a way to get out of shooting his own men. He could fire at the ground but they'd still have their sights on him. He'd be a defenseless target.

The first volley belched forth from the garrison with a loud roar. A cloud of smoke drifted towards him. Peter's heart tried to charge out of his chest. He gasped. Dulaney slapped him on the back.

Some of the rebels had their heads bowed, other shifted in their places. Peter wasn't going to fight his true comrades.

Peter ran hard. His ribs ached but he kept running. He didn't know where he was going, but it wasn't going to be to the fort. Sergeant Snidow overtook him, tackled him. Peter struggled, kicking, punching. The energy of a wildcat worked through his veins.

Snidow punched him in eye and his head snapped against the ground. "What's gotten into you, Burnett?"

"I-I don't know, Sergeant."

Snidow grunted. "You've never heard a cannon before?"

Peter didn't respond. Snidow had a tight grip on his arm. The sergeant dragged Peter before Captain Bane, the commanding officer of company D.

Peter sat in front of the gray viper, all his muscles tense. Bane had the look of a humorless man. His high forehead accentuated the start of his receding hairline. He had sandy-colored hair partly covering his ears, a long beard that went down to his breastbone and a mustache as rough as straw, just beginning to fade.

"This man should be court-martialed for cowardice in the face of the enemy," Snidow said.

"You've had it in for me from the day I joined, Sergeant."

"I'll oblige you, Sergeant Snidow, after this operation is over," Bane said.

"There's no need to go through all that trouble, sir," Peter said with a sigh. "I plead guilty."

"You plead guilty? Then you'd prefer me to give you a drum-head court martial?"

"Yes, sir. It won't make any difference."

"You have not distinguished yourself as a soldier, Burnett. I will not tolerate cowards in my company. I should make an example of you. I should have a C branded on your hip."

Branded? Peter's heart writhed in his chest. He remembered Abigail pressing the hot iron to his arm—the indescribable pain, burning smell. That scar was explainable but a C would be a permanent mark of humiliation.

Peter dropped to his knees. "I beg you to reconsider," his voice quivered. "This is my first offense and I am not trying to get out of it. I will not make the mistake again. I beg you for leniency."

Bane stared at him with narrow, brown eyes. "I can imagine that such a tattoo would injure the reputation of a gentleman. I am convinced you didn't know what you were getting into when you enlisted, Mr. Burnett. However, it's my job to turn you into a soldier."

He paused and Peter held his breath.

"I will accept your plea for leniency. This time. Sergeant, have a placard with coward written in large letters fastened across his back, and have him marched to and fro in front of the regiment carrying a rail on his shoulder."

"But the Yanks are—"

"I could still give you a C," Bane said, his voice hardening, eyes turning a shade darker. "Are you showing yourself to be a coward twice?"

"No, sir."

"The garrison's guns are out of reach!" Bane yelled, as Peter was led away.

Peter's face burned the sensation spreading through his body. His fingers sweated from the heat. Dangit. Why hadn't he thought of that?

Peter lifted the large rail on his shoulder and carried it like a musket. It was awkward but it didn't seem difficult. Peter closed his eyes when Snidow placed the coward sign around his neck. He didn't want to see the word staring back at him.

The word that his father called him freely. Coward. That might as well had been one of his nicknames growing up. Dread seated in his gut. His chest constricted making his breaths short and rapid.

"Yellow belly!" Lewry yelled.

Hale jeered, "Afraid of a little noise?"

"Gutless coward!" Johnson hissed.

Peter's flush reached the tip of his ears. He couldn't stand such ridicule. They didn't understand the verbal abuse he endured as a child...

Peter continued to be paraded through the regiment. Bane watched him with a smug smile. Peter wanted to crawl inside a tent and never come out. After making one pass through the regiment the rail became increasingly heavy and painful to carry. A line of sweat dripped down his forehead.

How many passes would he have to do? Ridicule and cuss words were fired at him relentlessly. Peter knew he deserved it for being so foolish. He'd been caught on the wrong side of the war for so long that it was making him jumpy.

In the future he had to be careful.

Captain Morton had said it was very important to win people over. Safety came from being liked. However, Peter was not doing a good job of establishing himself as a likable, respectable soldier. Captain Bane didn't like him. Sergeant Snidow and Sergeant Fry didn't like him. After being humiliated in front of everyone he was sure most of the regiment lost any respect they had for him.

Peter knew he had to salvage things the best he could. He asked to talk to Captain Bane. He was relieved when he was permitted inside the officer's tent. The captain motioned him to have a seat on the campstool.

"If you're here to give me a piece of your mind, you'd be wise to hold your tongue," he advised.

"Why would I do that? I'm grateful you spared me the branding iron, sir," Peter said.

Bane's eyes lit up and he smirked. "So the gentleman is humbled."

"Contrary to what you may think, I do not consider myself better than the rest of the ranks; actually it's the other way around. They know how to fight. I do not. You said it was your job to turn me into a soldier."

"I did."

"Then *please* teach me how to be one," Peter said. "I know how to use the musket and bayonet but if I can't distinguish myself on the battlefield those skills are useless."

"That is a fact."

"I do not believe in myself and the rest of this company doesn't believe in me either. How is that supposed to boost my courage? I was just acting how you and Sergeant Snidow had expected me to act."

Captain Bane rested his left elbow on his traveling desk with his chin cupped in his hand. He looked Peter squarely in the eye, brown pupils narrowed.

Peter held as still as a statue. The man was trying to determine his intentions. Peter only prayed he liked what he found.

"You know how to talk, Mr. Burnett," he said finally, "but there's truth in what you say. I just don't know how to teach a man to be brave."

Peter's face sagged along with his spirit. "I figured you'd say that. I'm just worried if I don't learn quickly I'll end up serving a term in Castle Thunder for desertion. I really want to avoid going to prison. A man's natural instincts are self-preservation."

Captain Bane stroked his beard. "You require a lot of work. Why are the rest of the ranks, common men, willing to risk their lives for the South and you're not? Isn't courage supposed to be valued by gentlemen?"

"In my defense the ranks are battle-hardened. The cowards already left. I do value courage, sir, I just don't possess it."

Bane laughed. "All right, you've convinced me. The first step to gaining courage is confronting your fear."

"I don't like the sound of that, sir."

"What are you afraid of?"

"Dying and getting shot are on the top of my long list."

"You've already been shot in the arm. The wound was still fresh when you arrived. How'd that happen?"

"Like I said, I'm from Fredericksburg. So when the Yanks came into the city I saw it was my duty to fight them. I was firing from one of the buildings when they invaded the city. I was lucky."

"You've survived one battle then. That should make the next one easier."

"A minor wound does not make me indifferent to the next minie ball which could cost me my life."

Bane opened his mouth and exhaled silently. "Colonel Kemper turned this brigade from young farmers, who knew nothing about the military, into soldiers. I guess I'm up to the challenge with you. Dismissed."

Peter blinked unable to believe the officer's words. It took him a second to recover. His heart rose and his words came eagerly. "Yes, sir. Thank you, sir."

"Burnett is beyond my help," Captain Bane muttered to himself. "I doubt he'll make a good soldier. I just hope he can make himself useful."

Peter's ears caught that private remark. He bounced a curled knuckle against his lips, his stomach cringing. He had tried to make amends for his actions and failed.

If he couldn't be a good soldier how else could he be useful?

CHAPTER 21

PETER PRAYED EVERY night that he wouldn't have to enter battle against the Federals.

The Confederate Army pushed their left flank to the Nansemond River and constructed a battery on Hill's Point. This closed the river to Union shipping. Union gunboats attempted to run the batteries upstream, but failed.

Peter hunkered down and gripped his musket. He couldn't see the Yankees hiding behind the trees and bushes in the distance, but he knew they were there. The air rushed out of his lungs. His palms were sweaty, his throat felt full of sand.

In the morning, he'd be ordered to charge them. The thought turned his stomach. Peter lit his pipe and allowed the tobacco to calm him. He had to get his nerves under control before he acted rashly again.

Another wrong move and I'll be dead.

Morning arrived too soon and Peter finally realized the time had come. The time to enter battle against the Union, fire at the ground, and pray he wasn't shot. Union artillerymen opened fire from hidden batteries. The ground shook as if by an earthquake. Cannon shot created a gruesome corpse.

Peter's muscles tightened, and his legs itched to run, but he refused to allow them to move. He wasn't going to run this time. Not again. If it was God's will he'd stand here and get blown to bits.

Sweat warmed his forehead, matted his hair. He heaved air as if he had jogged for miles, his heart rattling his ribs.

"A good run is better than a bad stand, me boys," Sergeant Fry's voice mingled with the smoke.

The cannon barrage continued. Peter's ears rang from the loud explosions. He put a hand over his eyes, willing himself to focus despite the intense headache pounding his forehead.

Dulaney grabbed Peter's arm, pulled him to his feet, yelled in his ear, "We're retreating!"

He ran, dragging Peter along. After a few minutes, Peter shook himself free of Dulaney's hand. Biting his tongue, he took long, quick strides. Lungs and heart pumped harder to keep up with his legs.

A ball grazed Peter's neck. It felt like a mosquito bite and barely drew blood. Thank God he was only nicked. It felt like years before they were out of range. Before the musket fire died.

After his first taste of fighting on the wrong side, Peter's hands trembled. Inside, his heart trembled to the same rhythm. With a deep breath, he unscrewed the cap of his canteen and took a long pull of water. The cool liquid slid down his throat, quenching his thirst. But it did not provide the calmness and reassurance he craved. He couldn't handle another incident of fighting those he knew as his true comrades.

Peter folded his hand into a fist and gently struck his thigh. Was his participation in this war going to be a waste? Was his suffering going to be for nothing? Wasn't there something he could do? Leaning against a tree, he tilted his head back and stared at the sky.

"Your prayers are always heard," a familiar voice said.

Butterflies hatched in his stomach, the fluttering sensation growing stronger. *Jack?*

Peter blinked to make sure he wasn't imagining his friend. No. The man walked towards him determination in his eyes.

"Some fight," Jack said, putting a hand on Peter's shoulder.

"The Yanks rooted us fast." Peter eased himself to the ground. The tree bark poked his neck.

Jack sat beside him, his short legs outstretched. "Seems like they knew exactly where to place those hidden batteries," he said in a voice scarcely audible. "The Confederacy does have to face adversity," he continued in a normal tone. "However, God's still smiling on the South. The loss of a few guns isn't going to break our spirit."

Peter knew he should smile and utter some secesh comment, but he couldn't bring himself to do it. He was too depressed to even fake being happy.

"What's bothering you?" Jack asked.

Peter looked him in the eye but didn't respond. That had been a stupid question. A squirrel scolded them and Peter looked up into the branches of the hawthorn tree. The tree was in bloom with lots of beautiful white flowers. The squirrel shook the branches as he climbed higher up the tree and flowers rained down on the men.

"I have news to cheer you up, Jeff. Your sister and your father are both well. That is, your father's as well as he can be. He's fighting his illness with all his strength."

Peter brushed some of the blooms off his head. "Good. I suppose Abigail's still holding fancy parties."

"As many as she can. You probably wish you were at one right now."

"Boy, do I." Anticipation and longing edged his words. "Have you heard from Molly?"

"No. But I wouldn't worry about her."

Peter rubbed his eyes. How could he not worry about her? That was like asking the sun not to rise.

"I need help," Jack said.

"*You* need help?" Peter exclaimed loudly, without thinking.

Jack nodded. "I need to know where my cousin Rodger Phillips is serving."

Peter looked at him, confused. Jack didn't have a cousin named Rodger. Slowly what Jack had said soaked in.

"I will ask around and try to find Mr. Phillips for you."

Jack offered a false smile that could have been detected a mile away. "Word is he's not faithful to the cause so to speak." Again Jack's voice dropped to a whisper. "He's a peddler."

Peter mouthed: you mean he's working both sides?

Jack gritted his teeth. "Yes, and if I get my hands on him I will tear him limb from limb. And you have permission to do so in my place."

Peter gave a quick nod. "We had a peddler come into camp once. I've never met your cousin Rodger. What does he look like?"

"He's my height with red hair and freckles. His left hand is lame. He can't move it."

"I see."

"Sound like the peddler you saw before?"

"Could be. The peddler I saw before was short with red hair. I had to stop Hale from nearly killing him. He was trying to sell us goods he had stolen from our camp."

"Hhmm. That wasn't a wise move. But if he needed the supplies to maintain his cover…"

"I'll ask around."

"You know the best source of information often—"

"Has colored skin," Peter said, finishing the sentence.

"Yes."

"I'll see what I can do."

An eagle soared overhead and Peter watched it glide until it was a speck on the horizon. If only he could fly away from here too, fly away from his duty. But he had responsibilities.

Jack opened his mouth and then closed it again. He rubbed his forehead.

"What's on your mind?" Peter prodded.

"I'm going to Tennessee soon to cover the war. I'll be there a while."

"The *Staunton Spectator* is sending you there?"

"That newspaper's going to be sending me several places it seems. Guess everyone wants firsthand information about what's happening elsewhere in this great Confederacy."

Jack was a likeable man, someone people were naturally drawn to. He could get away with saying things like that. But Peter knew he wasn't as lucky. Every word out of his mouth was heavily scrutinized.

"I'll look for your stories." Peter realized that "everyone" meant North and South. His own work in espionage wasn't getting very far. Hopefully, Jack could be successful.

"So with all your travels I won't be seeing you again, Jack," Peter said softly unable to hide his sorrow.

"Again? Oh no, I'm sure we'll run into each other sooner than you think. I can't stay away from Virginia too long. Miss Edmunds would kill me."

"I thought she wanted you to enlist?"

"Now she likes it better that I'm reporting on the war. She thinks it safer and equally as patriotic."

Peter extended his hand. "You do your part for the South and I'll do mine."

Jack grasped Peter's palm and shook his hand heartily like it was the last time he was going to see him. The thought made Peter even gloomier, plummeting his already low spirit.

"God be with you and may God protect the Confederacy," Jack said, before he left.

☆　☆　☆

They broke camp and marched further south. A brick mansion came into view and Peter's insides knotted. Each time he filed by a plantation he wished he had a torch to burn it down.

An elderly woman walked to greet them. Despite her advanced age her back was ramrod straight. The crinoline under her dress added fullness to her frail frame. She waved a white handkerchief to get their attention. "Help! Please help!"

Captain Bane rode over to talk to her. "What is the problem, ma'am?"

"I think my husband had a stroke." Her voice was desperate and tears made her green eyes glisten.

"Doctor!" Bane shouted, motioning with his arm for the man to ride up. In a few minutes the doctor was at his side. "The lady's husband—"

"Major Burton," the woman said.

"Major Burton needs your assistance. He might have had a stroke."

Doc dismounted and walked with Mrs. Burton into the house. "Hurry, please," she said, quickening her pace.

Captain Bane raised his hand and the column came to a stop. "We'll halt for a few minutes," he told Sergeant Fry. "For all I know her husband could be dead now.

The doctor walked back out and heaved a sigh. "How is Major Burton?" Bane asked.

"Alive. He can't talk though and his right side is paralyzed. Mrs. Burton is hysterical after I told her he'd likely never recover. I gave her something to calm her down." Doc raked his hands through his hair. "To show her gratitude she has extended an invitation for the men to bivouac in the clearing for a few days. They could use a rest."

Bane nodded. "But it's not up to me." He turned to Sergeant Fry who remained at his side. "Send a messenger to extend Mrs. Burton's invitation to bivouac here."

Sergeant Fry turned around and pointed at Lewry. "Go on. Deliver the message."

Lewry opened his mouth as if to protest. "Why do I get the long walk," he muttered.

"Because I said so! Move."

"Yes, Sergeant," Lewry said and started working his way through the other companies.

Peter put a hand over his mouth to stifle a laugh. Any extra work soured Lewry's disposition. Fry had picked him just to get a rise out of him.

Sergeant Fry acted more like a sergeant-major although he didn't hold the rank. He was definitely the captain's right hand man. And the rest of the soldiers gave him an extra helping of respect. Or maybe that was because they feared his Irish wrath.

To rest his feet Peter sat in his place. His aching muscles relaxed and longed for sleep. He yawned, hoping they would be allowed to camp here for the night. He didn't want to walk a mile farther.

"Anything we can do to help?" Captain Bane asked Doc. "After all I'd hate to leave that elderly woman…"

"She was mumbling incoherently about not being able to run things anymore. They don't have an overseer."

"Hmm. Does she have family who can come stay with her? Help run the place?"

"Yes. She said she has a cousin … he can be here in three days."

"Did her husband serve?"

The doctor shrugged. "I didn't ask. He's older … probably just shelled out enough money to clothe a regiment. The Confederacy has bestowed plenty of honorary titles."

"Either way we should help her. Sergeant Fry, I need to talk to Private Burnett."

"Yes, sir."

Hearing his name, Peter stood and walked over to the captain. "You wish to see me, sir?"

"I want you to stay here for a couple days and run things for Mrs. Burton." He gave Peter a warning stare.

Peter's eyed the fields. "You mean make sure the work gets done?"

"Yes, that is what I mean," Bane said as if he was talking to a child.

Peter winced. *Damn. This is not going to be easy.* He didn't have a choice though. He had already used up all of Captain Bane's goodwill. "Yes, sir."

"You're more than qualified for the job. I'm sure this will be a nice break for you. It suits you better than soldiering."

The captain grabbed Peter by the arm and turned him around to face the entrance to the house. "Come on. I will introduce you."

The two of them walked up the steps and Bane knocked on the door. A young negress, still budding, answered the door, wiping her eyes with the back of her hand.

"We would like to speak with Mrs. Burton."

"Please come in," the girl said in a soft voice. "I will go get her."

She disappeared leaving them standing in the entryway. Both of the men took off their hats. Peter gripped his kepi tightly.

A few minutes later Mrs. Burton appeared. "Captain."

"I am sorry to hear about your husband, ma'am. Private Burnett here has experience driving slaves and he would like to stay here until your cousin arrives."

Mrs. Burton's eyes brightened through her tears. "Oh Mr. Burnett, thank you! Without your help I know they would all run off and we wouldn't even be able to feed ourselves."

Peter swallowed the lump in his throat and started coughing.

Bane slapped him on the back and he finally stopped.

There was another knock at the door and the negress opened. Sergeant Fry stood under the frame outside, hat in his hands. "Captain, we have permission to camp here."

"Thank you, Sergeant. See to it."

"Yes, sir."

In the morning after breakfast Peter headed out to the field. Mrs. Burton had taken him to the barn and showed him where the necessary tools were and said that he'd need them. The workers were stubborn. Peter stared at the whip in his hand. He had never wielded a whip before, other than a riding crop.

This was going against every fiber of his being. He hadn't thought anything could be worse than donning a Confederate uniform. Peter Warren, temporary overseer. Acid churned in his stomach. The sun was just the right temperature to make the spring day comfortable. Peter surveyed the five acre field and wide rows of plants.

Many dark faces stared at him and he stared back, an unsettling feeling growing in his gut. For a tense minute they studied each other, sizing up the work ahead. A crawling sensation sped down Peter's neck, making his flesh goose pimple.

Finally, Peter cleared his throat and spoke in a commanding voice. "As you know, Mr. Burton had a stroke. I am in charge until Mrs. Burton's cousin gets here." He snapped the whip on the ground. "If you do your work we will not have any problems. I do not tolerate back talk or slow downs. As long as you do what is expected, I will treat you with respect."

None of the slaves moved a muscle.

"Now!" he bellowed.

The slaves started working at once cultivating the soil. The weeds were just as tall as the tiny tobacco plants. It was painstaking labor to make sure none of the tobacco plants were accidentally overturned.

As Peter expected, it wasn't long before some of the slaves slowed down. They were testing his authority. Just like children, his father had often said. They needed a firm hand. Peter gritted his teeth and tightened his grip on the whip. There was no way he could actually use it, but they did not need to know that.

Peter walked towards a youth who looked to be about sixteen. Only a half hour had passed, the youth was lagging and hadn't even broken into a sweat.

"You're not keeping up with your row," Peter said in a gravelly voice only an inch from the boy's ear.

The lad stiffened. "I's doin' the best I can, suh."

Liar. Peter grabbed him by the front of his shirt. "I know better," he growled. "Don't take me for a fool."

The youth's eyes were full of blazing cold anger.

Don't talk back, boy. Please. If he did that, Peter wouldn't have a choice but to skin him.

The slaves seemed to hold their breath—the field as silent as a deserted lot.

Peter lowered his voice so it only fell on the boy's defiant ears. "I don't want to hurt you. Don't make me." He raised his voice back to normal volume. "Do you understand me, boy?"

The man looked down at the ground. "Yessuh." He picked up his hoe and increased his pace.

Peter rubbed a hand across the back of his neck. He had jumped his first hurdle.

As the day wore on, the last conversation he had with Jack Selah kept playing in his head: The best source of information often has colored skin. Well, here was his chance. But it wasn't like he had their trust.

And he didn't have it in him to beat out any information…

Well, the best way to attract flies was with honey. Or something sweeter than honey.

The slaves stopped working for their noon break. They separated into little groups on the edge of the field to eat their share of grits. This was his best opportunity. Peter walked over to the first mess and the slaves jumped to their feet. Peter motioned with his hands for them to sit back down. "Relax, relax. I just have a question for you."

A plump woman in a tattered gray dress cocked an eyebrow and looked at him suspiciously.

"Has a peddler been by here recently?"

None of the slaves said a word.

Peter took a deep breath. He looked down at his worn uniform. It was still in better shape than the shabby clothes that many of them were wearing. A heaviness settled on his chest, making his words softer than he intended. "I could use another pair of shoes and a new shirt."

The plump woman eyed the rest of the group. She was clearly in charge and they would not speak without her permission.

Peter continued asking hoping his frustration didn't show. Flies flew around the sweaty slaves and landed on their plates of grits. Ants crawled on their clothes. The slaves didn't even bother pushing them away. That would have been a waste of energy.

Peter's stomach rumbled for the salt pork he had packed in his haversack. Of course the slaves might give him the information he needed if he offered them the meat… He went to the last group, about ready to give up.

"What's in it for me, suh?" the youth that had challenged him earlier asked.

Peter licked his bottom lip. He had never expected the insolent lad to be the answer to his prayers. "A day off."

"Dat ain't enough," the youth said. His eyes remained respectful but his challenging smile revealed his true feelings.

Peter's muscles tensed. His father's slaves always loved sugar, but he didn't have any. He opened his hand and closed it again. Civilian clothes. He had almost forgotten about John's clothes he had stuffed at the bottom of his knapsack. "If I get *all* the information I need, I will give you a brown coat. A good one."

The others in his mess gasped. The youth's eyes grew as wide as half dollars. "Deal."

"So," Peter said, dragging out the word. "Has a peddler been by here recently?"

"Yes, suh. 'Bout a week ago."

"Was this peddler short with red hair?"

"Yes."

"He have a lame hand?"

"Yes."

"Where did he head after leaving here?"

The youth presented his palm. "De coat?"

"I'll bring it to you in the morning."

The youth stood with his legs spread, back stiff. "Den I's tell yuh in de morning. Suh." He boldly thrust out his chin.

Peter folded his arms and stared at the lad, not wanting to back down too easily. That would give the wrong impression. "Fair enough. All right. Break's over. Get back to work!"

Peter clutched the brown coat as he walked to the field, hope rising with each step. This was just the first step towards taking care of the peddler. After he found him he had to… Well, he didn't want to think about that. He didn't want the blood on his hands. Perhaps there would be a way he could avoid doing the killing. Perhaps he could even convince the peddler to help him escape. Perhaps they could both get back to Union lines alive.

Peter toed the ground. He needed to stop letting his mind wander and concentrate on the task at hand. Being an overseer. He straightened, pushing his shoulders back, trying to exude as much power he could muster out of his small frame.

The slaves were waiting for him. Not working. Peter heaved a loud sigh. He could understand some of his father's frustration.

The first order of business was to find out about the peddler. The youth grinned like a fox who had just stolen a hen.

"So where was the peddler headed, boy?" Peter asked.

"He say he had family in Petersburg. Say he was goin' see him on his way to Richmond."

Peter took a step forward invading the slave's space. "Are you sure?" he asked, looking the lad over with a skeptic eye.

"Why does it mean so much to you? You can get some shoes at a shop."

"Fine," Peter said, taking a step back. "There's more to it than that. I have a score to settle with him. He wouldn't fight me on account of his hand. He just took off."

"Hmmm," the youth said. "I not be surprised if he bested yuh wid his one hand." A woman next to him elbowed him sharply in chest.

"Petersburg you say?" Peter said, his voice rising in volume.

"Yessuh."

Peter handed him the brown coat. The youth who had nothing covering his upper body except a threadbare shirt quickly put it on. "Thank yuh, suh."

Peter nodded. "Don't just stand there. Work!" Peter's voice was so loud it hurt his own ears.

The rest of the day passed in a daze. If one of the slaves had stopped working Peter didn't notice it. He had one thing on his mind: the peddler. Still, he had the presence of mind to listen to the chattering slaves. They spoke in whispers, but Peter had good ears. That night he wrote down what they had said about the Confederate Army on another small strip of paper and sewed it into the hem of his left pant leg.

Petersburg. The Mountain Boomers were marching in that direction.

CHAPTER 22

FOUR DAYS AFTER Mrs. Burton's cousin arrived Peter found himself in Petersburg. He been to the city for many years. Now that he was here, he couldn't even complete his mission let alone enjoy the sights. He was stuck in camp and there was no way he could find the peddler himself.

Suddenly it came to Peter, the peddler was a very money hungry man, perhaps he could use his greed to entice the peddler to come to him. Peter bit his lower lip. *Would it really work? If a cat offered a mouse a piece of cheese would the mouse be foolish enough to accept?* Considering the last encounter these men had with the peddler he wasn't sure if the man would take the offer or not, unfortunately it was the only play he had.

Peter counted out the Confederate bills he had in his pocket. Many men would go out of their way to make a profit. And the peddler was in the business to sell, after all. There was only one man in camp with the ability to slip through the lines and sneak into town—Big James.

Peter hadn't said a handful of words to the tall negro man. He had thought it safer that way. If he came across as too friendly it could spark suspicion. But he didn't have a choice. Big James was brushing the captain's horse, his son straddling the strawberry roan bareback.

Big James eyed Peter casually, his head slightly bowed. Peter straightened his posture and lowered his voice. "Can you deliver a message for me?"

"I doan wuk for yuh, suh," Big James replied curtly.

Peter took a deep breath. Bribery. It worked last time. "I'll give you five dollars."

Big James' expression didn't change—his suspicion and disdain palpable. "Deliver the message where?"

Peter's pulse increased. "In town. Can you walk into town?"

Big James' features hardened. "I can walk anywhere I likes, suh."

Peter swallowed, highly doubting that was the case. Still, it didn't seem that the captain kept a close eye on him.

"There's a peddler in town with red hair. His name is Rodger Phillips. Can you tell him to come back to camp? I would like to do business with him, and I'm sure the other soldiers would, too."

Big James nodded. "All right. But I want de money now."

Peter didn't want to give the money up-front. His eyes shifted from the note to Big James. Finally, he handed it over. He wasn't about to argue with a six-foot giant.

Big James' eyes gleamed. "Yuh doan trust me?"

"I don't trust my own brother," Peter muttered.

Big James lips parted and a booming laugh erupted. "I thought it was 'cause I's black."

Peter shook his head. "No. I'm just naturally wary."

"We have dat in common, suh." Big James lifted his son off the horse and onto his shoulders. "I's be back wid de peddler directly."

Peter grew more anxious with each passing minute, hour, and depressing thought. Did the colored man know the meaning of the word directly? He huffed and then realized it could be the peddler's fault that it was taking so long. Perhaps he had more important business. After all, his family supposedly lived in town. But, if the peddler had said no, then Big James would have returned without him.

Peter glanced around camp, looking for the captain. The man hadn't said a word about his missing slave. It seemed Big James was correct—he didn't need to be the least bit worried about getting in trouble. It seemed a strange master-slave relationship for these whereabouts.

In a way, Big James reminded him of Dan. He had many of the same build, mannerisms, and husky voice. Peter shook his head. It was getting late. Surely he was beginning to imagine things. Supper hadn't been much of an affair. It hadn't taken his mind off his coming confrontation with the peddler. He swallowed another sip of bitter chicory coffee.

The creak of wheels caused Peter's heart to flip. He sprang to his feet, spilling the lukewarm liquid all down his hand. Peter shook off the drops, silently cursing. The peddler drove into camp, the contents of his cart creaking and rattling.

Peter's joy was quickly chased away by thoughts of death. If he did his job, the short Irishman would soon be a corpse. Peter blinked, pushing that realization to the back of his mind. Before he could reach the cart, the peddler was surrounded by soldiers.

"Welcome!" Crawford said. "Got anything worth eating?"

The peddler chuckled and shook his head.

The peddler's eyes shifted constantly. He was clearly uncomfortable.

"I'm surprised you came back to our camp after that raw deal you tried to give us last winter!" Lewry said.

"That was just a big misunderstanding."

"Misunderstanding my fist," Johnson said, shaking his balled fist. "Ransacking a deserted town is one thing. Taking belongings from a soldier's tent is unforgiveable."

Johnson's words seemed to work the crowd into a fury.

"Hey, Rodger," Sublett called. "I haven't seen you for a while. Where have you been? Stealing from more of our comrades?"

"No. I have striven hard not to repeat that grievous error. I've been travelling. You know I can't stay in one place long."

"You better give us something good this time," Crawford said. "And at rock bottom prices. You owe us."

The peddler motioned with his good hand for the men to settle down. "Boy, boys, I am just trying to make a living here. I'd be fighting alongside you if I wasn't born with a lame hand."

"Sure you would," Lewry said, his timbre soaked with sarcasm.

Peter bit his lip, his stomach churning. If the soldiers ran the peddler out of camp he'd never get a chance to work out his deal. The deal for him to escape the Confederate Army.

"I came here to do business. Does anyone wish to buy something?"

"Got a pocketknife for sale?" Eaton's voice was hopeful. "I lost mine."

Peter lingered at a distance, waiting for the crowd to dissipate. The peddler climbed down from his cart and talked with the soldiers as if he was their best friend. A salesman. A true actor. The perfect spy.

Envy burned in Peter's cheeks. He rubbed them, willing the flush to fade. The sky darkened, swallowed his shadow, eased one of his constant fears—being recognized. Likely, in all his travels the peddler had seen one of the wanted posters with Peter's likeness.

The soldiers began saying their good nights and heading to their tents. It was time.

Here goes nothing. His hands in his pockets, Peter ambled up to the cart.

"Can I help you, sir?" the peddler asked. "A new pair of shoes, perhaps?"

"No." Peter motioned with his hand for the peddler to follow him. "I'd like to talk to you in private."

"Very well, sir," the peddler said. Despite his shorter stature he kept up with Peter stride for stride.

Once out of earshot of the rest of the company Peter stopped. "I know you're a spy."

The peddler froze his eyes wide, mouth in a small gape. "Yes," he said after a moment to recover. "I spy for the Confederacy." His fingers touched his lips. He drew a raspy breath. "Who told you?"

Peter patted him heartily on the back. "It is common knowledge around here. The whole camp knows."

The peddler sucked on his bottom lip struck speechless.

"See you're just the man I've been looking for. You can help me."

The peddler's eyes turned into flinty beads. He clearly didn't like the idea of being sought out. There was a long beat of silence before he finally spoke. "Help you how?"

"You travel freely through Confederate and Union lines. I want to get out of the damn army." Peter patted his pocket. "I can make it worth your trouble."

"That's asking for a lot a trouble. The price would be high."

"I understand." Peter's gaze darted from the peddler to see if any other soldiers were near and then returned to the peddler. "I'm desperate. I'm at your mercy."

"Exactly where do you want me to take you, sir?"

Peter dragged his fingernails down his cheeks. "I don't want to fight any more." He spoke in a small whisper, "To the Union. I want to give myself up."

"They will throw you in prison."

"At least I won't be shot at," Peter said, continuing to speak in a tiny voice.

The peddler nodded as if trying to process this offer. "Not cut out to be a soldier, huh?"

"I've already ran once. The battles … the corpses … I can't sleep at night. I'm going to lose my sanity." Peter grabbed the peddler's arm. "You have to help me."

"All right. All right. Settle down." Peter removed his hand, but his pleading eyes continued to drill the peddler.

The short man rocked back on his heels, his facial muscles tightened. "I'm not a soldier, but I know all about the horrors of war."

"Then you will help me?" Peter's voice cracked. "Please." Peter held his breath. The man held all the cards and he knew it. He didn't divulge his emotions, his thoughts. Silence smothered Peter until he gasped for air.

"You could lie down in the bed of the cart…"

"Yes."

"How much?"

"One hundred dollars in gold."

"Gold?" the peddler's voice increased in pitch.

Peter allowed himself a soft smile. Gold had much more value than Confederate currency. He pulled a small bag out of his pocket. He untying the bag and poured a few coins into his hand. "You get half now and half when I'm across Union lines."

The peddler grabbed a coin and bit it. No teeth marks.

"I'm a gentleman. I was half out of my mind with fever when they got me into this uniform," Peter said. "I just want out."

"We can leave tonight," the peddler said. "The Yanks are expecting me any day now."

"Good. Good."

Peter handed the peddler half the bag of gold coins, hoping his greed would keep his mouth shut. Peter returned to his tent to pack a few things. He shoved his pistol into the front of his belt, grabbed a section of rope, too, and stuffed it in his haversack. Molly's picture rested at the bottom along with his book by Shakespeare.

The peddler planned to stay here for the night, along with some other camp followers. So Peter wasn't in a hurry. Around midnight, he finally approached the cart. Candle glowing beside him, the peddler sat on the ground, back against one of the wheels, whittling with his good hand, the piece of wood wedged in the crook of his other arm. He motioned with his head for Peter to clamber up.

Peter's heart rate increased with each step. Once inside the bed there was no turning back. There was no way he could explain his presence if discovered.

Did he really want to do this? He scolded himself for having second thoughts. Without another second of hesitation he climbed in the back of the cart, praying that it would not be searched.

All was quiet except for the call of the sentries. The soldiers all knew the peddler so it made sense he would get a free pass—or at least a quick look over. And if they decided to do a thorough search Peter trusted that the peddler could think fast. Perhaps he carried some sort of proof that he was a spy for the Confederacy.

The peddler planned to tell the soldiers he was returning home to be with his family. Surely they'd let him through.

If Peter could get to Union lines, he would be safe and could just tell them to arrest the peddler. He wouldn't have to bloody his hands. But if that failed, he would have no choice but to kill him—strangle the peddler so it made no sound. The thought iced his blood and a frisson of dread knotted his insides like the loops in a noose.

The horse whinnied as the weight of the peddler settled into the front seat. He gave a low whistle, and the whip cracked. The cart jerked forward, jostling Peter in his hiding spot beneath tarpaulin, blankets, and dirty clothes. Hopefully it was too dark for anyone to notice.

Peter ran his thumbs over his fingernails. Nervous energy circulated through him, but he tried to remain still. It took five minutes to get past the sentries and out of the camp, and Peter didn't dare breathe easily the whole time. At any minute, he expected the blanket to be thrown off him, and his ass arrested.

Lieutenant Mullins' voice at the final stop on the way out of camp grated on his nerves so bad he clenched his teeth until he thought they'd crack. The usually uptight officer made inane conversation with the peddler for what seemed like forever. *Come on! Let's get on with it!* Peter thought strangling Mullins might be the better plan.

Finally, the cart began moving up the hill, and Peter relaxed – just a little – and stretched his cramped legs. There'd be few sentries to bother them for the next eight miles to Disputanta.

"We did it," the peddler called back. "You can take it easy now. We're on our way."

Peter allowed himself the luxury of uncovering his head and savored the cool night breeze. The stars up above twinkled merrily, unaware of the humans below and their struggles. He watched them, lulled by the gentle rocking motion of the cart, and the steady clip-clop, clip-clop of the horse's hooves.

He allowed hope to swell within him as he hid beneath the layers of various items. He closed his eyes and pictured Molly sitting beside him, with her arms embracing him. He could almost hear her sweet melodic voice telling him he would soon be home with her.

Peter wanted to have their wedding the day he stepped off the train. He didn't want to wait a minute longer for Molly Canton to become his wife. And after Springdale was no longer in existence he wouldn't be as ashamed of his last name. The evil memories, the ghosts that stalked the grounds, could finally rest.

Rest. His body yearned for rest even though he knew he should remain alert. His tense body relaxed and the lateness of the hour toyed with his eyelids. They grew heavier with each mile. He was tired, so tired of living in fear.

A gunshot jarred Peter awake. He sat bolt upright; his heart attempting to jump out of his chest. His fingers gripped tighter to the pistol he carried with him.

The peddler jerked back on the reins and the cart came to an abrupt stop. *Oh no. He's going to take the rest of the gold and turn me in for trying to desert.* Peter swallowed, praying he could talk the peddler out of this plan. There was no reason the Confederates would know that he helped him escape. Just get him to Union lines and they'd part ways. Permanently.

"Toss out your pistol," a deep voice ordered.

Peter looked at his piece, determined not to give it up. If things were going to come to blows right here, he was ready for a fight. He couldn't go back to the Confederate Army.

"Don't do anything hasty," the peddler said. There was a thud and Peter realized that the peddler had tossed his pistol on the ground. "I have a family. Don't kill me, please." The peddler's voice was strained as if he was holding back tears. "I have two little girls and a son that is only a few months old. They need me. They need me bad. They won't get along without me. I just bring in enough money to put food in their mouths as it is."

"Quit your babbling!"

Peter pressed his lips together. A tense silence followed.

"Step on down," the deep voice ordered.

"Are you going to search the cart?" the peddler asked, his voice loud enough to alert Peter.

"We're searching the cart for anything useful." Another voice laughed. Peter's breathing quickened. There were at least two of them.

"Money. We're after money," another male voice said.

"Shut up!" the first man told his partner.

Peter licked his lips. He lay back down in the cart and slowly pulled the blankets over his head. He was ready.

"I don't have much money with me," the peddler said in a remarkably calm voice. "I didn't make many sales today. I spent most of the day with my wife."

"You better make it worth our while. Got any guns with you besides this pistol?"

"N-no, sir. Just a couple pocketknives. You're welcome to them."

"Search the cart," the man with the deep voice ordered.

Peter held his breath. He sensed the man's body drawing closer and every breath grew increasingly louder. The tarpaulin covering him began to crinkle.

Peter's gut clenched. He squeezed the trigger. The bullet tore through the blankets and a man screamed. The horse whinnied furiously.

There was another gunshot. And then the sound of horses galloping away and a man cursing. Peter didn't move for several minutes, frozen by the fact he had at least wounded one of the highwaymen. At close range it must have left a gruesome hole.

The sound of a man moaning finally compelled Peter to peel back the layers covering him and investigate.

The peddler lay next to the cart, a hand holding on to a spoke of one of the wheels. His shirt was soaked with blood.

Without a second thought, Peter rushed to his side. "Rodger," he said. "How can I help you?"

The man's eyes rolled around like he was trying hard to focus. He spoke in raspy breaths. "They did me in. But you got one of them."

"Don't talk like that." He needed the peddler alive if he was going to talk his way through to Union lines. "I can get some of the blankets and try to get the bleeding to stop."

The peddler shook his head. "No. No use. Tell my wife and children I love them."

"I will."

Peter's throat constricted. It brought a sliver of relief that he didn't have to be the cause of his demise. If the peddler had started talking about his family, he doubted he would have been able to carry through with killing him.

The peddler pulled the sack of gold coins out of his jacket pocket. "They weren't the smartest pair. Went to search the cart before searching me." He offered a slight smile and then coughed up some blood. "Take the cart and continue on your way. But, get this to my wife Amanda. Amanda Phillips. This is all I have to leave her besides our shack."

Peter took the gold. "I promise." He felt the man's cheek. His skin was growing cold and he was still breathing. It twisted his insides.

"Put me out of my misery," the peddler pleaded in a thin voice. "The pain. I can't stand the pain."

Peter swallowed the uneasiness crawling up his throat. It was his duty to see him dead in more ways than one.

"Please," the peddler begged, tears spilling onto his cheeks.

Peter pulled the pistol out of his belt, pointed it at the man's heart. His fingers felt clammy and a tremor made his wrist shake. He held his breath to steady his aim and pulled the trigger.

The peddler closed his eyes and his head dropped to the left. Peter stared at the man's body. What had he just done? He had murdered the man. Blood oozed from the peddler's chest. Peter looked away and fought the wave of nausea rolling up his throat. "God, forgive me," he mumbled.

The peddler was a Confederate spy. Why then did he feel so rotten? His chest burned knowing the irony of his actions. Someone could be sent to kill him, too.

What was he going to do with the body? He couldn't just leave him here. But, it wasn't safe for Peter to stay on this road. He doubted he could talk his way through the rest of the sentries to make it to Union lines.

Damn. He had completed his assignment and ended his chance of escape at the same time. He sighed, his head suddenly heavy. Pain throbbed behind both of his eyes.

His best option was turning back. Of course slipping back into camp without being noticed was going to be an issue. If he had to be a Confederate soldier he didn't need to be known as a deserter. He was already known as a coward. That was bad enough.

Peter dragged the peddler's body up into the cart and then climbed into the seat and turned the cart around. His spirit sunk. He desperately wanted to head in the other direction. When he got close enough to hear the calls of the Confederate sentries he stopped. He placed the peddler in the driver's seat. The peddler slumped down. Peter used the rope he had brought with him to tie the peddler's hands to the reins—it was a miracle the horses hadn't spooked and ran away with the cart.

Peter climbed down and slapped the horse hard with the reins. The horse neighed and took off at a gallop. The cart raced towards the sentries. A guard ordered the cart to stop. It didn't. The order was given again and then a shot rang out.

Peter waited for the chaos to begin and then he started walking towards camp, hoping that the distraction would be enough for him to slip through unnoticed. He carried the full sack of gold in his coat pocket. He would pass the gold on to Mr. Phillips' widow if he could. The man was honestly going to get him to Union lines.

"You shot the peddler," a man said.

"He was charging at me. I didn't have a choice."

The guards kept talking and Peter kept walking.

"Hey, where are you going?" One of the sentries stopped Peter.

Peter stood still. His eyes darted from the peddler to the sentry. "I heard men yelling. I came to see what it was all about."

"All right. You've seen the corpse. You better get back to your tent."

"I'm going. I'm going."

"Sergeant of the guard!" one of the sentries shouted.

Peter took off running. He didn't want to be anywhere near when Sergeant Fry showed up. If Fry took one look at him and found the gold, he'd probably think he had stolen it off the peddler. Fry's opinion of his was equal to a spider. Fry yearned to squash him under his brogan.

Peter's chest burned by the time he collapsed inside his tent. He had made it back. Safely.

Back in the Confederate ranks. It had all been for nothing. A numbness spread through his body and his stomach felt hollow.

But it wasn't for nothing. The peddler was dead.

The Confederate spy could no longer pass information that could lose them artillery, kill Union soldiers, cost them battles. And while Peter was still breathing, he wasn't going to give up getting back to Union lines.

CHAPTER 23

PETER SAT AROUND the campfire smoking his pipe. Stretching his legs out and straitened his back as he tried to relax. The melodious song of a lark helped put him put him at ease. He puffed the tobacco and slowly worked the tension out of his shoulders. Peter finally felt like he had done something productive.

All his time spent in a Confederate uniform wasn't wasted. The peddler was taking a long dirt nap and couldn't spy for the South any more. Yet, Peter couldn't stop thinking of the peddler's last wish that his wife be cared for with his earnings.

The irony of that thought tangled Peter's stomach. A cold glass of milk and honey would be heavenly. He took his pipe out of his mouth and studied the smooth, polished wood. All he had was tobacco and the soothing properties of a smoke had deteriorated over the past months. Still, it was better than nothing.

He ran his fingers through the blades of grass at his side. It was a sunny day, the larks singing. It would have been the perfect day to take Molly on a picnic. Perhaps some day after this war Peter could show Molly around Virginia.

The drummer boy approached him. The lad, perhaps thirteen years of age, had the cleanest uniform in camp.

Peter tipped his head back to look into the boy's dark eyes. "Yes?"

"I was wondering if you had more of that tobacco."

Peter laughed softly.

The boy's face flushed. His eyes narrowed, a bright glint threatening to spark his reddish-brown hair. "I'm serious. I want to try a puff. My pa says that rich folks like you are smoking before you start wearing men's clothing."

Peter shook his head. "That isn't exactly true, but I'll let you have a taste." He patted the ground beside him.

The boy sat, cross-legged.

Peter handed him the pipe. "Don't inhale too deeply."

The boy took a puff and started coughing, his face scrunched. "That's awful. Why do men like that?"

Peter couldn't help but roar with laughter. His stomach started to ache. Dan's father had given him and Dan their first taste. He had been a lot younger than the drummer boy but had the same reaction.

"It takes some getting used to," Peter said. "Not all men smoke or chew tobacco. Some find it relaxing, as I do. Others just smoke because it is a sign of wealth."

The boy unscrewed his canteen and took a long drink. "I hope I can get the taste out of my mouth."

Peter slapped him on the back. "You still have some growing up to do."

The boy gave him a funny look. "I might not be very tall, but I'm a man. I saw my brother killed." The boy tensed, sorrow clouding his eyes. He poked a finger through a hole in his coat. "I nearly got shot, too."

Peter massaged his forehead, willing the twinge of a headache to disappear. He didn't know what to say.

That boy should still be in school. He should be swimming or fishing with his friends.

"Did you hear the news?" the drummer boy asked.

Peter tilted his head to the side. "News?"

"About the upcoming battle. I overheard Cap'n talking with some other officers."

"When is this next battle going to be?"

The drummer boy shrugged. "I'm sure we'll be ordered to march and head into another den of fire. It won't be long before everyone knows. I told you first."

Peter couldn't believe the boy had delivered news of another battle so casually. He must be numbed by what he had already seen. Too bad he couldn't have been numbed, too. Everything he had seen tortured him as much as his present misery.

The drummer boy stood and brushed the dirt off his butt. "Thanks, Burnett. You're not as bad as the men say."

☆ ☆ ☆

Peter stood and arched his back. These last few days in camp had passed as slow as molasses in a February freeze. Each day he endured the same rants and promises, the same threats and prayers, the same curses and headaches. With another battle brewing, the rebels were full of vigor, energized by morbid anticipation.

They had one thing on their mind—killing Yankees.

Their talk grated on Peter; left a festering wound in his soul. Was staying with the Virginia infantry what he needed to do to keep alive? Was it the best way for him to serve in the Union Army?

He had an equal risk of being buried six feet under for being a spy as he did taking that secret to his grave. The Union Army had benefited from him killing the peddler, but what more was there to do?

A spy needed the ability to move freely, and as a Confederate private he was not given that liberty. The Union Army needed him back in their ranks, needed his rifle and bayonet when charging the field, needed his knowledge of the South for further spying missions.

He had to find a way to escape. This charade had lasted long enough. Too long and for too little gain.

"You ready for the battle, Jeff?" Sublett asked.

"Of course. We've been out of the fighting long enough," Peter said; the confidence in his voice eased the tension in his chest. He stomped on a spider and ground it into the dirt with his heel.

Surprise flickered in Sublett's eyes.

"You didn't expect me to be eager for a battle, did you?"

"Truthfully I didn't know what to expect. You want to be honored for being a brave soldier, don't you?"

"Yes. Yes I do. I do not want to bring disgrace to my family."

Sublett grunted. "The code of gentlemen."

"It should be a code for everyone." Peter cocked his head to the side. "After all you've been through with your regiment you're still talking about honor and glory?"

Sublett shrugged strong and pronounced. "I know." He kicked a rock. "I don't feel or believe everything I say. I just don't want men saying things behind my back like they've been saying about you."

Peter took a step towards Sublett, invading his space. He spoke in a gravelly timbre. "What are they saying about me?"

Sublett's Adam's apple bobbed and he shifted up on the balls of his feet. "You know."

"No. I don't know. Tell me."

Sublett licked his lips. He glanced at Peter and then down at the ground.

"You've let this much slip," Peter said. "Out with the rest."

"They're saying you're a worthless coward."

Peter's insides untangled a couple strands and breathiness softened his voice. "That's all they're saying?"

Sublett shook his head. "Well, the newest joke is that you don't have the guts to be shot at even once," he mumbled. "That you would run away from a duel even if someone disgraced your sister."

Peter's face heated. He felt like a firecracker had been lit in his gut. But he couldn't let the fuse burn down. He wanted to curse; but gentlemen didn't talk like that. He took several deep breaths and the anger dissipated.

The corners of Peter's lips twitched downward, and with as much effort as it took to lug a saddle he pulled them up. "I will just have to prove them wrong," he said, then strode quickly to his tent.

He ground his teeth until his gums and jaw ached. The discomfort did not alleviate the hotness of his blood. He touched his forehead. No fever.

~ 249 ~

How dare he forget the true nature of the gray vipers! They were bloodthirsty brutes. A twinge of regret nagged him, persistent, pulsing, painful. By generalizing he was putting his brother-in-law and Mr. Scott in that category.

Still, he couldn't forget the slaves that had died at their hands too—from lack of proper nutrition and clothing. In their own way, in the guise of civilized gentlemen, greed made them bloodthirsty, too.

He'd have to risk the gray viper's venom if he was ever going to get out of its den.

Timing was everything.

And nothing seemed to have gone in his favor since he donned this stinking gray uniform.

Even he had to catch a break at some point.

Peter had to escape before the regiment was ordered to prepare for the coming battle. Right now the battle was just talk. Perhaps they were just rumors, but he didn't want to chance that.

Peter continued to keep his eyes open for a heavenly sign. It came weeks later while they were camped near Suffolk. Three soldiers from Company D deserted to the enemy. They had not been the first ones. There were numerous reports of soldiers deserting.

Peter's stomach flipped and his heart fluttered. Hope eased the heaviness that resided in his chest. *If they could escape to Union lines, I can, too.* He just had to wait for the right opportunity—his turn as picket.

That night he kept checking his watch, waiting for his turn to stand guard. Five minutes went by, then another three. He glanced around, hoping the other men didn't notice his nervousness. Finally, when it was nearly time to relieve his fellow soldier, he set off.

Peter walked down the road towards the Union garrison. He was making sluggish progress. Although his heart shouted for him to run, his head feared the noise would spark alarm. Instead, he resigned himself to tiptoeing in the shadows and timing his escape to avoid the other sentries.

Hopefully, by morning he would be close enough to the fort that a Union soldier would find him. He could walk faster once he had passed all the pickets. He wiped his sweaty palms on the sides of his pants. There was no way to get the permanent lump out of his throat. He wasn't going to have a second chance at this.

"Who goes there?" the sentry said, his voice wary.

Peter froze and replied, "Relief."

"Halt, relief." In the shadows all Peter could see were the green eyes of the dark-complexioned, dark-haired man. "Aren't you a might early?" The sentry yawned.

"I'm just following orders. If I am early, you should be grateful. You look like you're about to fall asleep."

The man yawned again. "I'm awful peaked and have been battling chills for the last hour. I'm not going to argue with you."

Peter took over the man's post, thankful he was ill. Peter remained there for only a few minutes before moving on. He prayed that the grand rounds would not come in the meantime.

He glanced up at the bright moon and cursed it under his breath. The beams shone through the leaves of the live oak trees and illuminated the ground. Why couldn't the sky be overcast? Peter continued his exit from camp at a swift pace, the sound of every step like a herd of mustangs, every breath he took like a rattling train. The distance between him and Union lines seemed painfully long. His right foot crunched some twigs. The crackling noise seemed deafening.

"Come back, Burnett, or I'll shoot!" Sergeant Fry's voice stilled Peter's feet and struck him in the stomach like a horse's hoof.

Peter's pulse raged pumping dread, anxiety, and fear to every muscle. Struggling to breathe, struggling to think, struggling to form words, he forced his legs to move. With mechanical steps, Peter turned around to face Fry. The sergeant's beady wolfish eyes were dead set on Peter. The chambers of Peter's heart iced shut.

"You're coming with me," Fry said, in a no-nonsense tone. He motioned with his musket for Peter to start walking.

"What's wrong? I heard a noise and was going to investigate."

Fry humphed. "You know you need to call for a relief before you leave your post."

"Yes, Sergeant. I wasn't thinking."

"Sure, I think you were 'not thinking' on purpose. I ain't falling for that trick. I've never trusted you. I've been waiting for you to desert."

Peter did as ordered, not wanting to test the sergeant's sincerity. A tiny sliver of hope kept Peter's tears at bay. *Desertion wasn't as dire a charge as spying—hopefully.*

Without any introduction, Sergeant Fry pushed Peter through the flap into Captain Bane's tent.

Bane visibly tensed, the lines in his forehead deepening. "What is the meaning of this?"

Peter's chest tightened and tightened and tightened, squeezing the last bit of air out of his lungs. He wanted to run, but Sergeant Fry stood behind him, blocking the exit. Sergeant Snidow had been the cause of his recent humiliation; now he imagined that Fry would be the cause of his death.

Big James sat quietly in the corner polishing the captain's rifle with ash paste. His head was cocked, an ear towards the soldiers, proving he was interested in the conversation. Peter touched the back of his neck. *Great. An audience for my downfall.*

Peter didn't let the sergeant state his crime. He did it for him. "Sergeant Fry has it in for me. I left my post, but I heard a noise. I went chasing after a shadow. A Yank could have been trying to get into camp."

"Did you see anyone, Sergeant?" asked the captain.

"No, sir."

"And this 'Yank' was by himself?"

"Yes, Captain. Or the darkness could have been playing with my eyes."

The officer grunted.

"I don't believe him," Fry said. "He was deserting. To the enemy."

"All right. All right. I was trying to desert. I am not cut out to be a solider. But I was *not* deserting to the enemy," Peter corrected. "I'm just trying to get away from here and I can't do that by running towards the rest of Longstreet's army."

"He was going towards Suffolk. That's an easy way to get noticed by the Yanks."

Despite his inner turmoil he forced his speech to be clear and calm. "I've been in one battle, and I'd like to keep it that way. Running from danger is man's way of preserving himself. Winding up in a Yankee prison isn't self-preservation; they are rat infested, disease pits. I'd have a better chance living here."

"Knowing your character and your record, I'm inclined to believe you," Bane said.

Peter's voice quavered. "I expect I'm going to get that branding iron now."

A smug glint lurked in the captain's eye. He spoke with self-satisfied fervor. "But the question is what to give you, a D for deserter or a C for coward? Maybe I should give you both."

"I know I can't talk my way out of it twice, sir. You could drum me out of the service."

Bane laughed at that suggestion. "That would make you the happiest man in the world!" he exclaimed in a booming voice. "And I am not going to satisfy you!"

Peter held his breath.

"I swear Captain, he was deserting to the enemy," Fry insisted. "I don't trust him, sir."

"All right. You're dismissed, Sergeant."

Fry saluted, drilled Peter with a hard smile, and left.

Captain Bane gave Peter a glare so cold it sent shivers racing to Peter's core. "If you have anything to hide, I'm going to find it."

"I don't have any secrets, sir," Peter said. To his surprise his voice didn't crack and lightning didn't strike him down. "I was just trying to desert. Look if you wish."

"Take off your coat and blouse, Burnett," Bane ordered.

Peter did as he was told. Bane emptied his pockets. The captain found the tintype Molly had given him, his pocket watch, and the sack of gold. Bane opened the sack, took out some coins and played with them in the palm of his hand.

"Please sir, I'd like to have that picture back."

Bane handed back the tintype, put the coins back in the bag, and began patting Peter's blouse.

"Sergeant Fry has it in for me. Do you think I'm a spy, sir?"

"No. I'm just making sure you're not. There's a difference. Take off your shoes."

They were empty. Peter shed his pants and now stood in his underwear. Once again, the captain went through his pockets finding nothing but tobacco and Peter's pipe.

"That's good stuff, home grown," Peter said.

Bane glanced up but did not say anything. He had taken out his pocketknife and was carefully cutting the blouse into strips.

"Men are wearing tattered clothes as it is and you're destroying my uniform. I cannot fight the Yanks looking like this, sir."

"After men die, they no longer need their uniform," Bane explained. "Big James walk over to the commissariat and bring back another uniform."

"Yessuh," Big James said. The tall man bent over and walked out of the tent.

When Big James returned a few minutes later, Peter quickly clothed himself. "For not suspecting anything you are conducting a very thorough search."

"It's nothing against you, Mr. Burnett. It's probably my own paranoia. But you have to see this from my side. If you were a spy and I missed it, I'd have an awful lot of blood on my hands."

"I understand, sir."

Peter's blouse did not display any secrets. However, nervous energy coursed through his body when Bane proceeded to his pants. Peter held his breath as the captain began cutting on them.

"I'm satisfied now," Bane finally said.

Peter breathed a lengthy sigh. His secret was safe for now. Gradually his pulse slowed. God had given him a second chance. Or actually a third chance.

Though, he still had to face the branding iron. His old wound in his arm burned reminding him of the pain ahead. He gritted his teeth to remain stoic.

"Wait a minute," the captain said, running his fingers over the hem of the left pant leg.

Peter's heart stalled. He coughed and it started again. A sense of doom dug deep into his lungs and wound its way into his intestines. He sucked in a raspy breath. The left hem was stiffer than the right one. *Damn. Where else could I have put the information?* It was too late now.

Time crept by painfully slow. The captain cut each stitch of the left pant leg. He pulled down the fabric revealing a strip of white. Unraveling the fabric more, he freed small pieces of paper from their hiding place.

Peter closed his eyes and Bane unfolded the papers. The crinkling noise sounded as loud as the roar of cannon. Peter winced and jerked backward as if to avoid the lead shower. The papers containing all his ongoing observations.

Instantly he forced himself to think of something positive, something to take off the edge. Peter drank in Molly's image, her arms embracing him, gentle fingers running through his hair. She made him feel safe, happy, strong. He wanted to bask in this reverie forever, but the slap of a hand hitting a desk snapped him back to reality. It was time to accept his fate.

The captain's eyes lit up, burning with an intense blackness.

Was it from pleasure or hatred? The air in the room felt thick and sticky. This was Peter's moment. He had to die valiantly, be a credit to the Union Army. At least that was what his head commanded him to do. His heart, however...

"I have to admit, you almost had me fooled, Yank!" The officer's brown eyes narrowed. "Who's in command of your regiment?" he demanded, a prominent vein on his neck bulging.

Peter's gut lurched. But he had been born with the deck stacked against him, and Dan had taught him to hide his fear. The Confederates had no idea of his inner strength. He wouldn't break.

"Who's in command of your regiment?" the captain repeated.

"Abraham Lincoln, the president of the United States," Peter replied, his chin jutted out.

Bane looked disgusted. "I mean, who's the general at your head?"

"Hooker."

"You know that wasn't who I was after. I know you're with the Army of the Potomac. Better yet, who's in charge of your company? What company and regiment are you from?"

"Why should I answer any of your questions? You think I don't know what happens to spies?"

Bane put his hand over his eyes. "What's the strength of your army?"

"I don't know, sir. I haven't had time to count." A smile slipped onto his lips. His cockiness would have made his father proud.

"You are beginning to anger me," the captain shouted.

"At least that will bring me some final satisfaction."

"I haven't even asked for anything important yet. I was working up to that," Bane growled.

"The importance of your questions is a matter of opinion," Peter said. "There's no point in giving you any answers. You're going to kill me anyway."

"Those are some pretty strong words for someone in your situation."

"You'll soon learn that I am a very strong man."

Bane laughed. "I'd like to see that! You've been nothing but a coward up to this point. If you don't want to talk now, maybe you will later. John!"

Peter shifted on the stool. Who was John?

"What do you want, Robert?" Lieutenant Mullins asked, sticking his head into the tent. A twinge of fear went through Peter like a sharp knife.

"This one is all yours," Bane roared. "For five months this spy's made a fool of us! Now he's too stubborn to talk."

Lieutenant Mullins offered a sympathetic frown, his eyes heavy. He said in a soft voice, "Is he now?"

Peter met his apparent mild-manneredness with a cold, defiant glare. His glare in turn was rewarded by having a pistol waved in his face. Peter's saliva dried up and he felt like his tongue was made of sand and it was impossible to swallow.

"It is a shame Mr. Burnett that you have forgotten how to be a soldier," the lieutenant said in a gentle rebuke. "You were making such progress, too."

Peter's blood chilled. He was used to people yelling at him. Yelling he could understand. Yelling was usually followed by ordinary pain. But the Lieutenant's voice promised something else. Something worse.

Peter had made up his mind. Mullins could yell all he wanted but he was not going to move. The officer got the message. Though he was stocky, he had plenty of muscle. He firmly gripped Peter's arms, picked him up as easily as if he were a sack of flour, and dragged him outside.

Peter's pulse pounded loud and violent. *If I survive this I will make amends with my sister, I will find a way to be in my niece's life.* A rock stared up at him, beckoning to him. Maybe he could grab it and … It was no use. Mullins was too strong. Even if he did break free and strike the lieutenant in the head, one of the other soldiers who had gathered outside would shoot him down.

Two large hands stripped Peter to the waist and pushed him onto his stomach. Bent over a large boulder, the rock jabbed his middle like a punch to the gut.

Lewry stood near Peter, pointing a pistol at his head. He pressed the end of the cold barrel to his neck.

Peter breathed short, rapid breaths. The rush of oxygen diluted the fear in his veins. A strange feeling seeped into his chest, leaving his insides tattered and tingly and numb.

The sting of a horsewhip jolted him. His eyes tightened, teeth gritted, muscles tense. He wasn't going to give the rebels satisfaction from hearing him cry out in pain.

Mullins seemed equally determined to make a Yankee squeal.

"Whip him harder," or "give him a stripe for me," men shouted. Hearing they were out for his blood, the chambers of Peter's heart clamped shut.

Mullins stopped. "Are you willing to cooperate now?" he asked. He sounded as if he had gravel stuck in his throat.

Peter exhaled deeply. He licked his suddenly parched lips, putting off answering for as long as possible. He didn't need any more pain. His whole life had been filled with pain. *Just shoot me and get it over with.*

And yet, he wasn't ready to die.

Death meant a cold body, an agonizing separation from Molly…

In a strong, raspy voice Peter said, "No."

His refusal earned him another taunting snap.

He bit his tongue and tasted blood in his mouth, reminding him of the blood trickling down his back. Tears escaped his tightly closed eyes, but he remained silent.

Hoof beats approached at a steady pace. Peter held his breath. It increased his wave of dizziness, his heart pounding with the force of a spike hammer. He couldn't continue the bravado much longer. He couldn't hold back screams. He couldn't keep from caving, turning into a blubbering fool. Tears burned the back of his eyes.

The hoof beats stopped. Peter felt the mounted man watching him, smelled the equine's sweat. Peter prayed it would be help—at least a Confederate with some decency, some humanity.

"I order this stopped!" The man's bellowing voice silenced the crowd.

Peter wanted to see who it was but the pistol pointed at him made him lie still.

"Who is responsible for this brutality?"

CHAPTER 24

THE VICE GRIPPING Peter's lungs loosened and he took slow, deep breaths. His pulse decreased until it pounded a normal rhythm.

The horsewhip fell to the ground.

"I took it upon myself, sir. He is—"

"Lieutenant," the man interjected sharply, "I don't care who the man is or what he has done. Your actions are not justified."

"Yes, sir."

"This is disgraceful to the army and to the whole Confederacy. You're a regular solider not a guerrilla. There are standards."

"Yes, sir."

"I'd like a tent where I can have some privacy."

"You can have my tent, sir," Mullins offered, his voice soft. "It's the least I can do."

"Fine. I'd like to talk to your prisoner," the man said, riding off.

"On your feet," Lewry ordered, continuing to threaten him with his pistol.

Peter reached over and picked up his hat. It took immense energy to stand up. His legs wobbled and for a moment he thought he'd collapse. *That officer's voice sounded vaguely familiar.* Peter rubbed his forehead. His mind was hazy and his head ached.

"Your torture might have ended," Mullins said, "but your fate will be the same."

"I figured that."

Peter slowly walked the street, a guard on either side of him. He couldn't believe they were worried he'd try to escape. It was all he could do to walk. Drops of blood continued to ooze out of his gashed flesh.

They stopped in front of the tent. "Enter," one of the guards ordered. Peter nervously pushed the tent flap up and went inside.

"Peter," Colonel Scott gasped, rising from the desk. He rushed over the campstool for him to sit on.

"I think this is what I have to call a bad day, sir," Peter said.

"Why in the world are you wearing a Confederate uniform?"

Peter's guts tangled into a string of knots, but he kept his face passive. "Abigail convinced me to switch sides."

Scott's brown eyes turned grave. "As much as I want to believe that, I don't. You're a spy, aren't you?"

The word, thrown back at him, felt like an anvil. He squeaked out, "*Was* a spy is more like it."

"Do they know who you are?"

Peter's eyes weighted with the threat of tears. He looked down at his lap, his hands clasped. "Is my father still alive?"

"Yes." Scott's Adam's apple bobbed and his voice changed to a whisper. "But who knows for how much longer."

Peter took a deep breath but it failed to ease his tightened chest. He raised his head but did not meet Scott's gaze. "Then I've done the right thing. I don't want this to tarnish my father's reputation. They know me as Jeff Burnett and I'd like to keep it that way."

Scott's eyes narrowed but were more contemplative than threatening. "You need to tell them who you are."

Scott's scolding tone made Peter cringe. The hollow feeling in his stomach grew. "Abigail told me I've disgraced my family and you've implied it. I will not disgrace them further."

"Your father has influence with Jefferson Davis, it might save—"

"I'm not hiding behind my name," Peter blurted. "Sure, everyone knows me. I'm the foolish son of one of the wealthiest gentlemen in Virginia who ran north and became an abolitionist. If my father's mind was corrupted with illness he'd give the captain a reward for killing me."

"So you want to hang?"

Peter's heart turned numb. "The rules of war are very clear."

Scott's voice hit tenor range. "You're crazy!"

Peter shook his head and it took great energy, his head felt as heavy as a bag of sand. "That's a matter of opinion, Colonel."

Peter didn't reply, his shoulders slumped. Colonel Scott stroked his golden mustache. "Why'd you become a spy?"

"My general ordered me to."

"Why'd you accept?"

"I wasn't asked; I was ordered."

"You could have found a way to back out."

Peter squirmed in his seat, his ears burning. He bowed his head. "No ... I was ... well, pressed into it."

"I don't want to see you hang. It might not make any difference but if you don't tell them your real name I will."

"Colonel!" Peter protested, fear edging his voice.

"You know I'll do it," Scott replied, his tone stern.

Scott's normally carefree nature had disappeared. From experience Peter easily read his friend's eyes; he was not giving an idle threat. Scott was forcing this revelation.

"I'll tell them," Peter said reluctantly, a heaviness settling on his chest. "But I want to write a letter first."

Colonel Scott took out a pen, piece of paper, and envelope from the traveling desk. Peter propped his check on his fist and stared at them. What was he going to write? He had to choose his words carefully, knowing it would be the last they'd hear from him. Molly would read the letter over and over again.

His eyelids pinched shut. The image of Molly gripping the letter in trembling hands, made his breath hitch, warm tears wetted his lashes. Molly crumpling to the floor of the post office, sobbing. Dan standing behind her, helping her to her feet, taking the letter from her hands. His brother supporting Molly back to the carriage and driving her back to the empty house.

Peter finally willed his hand to stop shaking and picked up the pen.

Suffolk, VA.
April 20, 1863.
My Dear, Sweet Molly,
Do not be saddened by this letter, but let it give you strength to carry on. I am writing you to say a loving farewell. This war brings consequences and causalities and tomorrow morning I will become one. I took an oath offering my services to the Union wherever needed. As you know, they appointed me a spy, which carries the penalty of death if discovered. Today, I was discovered.

My name has not been dishonored. I will be faithful to the Union to the very end. The United States of America has my heart and hand, as do you. You must keep your strength, faith, and courage. Molly, know that when the end comes you will be on my mind. Know that I will always love you, and as happy as I will be in heaven, my soul will not be content till we are together again.

Please marry. I want you to be happy. I also implore you to watch over Dan, Belle, and Rebecca. Once I'm gone, you are the only family they have there. My heart is heavy tonight, but it will be light once more tomorrow morning. I must bid you farewell. The light is so dim I can no longer write. Think of me as the years pass. The time I have spent with you has made me the happiest man on earth.

Your loving beau,
Forever and always,
Peter Joshua Warren

Peter handed the letter to Scott, the chambers of his heart clamped shut, a heavy sorrow settling in his stomach. *This will be the last thing I will touch that Molly will touch. This is our last connection.* "Please mail this to Molly. Here is her address."

Scott neatly folded the letter and tucked it into his inner coat pocket. "I will. I promise."

Peter stood and snapped to attention.

Colonel Scott stood and returned the salute.

Peter extended his hand.

The colonel shook it then pulled him closer and gave him a manly hug.

"It's a good thing no one's watching. I wouldn't want them to think I was a Yankee lover," Scott said, smiling. "I saw you the day you were born. If this is the last time we talk to each other, I want you to know I'm proud of you, Yankee and all."

"Thank you," Peter said, grimacing.

Scott removed his hand. "Peter, I'm sorry. I completely forgot about your back, and here I am touching your cuts."

"It was worth the pain to hear those words. I've been waiting my whole life for father to say them, but he never will, at least not knowing that I'm a Yankee."

"Your father is a stubborn man."

"That he is. If you don't mind me asking, what are you doing here? Stuart's cavalry isn't in Fredericksburg."

"I've been ill. Recovering at home is better than in the hospital."

There was a long moment of silence. Colonel Scott put on his hat. "Let's go," he said finally.

Peter didn't move. "I don't plan on making a run for it, but you better at least be holding your pistol."

"I never thought of that," Scott said. "This is a damn painful war. It makes a man threaten his friend with a gun. You know, if this doesn't end well, I won't wait around to watch."

"I didn't figure you would."

They stepped outside. Colonel Scott looked at the two guards who had been waiting, and then up at Captain Bane, who was approaching.

"I was coming to see if you needed anything, Colonel," Bane said.

"I'm fine, Captain. There's something the prisoner wants to tell you." Peter didn't say anything. "What do you want to tell him, Yankee?" Scott prodded.

"My real name is Peter Joshua Warren, sir."

The captain's mouth dropped open.

Peter held his breath. He could have said he was Abraham Lincoln and gotten the same reaction.

"I see you've heard about the Warren family, Captain," Scott said.

"One can't be in Virginia long without hearing of them. But he has to be lying!"

"Afraid not," Scott said.

"My father has a mole, by his nose on the left side," Peter said. "He was a major in the Mexican-American War where his right foot was crippled by shrapnel. He married my mother Hannah Marie Browning on June 20, 1830. They moved into Springdale two years later. My mother had two miscarriages before she had my sister Abigail May who was born August 25, 1836. My brother Frank was born a year later but he died at two. My mother died giving birth to me on Sept. 3, 1841."

Bane raised his hand for Peter to stop. Peter clamped his mouth shut, his pulse rushing in his ears. He eyed the captain for a reaction.

"I don't believe it," Bane shouted. "I heard what you said and I still don't believe it."

"I'm Peter Warren, sir, as much as I wish I wasn't."

"How'd you find out, Colonel?"

"I pried it out of him. He's ashamed of being a Warren."

Peter's cheeks turned boiling hot. He stared at his feet. There was truth to what Scott said. His pulse skidded faster. Maybe the poor farmers would cancel the hanging and choose to decorate him with feathers.

"When's the last time you talked to your father?" Bane asked.

Peter shifted his weight. How should he answer the question? After all, his father had been ill that last time they met and had not realized who he was. "I ran away at eighteen. So that would be over two years ago." His voice stretched so thin, the words tugged on his vocal chords.

"Any letters?"

"None, Captain."

"So it's true he's disowned you?"

Peter's heartbeat halted. He felt the blood draining from his face and the strength draining from his muscles. "Yes."

"Well, that takes care of that. His father won't interfere."

Peter closed his eyes. He had gotten his hopes up only to have them dashed. He clawed his palms to stop shaking.

The captain paused, his gaze sliding to his superior. "Unless you'd recommend stopping it, Colonel."

Peter inhaled; the cold air pricked his lungs. He looked at Scott with a silent plea.

"Why would I?" Scott said. "Hanging a Warren will make the papers. If anyone's head rolls for this, it will be yours."

"I know," Bane said. "But it's my duty to the Confederacy to proceed."

"Very well." Scott shrugged with such indifference, Peter's chest knotted and his gut clenched. Damnit. Scott hadn't made any promises, but he still felt betrayed.

Peter looked at his guards who had their rifles trained on him. Scott had said he didn't want him to hang, but he'd had the opportunity to stop it and passed it up. Peter wanted to scream his speech had all been bravado. He needed a way out; he needed freedom.

Or the freedom to die as an unknown person.

If he had to be a Warren, he'd rather live with the disgrace.

Without another word, Scott mounted his horse and kicked him in the ribs. He'd turned ghostly pale, perhaps feeling remorse over leaving Peter to die.

Peter ground his teeth together. He'd better feel remorse. But Peter held back curses. Despite their friendship, Scott couldn't think of anything but himself, couldn't offer to help him, couldn't bend to save an abolitionist's life.

Twenty-five yards away Scott reined his horse to a stop and looked back. "Yankee," he called back, with a slight nod.

"Colonel," Peter replied, his voice flat and unfeeling.

Scott looked at Peter, but he did not betray any emotion. Shadows from the tree branches masked his face. Peter had a fuzzy feeling in his chest. Scott likely stopped behind the oak tree on purpose. Knowing his friend tears likely swam in his eyes.

Peter sucked in his breath, his skin tightened, body stiff.

"I should continue riding through, Captain. By the way, there's a $5,000 reward for Mr. Warren's capture. You can collect if you deliver him to jail," Scott said and galloped off.

Peter watched his friend disappear into the darkness. When he was out of sight he strained to hear hoof beats.

Captain Bane put a hand on Peter's shoulder bringing him out of his daze. "I could tell by the look that passed between you and the colonel that you two know each other."

"Colonel Scott is my father's neighbor."

"Your neighbor," Bane said, his shock palpable.

Peter nodded. "He knows my whole life story."

Bane slowly strung his words together. "You really have that price on your head?"

Peter stiffened, his chest tight. He squeezed his voice out in a normal tone. "Yes. My father would pay you, sir, if you delivered me alive. I was involved in the Underground Railroad."

Bane stared up at the sky long and hard as if searching for an answer. "It's late. We're breaking camp and getting an early start tomorrow. We'll hang in the morning."

"Thank you," Peter said, his voice an airy whisper.

"What are you thanking me for?"

"For ignoring the fact my last name's Warren."

Bane shook his head. "I don't understand you. I'll walk with you to the jail."

"You mean the roped off square that just appeared near the latrine?"

The captain half-shrugged. "It's the best we could do."

"Do you think I could borrow a Bible, sir?"

"Yes. I'll find you one."

Peter stepped inside the square and eased himself onto his stomach. The breeze made his cuts sting. He was exhausted. The heaviness he felt seemed to push him into the ground.

"So you're Joshua Warren's son?" Dulaney asked. He'd been assigned as one of the guards.

Peter looked into Dulaney's brown eyes. They appeared confused not angry. Peter felt bad about deceiving him all this time.

"I am, but I don't want to talk about it."

The youth's eyes got big. "I'd give anything to be his son! Why'd you run North? You were so lucky!"

"Lucky?" Peter repeated then laughed. "I know that in the South there are special privileges for special born, but money isn't everything."

"What is your father like?"

"Please sir, I do not want to talk about my father or any of my family. I just want to go to sleep."

Peter closed his eyes and was relieved that Dulaney didn't ask any more questions. Peter was awakened by a shrill whistle. He cracked one eye and saw Doc standing over him.

"John sure cut you up," Doc said.

"Yes," Peter said, awkwardly getting to his feet.

"Do you want me to put salve on your back?"

"Don't bother. I won't live long enough to appreciate it."

"Suit yourself. You sure fooled me. I never figured you to be a spy." Doc gave a melancholy laugh. "I never figured you to be the son of Mr. Warren either. Heck, I was the one that encouraged Colonel Kemper to swear you in."

"I fooled everyone around here on both accounts and almost got away with it."

"But you didn't," Doc said solemnly. He handed Peter a Bible and the nub of a lit candle.

"Thank you. Where's the chaplain?"

"You'll be seeing him in the morning. Oh, if you're planning on a last meal, it's not coming."

"The Bible's more comforting than something to eat. It was a pleasure knowing you."

"Same here," Doc called back and walked away.

No sooner had Peter laid back down when he had another visitor, the little negro boy. Little James stood, his mouth agape. His expression made Peter feel uneasy.

"Is there something you want?" Peter asked to break the silence.

"I neber saw a white man whipped 'fore."

Peter laughed, biting his tongue to manage the pain.

The boy's father appeared, walking with long, determined strides. "James what yuh doin'!" he scolded.

The boy looked up at him. "I's done nothin' wrong, honest."

"I apologize dat ma son bothered yuh, suh."

"No need. I appreciated his company."

"Eben so, yuh needs to get to bed," Big James ordered. The boy took off, his father watching him for a moment.

Big James stroked his beard clearly contemplating what to say next. "Yuh really Joshua Warren's son?"

"I am."

"Yuh knows Aunt Ruth?"

"I sure do. The woman raised me."

Big James stared at the ground. He rubbed one foot against the back of his leg. When his head snapped up a dark shadow clouded his eyes. "Is she—alive?"

"Alive? She's as healthy as can be."

A lightness passed over Big James' face making him look ten years younger. "Thank God! I prays for my ma ebery night."

"Your mother?"

"Yessuh. Yuh's just a baby. I leave Fredericksburg when I's seven."

Peter gnawed on his bottom lip and struggled for words. "My father has a horrible reputation with his slaves, but he promised he'd never break up Aunt Ruth's family." *Of course I don't want to count how many promises he has broken. So why am I surprised?*

But why had this been kept a secret? Peter's heart ached. "Aunt Ruth," he said slowly, "and I were close, are close," he corrected. "She never told me about you."

James frowned, his eyes reflecting his hurt. "Likely she miss me and feel guilty 'bout agreein' to let me go. I knows what it feels like to lose chillun. I's lost three. Dey with de Lord now."

Peter pressed his lips together. So much loss and sorrow.

"I wasn't sold," James continued, "I's given to Bane," he explained. "When lil, he and what was to be his manservant took ill. He live but his servant didn't. The cap'n cry for days after. His family was friends wid yo' pa and dey was lookin' for a boy to take his place. Dat boy was me." Big James took a deep breath and ran a hand through his hair.

"I's see my ma often for de next couple years. Cap'n and me play at Springdale. We run 'round outside while my ma did her chores. Den we move lots of times and I huven't see her since. My ma tell me dat it best if I live wid Mr. Bane and lookin' back on it I agree."

"I'm glad my father did something right. If you happen to meet your mother after the war, please tell her what happened to me."

Big James nodded. "Is ma pa—?"

"He died ten years ago," Peter said. He hoped no questions would follow.

"Oh," James said. He shifted his weight. "Thank yuh for lettin' me know." Head bowed the man headed back to Bane's tent.

Peter wished he could have gotten to know Dan's brother before he died. But at least he got to meet him. Big James was a good man, Aunt Ruth would be proud.

Would she be proud of him, too?

The breeze kicked up into a strong wind. The cold ground chilled Peter even more. Half-clothed, goose pimples erupted on his flesh. He shivered. Mutely, Dulaney took off his coat and laid it over Peter's back.

"Thank you," Peter said.

Peter opened the Bible and turned to Psalm 23. He cupped his hands around the candle to keep it from blowing out and read in the glow of the flickering light.

Suddenly the candle went out. Peter closed the Bible. He didn't need it. He knew the Psalm by heart.

The words were just words. He believed in God. But now he had to trust in God's power.

Peter thought of the corpses of Henry Jackson and Andrew Silas. Their flesh was deteriorating, being devoured by insects. Soon their bones would not be distinguishable from one another. It would be impossible to tell who had been the quiet, shy stranger and which one had been the older, confident man who everyone called buffalo because of his shaggy hair. Peter rubbed his face with the palms of his hands. He couldn't think of that now. The body was not important. The soul lived forever.

Peter opened the Bible again and turned the pages until he found John 14. The dark made the print blur together. He strained to read the small print: *In my Father's house are many mansions: if it were not so, I would have told you. I go to prepare a place for you. And if I go and prepare a place for you I will come again and receive unto myself; that where I am, there ye may be also.*

Peter knew where he was headed. His mother would meet him at the gate. He closed his eyes and felt overcome with God's love.

Sleep crept over him like a shadow.

CHAPTER 25

SUDDEN PAIN IN his side jolted Peter awake. He opened his eyes and saw Sergeant Fry standing over him. It was still dark. When Bane said they were going to get an early start he wasn't joshing.

Fry motioned with his pistol, for Peter to walk ahead of him. Peter no longer feared death, only dreaded the last few moments of life. Instead of being directed to a tree he was led to the regiment in marching formation.

"You're not going to hang me?" Peter asked the question in a whisper.

"Not now," Fry said. "Pickett's division has been ordered to make a special reconnaissance of the Dismal Swamp and we're leaving in a matter of minutes."

This brought Peter a brief sigh of relief which he turned into a yawn. Fry handed Peter back his blouse. "I don't think anyone cares to look at your back any longer," he explained, not trying hard to hold back a smirk. "Your funeral can wait, besides I don't even think Colonel Kemper knows about you yet."

Peter rolled his eyes. "It would be awful if he missed my hanging."

"It will be a big event. Likely be in the papers."

His betrayal and death plastered across the front page of all the Virginia newspapers. Just what he didn't want. Why hadn't Colonel Scott understood? Peter shut his eyes and hung his head, hoping to hide the flush spreading across his cheeks. His father wouldn't be enjoying his pleasant delirium much longer.

Lieutenant Mullins showed Peter his position towards the front of the column. "I'm personally going to keep an eye on you." He patted the Bowie knife tucked in his belt. "I figure you can't run fast enough to avoid this. I have an excellent aim."

"I can see you don't trust me."

"Captain Bane made the mistake of trusting you, I never did. As the saying goes, keep your friends close and your enemies closer."

"A knife in the back might be a better fate than choking to death."

"Perhaps," Mullins said, his eyes gleaming. "I'd be happy to oblige you."

Peter was quiet. He recognized the lieutenant's smile. It was the same smile his father had when he was egging to be challenged. Peter was glad not to be six feet under. He kept marching. Committing suicide by making a run for it would have delighted the lieutenant too much. And Peter was determined to face death bravely, to die with dignity and honor.

Everyone complained about wading through the mud. It weighed men down, making the march slow and laborious. Some of the soldiers were unfortunate enough to have their shoes and socks sucked off their feet. The mud oozed forth an awful scent. The stench of decaying vegetation and meat was indescribable. It had such potency that it quickly overcame the column. Amidst the lovely sound of birds chirping were men cursing and vomiting.

Peter's stomach was empty, but bile swirled against its walls. To keep himself from getting sick, Peter imagined the smell of Aunt Ruth's sugar cookies sweet, sugary, buttery goodness. His mouth watered and he swallowed his saliva. In his state of delayed execution, Peter's nose breathed in a more pleasant smell of earthiness—the early scent of morning. It was the little things in life that gave man pleasure.

Peter felt like a fox caught in a trap. At least a fox used his cunningness to serve for his survival, gnawing on his leg till he amputated it and could scamper away before the hunter returned. Peter's heart sunk lower in his chest. He trudged through the mud with no hope of escaping.

Peter felt weighted down, his feet growing heavier with each step. He doubted he had the strength to escape even if given an opportunity. Hunger cramps and fatigue hit Peter like a bayonet slashing through his vitals. He doubled over in pain. A large hand grabbed the back of his shirt collar and jerked him upright. Lieutenant Mullins' expression made Peter think of a thug with brass knuckles. Doggedly Peter continued. With envy he watched Captain Bane work through the swamp on horseback, Little James holding on behind him.

Everyone started itching. Lice attached themselves to soldiers' scalps digging into their skin. The pests wove their way into Peter's shirt collar and arm pits as they fed upon his flesh. Peter scratched up his sleeves and around his neck but it didn't do any good. The graybacks were content sticking with him.

It took nine days to meander through the swamp. In that time, Peter had nothing but the occasional piece of cornbread to eat. The Rebs didn't get much more. Peter began to think of the Israelites. If they wandered around aimlessly would manna rain down from the sky?

Peter stared at the ground uncovered ground. No. God didn't work like that.

Once the Confederates reached dry land they halted. A hand gripped Peter's right shoulder. "Where do you think you're goin'?" Lieutenant Mullins asked.

Peter turned around and glared at him, but thought better of sounding a complaint. He hadn't made a move to go anywhere. With the gentle prod of a musket muzzle Peter was directed under a young pine.

He was being watched so closely he glanced up to see if buzzards were circling overhead waiting for him to die. One of his guards, a young corporal with messy brown hair, was barefoot. He untied one of Peter's brogans, yanked it off his foot and tried it on. Peter saw it fit and handed him the other one.

The soldiers tasked with cooking built fire and took out the pots, pans, and kettles. The pooled provisions of each mess were thrown together for the hot meal. Slabs of beef were put on a spit and roasted. A barbecue was the best meal the soldiers had had in ages and they were planning on enjoying it with every available fixing. Big James built a fire too and got busy getting a plate of beef ready for the captain.

The delicious aroma of the barbecued beef made Peter's hunger cramps excruciating. He looked over at the other guard, his old hut-mate George Johnson. The man was tearing apart the meat with one hand and firmly gripping his musket in the other. Peter contemplated snatching the meat away. He could have a last good meal before they hanged him.

Captain Bane saved him from his feat of desperation. "I'll watch the prisoner for a spell."

The two guards joined the nearest mess to finish their meal. Bane gave Peter a small chunk of beef on a tin plate.

Peter's savage hunger made him forget his manners. He devoured the meat in silence keeping his eyes on the man who controlled his fate. Bane sat beside him, a pistol in his hand. The officer tried to smile but the sides of his mouth would not curve upward. This war could do strange things to a man. It burdened soldiers with grief, pain, and bitterness.

Unable to take the growing silence between them, Peter was forced to talk. "What's on your mind? Being unable to do much else, I'm willing to talk."

"You weren't eager to talk a little over a week ago," Bane said.

"I don't mean talking about me. I mean talking about you. You can tell me anything seeing as dead men can't tell secrets."

"I'm not discussing military or personal issues with a Yankee."

Peter took off his kepi and clawed his scalp. "Suit yourself. I might be on the other side of the war but that doesn't mean I don't understand your cause. I'm from Virginia. As a spy I got out of possibly shooting my kin and old friends."

Bane frowned and stared off into the distance. "This war has split lots of families."

"My brother-in-law Jonathan is a first lieutenant in J. E. B Stuart's cavalry."

"With your friend Colonel Scott?"

Peter nodded, his hands still in his hair. "I figure a man is only good for one oath. I gave my heart and hand to the Union."

Bane's expression went from depressed to grave. "I'm not fond of killin'. We wouldn't need this war if the North would leave us alone. We're just defending our families and property."

The captain finally succeeded in forcing himself to smile, though his eyes remained sorrowful.

"I've quickly realized that when you behaved cowardly earlier it was an act. You are a strong man, a dedicated soldier willing to give his life for his country."

"Thank you, sir. Many of your men are just as faithful to your cause."

"It's only right that a battle between brothers would be a battle between equals. I have things to do." He stood and turned to walk away.

"Wait—I don't mean to complain about the company, I have no right to, but are you going to give me the same guards again?"

"That was my plan."

Peter's heart lurched. *No. I can't handle that.* He wetted his lips with his tongue. When he spoke his words flowed smoothly, his tone a conscious plea. "Captain, surely there's another way to insure I stay put."

"I can think of an easy way but it's painful compared to being watched. We could buck and gag you. You'd be able to be left alone. Within a couple hours we should be ready for, well, you know."

"I know." Peter took a deep breath. Even convicted murderers were able to sit in a jail cell without being watched every minute before their hanging. "If that's my only other option, I accept."

"You're an odd one," Bane said, shaking his head. "Crawford, buck and gag Mr. Warren."

Peter cooperated and he could tell that surprised his other former hut-mate. He drew up his knees, and then placed his arms around his knees. Crawford thrust a musket between Peter's elbow and knee joints, so he could not move, and then tied a bayonet in his mouth.

"Cheer up Yank, it will be over soon."

Peter closed his eyes. He couldn't tell if that comment was genuine or made out of spite, but he guessed the latter. As promised, he was left to his own thoughts. Not being able to scratch the pests infesting his clothes was torture.

Bane watched him. The captain tried to hide it, but Peter caught several glances. Being tied he didn't pose a threat. What had piqued Bane's curiosity? Perhaps he was having second thoughts. Perhaps he wanted the reward money. Perhaps he didn't like hanging a fellow man.

CHAPTER 26

PETER SWEATED PROFUSELY. It seemed like the two hours he had left to live had already passed. Worn out from trudging through the swamp, his muscles ached. He fell on his side, the sparse grass beneath him pricking his cheek. That shade of green reminded him of when he picked four leaf clovers and put them in his pocket before asking Molly to marry him.

He tilted his head to the sky. Fluffy clouds floated in the blue like wandering vessels on a vast ocean. Earth was so beautiful. He could scarcely imagine what Heaven would be.

But the end. Thinking of his last moments chilled the blood pumping in his heart and sent an iciness crawling up his back.

Frazier walked over to Peter, his eyes moist. He sat next to Peter, poured water from his canteen onto a handkerchief and gently wiped Peter's face, neck and hands.

Peter's eyes widened and his stomach flipped. Why would the slavery-justifying chaplain see to his welfare? Frazier's young face was riddled with grief, deep lines around his thin mouth.

Peter would have thanked him if he could speak. He hoped the man could see the gratitude in Peter's eyes.

"Death. All this death needs to stop." The chaplain's words were soft, but strong. They carried the weight and wisdom of a discouraged warrior.

Peter's heart sped up by a fraction igniting a glimmer of hope. This chaplain really cared about him. This man didn't want him to die.

The chaplain wetted the handkerchief again. Soothed by the coolness, Peter closed his eyes.

He dreamed of hugging Molly close, telling her his time was near. He took a deep breath inhaling her hair—lavender soap. They stood outside their finished house. The house where they were going to grow old together. A strong wind blew and made the leaves on the live oak moan.

Molly cried softly on his shoulder.

Peter brushed the tears out of her eyes. With two fingers under her chin, he gently guided her face upward and kissed her warm, rosy lips. "Shh. Our love will never die."

Peter was shaken awake. He blinked at the bright, spring sun. Sergeant Fry untied him and took the bayonet out of Peter's mouth.

"On your feet, Yank—it's time."

"Finally," Peter said, his voice cracking.

It was his turn to die.

His heart retreated lower in his chest and he wished there was somewhere he could retreat. But there was nowhere to run.

"I brung your horse right to you. How's that for southern hospitality?" Fry said then laughed.

Peter lovingly stroked the mare's nose. She nickered softly. Peter mounted Cloudy and spoke in a hushed tone, all the vitality stripped from his voice. "I appreciate it, sir."

She was pulling supply wagons. He read in her eyes that she yearned for a rider.

Fry tied Peter's hands so tight he could barely hold onto the reins. He led Peter over to a tall oak tree on the edge of camp. A large mass of rebels had congregated there. It seemed his death was a joyous occasion.

Peter's blood boiled, bubbling against his eardrums. He clenched his teeth against the eager, thirsty eyes of the rebels. Man had a morbid curiosity. Hangings always drew a crowd. Mingled among those eager to watch him dance were sober faces. Eaton and Sublett were not present.

"Who has the rope?" Fry shouted. Johnson threw him a weathered, thick cord.

Fry looped the noose with as much pleasure as a kid playing with a toy. Peter adverted his eyes. *Was that all this was to him? Having the winning card. Killing me. Did Fry see the difference?*

But they had an option about how to do their duty. They could have just sent him to prison for the rest of the war. Captain Bane could have collected the $5,000. What kind of man turned down that kind of money? He was a farmer. They were all farmers. They could split the reward and all have a wad of bills in their pockets.

Peter realized he had accomplished a lot in his few years. He had rescued countless people from slavery, he had seen Dan and Belle wed, was there for the birth of Rebecca, and had spent lovely hours with Molly. Yet, it hardly seemed like enough.

The hours he spent with Molly hadn't been enough. Would never be enough. They had planned to have children. Maybe even watch their grandchildren grow up. Fry and the other Rebs were robbing him of his future with the woman he loved. His chest burned, heart aching.

Fry threw the rope around a high branch and tied it to the limb. Though Peter's hands were bound, he was able to take off his hat. He watched it fall to the ground. Bareheaded, it made it easier for the sergeant to tie the noose around his neck.

Lieutenant Mullins' half-smile did little to lighten his hard features. In a stiff voice he asked, "Do you want your hat back?"

"No. It's disrespectful for a man to wear a hat in church; I better not wear one to my own funeral."

"Chaplain, talk to him so we can get this over with," Bane said.

Frazier stepped out of the crowd. He walked towards Peter, his eyes filled with sadness. "Would you like me to pray?" he asked quietly.

Peter nodded.

"Dear Lord," Frazier whispered, "we pray that Peter will be welcomed through your gates. We pray that his sins are forgiven and that those of us who have sinned against him are forgiven. We pray that his family will be provided for and that you may comfort them in their time of grief. Show us your grace, mercy and love in this hour of peril. You work in strange ways that we do not understand. We cannot change the plans you have laid for our lives. Let us take peace in your final judgment of us all. Amen."

"Amen," Peter echoed.

"Are there any last words you'd like to say?" Bane asked.

Peter bobbed his head, with closed eyes. He said the Lord's Prayer. Then he squirmed to feel the tintype of Molly in his pocket. He comforted himself with the knowledge he'd be able to look down from Heaven and watch over his family and Molly.

But, he would never make amends with Abigail. His gut twisted. He loved his sister, even though she was brought up as a proper southern belle. At least he had been able to spend a few more moments with Aunt Ruth.

He took a deep breath and opened his eyes.

"Let's get it over with!" Peter shouted.

Captain Bane gave the order. Sergeant Fry slapped the horse's rear and Peter felt Cloudy take off from under him.

His neck didn't break. Instead, he was running out of air. His heart charged at his rib cage again and again. The last desperate beats of his short life.

A white light replaced his dimming vision, easing his moment of terror. It reached out with lightning-like fingers drawing him closer. He had never seen such brightness. It was like a blinding August sun, pulsating prairie fire, and Helios' glowing chariot rolled into one.

The light grew closer and Peter noticed something else that was moving closer to him. Not something, someone, a woman. Abigail? Her hair the color of tanned leather cascaded in front of her shoulders, masking her breasts. She looked like she could be Abigail's sister and Peter instantly felt a familiarity with her.

She drew closer. Floating to him, her arms outstretched.

It wasn't Abigail. *Mother?* he said telepathically, his eyes burning with tears.

The woman's mouth didn't move, but he clearly heard her voice. *Dear, sweet Peter! I have watched you grow into a wonderful God fearing man! Do not be afraid my son.*

Just then it was like a dark hole opened up and pulled the woman away. No it wasn't her getting pulled away, it was him. Then the light disappeared, snatched away like a magician's cloth.

Peter landed hard on the ground. Stunned, he blinked. Doc stood over him.

Doc helped Peter to his feet and took the torn rope off from around his neck. Peter rubbed his throat with the back of his hands. The rope had left an impression, rough to his fingers. Was God teasing him or blessing him with five more minutes of life?

No, God didn't have anything to do with this. The rebels were the ones determining his time of death. Bile soured his mouth and he resisted the bitter words resting on the tip of his tongue.

Bane scowled. "I didn't expect that. Toss me another one."

"This one's new. It should hold," Johnson said, doing as he was asked.

The captain ran it through his hands. "I agree." He tied it to the same branch as the last one.

Adrenaline exploded in Peter's body like a Parrott shell and yet his feet refused to move. Lieutenant Mullins led Cloudy back to the tree. With Peter's hands bound, he needed help to mount her again. Doc assisted him. The gentleness in the man's aged hands calmed Peter's racing heart.

The order was given a second time. "May you fall without rising!" Sergeant Fry said, slapping Cloudy again. The mare took off. Peter's legs swung down. He desperately tried to breathe. The white light was getting closer and pulsated with inviting warmth.

Then his mother appeared again dressed in flowing white gown. The woman's caring green eyes softened Peter's fear, her gaze locked with his. Peter felt the strong mental connection snap into place.

Peter, I am your mother Hannah. I regret that I had to depart this world when you were a baby. I have been watching you grow into a man. A man that I am proud of.

But it is not healthy to hold onto hate. There is something you must know about your father. When I married him he was a depressed man. My love brought him out of many a dark hour. He drinks not only to drown his pain but to also to dampen a dark shadow that has plagued him since he was a boy. Do not die without forgiving your father and making amends with your sister.

Before Peter could think of a reply, his mother vanished.

Something snapped.

Peter clambered for breath. The air filled his lungs, slowly rejuvenating him. He lay on the ground, motionless, listening to his rhythmic heartbeat and feeling the rise and fall of his chest.

He was alive! He didn't know why, but the gates of Heaven had not yet opened. Perhaps the lock was jammed. The tree loomed above him, branches gently swaying, laughing. He didn't care that his head pounded and his arms and back ached from his second fall.

"I just don't believe it!" Bane exclaimed. "The damn branch broke! First the rope and then the blasted branch! If I hadn't witnessed it I never would've believed it."

Peter groaned. It was torture, pure torture. Peter's heart rammed into his throat. Twice he had cheated death and felt life again. Now he was going to have it taken away. Again.

"This does give you an opportunity, Mr. Warren," Bane said, business-like. "Have these near death experiences brought you to your senses? Do you—"

"No," Peter interrupted him in a hoarse whisper. "I already know what you're going to say and my answer is no." He kept his timbre as steady as he could. "I gave my heart and hand to the Union."

"All right."

A torrent of tears rolled down Peter's cheeks. He brushed them away and took several deep breaths. Damnit. He couldn't do anything right. He couldn't fight like a soldier, couldn't spy well, couldn't even die without making a fool of himself. "Please wait a minute and let me die like a man," he pleaded.

Thankfully, no one was laughing. Peter's cheeks burned. They all stared at him and the tree silently, wide-eyed and pale. Peter stood and gazed at the sky. "I'm ready."

The captain looked at him; his expression hard to discern. He glanced to the left and slowly licked his bottom lip. Peter could tell he was debating what to say. "Do you want to hang, Mr. Warren?"

"I'm not going to pledge loyalty to the South, sir. Even if I did I know that would mean a miserable existence in prison. You couldn't trust my word."

"That's not what I asked," Bane said, with a sly smile. "I asked if you wanted to hang. You said you wanted to die like a man."

Realizing what the captain meant, Peter nodded, once. "When I enlisted I thought that if I was to die in this war it would be because of a mortal wound on the battlefield. I would settle for the honor of facing the firing squad."

"Captain, may I talk with you for a moment?" Peter asked in a shaky voice.

"I'm listening."

The mob migrated with Peter, Sergeant Snidow glued to his side. Peter lowered his voice for the captain's ears only. "Can we talk in private, sir?"

"I guess. It will take a while to organize everything anyway."

"Thank you for the firing squad," Peter said, once in the captain's tent. "And thank you for taking the time to listen to me." His heart beat slow and hard, each thud sounding in his ears. He was in no position to suggest this. He didn't want to ask anything of the rebel bastards, but for his family he was obliged to try. He doubted the heartless man would grant his wish. "I would like to ask a favor."

"A favor! Well, you're not begging me to spare your life so what in tarnation is it?"

Peter glanced at the ground, swallowed, and raised his head. "I'd like my body to be returned to my sister."

"We're not in Fredericksburg."

"I realize that, sir. I didn't say it was a little favor." Peter paused. "You see, Abigail promised me that after the war we'd make amends. We missed two and half years of each other's lives. Her daughter, Sarah, barely knows me. I had plans of changing that.

"I love my sister dearly. Now that I'm not living to see the end of this war I know she'd appreciate my body. We could still make amends."

"Taking your corpse to Fredericksburg would cost time and money not to mention the particulars involved in such a peculiar business."

Peter licked his lips. "I know I am asking a lot, sir. But you won't be out anything." His voice carried his urgency, his tone a soft plea. "My sister would reimburse all the costs when my body was delivered, Captain. Likely, throw in extra for your trouble."

"And who would be paying for it on the way down? Me? It doesn't benefit me to solve your personal problems."

Peter lungs tightened, causing his heart to race. Warmness surged up his throat. He gritted his teeth to keep his tears at bay. "I had a hundred dollars in gold—"

"Which you stole off the peddler after you killed him. I am sending that money to his wife."

Peter swallowed a ball of uneasiness. Well, that was good. "I wish I had more money to give you, but I don't," he said. Then suddenly he had an idea. "What if I worked a few days to pay for it?"

Bane's dark eyes brightened and he cocked his head to the side considering this. "I reckon we'll be headed to Fredericksburg soon."

The silence tugged at Peter's heartstrings and his upper body swayed side to side. That was all he had to offer. The captain was honorable, had been just with him. *But would he accept?*

"You'd do that just so your sister would get your body?" Bane asked, with raised eyebrows.

"Yes, sir. I can't repay my sister for the time we lost. Now this is all I can do."

Bane continued to study Peter. "All right," he said, "it doesn't really help me, but it's all you have to offer. If this means that much to you, I'll do it."

Peter took a deep breath, his shoulders lifting and his face erupted in a grin. "Thank you, sir!"

"You realize I'm still going to kill you?" the captain asked, as if he was talking to someone slow in the head.

Peter nodded, feeling for the first time his mother was truly with him. "I know. But I feel my last act will make a difference. I'll start working right away if you tell me what to do."

The captain laughed. "All right. I can't believe you're so eager."

"What are you smiling for Yank?" Sergeant Snidow asked.

"Maybe because he's not dying today," Bane replied.

"What!" several men in the mob of soldiers exclaimed.

"We'll fill him with lead in a couple days."

"This is ridiculous. With all due respect, Captain, I think you're going soft," Snidow said.

"Don't worry; we will fill him with lead," Bane assured him. "But right now I want people to volunteer to watch him." Several men raised their hands. "Yankee, you can pick your medicine."

Peter chose Lewry and Dulaney. They wouldn't make his life miserable. Now that he had some extra time, he figured he could tell the boy what it was like to be a Warren.

"All of you get shovels and an axe and help him bury that dead horse," Bane ordered.

"Help him!" Lewry protested.

"Does this job need to be supervised?" Bane asked.

"No," Lewry said. "But you can't expect just the three of us to bury that horse. It takes a lot of work."

"Fine. I don't care. Yankee you can pick another unlucky man. That way I won't be the target of profanity."

Peter looked around for Eaton and Sublett but neither was present. "Hale."

"What? I didn't volunteer," he grumbled. Hale glanced over at Bane, "But I don't mind doing it," he added.

"You never said we had to work," Lewry complained. "I wouldn't have volunteered if I had known. Get someone else."

"You never volunteer for any duty," Bane said, his voice sharp and dry.

☆   ☆   ☆

Peter smelled the rank, spicy aroma of the carcass. Clearly the beige stallion had been dead several days. Peter lifted out his first shovelful of dirt and glanced around for Lewry. He'd already found himself a comfortable spot under an oak tree. The corners of Peter's lips turned slightly upward. To think they thought he was going to be a beat.

"Dulaney, you still want to know what its like to be a Warren?" Peter asked.

The lad nodded, his face already pale green.

"Well," Peter said, digging his shovel into the ground close to the horse, "my father was not involved in my life. We lived together and that was it." Peter tried to keep from breathing through his nose. Mouth open he sucked in air and then spoke with a strained voice. "My mother's servant, Ruth, raised me and my sister, Abigail. My mother died giving birth to me and my father blames me for it.

"He's been a raging drunk for as long as I can remember. I didn't see him much as a toddler because he was in the army. Later, he re-enlisted for the Mexican-American War. When he came home wounded he drank more than ever. I would take his abuse to protect everyone else in the house." Peter paused, rose, and rubbed his back.

"It couldn't have been all bad," Dulaney said. "What about the privileges?"

"Privileges?" Peter exclaimed, and then laughed. A wave of decaying flesh wafted over him and his stomach roiled. He held his arm over his nose. "They were few. I was invited to plenty of fancy parties, balls and such. I never worked a day in my life until I left home. I never had to want for anything, material-wise that is; but I always wanted at the least a sincere smile from my father; not one out of hatred."

Peter took a deep breath. It was hard to talk and hold his breath at the same time. They didn't want to hear about his trouble with his father.

"I rode into Fredericksburg to attend a private school. Father wanted me to have a tutor at home but I wouldn't stand for it. At that rate, I'd never leave the plantation. I ran away a week before I was supposed to become a cadet at the Virginia Military Institute. My father had always wanted me to join the army. After serving my time, I probably could have worked into politics. Father had many contacts but I would've had to change my stance on slavery."

Dulaney, wide-eyed, hung on his every word. He bit his lip, and bent over, his face graying.

Peter tried to think of more to say. He'd explained everything, matter-of-factly, but everything nonetheless. The shovel handle rubbed against his skin and gradually tore the palms of his hands. The pain caused Peter to think of his father's field hands toiling away amongst the tobacco plants at Springdale. This bit of labor was nothing.

"My sister, Abigail, and I were very close. She always tried to calm father down when he got worked up so I didn't end up with a split lip or a black eye. I had many friends, but I always knew it was because of my money. The only one who valued me as a person was Dan."

"Who's Dan?" Dulaney asked.

"My manservant."

Hale sneered, the playful glint in his eye turned more sinister. "Then he wasn't truly your friend either."

Peter ignored the comment. "So you see Dulaney, money doesn't make life perfect."

Doc walked out to the work crew, pinching his nose with one hand and holding a small jar in the other. He had a canteen draped over his right shoulder.

Standing over the dead horse for so long the odor doubled in potency. Dulaney gripped his stomach.

"This canteen is for you," Doc said, handing it to Peter. He stood so close to Peter their shoulders almost touched.

"Thank you." Peter took a long drink, holding an arm over his nose. It did little to block out the pungent smell.

"I am going to put this salve on your back whether you like it or not." His nose still pinched, Doc's voice was nasally and flat.

Peter shrugged. "I'm not going to fight you over it."

"You mind telling me why the captain's put you to work?" Doc asked.

Peter lowered his voice as if telling Doc a secret. "It's a personal matter. I'd like to keep it private."

Rubbing salve into Peter's cuts, Doc did not respond. He scurried away from the horse carcass.

Dulaney scrambled out of the hole, bent over, and vomited. This caught Lewry as funny and he burst out laughing. Peter took a concerned glimpse at Dulaney who was now doubled over on his knees.

"Shut up!" Peter bellowed at Lewry. He stabbed the ground with his shovel so it would remain upright and went to confront him.

Lewry's face, already red from laughing, turned rigid. "And you have no right to talk to me like that, Yankee!"

"What are you going to do about it? You're too lazy to fight!" Lewry stood and took a few determined steps forward. "You move awful slow in all those clothes," Peter said. "I could whip you with only one hand."

"How dare you! You impertinent rat!"

"Rat?" Peter said and then laughed so loud his gut ached. "That's the best you could come up with? You need to take some lessons from my father. He can spout every derogatory word in the dictionary."

Lewry came closer. He was figuring how best to strike first.

"Don't fight on my account," Dulaney urged.

"It's not about you. That's just an excuse," Peter said. "I've wanted to do this for a long time. Seeing as how my time is running short this seems like a good occasion."

Lewry tried to jab Peter's throat, but Peter grabbed his arm and stopped him. With his other hand he worked on ripping off Lewry's coat. "Don't you know how to fight? You need to strip down."

"You're going to get in trouble for this," Lewry threatened.

"Only if you squeal on me like a child." Still holding onto Lewry's arm, Peter twisted it behind his back and walked him towards the hole. "You give up easily," he said. "That's what I expected."

"Hale aren't you going to help me?" Lewry pleaded.

"Help you with what? *I* didn't see anything," Hale said, with a wide smile.

"You're enjoying this aren't you? Don't just stand there!" Lewry shouted, desperation flashing in his eyes. "Go tell someone what is happening!

"You're a pitiful excuse for a man, let alone a soldier," Hale said. "Besides, I think the brass would be on his side."

Peter let go of Lewry's arm and pushed him into the hole. "Take Dulaney's shovel. Start digging."

"I don't take orders from you," Lewry said, picking himself up off the ground.

Peter grabbed his shovel and held it above Lewry's head. "I'll give you a choice. You can either get hit with a shovel or dig with one."

Lewry looked nervously at the shovel above him. He glanced over at Dulaney and Hale. They weren't offering to help him. He reluctantly reached for Dulaney's shovel. "I'll dig," he mumbled.

"You'll what? I didn't hear you?" Peter said.

"I'll dig," Lewry yelled, his free hand balled into a fist, knuckles white around the shovel handle.

"I'm pleased you've decided to help," Peter said.

He sighed as he went back to work. Thinking about his funeral had drained his energy. When the hole was finally big enough he was drenched in sweat, ready to collapse from exhaustion. Hale worked alongside Peter without saying much. His face remained somber almost the entire time. Was that was from the loathsome duty of mourning the equine or if it was because of him?

"Lewry, Help roll him in," Hale ordered.

Lewry grudgingly accepted this chore. The horse's legs were sticking up in the air. It was a pitiful sight. Peter felt for the poor animal. He had been an officer's mount, but he broke his leg and was shot. Peter took the ax and broke its legs. Dulaney winced at hearing the bones crack.

Once the grave was filled Peter was escorted back to his quarters. To his surprise, Sergeant Fry brought him a plate of food and returned his coat. "If you're going to work you need to eat."

"Thank you." Peter was very grateful even though it was just another small brick of cornbread and tiny piece of raw bacon.

"I didn't know what the captain had in mind, but I definitely approve. Mr. Warren's son put to work burying a dead horse," Fry said. He laughed, shaking his head. "The irony of it."

"This isn't the first time I've buried a horse," Peter said.

"If you hadn't run north you wouldn't have had to do it at all."

"It's not that bad."

"I wish everyone around here agreed with you. No one wanted that job. Everyone whined that the cavalry should have to do it but there's no cavalry here. If you were fighting for the South, I know you'd be an officer," Fry said, changing the subject, "but I doubt that they'd make an officer a spy so what rank did the Union give you?"

"Sergeant."

"That don't make us equals," Fry said, his voice a warning. "If you don't want an earlier death than Bane is planning, you best remember that."

CHAPTER 27

"I THOUGHT THESE graybacks had enlisted for the duration of the war," Peter said.

Big James shook his head. "Boilin' yo' clothes always gits rid of 'em." He, his son, and Peter all stood naked. Their clothes were wadded up into a ball and he stirred them around the pot with a long stick. Indecency was not an issue when you were being eaten alive by lice.

Billows of hot steam caused a line of sweat to drip down Big James' stomach. Peter's skin was uncomfortably warm. Hoping the steam wouldn't roll in his direction, he took a step back.

Peter sneaked a glance at the negro man's back and was pleased to only see a few small scars. Peter put his hand on the man's bicep, a touch of affection he and Dan shared. Big James man stiffened, his lips pressed together. Not wanting to make him uncomfortable, Peter removed his hand. "You remind me a lot of your brother. He always knows how to fix the problems I can't."

"I'd sure like seein' Dan 'gain. When I lef' Springdale, he's just a baby. I doubt Hattie 'members me eider."

"I have a feeling you will see them." With both hands, Peter itched his scalp vigorously. "How do you get the pests out of your hair?"

"Shave yo' head."

Peter laughed in a melancholy tone. "I refuse to die bald."

"Warren!"

Peter turned around and was nose to nose with Lieutenant Mullins. His blood chilled, keeping the flush out of his cheeks. "I say this respectfully, sir, please don't call me Warren ever again."

"Fine. If you're ashamed of your name then I won't call you by anything. You can help clean up around here, Yankee," he sneered.

Peter nodded. That would do.

Big James handed him his clothes. "Dey keeps yuh busy and I've nothin' to do," he said, and then chuckled.

"How do you get the graybacks out of your hair, Lieutenant?" Peter asked, putting on his blouse.

"As far as I know you can't."

"You're as bad as these lice. You haven't left me alone yet," Peter said. The lieutenant ignored that smart remark.

Peter walked over to join other soldiers also given the task. He was disheartened when he realized that cleaning up camp meant filling in the latrine left by the last soldiers who had passed through the area.

On the way back, a tan-haired rabbit rustled in the brushes. Peter raised his hand for Eaton to hold still. Peter struck the rabbit on the head with his shovel. It lay motionless. Peter picked the rabbit up by the ears. His eager stomach caused him to break out in a mouth-watering grin.

"Looks like I'm going to have a feast tonight," Eaton said, grabbing the rabbit.

Peter inhaled sharply.

Eaton stopped walking and turned around. "I figured you'd protest."

"You've given me enough food to more than make up for it."

"No need for such a heavy voice. I was just teasing." Eaton gently punched him in the arm. "I'll cook it and bring you a share."

"Thank you."

Peter continued walking to his square. He wasn't guarded, but he sensed eyes watching him. He saw the chaplain and found himself being pulled in the man's direction. The strong feeling did not stop until he stood in front of him. Frazier's eyebrows rose and he waited for Peter to state his business.

"Chaplain…"

"Yes?"

Peter stared silently at the ground for a long time. Frazier's eyebrows lowered.

"Chaplain," Peter repeated, "I was wondering if I was still welcome to attend your nightly devotional."

"Of course you are. Everyone is welcome." He reached over and grabbed Peter's left shoulder. "We're all brothers in God's eyes."

"Not all chaplains would think that way," Peter replied softly. "Not now."

Frazier gave a slow nod. "Many let their personal feelings get in the way of God's word." He paused. "I will see you tonight then?"

Peter arrived late to devotional with his guard, Lewry. It had taken Peter ten minutes to convince him to make the extra effort to walk to Frazier's quarters and sit through a short sermon. When they walked in, everyone in the tent looked at him. Peter's face flushed. He wanted to crawl under a rock and hide. Most of the men failed to conceal their spite.

All the seats had been taken. Peter looked around for another stool or even a barrel, but didn't see one. Frazier stood and gave up his chair. Lewry walked over and sat. Peter offered Frazier a shrunken smile.

"I do not mind standing, Chaplain," he said, forcing the tone of his voice to remain pleasant. "Continue with devotional."

"You're not standing by the tent flap," Lewry said, his voice curt, eyes bright.

Peter walked over and stood behind him. He could feel everyone watching him. He used every ounce of determination to maintain a stoic expression throughout the sermon, concentrating on Frazier the entire time. He looked like a slave standing behind his master to wait on him while he ate. Despite what the rebels might think, he was entitled to prayer and to hear the word of God.

"Let us bow our heads and pray," Frazier said. "Lord, in this time of war, we need your help and guidance more than ever. Let us be strong of faith and not question your will. Thank you for the blessings you have given us today and for the promise of salvation. We humbly ask for your protection tonight. May you also protect and guide our President, Jefferson Davis. Amen."

"And may you also protect and guide Abraham Lincoln," Peter added.

A man with blue eyes and brown wavy hair stood abruptly as if he had been struck with a hot poker. He glared at Peter. A vein protruded on his forehead. "How dare you say that," he bellowed, shaking his fist in Peter's face.

"I will not have a fight in my tent," Frazier said, emphasizing every word, his tone firm. "It is a place of God. He has the right to pray as he wants."

"We need to skedaddle," said a wiry man with a blond mustache, dragging the enraged soldier out of the tent. "We don't need to get arrested again for not extinguishing lights."

Walked back to his roped off square Peter struggled to hide his emotions.

Lewry glanced at Peter with a mocking smile. "I'm glad you convinced me to go to devotional, Yank."

Peter gritted his teeth. Lewry didn't care a tinker's cuss for the sermon. He just cared about humiliating him.

Peter didn't plan on attending devotional again.

☆   ☆   ☆

The 7th Virginia struck camp and marched through the swamp en route to Richmond. The Confederate capitol. Peter thrust out his chest his breathing growing louder. Even the soldiers did not seem pleased going to the heart of the Confederacy. Or at least the march there. Cold mud squished between Peter's toes. Soon they turned numb. A chorus of complaints trickled down the line.

One man, not much older than himself, muttered under his breath just loud enough for Peter to hear, "Hell itself couldn't be worse than this." Many of the men felt the same way.

Peter grunted. If they thought that was bad he would love to see them walk a mile in his shoes, if he had any. Peter shook his head with a tight smile.

Big James, also barefooted, trudged through the swamp with his son perched comfortably on his broad shoulders. Now knowing that Big James was Dan's brother, Peter watched him with increased interest. Big James spun yarns for his son covering everything from steamboats to Africa. After each story Little James asked his father lots of questions and Big James answered them the best he could. Mostly he made them up.

Big James reminded Peter a lot of Dan's father. His heart lightened with the memory of the man telling stories outside the line of slave cabins. He waved his arms and used unique voices for all the characters. He had all the children hanging on his every word— including Peter.

Dan on the other hand preferred to retell stories he had memorized from books. The books he could read, but Peter had to read aloud to him for appearances. Peter's stomach tightened thinking of his colored brother.

Aunt Ruth loved her family and would have given up her life for them. Peter had a hard time wrapping his head around the fact that Aunt Ruth had let one of her children go—especially while his mother was alive. There must have been a damn good reason.

Peter's attention was drawn to a lad who couldn't have been more than five-foot-three, struggle through the swamp. His legs kept giving out, and his comrades helped him along as best they could. Peter felt sorry for him when he took a wrong step and landed face first in the bog before anyone could catch him. When they pulled him out he was naked from the waist down.

The men erupted in a roar of laughter. The poor fellow turned the air blue with curse words before he continued forward. He cursed his rotten luck and the Confederate Army and everything else he could think of. The stern words sobered some men, but not many. Peter bit his tongue remembering the scorn he had endured from the same men not long ago.

The march halted once everyone made it out of the swamp. "Give up your trousers, Yank," one of the soldiers ordered.

"They're going to be huge on that bitty fella," Peter protested.

"He's not in the position to be choosy. Take 'em off."

Peter obeyed, his cheeks warming. He marched into South Quay in his red underwear. There the Mountain Boomers heard of the great Confederate victory at Chancellorsville. "Huzzahs" erupted from the men. Watching all their excitement, a gloom settled over Peter. The only news he was looking for was for the war to be over.

Since there weren't enough railcars to transport Pickett's division, they marched on the Jerusalem Plank Road to Petersburg. The wagon wheels, horse hooves, and tread of soldiers' feet hammered the planks like a drum. The lad, wearing Peter's trousers, arrived at Petersburg in a wagon. Some illness had seized hold of him. The following morning, he didn't wake.

Peter grumbled as he dug the man's grave. It was hard to believe he was gone so quickly. One moment the man was alive. The next he was dead. "Life was blasted short."

Peter debated whether he should take his pants back. There was no way to know if what the soldier died from was catchy, but he didn't like walking around half-clothed either. What did it matter if he took ill? He was being silly. He was going to die soon enough anyway.

Peter didn't want to touch the cold, stiff body. He grabbed the bottom of the pant legs, which were past the short man's feet. With one swift motion he pulled them off. He dragged the man by the shirt collar into the hole. Peter closed the man's green eyes but the lids wouldn't stay shut. Peter shivered. The man's soulless eyes stared at the sky blindly.

Peter took a deep breath. Soon his eyes would be soulless, too. How would his sister react to receiving his body? Would she bury him with kind words next to his mother or somewhere else in a pauper's grave? He dropped a shovelful of dirt on the soldier's head. He didn't want to see those eyes staring up at him.

Sweat made Peter's clothes cling to his body. He wiped his forehead and exhaled loudly. Finally, the six-foot hole was done. He took off his kepi, wiped the sweat off his forehead, and bowed his head.

Other soldiers had gathered round to also pay their respects. Frasier read over the body.

Then the drummer boy played a solemn tune, a mournful expression on his face. The music caused Peter's arms to goose pimple. Sadness weighted on Peter's chest. He realized that even though he had served his country faithfully he wouldn't be given a ceremonial burial.

It seemed ironic that people played depressing music over the bodies of the deceased.

God would have the angels play triumphant music as he marched through the gates of Heaven. He was entitled to that.

CHAPTER 28

PETER DIDN'T FEEL like he'd gotten any rest. It took great effort to keep his eyes open, his head pounded. With sheer determination he kept walking. They pushed ahead through Petersburg to Chester Station. Peter yawned thankful they were camping here for a few days.

Walking to his roped off cell, Peter's mind again wandered to Molly. Colonel Scott had mailed his letter. Hopefully, it would reach her. The war made the mail delivery unreliable, especially a letter from the South going all the way to New Hampshire.

Johnson held up a hand and Peter stopped.

"Bluebelly, you can help police the campsite."

"Yankee," Sublett called from a distance as he ran towards him. "I'd appreciate it if you took my place on the fatigue detail."

"I wouldn't mind at all, Sublett," Peter said quickly.

"Hey! I asked him first," Johnson yelled.

"It sounded more like an order and either way I was not informed of a rule stating my services went to the first person who asked."

"You two better get over there," Sergeant Snidow said. "The fatigue party's lining up."

"I'm taking Sublett's spot," Peter informed him.

"But I asked him first," Johnson complained.

"Along with calling me a bluebelly. I prefer Sublett's manners."

"Maybe next time you can bribe him with tobacco, Johnson," Sergeant Snidow suggested then laughed.

While they walked over to join the rest of the party, Johnson aimed a long line of stiff words at Peter and the rest of the damn Yankees.

"You better stop between those words," Peter advised, "or you might run out of air."

Suddenly the back of Peter's head hurt. He turned around expecting to see Johnson's fist in his face. Instead he saw a thin, wild-eyed rebel waving a pistol.

"What's goin' on here?" Snidow demanded.

"It's Yankee's time to die," the rebel said.

Peter sucked in his breath and looked off to the side, not wanting to provoke the soldier. He stood stone still, beads of sweat popping his forehead.

The fatigue party silently looked at Peter and then to the man who was threatening to kill him. Snidow glanced at his men. None of them moved, let alone offer to help.

"If the captain had decided that Yankee's time was up, he'd have sent more than just you." Snidow said, taking a step towards the soldier. "Put the gun away."

"It's not the cap'n's idea, it's mine," the man said, continuing to point the pistol at Peter. "A rider came through and said General Jackson died."

This news elicited a collective gasp from the fatigue detail.

"Stonewall's dead?" Snidow exclaimed. He stepped directly in front of Peter. "What happened?"

"I didn't wait to find out. I'm guessin' the Yanks had something to do with it. The rider's talkin' with cap'n now."

The soldiers assigned to the detail took off running to hear the news.

"Stop waving that pistol around," Snidow ordered. "I don't want you to accidentally shoot me."

"I'm not going to shoot you. I'm going to kill him," the man said, with tears in his eyes. His gun hand began to quiver. "Get out of the way, Sergeant."

"I can't do that."

"He shouldn't be alive," the man shouted.

"I agree, but revenge for Stonewall's death isn't the reason."

"Why not?"

"Stonewall was a devout Christian. He would not approve of murdering for revenge."

"I don't see anything wrong with it," the man said in a shaky voice.

"Put the gun away," Snidow repeated.

"If I shoot a Yankee spy I won't be charged with murder."

Snidow rubbed his chin. Peter's heart pounded so loudly he could barely hear the sergeant's response.

"If we get a firing squad together later I guarantee you'll be on it. Now if you don't put that gun away I'll have you arrested for disobeying orders."

"I'm going to hold you to it." The soldier finally put the pistol back in his belt and walked back to the growing crowd.

"Come on Yank, we might as well join them."

"Y-you saved my life," Peter said.

Sergeant Snidow leaned over and spat tobacco juice on the ground. "Don't go spreadin' it around."

☆   ☆   ☆

From a distance, Big James and Little James listened to the speech honoring Stonewall Jackson. Peter stood beside them. They were busy cutting a long piece of black fabric into strips. Big James took one of the strips and tied it around his son's right arm then tied another one around his.

When the speech was finished the soldiers seemed stunned, frozen in place. Peter eyes shifted from soldier to solider. Would they come back to life if he snapped his fingers?

"I can't believe he didn't die in battle," Crawford said.

"Pneumonia. Struck down by pneumonia," Johnson said.

Crawford rubbed his cheek. "What are we going to do now?"

"Keep fighting."

Big James gave his son a handful of strips. "We can hand the armbands out now," he said softly.

The boy ran up to the crowd. He didn't smile, but he handed the black bands out eagerly.

Big James sighed and slowly got to his feet, unfolding his long limbs. His son didn't realize the magnitude of the situation. Big James walked over and put his hand on Bane's shoulder.

"To think Stonewall would be struck down by pneumonia," the captain said. He tied on his armband. "It's a sad day, James."

"Yessuh, it is."

The crowd gradually dispersed. Bane was still talking to Big James. Peter took a deep breath trying to calm himself. He had an anxious feeling in the pit of his stomach.

"Do you have an extra armband, James?" Peter asked.

Big James glanced down at the black material between his fingers. He handed it to Peter.

Bane looked at the Peter, his eyes wide, but did not say a word. While Peter tied on his armband he hoped someone would speak. The silence worsened the anxious feeling in his stomach. He looked at Big James and then the captain. "Are you busy or can we talk, sir?" Peter asked.

Big James cleared his throat, his eyes darting from Bane back to Peter. "I's just leavin'."

"Captain, I was wondering when I should plan on the eternal sleep."

Bane rubbed his eyes with his left hand. "Why are you in such a hurry?"

Peter stared at him dumbly. He didn't have a response. Bane took the moment to study his prisoner. Peter's skin crawled, and a shiver worked its way down his arms. He didn't like being examined like a cow at market.

"You can't be late to your own funeral. This just makes it easier for me to keep my word. We're headed closer to Fredericksburg."

"You're really going to, sir?"

"Yes. So be patient. Go to your square and stay there," the captain said gruffly. Then he added, "I don't want anyone to get the private privilege of killing you."

Stonewall Jackson was dead. Peter couldn't believe it. The general had seemed invincible. Some people had claimed that the hand of God was on him. Peter reached down and picked up a small, smooth stone. He ran it through his fingers and pondered the general's death—pneumonia.

Hearing the name Stonewall Jackson evoked fear in hearts of Union soldiers. The general understood military strategy and implemented it well. Peter had never heard of his troops retreating from the field. General Jackson was nearly as famous as Lee. He was Lee's right hand man. Peter thought about the distraught soldier who had threatened to kill him. Stonewall was more than that, he was a hero, and now a martyr.

Peter dropped the stone. He couldn't understand how the Lord could take such a man and allow him to live a little longer. Peter hoped that Stonewall's death would give the Union an edge that they could exploit quickly.

"What are you smiling for Yank?" the gangly guard's voice was gruff. "We're all in mourning."

"I'm not sir," Peter replied, his jaw set. He knew better than that.

"Don't look at me cross either. I'm not in the mood to put up with you."

"I'm not," Peter stopped what he was going to say. He saw the hatred mixed with grief burning inside the man's green eyes and the loaded musket he was clutching. He took a deep breath and adverted his gaze. "I mean, I'm sorry."

"That's better. I'm guarding you because I was ordered to but I don't like it none."

Peter lay on his stomach, his feet towards the guard, so that the man couldn't see his face. He kept silent. He sighed and closed his eyes.

☆　☆　☆

The Mountain Boomers were called into marching formation again. Peter was positioned in front of Lieutenant Mullins. The man pulled out his Bowie knife, the blade glistened in the sun.

Peter gulped air and nodded. He wasn't going to run.

Mullins shoved the knife back in the sheath.

Peter's feet burned with the passing miles. His soles blistered. Legs sore.

At Richmond, Pickett's division was divided with two brigades left behind to defend the capitol. Kemper's brigade continued on to Taylorsville, much to Peter's pleasure. Though, he realized, a new location meant making camp. He groaned when he saw Mullins approaching with a shovel. There was no way the lieutenant planned to use it.

"More graves?" Peter asked in a weary timbre.

"You'd like that wouldn't you?" Mullins replied sharply. "No. This time you can dig a latrine."

Did they think all he was good for was breaking his back with a shovel? Peter laughed inwardly. Maybe they didn't trust him with an ax.

Sergeant Fry glared at Peter as he approached. "You're late."

Peter looked away. "Yes, sir," he said in a half whisper.

He stabbed the ground hard with his shovel fully expecting Fry to utter a bunch of scathing comments. Peter held his breath and exhaled when none came. However, he felt several pairs staring at the back of his head. Peter's neck crawled with anxiety and his stomach crawled with hunger. He stared at the ground as he mechanically lifted one shovelful of dirt after another.

"Gentlemen ain't used to workin' to the bone like us farmers," a stout fellow with a bushy, brown beard said.

He leaned over and spat on Peter's foot. Instantly Peter's face turned hot and his temples pulsed. He gripped the handle tightly in an effort to restrain himself from retaliation.

He hated meekly enduring their harassment. He had endured his father's abuse for eighteen years. But he didn't have a choice. Peter wiped off his foot by rubbing it in the dirt. Then he slowly uncurled his fingers from the handle and watched them turn from white back to tan.

The bushy bearded soldier looked over at his comrades. They smiled. The man waited for Peter to relax and spat on his foot again. This time Peter didn't seem to notice. He continued digging, letting the sun dry the saliva to his skin.

He paused and rose to stretch his back, the man sneered. Ignoring him, Peter unscrewed the cap of his canteen. However, before he had taken a drink the man batted it out of his hand. Peter reached down to pick it up and the man kicked it as far away as he could. Peter didn't bother to see where the canteen landed. He wet his lips with his tongue and resumed shoveling.

"Don't you want your canteen?" The bushy bearded man asked, a baiting tone to his voice.

Peter nodded without looking up. "I want it but I don't have the energy to get it."

"Aren't you thirsty?" the man drawled.

Peter swallowed trying to make the dry lump in his throat disappear. The man refused to be ignored any longer.

"I am thirsty," Peter said, looking his adversary in the eye. "But as a prisoner I'm dependent on the kindness of my enemies. I'm grateful to have had coffee and breakfast this morning."

The man blinked dumbly at Peter. After a long minute he went back to work. Peter exhaled.

Talking about food made his stomach grumble. Breakfast had been the usual cornbread and small slab of raw bacon.

Peter gently touched the back of his neck. The sun had turned it hot and tender. Sweat caused his clothes to cling to his skin. Peter shed his coat but it brought little relief.

Peter looked back at camp as he stretched his arms. A long line of tattered, conical tents had been erected. Outside the tents were rows of muskets, neatly stacked together into a teepee shape, six to a pile, the bayonets crossed at the peak. Many of the rebels were swapping jokes and telling stories. Not long ago Peter would have been doing the same. He didn't realize how much he'd miss being in the Confederate ranks.

"Yankee! What are you doin' resting?" Sergeant Fry said, loud and sharp.

Alarmed, Peter jumped. The men erupted in laughter. Peter closed his eyes and waited for it to pass. In the back of his mind he could hear his father scorn him: men don't startle as easily as a high-strung pony.

Fry's eyes narrowed into threatening beads. "Keep shoveling or you'll be scooping the dirt out with your hands."

Peter wanted to say a few choice words but that would've escalated things. Once again, he forced himself to dig.

As he worked, he was aware that some of the soldiers would take a break from reading an old newspaper, their card games, or writing a letter home and watch him with smug faces. His skin tingled. He tried to ignore the onlookers. Captain Bane kept a close eye on him, too. Apparently, watching the Yankee prisoner sweat was good entertainment. It wasn't just watching a Yankee prisoner they were interested in, it was watching Joshua Warren's son do manual labor.

With a determined set of the jaw, Peter kept shoveling. He'd show them that he wasn't a rich, spoiled youth. He was a man who knew how to work. Peter didn't complain despite the fact he felt lightheaded. When he rose to stretch again he was unsteady. He leaned heavily on his shovel to maintain his balance.

"It's not funny anymore, John," Dulaney said. The boy picked up Peter's canteen and handed it to him. "I'm afraid half of it spilled out."

"Thanks." Peter took a long swig of water. He took another drink. It wasn't enough to quench his thirst or cool his burning throat but he screwed the cap back on. If he drank much more he'd make himself sick.

Dulaney looked at Peter, flecks of respect in his brown eyes. "I can't imagine working that long without something to drink."

Peter spoke soft, his words heavy. "I hope you never have to."

The following morning, Peter was woken by four armed guards—unwelcome visitors to his roped off cell in the center of the Confederate camp.

"So today's the day," he said, low, solemn.

Slowly he got to his feet, his chest weighted down by the heaviness of his heart. His back, shoulders, and arms ached. He stretched his arms above his head then bent over and grabbed his toes. His muscles protested the slightest movement. Never before had he been grateful for misery. But it reminded him he was alive.

"They wear me out then they kill me," Peter mumbled, as he was marched to Bane's tent.

He looked at his guards. They all had expressionless faces. Their eyes frozen, looking ahead.

"I guess this is how people look when they're about to attend a funeral," Peter said with a tiny laugh. He stepped inside Bane's tent, snapped to attention, and saluted.

"You never cease to surprise me," the captain replied. "There's still a hint of a southern gentleman in you. Not how I'd imagined Joshua Warren's fugitive son to behave." He stroked his wiry beard, his dark eyes focused on Peter's face.

Peter's hands burned, tingled. He gripped his sides. He couldn't weaken his resolve. His voice must sound strong, determined. "I figured you're going to tell me it's time, sir," Peter said.

Bane nodded. "It is time."

Peter bit his lip, his pulse quickening.

What would Abigail do with his body? Would Molly visit his grave after the war? Would Dan? Those thoughts sent a jolt of melancholy through his body, landing in his stomach like a rotten apple. He swallowed hard, but his mouth remained parched.

His mouth twisted into a tight smile. He had done all he could to help the Union. He was doing the best he could to make amends to his sister, though it didn't seem enough.

He took a deep breath, loosening his lungs. Now it was time for him to die bravely.

Bane put a strong hand on the middle of Peter's back and spoke directly into his ear, slow and deep. "The firing squad is waiting. Or you can take a pledge and I will offer you parole."

Parole? Peter's heart rose and his stomach fluttered. This had to be a trick. He had prayed for a way out and this was it. But could he do it? Could he continue to wear a Confederate uniform?

Then again, if he was dead, his cause would die with him. He'd be no good to anyone. Bane had offered him a chance. A chance to live. Was a pledge different than an oath? Was he just splitting hairs?

Still, he wasn't about to betray the Union even if it meant staying alive. He had been running from death since he was eighteen. Now he was finally ready to face it, embrace the fact that he couldn't escape death forever. No one could. Under the best circumstances a man could decide when and how he died.

Peter swallowed to ease the rough lump in his throat. "That depends, sir. What kind of pledge?"

"A pledge not to escape. Damnit. I'm giving you a way out. Don't let your high morals cost you your life."

The captain's voice sounded slightly like a plea. Caught off guard, Peter blinked. Was the captain having second thoughts? Or would the man save his life only to collect the $5,000 reward.

Sure, he'd be alive, but life in prison wouldn't be much of a life at all… That decision was easy. Besides, the hurt it would cause Molly to see him in jail, he'd never forgive himself for causing that pain. "As I said before, I won't be bullied into fighting for the South."

Bane leaned forward and brushed all the papers off his desk. "Yes. I know. You're a brave man. You're fighting for the North. You've risked your life for the North. But that doesn't mean you have to die for the North."

Perplexed, Peter unconsciously held his breath, and his thoughts raced back to New Hampshire. If he didn't take this pledge he'd never see Molly or Dan again. He needed to be there for them. He needed to have a future with his family, with the ones he loved. But it had to be on his terms.

Peter stuck out his chin, his eyes fixed on a point behind Bane. "I won't go to jail either, if that's what you're thinking. I'd be better off with the gallows."

ABOUT THE AUTHOR

Haley Whitehall has been obsessed with telling stories since the age of four. While most little girls go through phases wanting to be a ballerina or doctor Haley has always wanted to be an author. She grew up watching western movies and spending pleasant weekends on her grandparents' ranch.

Haley's interest in the Civil War was sparked in elementary school after reading *Rifles for Watie*. The more she learned the stronger her addiction to the Civil War became. She has tintype, button, and bullet collections as well as an extensive Civil War library.

Haley earned her B.A in history from Central Washington University in 2009. Pairing her two passions, she writes historical fiction with a touch of faith. She gives a voice to the underdog with her two cats Tom and Pippy supervising. Mark Twain serves as her writing mentor.

Check out Haley's weblog to read exclusive extras on *Grits and Glory* and learn about the next book in the Plantation Shadows series.

Connect with Haley online:

Facebook: http://www.facebook.com/HaleyWhitehallAuthor

Fan Page: http://www.facebook.com/LightonHistory

Goodreads: http://www.goodreads.com/user/show/5752668-haley-whitehall

Weblog: http://haleywhitehall.com

Twitter: @HaleyWhitehall